PENGUIN

The Wedding Game

Elle Cook worked as a journalist and in PR before becoming a full-time novelist. She is the author of contemporary romances: *The Man I Never Met*, *The Last Train Home* and *The Wedding Game*.

Elle is also the author of six historical timeslip novels under her real name, Lorna Cook. Her books have sold over 400,000 copies combined. She lives in coastal Essex with her husband and two daughters.

THE WEDDING GAME

ELLE COOK

PENGUIN BOOKS

PENGUIN BOOKS

UK | USA | Canada | Ireland | Australia
India | New Zealand | South Africa

Penguin Books is part of the Penguin Random House group of companies
whose addresses can be found at global.penguinrandomhouse.com

Penguin Random House UK,
One Embassy Gardens, 8 Viaduct Gardens, London SW11 7BW

penguin.co.uk

Penguin
Random House
UK

First published 2025
001

Typeset in 10.4/15 pt Palatino LT Pro by Jouve (UK), Milton Keynes
Printed and bound in Great Britain by Clays Ltd, Elcograf S.p.A.

The authorised representative in the EEA is Penguin Random House Ireland,
Morrison Chambers, 32 Nassau Street, Dublin D02 YH68

A CIP catalogue record for this book is available from the British Library

ISBN: 978-1-804-94699-2

MIX
Paper | Supporting
responsible forestry
FSC® C018179

Penguin Random House is committed to a
sustainable future for our business, our readers
and our planet. This book is made from Forest
Stewardship Council® certified paper.

For my mum,
because of everything.

Chapter One

Lexie

August 2022

'Get off with the *groom*?' I squeak the words in shock as I read out the dare my best friend Scarlet has set me.

'Sorry. No. That's meant to say *best man*.' She chuckles at her own mistake while we take our seats at the wedding breakfast. 'Get off with the *best man*. Don't get off with the groom, for God's sake.' She leans over, crosses out *groom* and replaces the word with *best man*.

I murmur 'hello' and nod a greeting to those already seated at our table, who are attempting polite conversation with those next to them. We'd been stuck at the back of the church because we'd arrived late, as per usual, so I have no idea what the best man actually looks like.

'What if he has a girlfriend?' I ask quietly as we sit.

'Don't do it then,' Scarlet mutters. 'Obviously.'

Obviously. My instruction to get off with the best man is less of a dare and more part of what Scarlet and I have dubbed *wedding bingo* – a game we've developed for a bit of fun to pass the time at the *many* weddings we've been invited to over the past two to three years. I compile a bingo grid for myself, Scarlet writes one for herself and then we give each other one 'out there' instruction that's meant to scupper either of us from getting a full house.

It's usually just a giggle, but as we sit here in the ornate Georgian country-house banqueting hall at our table full of eight other strangers tucking into their starters, I scan my wedding-bingo sheet to see what I can tick off so far. With the instruction to get off with the best man, I'm now a bit concerned we're venturing out of my comfort zone. Although, in fairness, I've given Scarlet an almost equally disarming instruction to get a waiter's telephone number. Now that I compare our bingo grids, I think she's been unfair with my instruction. Or perhaps I've been too light with hers.

This is the last one: the final wedding of the summer and so we've upped the ante. There are prizes to be won.

This is Georgia's wedding – Scarlet's friend from university, who I've met once or twice over the years, although Scarlet's not seen her in ages. Georgia's wedding, with its big country-house setting and elegantly sober but soon-to-be-drunk early-thirty-somethings, carries all the hallmarks of almost every wedding that's come before it, for us anyway.

Because weddings are all the same, aren't they? And they really need not be. A cut-out-and-keep version of one wedding can so easily be transferred over to the next bride and then the next, and the next. I suppose that's why, when the bouquet is caught, we all acknowledge that it heralds the turn of the next woman to go through the same motions as the girl who's just thrown the flowers in her direction. That bouquet might as well be a relay baton.

But maybe this wedding will be different. Perhaps it heralds the *start of something*, either for Scarlet or for me. Or, even better, for both of us.

I sip my water, freshly poured by a silver-service waiter. It's a hot summer's day, but at least we're indoors with the wide sash windows thrown open, allowing a much-needed breeze to travel through – rather than being stuck in a stifling marquee, as has often happened at other weddings this year.

When we plan our dream wedding (not to each other), Scarlet and I have agreed that marquees are merely glorified tents and, if we're going to get married in a venue fresh out of a costume drama, then we're dancing the night away in the location of our dreams rather than in a sweaty tent.

Scarlet looks round for the handful of her old university friends we'd spotted in the church earlier, but they've spread out around the room. I've met a few of them at various weddings over the past couple of years and they all fade into a series of lookalikes with whom to make small talk.

Scarlet and I met just after we'd both graduated and I answered an ad to flatshare with her in London. We've been flatmates ever since. Nearly a decade. Of the wedding invitations that have fallen through the letterbox over the last few years, this is our tenth together in eighteen months. Or maybe it's the eleventh? I've lost track now. But it's the final one to be ticked off the calendar before normal service resumes and my weekends stop being about country-house nuptials, heeled shoes that slice through damp churchyard soil and roast chicken for the sit-down dinner. Although saying that, Scarlet and I could easily get home tomorrow to find another wedding invite has landed on the mat in our absence.

At this wedding I am the plus-one, the wingman to Scarlet, who is the real invitee. She's been my plus-one, I've been hers. Back and forth.

Until one of us dies of old age.

I'm sure one of us will find a romantic partner to go with eventually but, until then, we've stayed strong and accompanied each other. Casual five-dates-in guys have not been permitted to attend any weddings as plus-ones, because it is traumatic for everyone involved when it comes to an end and you have to hastily ring a bride and beg her to scratch a name off a table plan that's already been printed. We don't bother any more. Regulars at these events have started assuming Scarlet and I are a couple. Scarlet and Lexie. Lexie and Scarlet. We are the last two left, the final bastions of singlehood.

Practically everyone we each went to university or college with decided that this was the summer to tie the knot. Almost every other weekend from May to September has involved a wedding. And those who haven't done it this year are doing it next year. I'm exhausted.

'Why is it always chicken?' Scarlet whispers as she glances from the bingo sheet I've handed her to the elegant calligraphy-written menu placed in front of us.

'It's chicken,' I tell Scarlet, 'because it's always chicken. Because chicken is safe. Easy. And because no one really cares what they eat as long as they get fed.' We both tick a 'chicken' square on our wedding bingo cards.

4

Prior to the reception, I'd also ticked off a reading from *Jane Eyre* during the ceremony. Scarlet reluctantly sanctioned my double points because it was 'I have now been married ten years' and I was very specific about which reading from *Jane Eyre* it would be. I often score a full house long before Scarlet. She refuses to believe people can be *so* predictable time after time.

'So do I actually have to *snog* the best man?' I ask.

'Yes or you can't win. And you remember what happens if you win?' Scarlet asks.

I straighten my back, sitting up excitedly. 'I do. I get a spa day, including treatments and dinner, with you – all paid for. By you,' I remind her.

'This is correct,' she says. 'And if I win,' she reminds me, 'you have to buy me a pair of Christian Louboutins, because I am sick to death of wearing shit shoes to these weddings.'

'I cannot believe a pair of Louboutins is the same price as a spa day, treatments for two of us *and* dinner.'

When we set the outlandish financial cap on what each of us might win, I'm not sure I chose too wisely. At least Scarlet gets to enjoy some of my winnings by accompanying me to the spa. I don't get to enjoy wearing her shoes. We're different sizes. Although for Louboutins, which I don't think I will ever be able to afford, I would willingly squeeze my feet in and endure the agony.

'You chose badly,' she decides.

'Mmm, maybe,' I agree.

She eyes her instruction from me and then scans the room hungrily for a suitable waiter from whom she can extract a mobile number. I watch her laser-beam onto a blond waiter channelling his inner Kurt Cobain, all jawline and a bit too much stubble for this silver-service location – blue, tired eyes pale against his tanned face.

'Oh, this is almost too easy,' she says, salivating. 'I've basically already won.'

I scout around for anyone who might be the best man. How soon is too soon to snog someone? I didn't really get a good look at him, given that Scarlet and I were at the back of the church *and* are now sitting at the 'randoms' table, placed at the rear of the room with a view of the kitchen door swinging open and closed as waiters pass in and out. She looks at the tight-fitting trousers of the waiter she's got her eye on as he walks into the kitchen. The guests at our table pay no attention to us nattering away. They're deep in various conversations, enthusing wildly about the venue and the food.

'On my bingo card I've got "sitting at the back of the room for the sit-down dinner",' Scarlet reminds me after the waiter disappears.

'I know,' I bristle. 'I saw.'

'This is how we know we're fillers, invited to the day because they've booked a one-hundred-guest package and didn't quite have enough real friends to fill the space.'

Ouch. 'Bitchy but true,' I agree. I wish I'd included this on my grid. I thought this time we might be in the middle of the room at least.

She ticks that particular bingo square with glee. I'm starting to twitch about losing my spa day.

When we've run out of small talk with those around us

6

and the dinner finally ends – both of us ticking off 'bride cries during her father's speech' and 'best man tells rude in-joke involving stag-do' – Scarlet downs the rest of her wine, wishes me luck and makes a beeline for the Kurt Cobain waiter lookalike. The wedding party is invited to go through to the library and adjoining snug, for yet more complimentary champagne as we wait for the evening guests to arrive.

I wonder how I'm going to do this. I know vaguely what the best man looks like, now he's made his speech, but I could hardly stand up from my poor position at the back of the room and stare right at him, so I'm not totally sure I could even identify him in a line-up. The odds are against me, and I wish I'd made Scarlet's bingo instruction slightly less attainable now, although I do want her to meet someone eventually. But today . . . the stakes are too high financially for me to lose. I don't have a job at the moment, I'm living off my tiny inheritance from my gran and I'm still knee-deep in student debt. I can't afford Louboutins. I can barely afford to eat. I'm going to *have* to snog the best man.

I hope he's good-looking.

And that he doesn't have a girlfriend.

I haven't seen Scarlet for about an hour and I assume she's got lucky with Kurt Cobain. I've been making small talk with the bride's gran for ages. She parked herself on a stool next to me at the bar and told the bartender she'd be here drinking sherry until the bitter end and that he was to 'keep it coming'. What a woman! But her attention has been taken up by the return of her husband, and I need some fresh air. I might have drunk a bit too much over the past hour, so I slip off the bar stool and sidle past people talking and milling about, waiting for something to happen.

A group of classical musicians has taken up residency in the corner. I grope around in my bag for my bingo sheet, so I can tick off 'string quartet'. Soon they'll cut the cake and the dancing will begin, at which point I'll have to start my search for Scarlet. We're staying overnight and she took the key after we dumped our weekend bags in the room. I should check my friend's not dead, but I'd also really like the key to the room at some point in the next few hours.

I stand on the terrace, leaning against the stone balustrade and looking out over the immaculate lawn while classical music emanates from the room behind me. The sunshine is blinding. I can't remember if I have 'fireworks on the lawn' on my bingo card. I glance at it and see that I don't. Given the space out here, there probably *will* be fireworks later.

'Bugger,' I say loudly.

'Hello,' a man's voice says.

I scan further along the terrace. 'Hello,' I reply, looking into the obviously amused face of a rather good-looking man. From his facial expression, he's definitely heard my loud swearing. 'I thought I was the only one out here,' I admit.

'Clearly,' he replies, smiling warmly. He looks about my age and is wearing a navy suit, the same as the other men in the bridal party.

'Are you the best man?' I ask hopefully, because he's got the same dark-brown hair, which is the only part of the best man I could see from the back of the room. If this very handsome guest *is* the best man, and also single, then I owe Scarlet some serious thanks for setting such an outlandish bingo instruction.

'No,' he says, as if I really should know who the best man is by this point in the day. 'I'm a lowly usher.'

'Damn,' I mutter and realise that's an odd reply. 'Sorry, I was sitting at the back during the speeches, I couldn't see who was talking. I thought you might be the best man, given the suit.'

'Nope. Not guilty. What did you do to get stuck at the back?'

I turn to face him fully, unsure *quite* how to respond to this very direct question.

He laughs at my expression. 'I'm usually stuck on the back table at weddings too. Being single is my only crime,' he deadpans.

'Do you think that's what it is?' I ask. 'My friend Scarlet and I double up at weddings, but we didn't think we were at the back because we were single,' I say, pondering this. 'We thought it was because—'

'Because?' he prompts as I stop.

I realise what I'm about to say might be quite offensive and, given that he knows the bride and groom well enough to be an usher, I *might* need to stop talking here.

'Go on,' he prompts again. He's walking towards me now, the sunlight filtering down on us through a wisp of cloud.

'You can't tell the bride or groom, because it might be a bit rude.'

'I won't,' he says. 'I'm curious now, though.'

'We think we're fill-in guests.'

He narrows his eyes; they're brown – like mine.

'You know the drill,' I say. 'You're a bride, you've bought a one-hundred-seater guest package, but you don't *quite* know enough people . . .'

He laughs. 'Oh,' he replies slowly, 'that *is* quite rude.'

'But true?'

He laughs. 'Yeah, probably.' He sips his glass of champagne. I sip mine.

'I'm Chris,' he says and offers his hand to me. His eyes are warm, his skin tanned and his suit fits him very well.

'Lexie,' I offer in return and feel the softness of his skin as his hand grasps mine for a second before he lets go.

'So, Lexie,' he says, 'what do you do when you're not crashing weddings?'

'I don't *do* anything currently.'

'Are you a Lottery winner?' Chris asks with a mock-serious expression.

'Sadly, no. I'm . . . between jobs.'

'From what to what?'

'Pardon?'

'What job have you left and what job do you want next? And . . .' he says, leaning in conspiratorially, 'is this the most boring conversation you've had all day?'

I laugh loudly and he does the same.

'Sorry,' he goes on. 'I'm not very good at small talk. That's why I've escaped out here.' In saying that, he's endeared himself to me even more – and he's already good-looking in that boy-next-door-grew-up-fit kind of way that men are prone to.

'You're doing fine so far,' I confide. 'As an usher, have you had to engage in lots of inane small talk today with people you'll never ever see again?'

'*So* much small talk,' Chris agrees.

'So, let's not do small talk then,' I say. 'Let's do . . . Big Talk.'

'Big Talk?' he queries with an uncertain laugh, then plays along by starting first. 'OK. Are you married, Lexie?'

'We're going straight in, are we?'

'Yep. It's quick-fire Big Talk,' he declares. 'Round one.'

'You're good at this,' I tell him, then I fall into line. 'No. I'm not married. We've just established I'm single, and parked at the back of the room for that very reason.'

'Or because they don't have enough real friends?' Chris reminds me darkly, and I laugh.

'Why aren't you married?' I fire back.

'I've never met the right woman. But if I did, I'd probably propose to her within minutes. Lock her down, there and then.'

I love this. It's so silly.

'Within how many minutes of meeting someone would you propose?' I ask.

He puts on a thoughtful expression. 'Seventeen.'

'What?' I chuckle and then adopt my serious expression. 'Seventeen? Why such a random number?'

'Fifteen's not enough time – you can't establish whether someone's a total psycho in fifteen minutes. Twenty minutes is too long. You've missed the boat at twenty minutes. They've married someone else at that point.'

'Seventeen is the sweet spot, is it?'

'Got to be.'

I laugh. 'So you're getting married at seventeen minutes. How soon after that are you having kids?'

'Nine months, obviously,' he's quick to say. 'You can't do it any faster than that. It's not medically possible.'

I really laugh at this. 'OK, genius,' I reply, 'how many kids do you want?'

'Two,' he says without thinking. 'Two hands to hold two kids. Don't want a third one scurrying off in the wrong direction. Too much hassle. What about you?'

'Two is a good number,' I concur. 'I hadn't really given it much thought, but now you've mentioned the potential scurrying, I'm sold on two.' I dive around in my conversational brain to find something to ask. 'Have you ever been in a fight?'

'A *fight*?' His eyebrows shoot up. 'Like a real one?'

I nod.

'No. But I broke up a fight at a wedding last year and I'm ready to step up again, should the need arise.'

'You broke up a fight. At a *wedding*?'

Chris nods sagely. 'All good weddings end in a fight.'

'All good weddings end in a fight? Oh my God,' I laugh. 'You have to be joking.'

'You watch . . . You might be surprised yet. The bride's mum *hates* the groom's mum. Could be worth sticking around. OK, my turn. Round two: what's your crazy quirk?' he asks and, because I give him a confused expression, he elaborates. 'Everyone has one. Mine is cleaning. I clean like I've got shares in Dettol.'

'Do you?' I ask. 'Really?'

'Yep. Can't help it. Love cleaning.'

'Love it as in . . . really love it? Or you're obsessed with cleaning?'

'I just really like a clean apartment, then it's done and I can relax.'

'Apartment? That's a very American phrase. Is your other crazy quirk that you watch too much American TV?'

'No,' he replies. 'I do live in New York, though, and every now and again a US phrase falls out of my mouth.'

'You live in *New York*?' I ask slowly.

'Yep. For now. Where do you live? Careful, though, we're bordering on small talk again.' He sips his drink.

Why has this information made me pause? Why has learning that this man lives nowhere near me stopped me short? 'London,' I say.

'Did you have to think about it? Did you forget where you live? Or are you making it up to throw me off the scent?'

I smile. He's very quick. 'No, I really live there. How long have you lived in New York?'

'About three years.'

'Why?'

'Why do I live there or why have I lived there for three years?'

'Both,' I clarify.

'We're really in small-talk territory now,' he says. 'I got a job there.'

'Doing what?' I fire back.

'Property.'

'I need more information.'

'I work for a boutique-hotel chain,' he says.

'Still more detail needed . . .'

A smile lifts the corners of his mouth. 'We do up old properties and turn them into boutique hotels. I fit them out.'

I stare. 'That's my dream job.'

He frowns. 'For real? That's no one's dream job.'

'Interior design.'

'Oh, that's not what I do. I do the technical bit.'

'Ohhh,' I draw out the word. 'You do the boring bit.'

'Ha! If you like. So you're into interior design?' Chris asks.

'I'm absolutely into interior design. I'm desperate to get an interior design job.'

'Huh, well, I know people who could help,' he says cryptically.

'Interior-design people?' I ask hopefully.

'I know *an* interior designer. Does that count?'

'Maybe,' I muse. 'Although it doesn't matter, because I'm not actually an interior designer, so no one would hire me. You're of zero use to me. It was nice to meet you, though. Bye.'

He laughs. 'You want to be one, though?'

'I do. When I become a proper adult.'

'Ha! How old are you?'

'Thirty-one. You?'

'Thirty-five.'

'Hmm, not married by thirty-five,' I comment with a suspicious expression.

'I wasn't aware there was a time limit.'

'Of course there's a time limit. Dating seriously at twenty-five, married at thirty, babies by thirty-five. Divorced by forty.'

'Jesus Christ! In that case, I'm massively behind.' He looks out over the lawn and then glances back at me and his gaze holds mine for a second, two seconds. It's magnetic. I can't look away. I don't want to.

'Me too,' I say softly.

He checks his watch and I feel my stomach lurch in disappointment that he might be leaving. 'Have you got somewhere to be?'

'I'm just seeing if it's been seventeen minutes yet.'

I laugh at that. 'Oh, that's funny.' I realise I like him. A pity he's not the best man, though, because I should really be on the hunt. I can feel this spa day slipping away.

Chris drains his drink and I see my glass is empty too.

'Would you like another champagne?' I ask.

'Sure, I can go and—'

'I'll do it,' I say, not wanting to risk losing him inside to the crowd. 'I'll grab a couple of glasses and bring them out here? If you don't feel our Big Talk has run its course, that is.' I don't want this to finish. I'd like to stay out here with Chris, talking and laughing and flirting.

'Stay out here, chatting Big Talk with you and avoiding the small talk in there? Sounds perfect to me.'

'I'll be right back then,' I tell him, taking his empty glass.

'And I'll be *right* here,' he replies. He leans against the balustrade, folding his arms across his chest and watching me go. I turn at the door and give him one last look, smiling. He smiles back, then I go inside.

Chapter Two

'What can I get you?' the bartender asks as I reach the front of the queue after a long wait.

'Two glasses of champagne, please.' I say politely, handing over our empty glasses. He takes them away and pulls out two fresh flutes, popping the cork on a new bottle of fizz. 'And can you fill them right the way to the top, so I don't have to queue again for a while?'

The barman pauses pouring, looks at me.

'I'm not joking,' I say. 'No half-measures.'

His eyes widen and he continues to pour. 'Fair enough.'

'Thirsty?' the man queuing next to me asks as I watch the bartender pour.

'They're not both for me,' I reply, turning to him.

'No, I meant . . . all the way up to the top. Never mind,' he says, blinking away his comment.

'Oh, I see what you mean. I've just queued for what feels like for ever,' I tell him, 'and I don't want to have to go through it all again in twenty minutes.'

'That's a good plan,' he agrees thoughtfully. 'I might steal that idea.'

'Especially since the drinks are free,' I whisper.

'They're not free any more,' he says. 'They hit the limit

behind the bar a little while ago, and now it's every man for himself. I didn't manage to get a refill in time, either.'

'Oh, shit,' I say as the bartender presents the glasses to me and tells me the astronomical sum I'm expected to magic up now for two glasses of the most expensive champagne ever. I've turned cold at the thought of my next credit card statement. I produce my card and hold it out to tap.

'Sorry, it's not gone through,' the bartender tells me. 'Do you have another card?'

'No,' I say ever so quietly.

The man next to me sees my concern. 'I'll get these,' he says smoothly.

'There's no need,' I protest. 'I'm sure I can . . .' But I've hit my credit limit. I can't do anything.

The guy continues to look at me, waiting for an instruction as he holds out his card. I can't pay. Oh God, this is so embarrassing. I nod reluctantly and he turns to the bartender. 'Can you put two pints of Guinness on there too, before I forget the reason I'm queuing here in the first place.'

'Thank you,' I say, 'um . . . ?'

'Josh,' he says. 'You *were* asking my name, right?'

'I was. I am. Thank you, Josh.' We stand for a few seconds and I realise this man is wearing the same-colour suit as Chris and is sporting the same yellow flower in his buttonhole. But he's wearing that suit very differently. He's both well spoken and well built, like a rugby player. His eyes are blue, speckled with lines of grey and a hint of amusement.

'This is the bit where you tell me your name,' he prompts, when I don't immediately speak.

'Lexie.' I reply, preoccupied by my mission and the stubble around his jawline. He has dark hair, lighter than Chris's, but I venture, 'Are you the best man?'

He nods.

My eyes widen, while internally I silently shout, *Yes! Yes!*

'I made a speech for about five minutes, which I'm guessing wasn't very memorable,' he says, putting on a pretend insulted face.

'The *speech* was memorable,' I fib.

'But I wasn't?' Josh teases, and I smile.

'You're memorable *now*.'

He chuckles as two pints of Guinness are put in front of him. 'Is that because I came to your rescue?'

'It is,' I reply. 'If there's anything I can do for you in return, other than transfer you some money, obviously . . .'

'No need,' he says softly. 'Honestly.'

'Really? I feel bad now.'

Behind us the DJ announces, 'Now it's time for the bride and groom to have their first dance. And,' he looks down at the note he's reading, 'they request you to join them on the dance floor as soon as possible, because the groom is nervous and doesn't dance in public.'

A few laughs and rumbles of 'Aaah' and 'Oh, isn't that sweet' emanate around the room. It is actually quite sweet.

'Dance with me?' Josh asks, looking nervous, as if he can't believe he's just said it out loud.

'Sorry?' I say.

He nods his head towards the dance floor as the bride and groom cling to each other, shuffling their feet.

'Shall we save them? One good turn deserves another and all that,' he points out.

'You mean you saved me, so now I need to help save them?'

'Exactly,' he replies, his blue eyes connecting with mine. 'What do you say?'

The DJ helps the newly-weds slow-dance together, reiterating his request for couples to join the dance floor.

Josh holds out his hand. 'Shall we?'

Chris! Oh my word, I suddenly remember Chris. I've left him out there, waiting for a drink and my return, and neither of these things has happened. I've lost track of my mission.

Although, now I think about it, my mission is to get off with the best man, who is standing in front of me, asking me to dance. If I pursue that, I win the game *and* my financial woes are gently alleviated for a very brief period of time, as I won't have to fork out for a pair of expensive shoes. I also get a spa day. I'm torn. I should turn, make polite apologies to Josh, take Chris's drink to him and continue enjoying our time together, no matter how brief it's going to be. Because it *is* going to be short-lived. He lives in New York. I live here. Though there's something about him.

'Are you single?' I ask Josh, cutting to the chase because there's no point prioritising this gamble if he's not.

He blinks, laughs in shock at the directness of my question. 'Yeah. Are you?'

'Yeah.' His stubble gives him that *I might have shaved this morning, I might not have*, devil-may-care look I've always liked. I don't know what to do. I'm not the kind to stand up a man. And there's a connection with Chris. I feel it. It's tangible, despite having spent only a fraction of time with him. I know it's real. I know it's there. But he lives so far away and . . . Josh, well I don't know where he lives, but I'll be honest with myself: wherever it is, it has to be closer than sodding New York.

'I . . .' I trail off, glance at the two champagne flutes still on the bar, the bubbles rising to the surface, condensation trickling gently towards the base of each glass.

'We can leave them there. I think they'll be fine, if we ask the bartender to keep an eye on them?' Josh points out helpfully as my gaze settles on the drinks while I debate what to do.

Couples are making their way onto the dance floor, and the bride and groom look relieved that help has finally arrived.

Josh's hand is still outstretched, his hopeful expression cutting into me. I can't leave him hanging any more, so I take his hand and let him guide me onto the dance floor.

The space is popular, as nearly everyone jostles on to support the couple, and Josh and I are pushed together as he holds me and we sway to Taylor Swift's 'Gold Rush'. It has quite the beat, so is easy to move to. Josh is polite; one hand remains in the small of my back and he never once tries to move it south. He glances down and smiles at me briefly as we move to the music. If I wanted to snog him and win, now would be the time, even though it might be a bit inappropriate and out of the blue. He swirls me around and pulls me back towards him. He's getting into the groove, and so am

I. But after three minutes the song comes to an end, and we join in with a round of applause for the bride and groom.

'Thanks,' he says.

'You're welcome. You're quite the dancer.'

We stand for a moment and then, feeling so pulled back towards Chris, I say, 'I'm really sorry, but I have to get that drink to someone.'

'Of course. Yeah.' Josh lifts his hand to wave and then follows a little behind me on the way to the bar, so he can scoop his drinks up and head back to the dance floor.

I've been gone so long, I really hope Chris is still outside.

Chapter Three

Chris greets me by pushing himself away from the balustrade, a wide smile on his face as he says, 'For a while there I thought you weren't coming back.'

'I'm so sorry. I got held up. I had to help save the bride and groom from embarrassment by joining in during their first dance. I boogied briefly with the best man, Josh.'

'Oh, damn, I missed the first dance,' Chris laments with an anxious expression.

I wonder briefly what it would have been like to dance with him instead of Josh. 'But look,' I say quickly, gesturing to the two full glasses.

'Well done,' he replies, taking one. 'Thanks.' His smile is so warm, infectious.

'You are very welcome.' I don't tell him that it wasn't me who paid for them. 'I hope they're not too warm by now.'

'How was your dance with Josh?' Chris asks warmly.

'Quick. Easy.' There was no more to it than that. *I was preoccupied, willing it to finish, so I could get back to you.* 'It was a very short dance. The couple chose something fast, so we'd finished before we'd even got started.' I laugh.

'He hates dancing,' Chris says.

'Josh?'

'Dan.'

'Who's Dan?' I query.

Chris smiles. 'The man who got married today. You're at his wedding.'

'Oh God, yes, of course.'

He laughs. 'I have no idea whether Josh hates dancing. I don't really know him.'

'No?'

'We only just met on the stag-do a few days ago. He seems nice, though. I'm friends with Dan from uni, and Josh knows him through school, so . . .' he trails off, nowhere left to go with that small talk. Then Chris lifts his glass towards mine. 'Cheers, Lexie.'

We clink glasses and then he devastates me by saying, 'Um, so . . . you were gone ages and I hate to do this, but in about five minutes I'm going to have to go.'

'Go where?' I ask.

'I need to head inside and say goodbye to Dan, and then I've got a taxi coming.'

'And then you're leaving?' I ask. I can't help but feel disappointed. I'm enjoying this too much. Or rather I was, until I ruined it and went inside, danced with Josh, when I could have been out here with Chris.

'Yeah. I don't want to go quite so soon, but my flight is in a few hours.'

'Your flight? Are you going back to New York *now*?'

'It was the only flight I could get that didn't cost a million pounds, and I have to be at work on Monday morning. Dan understood, so I figured I'd go for it. It meant a lot to him that I came over for the stag-do and the wedding and was an usher, so . . .' he trails off again. 'I'm babbling,' he finishes with a smile.

I breathe in deeply, breathe out. 'How often do you make it back here?'

'I don't really,' he says sadly. 'Work is kind of intense and . . .'

'Oh.'

'Do you ever get out to New York?' he asks hopefully.

I shake my head. 'No, sadly. Especially as I don't have a job at the minute. Although I went to Miami with my ex-boyfriend about eighteen months ago,' I add pointlessly.

'OK,' he says. 'Fuck!'

I laugh. 'Say how you really feel,' I joke.

'OK,' he says again, taking me literally. 'I will. You're fun and I'm having a good time out here with you. We've got . . . probably four minutes now, so we need to fit in as much *Big Talk* as we can. Let's make it count.'

'Round three?' I suggest.

'Round three,' he agrees. 'Why did you and your ex break up, and how long ago?'

'Really?' I query. 'Four minutes to go and that's what you want to talk about?'

He nods. 'Go for it.'

I take a deep breath. 'It was about a year ago and he cheated on me.'

'Shit,' he says. 'I wasn't expecting that.'

24

'What were you expecting?'

'The usual story. Incompatibility – something like that.'

'We were incompatible enough for him to cheat on me after only eight months,' I point out. 'Now you. When was your last relationship and why did you break up?'

'She dumped me. It was a couple of months ago.'

'That's quite recent, isn't it? Did it hurt? Does it still hurt? Why did she dump you?'

'That's a lot of questions all in one go. It doesn't hurt. It did for a while. But y'know . . . time heals, I guess.' He gives me a shy smile, as if he's not sure of his own words. 'We got together pretty soon after I arrived in New York. I didn't know many people. I sort of clung to her like a life-raft. For quite a while at the start she was dating me and a few other people at the same time, so we weren't really serious. She was keeping her options open, which worked for her, but not for me. And after I thought we were moving in a good direction, it kind of went back to how it was at the start. I realise now she was looking for a way out when she suggested that we start seeing other people, to find out if we missed each other – to see if we really were destined for each other. I said no. She ended it.'

Chris defuses the seriousness of what he's just said by chuckling at my expression. At some point during this short tale my mouth has fallen open.

'Wow' is all I can say, followed by, 'I got cheated on in secret, and your girlfriend flat-out *told* you she wanted to cheat on you. That's . . . another level.'

'Yep,' he replies. 'It's also embarrassing. I couldn't comprehend it – any of it. We obviously weren't right for each other. Serial dating is crazy. I don't have the time, or the energy.'

'Me neither. Serial dating is the worst,' I say.

'Dating in general is pretty dire,' Chris observes. 'But how will we ever meet people if we don't date?'

'You should be able to meet people *before* having to endure a date. Like in a normal way,' I say.

Chris nods enthusiastically. 'You go on a date with *someone you've never even spoken to. Or met!* I can't get how we've normalised that.'

It's my turn to enthuse. 'You turn up, a bag of nerves, and you wait. What if they don't turn up?' I ask.

'Or what if they do and they don't look like their profile picture. Or they've lied about everything you thought you had in common with them and it turns out they have *zero* hobbies,' Chris goes on, rising to the point.

'Or,' I continue, 'it was fantastic when you were typing cute flirty messages to each other, but now you're sitting face-to-face across a table, nursing a warm glass of wine, and it turns out there is *no* chemistry whatsoever. There are so many things that can go wrong. And you're there for an hour minimum, watching the sand-timer of your life run out, waiting for it to end so you can try it all again with someone else a few days later.'

Chris stares at me, takes a deep breath. 'That's dark, so you've obviously had some bad experiences. I've not been missing out by being in a quasi-relationship with someone who just wasn't into me.'

'You have not,' I confirm.

'See, that's why I don't do online dating,' Chris answers, as if reminding himself of the multitude of reasons why it's bleak. 'And *this*,' he says, gesturing to the invisible but new connection between the two of us out here on the terrace, 'is the reason why I don't bring plus-ones to weddings.'

'This?' I question.

'You and I just met on a terrace at a wedding, because I was out here catching some air and *not* ushering a plus-one around. It gave me room to meet you and have a great conversation, and that doesn't happen very often.'

I think about Scarlet, not ushering me around a wedding as her plus-one, but instead probably snogging the face off the blond waiter. I'm glad I met Chris, out here like this, even if he is about to leave.

His thoughts must echo mine because he says softly, 'It's a shame I'm leaving.'

'It is,' I reply quietly. And then, because I've got nothing to lose, I continue, 'Of course I meet a really nice man and he lives nowhere near me.'

Chris holds my gaze and it feels so real, so natural. It's the kind of look I've been desperate to experience . . . for years. And this man, out here, who is getting on a plane and leaving London in a matter of hours, is giving me *that* much-longed-for look.

I smile and, knowing the connection and the chemistry

between us are real, I risk saying, 'There's not too much we can do about this.'

'Perhaps online dating *is* the answer after all,' he sighs.

'Don't do a U-turn on me now.'

'Dating apps would never have shown you a guy who lives in New York,' he counters.

I laugh. 'True. I've widened my search criteria, but not by *that* much.'

He laughs in return, and then somewhere in the recesses of his pocket his phone alarm goes off. 'That's my cue to get moving.'

My chest tightens. 'It was a lovely four minutes,' I tell him.

'It wasn't long enough,' he says meaningfully. We stand for a beat, just looking at each other, and then he continues, 'I need to say bye to Dan and grab my luggage from reception. Come with me? We might be able to squeeze in some more Big Talk.'

I smile as we walk away from the terrace and into the house, where the slow dancing has long since ended. The retro beat of Pulp's 'Common People' blasts out, and the dance floor thrums under our feet as people bounce around us. I momentarily lose Chris and he turns, touches my fingers and holds my hand, sending a jolt through me as he leads me through the crowd. He finds the groom, says something I can't hear and embraces him in a bear hug. I see Josh and he turns to look at me, giving me a quick smile. I return it and then he looks away, singing along as the chorus plays, while jumping up and down with his friends.

Chris and I make our way through the library and, in the corner of the room, Scarlet and the waiter are standing by the books, talking and smiling. I'm relieved I've found her. The waiter's holding a tray of dirty glasses, but isn't making any signs of returning them to the kitchen. Instead he's laughing at something she's said. In the quiet of the flagstone-tiled reception area Chris walks towards the desk and asks for his luggage and, when he's collected it, turns to me.

I stand there, knowing this is almost it. It's too fast. It's all moving too fast. Meeting someone, flirting, realising you like them . . . then they leave to go back to where they live, very, very far away. It's not supposed to happen like this, surely.

Chris starts to speak, but he's cut off by his phone. 'Hang on,' he tells me and lifts it to his ear. 'Thanks,' he says to the caller. 'I'll be there in a second.'

'It's my taxi,' he tells me as he hangs up. 'Shit,' he goes on, looking at me with a sad smile. We walk together towards the large double doors, open because the welcome breeze of the day has long since left and the evening air is warm, still.

As we cross the threshold and stand on the steps I ask, 'Do you maybe want to . . . um . . .' I trail off.

He steps forward. 'Do I maybe want to what?'

I get brave. 'I was going to say do you want to swap numbers? Just for when you might be back in town again? Although I know you said it's not often, so . . .'

'Yeah,' he replies uncertainly. 'We could do.'

I realise, from his tone, that I've misjudged the situation

dramatically. 'No, don't worry.' I try to claw back my dignity, but fail. 'Sorry, I've totally misread—'

'No, you haven't,' Chris says quickly. 'You haven't misread *anything*.' He stands for a second, weighing something up. 'I think I'm about to do something . . . unprecedented.' He glances at his watch.

'It's been longer than seventeen minutes, by the way. You've missed the boat on proposing,' I tease.

'Damn,' he laughs and then looks at me. 'Bear with me, because I'm about to do the most random thing I've *ever* done.'

I narrow my eyes, no idea what he's about to say.

Chris opens his mouth, pauses and then says, 'Come with me.'

'Come with you? Where?'

'To New York,' he says simply. 'I know it's ridiculous. I know we've just met. But I also feel as if you should. I feel as if you should come with me.'

'You feel as if I should come with you *to New York*?' I ask in a high-pitched voice.

Chris is laughing now. 'Yeah. I don't understand what I'm doing, either. I've never moved this quickly in my life,' he tells me. 'Maybe that's where I've been going wrong all these years. Lexie, I like you. And unless I am totally misreading things . . . I *think* you might like me.'

I smile shyly and nod. 'I do.' What is *happening*?

'So,' he goes on, and he breathes in, breathes out, 'come with me to New York.'

I open my mouth and pause. 'You're serious?'

He laughs, clearly shocked at his own behaviour. 'Yeah, I'm serious. It would be like . . .' He grasps around for a comparison. 'It would be like continuing this evening long into the early hours of the morning, which is probably what we would have done if we were both staying at the venue, instead of one of us rushing to catch a flight. We'd wake up here tomorrow, find each other over the breakfast buffet, talk again over coffee and then make plans to continue seeing each other. This is sort of like that. But . . . on a plane and in a different city.'

I think. 'Really? Are you being serious?'

'Maybe,' Chris replies. 'I think I am. Yeah. Why not?'

'I . . .' I can't think of what to say. I like Chris. I liked him immediately. He's lovely, funny, charming, handsome . . . And how often does this happen? How often do I meet a man like this and experience such an instant connection? Never. Not like this. *This* has never happened. This seems fated. Chris asking me to go with him – because he feels it too. This must all be happening for a reason. What if he's the one?

I'm not speaking and he continues, nervously, 'I know it's a ridiculous thing to suggest, but . . .'

'It is ridiculous, yeah,' I say absently as I try to think it through. I can feel excitement brewing inside me. I love this idea. I love the idea of being with Chris, even for a minute longer, so the idea of being with him in New York for a few days: yes, please. I don't exactly have a full diary this week, being unemployed. 'It's my turn to clean the flat,' I say out loud, realising immediately how boring that sounds.

Chris nods, a knowing smile on his face. 'I hear you. I

love cleaning. Cleaning is important. I respect your decision-making process.'

'Shh,' I say, thinking. 'Are you being serious?' I ask again, because I can't help thinking this sounds fun, incredible. 'How?' I ask uncertainly. 'How would we do this?'

Chris blows air out of his cheeks. 'I don't know.' But his face betrays the excitement that is clearly rushing through him too. 'How about this,' he suggests, with laughter in his voice. 'Just come for a few days. Then, if it turns out I have zero hobbies, we've got no chemistry and you don't fancy watching the sand-timer of your life run out . . .' he repeats my words and I can't help but laugh, then clamp a hand to my mouth as excitement bubbles over. 'Then you're only a taxi ride away from the airport,' he finishes.

'What if I decide it's a terrible idea after having spent . . . however long the flight is with you? I'll be stuck.'

'Eight hours,' he says. 'It's only eight hours. And if we land at JFK and you think, *This man's an idiot. No way. I'm out of here*, then you're already at an airport, so you can go home. It's almost *too* easy,' he ends with a grin.

It *is* almost too easy, isn't it? He's quickly scrolling online, saying that my ESTA will still be valid, as I went to Miami less than two years ago, and that we might just have time to book a flight *and* drive to my flat to grab some clothes and my passport.

I love this idea. I love it so much.

But then this dream-like trance that I'm in is replaced by a jolt of reality. How will I pay for all this? I can't afford a plane ticket to New York. I couldn't even afford drinks at the bar. I can't afford anything.

Could I use what's left of my gran's inheritance? Something tells me I can't, or rather I shouldn't. She was a pragmatic woman and would never have done something like this. Blowing her money on a ticket to New York to be with a man I've known for such a short time – it's too crazy. The guilt would consume me.

Chris is scrolling for flight info and I have to stop him. I say his name and he looks up from his phone. His expression falls when he sees my face. He knows I'm going to say no – he can see it in my eyes. I must look sad. I feel it.

'This isn't what people do, is it?' he mutters softly, obviously sensing I'm about to say something similar. 'Normal people don't invite women they've known for an hour to get on a plane with them, do they?'

'Oh, I don't know,' I reply, keeping firmly to myself the real and embarrassing reason why I'm saying no. 'For a very long moment I was seriously considering it.'

'Really?' he asks.

'Yes,' I breathe. 'I was very nearly there. Despite the fact that it would have been the most outrageous thing I've ever done.'

Chris nods, smiles, looks at the ground and then at me. 'It would have been amazing.'

I swear my heart rate is well into the hundreds. 'I know,' I say, because I believe him. *I think it would have been . . . everything.* 'I'm sorry.'

'There is absolutely no need to apologise,' he tells me. 'It was either the most romantic gesture I've *ever* made or I am massively unhinged.' Chris smiles and his gaze connects with mine as he puts his phone away.

'I guess I'll never know now,' I say.

He's so nice, so attractive, so funny, so warm and I've just said no to the most romantic offer I've ever received. Am I making a mistake? I could have borrowed some money from Scarlet maybe, *again*. I don't know much, but I do know this: Chris is right. Normal people don't ask women they've known for less than a day to get on a plane with them. But maybe this isn't a normal situation . . . I groan inwardly. Oh, finances be damned, because practicality tells me saying no *has* to be the right decision. Or else why am I doing it?

His phone rings again. Chris pulls it out of his pocket as we stand on the steps.

'It's my taxi again,' he says, looking round for a vehicle that isn't there. 'I wonder if he's in the car park. I should go and find him.'

'Can I walk with you?'

He nods, picking up his luggage. 'I'd like that.' The warmth never leaves his dark-brown eyes.

Oh, what am I doing by not going with him?

'Can I just say . . .' I start, as we enter the large gravel car park, with the house behind us. The taxi is in the distance and pulls out of a front-line space on seeing us. 'That I am genuinely really annoyed you live in New York.'

He laughs. 'So am I, at this moment in time.'

Gravel crunches underneath as the taxi pulls up. The

driver pings the boot open and Chris loads his luggage into the car. I feel strangely bereft with every passing second.

'Can I get your number? Just in case . . . ?' he asks, closing the boot and turning to me, although his defeated expression says everything. We'll swap numbers, sure, but we won't message each other. Why would we?

'Just in case I ever move to New York?' I tease.

'You never know,' he replies and, because he's so lovely and now so utterly unavailable to me, I torture myself, cave in and give him my number. Chris saves it into his phone and then says, 'This isn't the way I saw this day going at all.'

'Me neither,' I reply, and I make myself a little taller and kiss him on his cheek, lingering for a moment, two moments. I hear Chris breathe. I close my eyes, for a second, lingering in this moment. It's so joyous, but bittersweet. I could turn and kiss him properly. He could do the same. I'd let him. I want him to. His skin is warm and soft and he smells of euca-lyptus, lime, sunshine. But neither of us makes any kind of move and I open my eyes and step back.

Eventually he says, 'Bye, Lexie. Another time, another place.' He smiles again and my insides melt.

'Bye, Chris,' I reply softly, screaming internally for letting him go like this. But what else am I supposed to do?

And then he's in the taxi, the door closes and it pulls away. The gravel scatters underneath the tyres until the car dis-appears through the open gates and turns the corner. I watch it until I can't see it any more and then, when Chris has gone, I look up at the sky, trying to process what has happened.

It's only just beginning to get dark and a hazy, twilit-blue colour enters the atmosphere ever so slowly. Through all of that I hadn't even noticed the evening fade away. Soon the sky will turn a shade of black and will be full of stars.

My mind is full of regret. In a matter of hours Chris will be up in that sky, passing overhead on a flight back to New York. And as fireworks start behind me, there's a huge part of me that wonders if, by not going with him, I've altered the course of my life in some way.

Chapter Four

Scarlet greets me on the crowded terrace by producing her bingo grid from her clutch bag.

'Fireworks!' she says gleefully, having already ticked it off.

I look up listlessly and watch them shooting into the darkening sky, the bright shards of light defying gravity briefly, before falling down towards Earth and disappearing long before they connect with the ground. I can't feel the enthusiasm of the crowd. Scarlet has no idea what's just happened to me or, rather, what hasn't. Something incredible and then . . . nothing at all. Chris has gone, and that's that.

'I've only got one square left,' she says, showing me.

'Which one?' I take a look. 'You *still* haven't got the waiter's number?'

'Not yet. He's playing hard to get.'

'Really?' I'm confused by this. 'You were wrapped up pretty tightly in conversation earlier.'

'Yeah, I get the impression he only wants to sleep with me and not *actually* have to see me again.'

'Oh my God,' I say, turning to her. 'What is wrong with people?'

She shrugs, looks up. 'I'm not worried. You haven't snogged the best man yet, so I haven't exactly lost.'

'No,' I agree, thoughts of all *that* long forgotten. 'No, I met someone else who was . . . perfect. But, sadly, it's not to be.'

I'm not sure Scarlet's listening as her gaze is skywards.

'And I did meet the best man, though I didn't kiss him,' I say, refocusing on our bingo game as I too stare up at the sky. Colour merges into colour, explosion into explosion. We're surrounded by guests who've spilled out to watch, their gazes firmly tipped up.

'That doesn't count as a win. You have to kiss him, if you want that spa day.'

I think of Josh and me on the dance floor – as fleeting as the dance was. There wasn't much time for sparks to fly, but he was nice, saving me like that at the bar. And there's no denying he's good-looking. 'I suppose he's actually quite kissable,' I think aloud, attempting to make light of it all. 'You could just have pretended to have got the waiter's number, you know – made something up, put a random number in your phone. I'd never have known.'

Scarlet swears. She's obviously not considered this. 'Same thing applies. You could just have told me you'd kissed the best man.'

'Oh, yeah,' I say slowly. 'Damn it.' I sip the final dregs of my now-warm champagne, pondering this.

A man standing behind us, watching the fireworks, leans in. 'Why is it you have to kiss me?'

I look back and realise I'm staring straight into Josh's eyes. 'Oh God,' I say, coughing on my champagne.

'You all right?' he asks as I recover.

'Yep.' I don't know where to look, but I can't help but be drawn up towards his blue eyes, crinkling at the sides with laughter. He smiles and looks confused at the same time.

'Am I a *bet*?' he asks in disbelief.

'No,' I say at the same time as Scarlet replies, 'Yes.'

'I've *never* been a bet,' he says thoughtfully.

'That you know of,' Scarlet responds under her breath, but loud enough for us to hear.

Josh's eyebrows lift in surprise and he looks from Scarlet to me. 'Is the bet kissing me? Is that what I overheard?' he asks as the fireworks build to a crescendo.

'It most certainly is,' Scarlet says.

'Are you *drunk*?' I ask Scarlet. 'Stop talking.'

'I'm a little bit drunk, yeah. Plus I want to see how this plays out.'

'You have to kiss me for a bet?' Josh clarifies. I can't tell if he's angry or not. He still looks confused. It's quite endearing.

Oh, please somebody make this stop. 'I have to . . . um . . . Yes, is the simple reply. I have to kiss you, for my bingo grid.'

'For your *bingo* grid?' Josh asks, but the smile doesn't leave his face. 'Bingo? Are you secretly ninety years old?' he teases as Scarlet launches into a slightly slurry explanation of our game. He watches her with narrowed eyes as she explains our challenges, and then his gaze lands back on me. Josh sips his Guinness thoughtfully as, around us, people start drifting back inside the house or off to lean on the terrace balustrade as the fireworks draw to a close.

'And how close are you to winning this bingo game?' he asks.

'One square left, so quite close,' I say in fast, clipped tones as my mortification deepens. He just needs to go now. *Off you go, Josh. Walk away.*

He stays put, sips his Guinness thoughtfully. 'OK then,' he says.

'What?' I ask.

'I said OK. If you need to kiss me to win, I offer myself as tribute,' he jokes.

Scarlet's eyes swivel back and forth between Josh and me as if she can't believe it. *I* can't believe it.

'No, thanks,' I reply. Minutes ago I was on the verge of saying yes to Chris – of getting on a plane with Chris, who I really, really liked. I'm not about to *kiss Josh*.

'No, thanks?' he asks in disbelief. 'You don't want to win? You don't want to kiss me?'

I can't even speak over the rush of blood that's entered my head. I laugh because this is ridiculous.

'Let me get this straight. You've got one square left to tick off and it's kissing me. And your friend's got one square left to tick off and it's getting a waiter's number.'

Scarlet nods, eyes still wide, disbelieving smile even wider. Josh turns to her. 'So if you run into that kitchen right now and grab a waiter's number, what do you win?'

'Shoes,' she immediately replies. Her eyes slide towards me triumphantly, as if she's already won. 'Really expensive shoes.'

'And if you kiss me,' Josh turns to me, 'you win . . . ?'

'A spa day. And not having to buy her the expensive shoes. But I'm not going to—'

Scarlet cuts me off, turns to me. 'I'm going to do it,' she tells me. 'I'm going into the kitchen to get his number. I'm going to win.'

'Don't you dare move,' I hiss.

'Too late,' she says, backing away. 'I'm about to win. You're about to lose.' She makes the L sign with her finger and thumb and holds it against her forehead as if we're teenagers. She looks at Josh, thanks him for the suggestion and makes a dash for it.

I stare at Josh. 'What did you just do?'

He laughs. 'I cleared the path for you to win. But I don't think you've got long. Seconds at best. Isn't it about who wins? Who gets the square marked off first? Isn't that how bingo works?'

'You're joking surely?'

He shakes his head slowly. The smile is still on his face. He's enjoying this.

'We could simply *say* I kissed you,' I suggest.

'You want me to *lie* for you? I'm not doing that. I've only just met you.' His smile widens.

I think I'm smiling too. What is happening?

I down the rest of my warm champagne, step forward. *I'm going to do this. I'm going to win.*

'Fuck it!' Goodbye dignity, hello spa day. I tip my head up towards Josh and he leans into me; his smile wavers until he's not smiling any more. Instead his expression is one of surprise.

'Bloody hell,' he murmurs, 'Are you actually going to kiss me?'

And then he can't say anything because my mouth is on his and I find myself pressing against him. His chest is hard, and his hand that's not holding a pint of Guinness finds its way onto my back, pulling me towards him gently. His eyes close as our tongues meet, and I can't stop myself kissing him softly and then harder. I can taste cold Guinness on his tongue and it's kind of sexy, as is the way he kisses me back – once he's realised this is actually happening – stroking my tongue with his. I hear someone cough as they enter the terrace and, as if I'm only vaguely aware that we're making out in a public place, I break away first and look at Josh with a stunned expression. He looks at me, equally stunned in return. That was hot. We both know it.

I touch my lips. Neither of us speaks, but I'm still so close to him. Josh looks like he wants to kiss me again. I think I want him to. And then Scarlet appears at our side, wailing, 'I can't find him! I think his shift's ended and he's gone home.'

'Oh,' I reply, still looking at Josh.

'That's a shame,' he says, still looking at me.

Oblivious to what's happened, and obviously assuming I'd never do what I just did, Scarlet announces that she's going to grab another drink and offers, 'Do you guys want one?'

'Sure,' we both say as she disappears.

Josh drinks the rest of his Guinness and then laughs. 'That was unexpected.'

'What do you mean, *that was unexpected?* You literally *goaded* me into kissing you.'

'I didn't actually think you were going to do it,' he confesses. 'It was hot, though,' he adds.

'Maybe,' I say.

'Maybe? Don't lie.'

'Yeah, it was hot.' I'm so embarrassed I can't even look at him.

We're both quiet, both smiling, both avoiding eye contact. 'So now what?' he asks.

'I don't know,' I answer, forcing my eyes to connect with his.

'Can I get your number?' he asks.

'You move fast,' I declare.

'Look who's talking. You just *kissed* me.'

'It depends. Do you live in New York or somewhere that involves a plane ride?' I ask warily.

'What? No,' he replies, as confusion finds a path to his face. 'Is there like a postcode criteria or something, if I want to take you on a date?'

'You want to take me on a date?' It must have been about six months since I last went out with a guy, and that was a swipe in the wrong direction.

'Yeah. Is that OK?' Josh asks, suddenly shy.

That kiss. 'Yes.'

'That was a fast response,' he says. 'Something to do with how well I kiss?' he teases, no longer shy.

He *is* a good kisser. Once he'd got over the initial surprise, it was inappropriately hot. I give him a look as he laughs, pulls out his phone, unlocks it and hands it to me. I haven't given a man my number in ages and incredibly, for the second time tonight, I enter it into a second man's phone, add my name, hit save and hand it back. Josh's hand touches mine as he takes the phone from me and, as if I needed any more proof that there is something there, a charge of sexual energy passes back and forth.

Scarlet returns with our drinks. Josh takes his from her, says thank you and offers her some money, which she politely declines.

'So I'm going to head back inside to catch up with the guys now,' he tells us. 'But it was very nice to meet you both. Lexie,' he says turning to me, 'if I don't catch you later on, I'll message you?'

I nod, smile.

'Oh and, Scarlet,' Josh says as she looks up at him curiously and he gives her a jubilant look, 'your friend won the bingo.'

Chapter Five

'I still can't believe you actually did it!' Scarlet says, not for the first time, as we arrive home to our badly-in-need-of-a-refurb rented first-floor flat in North London the next afternoon.

'Neither can I,' I mutter yet again, sifting through the post that came while we were away.

I feel kind of strange for doing it – for kissing a man I'd only just met, directly after I'd experienced such a strong connection with another man. It was kind of risky, but also kind of exhilarating. It was a good kiss – so good I gave Josh my number. I gave Chris my number too. But the connection between us was less sexual, more . . . deep, conversational.

I wonder what would have happened if I'd said yes to his suggestion that I get on the plane. I think about it for the rest of the weekend. I gave Chris my number because I experienced a real spark, a feeling that I can't name. It was a connection that I've never had with anyone before, even in past relationships. None of them have been successful. They've all either been short-lived and have fizzled out quickly or, in the case of my last relationship, they go on for too long.

I didn't see it coming – the cheating. I wish I had. It blind-sided me because everything had been so *good*, so easy, or so I'd thought. I'd been the epitome of a chilled-out girlfriend, but my then-boyfriend Simon had been ready to move on for some time, he'd eventually told me. He'd been messaging other people in his downtime between seeing me, his phone constantly pinging away. Until messaging turned into something else entirely and a photo message lit up his screen briefly while he was holding it. It was of a woman wearing hot-pink lace underwear. I thought I was going mad, refusing to believe what I'd just seen. And then Simon swiped it away so fast he almost dropped his phone.

So . . . I feel Chris's pain. Having someone you trust, someone you're invested in, 'keep their options open' cut my heart wide open. I should probably be wary of it happening again, and I am, to an extent. But I'm also a firm believer that lightning doesn't strike twice and that you can't tar all men with the same brush. There are good ones out there. I simply don't seem to find them. But Chris – meeting him knocked me sideways. He'd been the highlight of the wedding, our conversation had been so *special*. And then there was Josh, and although we didn't have quite the same, immediate connection, there was *something* between us.

'So you won the bingo-to-end-all-bingos,' Scarlet reminds me. 'Any particular spa you want to go to?'

'You don't have to take me on a spa day, honestly,' I reply somewhat reluctantly, because it's the right thing to say, but actually I'd love to go on a spa day. And I definitely can't afford to pay for it myself.

'No. Fair's fair. We're going.'

'Thank you,' I tell her softly. 'You choose.'

I flick through the mail, while she online-browses Champneys spas. The post is mostly leaflets. Thankfully our joint bills arrive by email now, since Scarlet streamlined it all, which makes ignoring them so much easier than if they're made of paper, edged in red and propped up by the toaster, like they were this time last year.

'One for you,' I say, throwing the rest in the recycling and kicking off my shoes.

'Posh wedding invite: four hundred and fifty gsm,' she says, ripping it open and identifying the paper quality.

'You are the geekiest person I know,' I tell her.

'I work in graphic design. I'm allowed to be geeky about paper quality. When you're an interior designer, you're going to be all geeky over Egyptian cotton thread-count or sofa-cushion placement or whatever.'

'I'm already quite geeky about that,' I admit. 'Who's getting married now? I thought we were done for a while.'

'It's not until February. A Valentine's Day wedding – that'll be nice. Be my plus-one?'

'Obviously,' I tell her. 'I'm sure I'll still be single then, as per usual.'

'Me too,' she replies.

Although now I've agreed to it, I wonder whether I'll be able to afford to stay overnight anywhere, even if it's all the way off in February. I silently pray it's nearby in London and not somewhere far away that requires a hotel room, such as . . .

'Edinburgh, that'll be nice,' Scarlet says, casting the invite to one side as she goes off to her bedroom to unpack.

I sigh. How much are hotel rooms in Edinburgh? I need to sort out my life. I can't go on like this, cruising aimlessly. I'm not even cruising any more. I'm drifting. Away from my dream of being an interior designer, and away from the reality of any kind of gainful employment. First thing Monday morning I'm going to get back on the job hunt. I have to lower my expectations about what kind of job I'm qualified for, which is – pretty much no job at all. Since leaving university I've worked in admin, or on receptions, or as an assistant. The last proper job I had was essentially laminating security badges and handing them out to guests at a TV production company. I'd thought this was a step up from the usual admin roles, and it came with a snazzy made-up job title that didn't turn out to reflect the role I was doing at all. But everyone told me to stick with it, because it was a precious job in TV and 'Do you know how many people would kill to be in your position?'

It was fine while I worked out what I really wanted to do. And then the Fates decided for me. I got made redundant and all bets were suddenly off. I felt so low. It was like going back in time on the job-hunt front. Then too much time passed, the window between jobs widened and now my CV is a mess. Temping on and off for a year at my age – it's a hard one to explain to potential employers.

My parents told me that, in their day, working in the post room or on reception was a sure-fire step to one day becoming CEO, but I'm pretty damn sure those days are over, and that these days working in reception leads to . . . continuing to work in reception.

But that's how it's got to be, and I need to suck it up. I

have a history degree and I don't know why I chose it, on reflection. I just needed something to justify three years of university partying. But it's always proved pointless when it comes to job hunting.

Perhaps it's something to do with having to decline an invitation to New York with Chris because I'm broke – an invitation that could have been life-changing – but I am now feeling determined, and the Monday after arriving home from the wedding I start to fix my situation. I need to get out of the endless rotation of temping jobs and find something concrete in an industry I want to work in. I send out CV after CV, doctoring bits of it here and there, depending on the job I'm applying for. I nudge all those recruiters who months ago promised me the world, but delivered nothing. I will take anything at this point. While I wait to hear back from the design jobs, I've been placed on a two-week temporary agency contract that required no interview, thankfully. The temping role involves turning up and covering the reception phone lines for someone's annual leave. But after two weeks I'll be back in the wasteland again.

The only good thing about these temp jobs is that very little is expected of me, so I can sneakily snatch moments throughout the day when no one's watching my screen to work on my mood boards and portfolio – such as it is. I redecorated and designed my parents' house when they refurbished earlier this year. I managed to make a sixties semi-detached three-bed look like it belonged in *House & Garden*.

And then there was my grandmother's house, a quintessential English country cottage that we had to bring out of a bygone age in order to get potential buyers interested, when it had to be sold. It turns out Londoners looking to buy into that second-home lifestyle don't want to do any of the work themselves, so I had a go at sprucing it up. It wasn't a total renovation: the local council doesn't like it when you attempt to gut a Grade II listed property, so instead I made good with what was there, worked with the original features and built a fresh look. And all on a very tight budget.

Now I've finally got the time to edit my scant portfolio, although I'm not sure what I'm going to do with it, given that I have zero interior-design qualifications and know no one in the industry. A foot in the door, that's all I need. But I can't even get a job as a PA or a full-time receptionist. Becoming an interior designer – a proper one – feels so out of reach. Still, it's nice to have a focus.

My phone pings next to me and a message flashes up on my screen from a number I don't recognise.

How was the rest of the wedding?

Who's this? I wonder.

And then the answer. **It's Chris, by the way.**

I breathe in sharply and then smile. He's stopped typing, but he must see I'm online.

'Oh my God,' I say quietly. My fellow receptionist looks over at me. She's discreetly scrolling on her phone and glances back down at it again, when it's clear I'm not going to divulge more.

I'm so pleased he's texted me. I'm more than pleased. But I genuinely wasn't expecting him to. I rub my finger across my top lip while I work out what to type. Should I play it cool? Should I tell him how excited I am he's messaged? I should probably do neither of those things. He's opened up a conversation by asking a question. I'm just going to answer it.

The wedding was great. There were fireworks. I pause before hitting send. I want to say something funny. **But sadly no fights,** I finish with.

Chris sends back a laughing emoji.

I wait for more, but there's nothing, so I wonder if he's waiting for me to keep going or if he also can't work out what to say next.

How was your flight? I ask.

You made the right decision deciding not to come, he writes cryptically. I wait while he continues typing. **Two solid hours of pure turbulence midway across the Atlantic.**

Ugh, I reply. **I don't love turbulence.**

Neither does anyone sane, he says. **It might have been a bit of a mood-kill for you and me. Also, the woman in front of me threw up.**

Delightful, I reply, but I'm enjoying his mind's process, the reminder of romance that he's introduced between us – **you and me . . .** – a few days after we met and then had to immediately say goodbye.

He carries on. **I was watching *Sully* throughout the turbulence. You know, the Tom Hanks film where he's a pilot carrying out an emergency landing on the Hudson River? It was like being on a far-too-realistic flight simulator. I had to switch over to *Friends*.**

I laugh and then type, **Wise move. I did feel this deep sense of regret after I said no, but I hate turbulence and people throwing up near me, so you've reassured me now.**

Did you? he asks. **Feel regret? Really?**

Yes, I reply honestly. **I wondered . . . what if?**

Chris doesn't immediately reply and I stiffen, panicking I've said the wrong thing. I can't see his reaction. I'd have said that to his face, if we'd have been having this conversation at the wedding. But now I'm scared I've been too honest.

Me too, he comes back with. My body gives up its stiffness at his reply and I lean back into my seat. How far can we take this? I don't even want to consider that there's no point in this. I refuse to consider it. If there's no point in it, why are we doing it? I haven't even kissed this man and yet I'm wrapped up in him – thoughts of what it would have been like if I had gone with him. I'm so wrapped up that I don't notice someone standing in front of me, attempting to check in for a meeting. I put my phone down to deal with the enquiry, but when I pick my phone back up again, Chris is no longer online. He must be at work too, although hours behind me.

I don't know how to restart the conversation. And if I do restart it, where this might go? Might we talk more, video-call? Might we make idealistic plans that we can't actually see through to their conclusion? Might it hurt me more doing that than if I do nothing at all?

Chapter Six

Chris

I tap my fingers on my desk as my screen goes blank. I waited a few seconds for Lexie to reply and, when no reply came, my phone locked. **I did feel this deep sense of regret after I said no.** Her words played in my mind while I waited. I wasn't expecting that.

I'm grinning from ear to ear. I wonder what she's up to. I might leave it a while before I start a conversation back up again. I don't want to look too keen. Although I've already shown how keen I am by inviting her to get on a plane with me. In hindsight, this was the act of a crazy person, because I am not that impetuous – ever. I'm thoughtful and methodical. Lexie caught me off-guard. How I felt in her company was something I'd never experienced before.

Asking her to come with me to New York was a strange choice, but it felt so right, *so right.* Though I'm at work now. And having to go to work was a detail I conveniently forgot when I was casually throwing around overblown romantic gestures. Although it wasn't casual, not really. I meant it.

This feeling is so new to me. And maddening. Not least

because Lexie is halfway across the world, but also because having only just been dumped a few months ago and getting over the general bafflement of that, there are things I had planned here, places I wanted to see, things I wanted to do, a life I wanted to build. It was a life I had envisaged for myself when I moved here, but it didn't happen. I fell into a relationship, of sorts, too quickly. And that meant falling into step with another person's life. Evenings spent with her friends because I had yet to make any. Weekends doing what she suggested because I didn't know my way around the city enough to scout out the kind of places I might like to visit. I didn't really know what I wanted to do. I still don't. Not really.

It's easy to be led when you're in a couple. And can you truly know who you are when you rely on another person so heavily? Then there was Big Talk with Lexie. Having a plus-one on my arm would have inhibited me from meeting and spending time with her. I need to be by myself for a while. It's essential for my own well-being.

But I also needed to connect with Lexie again. Just to say hi. I couldn't stop myself, even though I know falling for Lexie feels like it's not supposed to happen now – not from such a distance. And especially not when I feel so unsure of my life here in New York. I told her another time, another place, and I meant it. We left each other at the wedding knowing it was a non-starter or she'd have come with me, right?

So now is my chance. I'm going to live my life how I want to. Just for a while. I'm going to book in activities at weekends and after work and, finally, I'm going to work out who *I* want to be.

Chapter Seven

Lexie

It's Tuesday and I've only got three days left before the weekend. I can't wait.

I've been trying not to pick up my phone too much as I don't want to look like a slacker, but I'm on my own, as the girl next to me is on her lunch break. I grab my mobile and half-heartedly search for jobs, but I'm distracted as the screen lights up with the words: **Lexie, it was good to meet you at the wedding. This is my number. Do you fancy lunch with me on Sunday? Josh.**

Oh my word, what is going on? When I saw the text come through, I hoped it might be Chris. But it's not. *Josh* is messaging me. I don't know how I feel about this. Flattered, I think. But lunch feels like a strange first date. Surely evening drinks, or even dinner, is the norm for a first date. I've never been asked out on a first date in the middle of the day on a Sunday. I look at the message for a while, then put my phone away.

It's only when I get home later that night that I decide to reply, because I wasn't sure if I wanted to go on a date at all.

Dates can be torture. *Warm wine, zero personality*. Although I know Josh has a good personality, so that's that box ticked. He's also hot, and a great kisser . . . There is, however, this slightly odd feeling that what I'm doing with Josh is some form of betrayal, coming as it does on the back of what went on between Chris and me, or rather what is still going on between Chris and me. Chris was there and then he was gone. I thought that was it. But now we're talking across the airwaves and that feeling from when we first met . . . it hasn't gone away. It's intensified.

I wondered . . . what if?

Me too.

It's hard not to feel totally alive after that conversational connection. But Josh is the one who's here, and he's kind – saving me at the bar as he did – and funny. And attractive. What if I don't take the possibility of Josh seriously? I might be throwing something away that has potential, because he is here, right now, on this text message, asking me out. And Chris . . . is not.

Oh, Lexie, just get on with it. Take a chance. Get on with your life.

All right then, I reply and then hit save on his number.

All right then? he echoes immediately. **What kind of reply is that?** He adds a laughing emoji.

I'm quick to type back. **Why lunch?**

I'm quite tight on time on Sunday. Lunch is all I can squeeze in. I've got a few hours, though. Any good?

And there was I, thinking *I* was playing it cool. But it's Josh who's squeezing me in around other events, other things going on in his life. Now I want to know what he's fitting me in around. Well played, Josh.

I agree to our day-date and Josh says he'll message me a location later on. That evening he sends me the link to a venue, which turns out to be in the far reaches of the West End. He asks if I can get there with ease, which I can, although it's a bit of a journey from where I live in Edmonton Green. I am now curious about Josh – where he lives, what he does and why he's tight on time on a Sunday. That's good, isn't it? To have a level of curiosity about someone you've already kissed, someone you've already stripped away a layer from.

I climb into bed later that night and pick up my phone. I look at Josh's messages again, the easy exchange we had, the speed at which we settled on a location and a time.

I'm single and in demand. I should just roll with it – roll with all of it, see what happens.

It was easy to get caught up in the moment with Chris. But I feel more vulnerable in the relative safety of being a keyboard warrior than I would if he was standing in front of me. If he was here with me, I feel as if I could say anything. How did he get me to feel that so early on? As if the universe hears me, a message from Chris lands on my screen, a simple **Hi**, which does things to me it shouldn't.

It's early evening in New York, so I'm guessing he's just finishing his working day. I wonder if he's already eating dinner or catching a train or a bus home from work. Perhaps he's in a bar with some friends or still at his desk and has chosen this moment to break free for a minute, to message me.

I didn't scare you off with my 'what if' comment? I test.

Why would you scare me off? he replies. I was feeling the same thing. Still am.

And although his words are so simple, my world fills with colour. I'm placing too much on our connection, I'm sure of it.

I worried I'd scared you off by inviting you out here, he continues. Although I have since realised we'd only have had one day together before I had to go to work. I was a bit cavalier with my invite.

I like cavalier, I say. Go on, taunt me with all the fun things we could have got up to in New York before you'd have cruelly left me to my own devices.

He's typing for ages and I watch, inhaling deeply in anticipation. The message lands in one big paragraph. I'd thought about this. We'd sleep off our jet lag, although I'm a pro now, but I'd have been patient while you slept. Then brunch. I've been trying to really discover the city, making a point of finding places I like, rather than going where everyone else goes or where I've been used to going. We'd have been for a walk in the park. Right down The Mall, with all the trees. I admit that's where everyone goes, but I really like that walk. I think you'd have liked it too. A stop for coffee. If you wanted to see anywhere else, we'd have factored that in. Shops, or whatever. I'd have given you carte blanche to be a tourist. I'd have been happy just being in your company.

I smile at this. He'd have been happy just being in my company. My heart! What is he doing to me? The day sounds perfect, I reply. Minus the shops. I would love that, but shopping in New York would have been financial suicide. A girl

can dream, though. All of it's a dream really. New York with Chris was a lovely idea, but not a reality. I can play along, though. **And then what?**

I'm not sure I thought much past that, he types and I suspect he's not telling the truth. He must have given sleeping arrangements at least a passing thought. **Dinner,** he says. **And then . . .**

He leaves that opener there.

How many bedrooms does your flat have? I ask, probably a bit too suggestively, but now I like that he can't see me and I can't see him. There is safety in hiding behind a keyboard after all.

One, he replies and then says nothing.

I say nothing. I'm smiling, though, and the silence from him is killing me. I won't be the first to break. I stare at the phone. Still nothing, so I cave. **Where would I have slept?**

Perhaps I didn't think about that part, either, when I threw that invite out there. Where would you have wanted to sleep? he asks.

That's not fair, turning it on me like that. Although I am the one who started this line of questioning. I put a laughing emoji, so Chris knows I'm being light-hearted.

One of us would have been on the sofa, I'm sure, he replies. He's at least insinuating that he would have been a gentleman.

Are you sure? How big is your sofa? I ask.

Not that big. And not that comfy, either, he says. **Not very good for sleeping on.**

I chuckle. **I wonder what we'd have done about that?** I dare, because I'm not a nun, and Chris is gorgeous.

He puts a laughing emoji. And then he's offline. What? Where's he gone? A minute passes, two minutes.

And then he's back and my screen lights up. **Sorry,** he says. **The designer just came over to get me, as we're heading out the door to someone's leaving drinks, and I couldn't get my phone out of his eyeline quick enough. I have no idea how much of that he saw!**

You're still at work?

I'm leaving now, he says, **though I'm a little hotter under the collar than I was before we started talking.**

It's my turn to put a laughing emoji in our chat.

Speak tomorrow? he asks.

Yes, please.

Chapter Eight

On a sliding scale of one to ten, how hungover are you? I message Chris as I'm walking to the Tube station after work. I'm meeting Scarlet at Oxford Street to go shopping for her mum's birthday present. Then we're treating ourselves to a few drinks in a new bar. Scarlet worked on their logo, but I can see my entire day's earnings being spent on a round of drinks and some nibbles unless Scarlet can wangle us some freebies.

I've hung on all day to message Chris. I don't want to look too eager and he wouldn't be awake until a few hours ago, so I'm playing it cool, safe.

One is his reply to me. It was a midweek drink with very uptight New Yorkers. I'm afraid they don't do leaving parties the way we do.

I did wonder, I tell him. A leaving party not on a Friday isn't a leaving party, is it?

Amen, Chris replies. Where in London are you right now?

Oxford Street. I've just left work.

Oxford Street at night. That whole vibe makes me miss London, Chris writes. Tell me all the things you can see. (Leave out the rubbish bits.)

I laugh and someone jostles into me as I slow on the

pavement to type my message. I stand near a bus stop to keep out of the way of busy pedestrians with no time for dawdlers. I tell Chris all about the lights beaming out from the shops, and the early diners enjoying pre-theatre dinner, the office-types heading into bars and sushi joints.

A lot like New York, no? I ask.

A bit, he says.

I've got time to kill until I meet Scarlet, so I wander into Selfridges. I'm not really paying attention to the perfume and cosmetics counters and I find myself meandering aimlessly, glancing up every now and again from my phone as Chris and I message back and forth about our days, and our lives. Chris takes a selfie in his office and sends it to me. The office is open-plan, and bright-eyed workers look busy at their desks, unaware he's snapped them and inadvertently sent their images to a woman in a busy London department store. He looks good. Exactly as he did at the wedding, although the suit he's in is less formal. He has a slim build, like a runner. He's smiling and seems relaxed. I zoom in on his eyes, which are wonderfully intoxicating, a smooth nut-brown.

I reciprocate with a pic of me in the Selfridges shoe department, tilting the phone to get my best angle. I applied a ton of make-up before I left my desk, so I should look fairly presentable. I zoom in on my own eyes to check my mascara is exactly where I put it less than an hour ago. It is and I hit send.

It's nice to see you again, Chris says.

And it's nice to see him too. This is easy. Too easy. And given the fact we've only met once, I wonder if it shouldn't be. Surely this should be harder? Weirder? But it feels none of those things.

I've got to step into a meeting now, Chris types. **Just in case you wonder why I've gone silent.**

I've got to go and taunt my best friend about shoes, I reply. **Just in case you wonder the same.**

Er, OK, Chris says. **You can explain that one later. Bye for now x**

Bye x, I answer.

Then I take a pic of a pair of Louboutins, send it to Scarlet, make a joke about how there are no prizes for coming last and wait for the fallout.

Chapter Nine

Chris

Hamilton? Lexie messages after I told her how I spent last night, which involved buying spur-of-the-moment discounted tickets to the theatre. I think it was her mention of a pre-theatre dinner. It made me realise I've not seen a show in . . . for ever.

I'm so jealous, she types. I haven't seen it yet. Theatre in London is getting so expensive. What did you think?

Loved it. Didn't think I would, but I wanted to see.

Why didn't you think you'd like it? she asks.

It's a musical.

Yes, it is. You don't like musicals?

Not really, I reply.

I love them, she says. The singing, the dancing, the sets, I can't get enough.

Well, now I know I like them too. Or, rather, I like *Hamilton*. I'm not sure about the rest.

Maybe you should do them all one after the other. *Wicked* next week, *Phantom of the Opera* the week after . . .

I might not do that, I think. Working out what I do and don't like is costing me a fortune, and fitting it in around work projects is proving tricky. I like one musical. So far. Let's tick that box and move on.

I glance down to see another message has landed. **Who did you go with?** she asks.

I don't answer for a second. How do I explain this? How do I explain that it was really all our Big Talk that inspired me to expand my horizons. Hmm, I'm not sure how to do this, so instead I type, **I didn't go with anyone. Fancied a night out by myself.**

She's not typing.

Am I coming across as weird? I ask.

No. It's cool. I've never done that before: a night out by myself.

You should, I tell her. **I'm sort of** . . . How do I say this? **Trying to see what I like and don't like. Letting myself discover who I am.** I cringe, hit send, wait for the inevitable laughter emoji.

But there was no need to be concerned about what Lexie thought as she replies with a little smiling emoji and **What's prompted this?**

I like Lexie. I don't want to lie, but I'm not sure I want to pour my heart out via a messaging system. I don't want to say: **It was you.** I don't want to say: **I've realised, since meeting you, that the reason my relationships fail is because I never take the lead, or the initiative to discover who I really am. And if I don't know who I am, then how the hell is**

anyone else supposed to? I condense this down into something less manic.

I think it was our conversation – our Big Talk about past relationships. It nudged me in this direction. And then my internal monologue when I got home nudged me even further.

It sounds like a fun direction in which to be nudged, she types. **Taking yourself out for dates and doing all the things most of us don't get time to do, because we're wrapped up doing what other people want us to do or need us to do. Are you enjoying it?**

She gets it.

I think about her question for a second. I haven't asked myself this. **Yeah, I suppose I am. It's not every night, and I can always go for drinks with friends and workmates if I want to. I'm just choosing to be a bit selective socially while I figure all this out. And I don't want to take people on dates, or swipe endlessly on women's profile pictures and interests.**

I don't tell her that it's also because I want to be single. I'm not sure why. I wonder if I'd have said that if she'd been here, with me in my apartment. Of course not. We wouldn't be having chats like this if she'd been here. We'd be . . . what would we be doing? Falling for each other? Big Talk, but not the kind where I tell a woman, to her face, that I really, really like that I'm happy being single.

Which is why it's good Lexie's in London and I'm here. It makes my mission to be single easier *and* I still get to talk to her. This is almost too perfect. So why is my mind a mess?

We sign off our chat, and once again I notice that even though I've held back a bit, it's fallen into Big Talk.

We have a habit of doing this, Lexie and me.

What I learned about myself this week: I do not like modern art. In one of my lunch breaks I took myself off to a nearby gallery. I'd seen a post on Instagram about the exhibition and, instead of asking someone in the office if they wanted to come with me, I thought I'd give it a go on my own, keep this solo life going. I enjoyed *that*, but the gallery itself was not my thing at all. But recognising this is positive. I learned a couple of new things about myself this week and I see that as an accomplishment.

In bed last night I browsed a bunch of artists online and discovered I like Edward Hopper, John Everett Millais and the photographer David Bailey. I realise this is an eclectic mix of media from across the ages, but discovering what I like and don't like – and doing it by myself – is my new project.

I message Lexie during the day, although it'll be the early hours of the morning for her, so I hope she switches her phone to silent during the night, as I don't want to wake her up.

Big Talk round four: if you could only take one piece of art with you to a desert island, what would it be? I'll start. John Everett Millais's *Ophelia*. I just discovered him and think he might be my favourite artist.

Three hours later, Lexie replies. **This is some Big Talk for first thing in the morning,** and she attaches a laughing emoji. **Unpopular opinion, but I don't really like *Ophelia*. I do like Millais, though, before you decide never to talk to me again.**

I went to a museum in Cambridge and far and away the most interesting picture was one of Millais'. I can't remember what it's called, but I stared at it for ages. I was captivated. Hang on, I am going to have to do some googling to find this thing.

I smile and wait. I'm sitting at my desk and am now intrigued.

The Twins, Kate and Grace Hoare is the most unimaginative title ever, but that's what it's called, she types. I just looked at it online and I still love it. They're identical twins, but look at their expressions. I don't know which one is which, but the one on the right looks so anxious, so pensive, but the one on the left looks so calm, serene, open. I think he's so clever to make two women who look identical look so different. I love it.

And this is the one you want to take with you to your desert island? I ask, and then I click off our chat and go and look. Lexie's right. It is a captivating image.

She's offline and I catch myself tapping my fingers on my desk waiting for her reply.

It's 6.30 a.m., she says, so I feel any decision made before coffee might not be the best, but . . . OK. I'm all in. I'm taking this one with me. It's fabulous and it's also a huge canvas. The women are almost life-sized. I'll let you keep *Ophelia*.

What do you have against *Ophelia*?

She dies.

What? I ask.

She dies, Lexie types again. And in a case of life imitating art, or whatever that phrase is – Lizzie Siddal, the model who posed for it in a bath of water, caught a chill afterwards and got quite sick. So . . . there's that.

How do you know so much about this? I ask.

I went to an exhibition, she replies. **Although I haven't been to one in ages. And now I need to get up, get dressed, get coffee and go to work.**

I can feel your excitement from all the way over here, I tell her.

Ha! She puts a laughing emoji. **It was nice to wake up to a message from you, though. This time zone thing is quite good for that.**

Yes, I tell her. **It is.**

Chapter Ten

Lexie

Josh stands to greet me when I arrive at the gastropub he's suggested. He looks good, his blue eyes twinkle when I arrive and he's wearing a very lovely fitted white shirt tucked into pale-blue jeans. Men just manage to nail smart-casual so much easier than women. I'm in a wrap dress and flats, because I had no idea how casual the venue would be. It's in Marylebone and it's pretending to be a relaxed boozer, when it is in fact a staggeringly expensive gastropub. I've caught sight of the menu and am desperately hoping Josh remembers my credit card is maxed out or this could get embarrassing. He leans in to kiss my cheek and I kiss his in return.

'You look . . . great,' he says, ushering me next to him in our semicircular booth-style table. The pub is busy, exuding a hint of glamour played down with antique curios. It's good to have the sounds of other revellers drowning out what I sense might possibly turn out to be an awkward first date. It was all fine and easy when we were a few drinks in and bantering about wedding bingo. But I wonder now, sober and in the middle of the day, if we'll have enough to talk about. I'm not sure how I feel, being on this date. Part of me regretted saying yes this morning and I thought about cancelling. But I've got to put myself out there a bit more, say yes to things.

'Thanks. You look good too,' I reply.

'I didn't think you were going to come,' Josh says with a laugh. He's not wearing his devil-may-care-stubble today – he's freshly shaven and I'm not sure which version of him I prefer.

'Why did you think I wasn't going to come?' I'm surprised at his confession, while also wondering if he somehow magically sensed my hesitation.

'I don't do this kind of thing often,' he says. 'I'm not sure what the protocol is. When people – women – say they're going to turn up for lunch, if they . . . really will turn up. It was a bit of a surprise when you walked through the door. A nice one. I genuinely didn't expect you to.'

Well, now I feel guilty about considering cancelling. 'The same way as when you goaded me into kissing you and I did, you didn't expect that, either,' I tease.

He smiles. 'I should probably stop underestimating you.' There's something in his expression that sends a light tremor of excitement through me.

'Might be a good idea,' I say, mock-seductively.

A waitress takes our drinks order, although we've not looked at a wine list yet, and so I suggest a bottle of house red and Josh agrees.

'Did you *honestly* think I wasn't going to turn up?' I ask.

'I don't know,' he replies. 'I'm glad you did, though.'

I'm starting to feel more curious about Josh and ask him, 'When did you last go on a date?'

He pauses, and his gaze moves gently to the side as he works it out. 'A proper one? Like this?'

I nod.

'Maybe two years ago.'

'Two *years* . . . ? You're joking? Have you just been released from prison or are you freshly divorced?'

'No,' he answers, laughing. 'Neither of those things. Do I look like enough of a bad boy to have been incarcerated? I'm not sure how to take that,' he says with a shocked grin.

'Why so long, then?' I ask.

'I've dated – sort of – but I'm so busy with work and life and . . . all that stuff. You know?'

No, I think. I *wish* I was so busy with work that I'd lost the ability to date. I've dated a bit since my last disaster of a relationship. A swipe here and a swipe there. But it's been one and done, with each of them. Soulless guys in soulless bars. All of them combine into one immemorable man – the cut-out-and-keep proverbial bad date.

The waitress saves me, returning to take our order. We both opt for fried courgette with flaked truffle to start, followed by roast beef.

'Is it boring that we're both having the same thing?' he asks.

'Nope. It means we're in sync, food-wise,' I say and lift my glass of wine. 'We'll have to choose different puddings, though.'

'Cheers,' Josh says and we clink glasses. 'I thought a

roast dinner was probably an OK suggestion for a Sunday, especially given it's not too hot out there. Sort of autumnal enough today, now it's almost September, to get away with being indoors for lunch.'

'You know summer's over when there are no more weddings. Well, for now,' I say.

'Have you had a lot?'

'Too many. It's all got very expensive. But I am seeing a lot of the UK.' I tell him about Scarlet and me being each other's plus-ones throughout the wedding season last year, and again this year. 'They all sort of merge into one. Hence why we initiated the bingo game.'

I watch Josh smile, dip his gaze down and then back up to me again. 'Oh yeah,' he says slowly, softly. 'The bingo game. I must admit that worked out well for me.'

'I didn't do too badly out of it, either,' I say as our starters are placed in front of us. 'Although it is all a bit upside down, this way round, isn't it? Kissing first and then going on a date.'

'Do you know,' Josh says, 'I think everyone should kiss first, date after.'

'Really?' I ask, my fork halfway to my mouth.

'Hear me out,' he continues. 'If you and I hadn't kissed, we wouldn't be here right now, would we?'

'We might,' I say. 'You asked me to dance, remember. If I hadn't had to rush off to hand someone a drink, who knows where that might have led.'

He looks at me as if he's not quite sure what I'm insinuating. Am I being suggestive? Is he? I quite like this.

'You tried to turn me down?' he says. It's a question, not a statement. 'Don't think I didn't notice. You didn't initially want to dance with me, but you *did* want to kiss me?' He draws out the next word: 'In-ter-esting.'

'Perhaps it was the dance that sealed the deal for the kiss?' I suggest. 'You asked so sweetly as well, but I'd already agreed to go back to the terrace with drinks for someone else. I left them standing alone for ages so that I could sway awkwardly with you.'

Josh laughs loudly.

'But as if I could turn you down. Especially as you paid for the drinks.'

He smiles and looks thoughtful. 'I'd forgotten about that.'

By the time we reach our main courses we've drunk most of the bottle of wine and have agreed to order a second.

'You don't have to drive then?' Josh asks me as two plates of roast beef and all the trimmings are placed in front of us. There's so much food, but I'm starving, and I haven't lined my stomach enough for the amount of wine I'm drinking. I'm having a really nice time. Josh is so easy to talk to; he's kind of sweet too, sort of unsure of himself, but handsome enough to carry it off.

'Drive? In central London?' I ask. 'Of course not. Do you?'

'No, but I've got to get up stupid early in the morning.'

'Well, yeah, it is Monday tomorrow,' I say. 'How early is stupid early?'

'Five-thirty a.m.'

'Ugh! Why?'

'Work,' he replies and then asks me, 'What do you do?'

74

I tell him I'm temping while I work my way towards something better, although I'm not really sure what that *better* actually is. I tell him I want to be an interior designer one day, and then I wait for the inevitable advice to be dispensed, but Josh doesn't offer any, simply saying, 'Great. I've no idea how office jobs work. Is it an easy leap from temping on reception to interior design?'

'Of course not,' I say. 'Oh, wait, you're taking the piss.'

'A little bit,' he replies and leans forward to top up both our glasses. 'Do you . . . have a plan as to how you can become an interior designer? Can you temp and study for it at the same time?'

'The thought of doing another degree fills me with dread, but now that I know I really do want to be a designer, I've started thinking about courses that won't suck three years of my life out of me.'

'Can you do an online one or an evening one, or . . . I dunno how it works.'

'I suppose I'm having so much trouble actually finding a *normal* job that it didn't seem realistic to take my fantasies about my *dream* job any further right now. I've been focusing on working on my portfolio and hoping an internship in a design company might crop up.'

Josh nods, but looks unconvinced. I'm sure I do too. 'I might have another little look at courses when I get home later,' I tell him. And I will, although I need to get a proper job in order to fund a course. I shudder inwardly.

I direct my gaze fully at him, noticing again those little flecks of grey within his blue eyes, a little frown line running vertically in between his eyebrows. He looks a little rough around the edges, kind of rugged, not too perfect.

He looks back at me and there's a quiet moment between us until I think we both realise we're looking at each other for far too long. I take a mouthful of the delicious roast beef in order to avert my gaze. I still haven't started on the cauliflower cheese yet, but I fully intend to. I might not eat this well again for months.

'How's your food?' he asks, gesturing to my plate.

'It's incredible,' I say. 'I think it's the best beef I've ever had. I regret drowning it in so much gravy now. It's like butter, does that make sense? Like if silk was a food.' I start on the cauliflower cheese.

He laughs. 'If silk was a food,' he echoes thoughtfully.

'Where do you live?' I ask, putting my knife and fork down for a bit. I want to look polite and not as if I'm eating for survival – which I am.

'Somerset,' he says.

I frown. 'Which bit of London is that?'

He laughs. 'It's not,' he replies. 'It's just at the bottom of the Cotswolds.'

'Oh,' I say, and I'm sure my mouth has dropped open. 'You live in *the Cotswolds*?'

'Yeah.'

I sit back, stare at him. 'Really?'

It's his turn to frown, to stare back at me. 'Yeah.'

'Oh,' I repeat, wondering why we're here, having this date, if he lives nowhere near me? I'm reminded of Chris and his early disclosure that he lives in New York. It's happened to me again. I can't believe this.

'Hang on,' I say, hazily remembering our chat at the wedding. 'I asked if you lived in London and you said yes.'

He recoils a bit. 'No. No, you didn't. You, rather weirdly, asked if I lived somewhere that required a plane ride to get to.'

I look at Josh directly. I feel I've been duped and I'm not sure why. 'I just assumed you lived in London,' I say rather pathetically.

'Does it matter?' Josh asks. 'Have you got an aversion to anyone who lives outside the M25?'

'No, of course not,' I tell him. 'But . . . how long does it take you to get into London from Somerset?'

'About two hours, as long as the trains aren't running late. I've got a bit of a drive at the other end as well, but today my mate's picking me up later, so I could have some drinks with you.'

'Oh my God,' I say loudly. 'You live for ever away.'

He laughs. 'Well, not really. I mean, it's a bit of a drive or – you know – the train.'

'I'm totally thrown by this,' I tell him honestly.

'I can see that,' Josh replies and his shoulders rise and fall briefly as he chuckles. 'In a way I should probably take this as a good sign: you being a little miffed that I live quite far away. If you didn't like me, you wouldn't care.'

I narrow my eyes, but I can't help smiling. Maybe he's right.

I lean forward, take up my wine glass, sit back and think. 'What do you do, all the way out in Somerset?'

'I'm a farmer,' he says and I actually cough on my wine. The surprises keep coming.

'You're a *farmer*? A real one?'

'A real one,' he confirms.

'I can't tell if you're pulling my leg.'

'I'm really not. I'm probably one of the most honest people you're ever going to meet. To a fault. I live in Somerset and I'm a farmer.'

I look at this man. slightly rugged, very tanned and, dare I say it, handsome and I can see it. I see that he's not like everyone else in this restaurant. He's different. Earthier, raw, but in a good way.

'What do you farm?' I ask, determined to catch him out. 'Or are you actually a stockbroker, and any second now you're going to cave in and confess you live in Islington?'

'Beef and dairy,' he replies. He's enjoying this, I can tell. 'I farmed the lunch you just ate. That's why I chose this particular pub. I'm one of their suppliers.'

My mouth opens in surprise and I feel it move into a smile. Josh is refreshing, in so many ways.

'Well,' I say, failing to mask my disbelief. 'This city girl is surprised. I didn't see that coming.'

'I can't tell if it's put you off,' Josh says, sitting back. 'If I ask you out again . . . ?' He leaves that question there.

'How would we do that?' I ask, as I can't see how the logistics of this are going to work. But . . . I am interested in seeing Josh again. This revelation surprises me. I didn't see it going past this one date, which is why it felt fine to book it in the first place. To put myself out there.

But at the back of my mind is Chris. It felt wrong to be seeing Josh when I'm messaging Chris. I know this is how it works these days. I know we all need to keep our options open in the early days – only make decisions when decisions need to be made. But it just feels a bit seedy. It's having been cheated on; I know that's what's making me hypersensitive to the possibility of hurting someone else. And getting hurt myself.

'I get Sundays off. Or, rather, I force myself to take Sundays off while someone else from my team looks after the animals. I could come back into London again next week, late on Saturday, and get a hotel for the night, spend the evening with you, all of Sunday if you want – it could work. But how about . . .' he says teasingly, 'how about we see how the rest of the lunch goes? I might yet change my mind.'

I play-thump him on his arm and Josh winces, laughs.

Conversation flows so easily as we learn more about each other. And, in contrast to how it was with Chris, there is so much small talk. It's the details, the tiny little nicks and cuts of a human that make them who they are, and I like finding out these things about Josh. By the time we've finished lunch, opting for coffee over dessert, we decide to walk off our food. I'm reluctant to leave the dark and moody surroundings of the pub; it's a little bubble where Josh and I have dined and laughed, talked and drunk. We sidled a little closer to each other when coffee came, and I could feel the heat emanating from his arm as he showed me pictures of his farm on his phone. I told him I needed some sort of proof.

Exiting the pub, we're confronted by the bright glare of the late-summer sun 'It feels later, like it should be night-time,' I say, fumbling in my bag for my sunglasses. Josh hasn't brought any and I can see white lines around the side of his eyes where the sun doesn't get in, as he must wince in the glare when he's working. We walk for a while as I grill him about farm life. I'm enjoying hearing more about this man and, as we cross the road, his hand rests on my back to escort me towards Kensington Palace Gardens.

'You're quite the gentleman, aren't you?' I say as we enter the lush green space.

'I'm well-trained,' he replies. 'I always forget London has such huge parks.' People ride bikes past, and families with small children meander next to us. 'It feels like the countryside.'

'Do you want to be a tourist and get tickets for the palace?'

'I can't,' Josh says reluctantly. 'I have to go soon.'

My eyes widen. 'Already?' Men keep running out on me.

'Sadly,' he says. I think he means it. 'I didn't like to auto-matically presume this would go well, so I booked a return ticket and I haven't got long.'

'Oh,' I reply, sadness sweeping me up in its grasp. That has to be a good sign, because I don't want him to go. I wonder briefly if he's going to do a Chris – invite me to go with him. But Josh doesn't.

We're on a tree-lined avenue with cherry and magnolia

glades on either side and, as we naturally come to a stop, Josh says, 'Can I see you again?'

'Yes,' I reply meaningfully. 'I'd like that.'

'Next weekend?' he suggests and I agree.

'Can I walk with you to the station?' I ask.

He glances at his watch. 'I genuinely think I'm going to have to break into a run or I will miss my train. It's not going to look effortless or cool, but I've got no choice.'

'Oh, OK then. Quickly. Go!'

'But first,' he says and dips his head, brushes his lips against my cheek, withdraws and backs away.

'No proper kiss this time?' I call after him.

'Something to look forward to next weekend,' he calls back, laughing from a few feet away. And then he changes his mind, comes back to me, pulls me towards him and kisses me. I love how his body feels pressed against mine, how his mouth feels against mine, how we feel in each other's arms – here, like this. It's so hot and so unexpected. All of it.

He pulls away, brushes my lips with his once more, lightly, which is far too seductive for this time and place. 'OK, I *really* need to go now,' he says. 'I'll call you?'

'Yes, please,' I reply.

He turns and jogs away, raising his arm in the air to wave, and I can't help laughing because Josh was not at *all* what I was expecting.

Chapter Eleven

'A farmer? A real one?' Hours later Scarlet echoes the exact words that I spoke to Josh, when she walks through the door after a day spent shopping and I tell her how my date went.

'It was the oddest date I've been on in ages,' I reflect.

'It's the *only* date you've been on in ages,' Scarlet points out. 'Why was it odd?'

I pause and think. 'I'm not really sure. I just felt odd. But *good* odd . . . you know?'

She gives me a curious look. 'Do you like him?'

I think about this for a second. I do like Josh, and getting to know him is going at a slower pace than the quick-fire Big Talk way I've got to know Chris. I've got the luxury of time with Josh, but I'm in a bit of a quandary because I like Chris too. So much.

I wondered . . . what if?

Me too.

'Yeah,' I say slowly, thinking about it. 'I do like Josh.'

'And you like him despite the fact he lives in a part of the country you'd never heard of?' Scarlet teases with a roar of laughter, following it with, 'I can't believe you thought Somerset was a London borough.'

'He caught me off-guard. I wasn't expecting to be told

he lives in the Cotswolds or the West Country, or whatever you call it.'

'Nice part of the world,' Scarlet says absently. 'Lots of celebs live there. Went to a wedding there once.'

'I've never been,' I tell her.

'You might get the chance,' she replies. 'You might end up shacking up with a farmer . . . Stranger things have happened.'

'I doubt it. It's probably a two-date thing,' I say. Although I'm reminded of that kiss and how lovely Josh is, and handsome, and rugged . . . in a farmer-way that makes sense, now I know he is indeed a farmer.

'When are you seeing him next?' she asks.

'Saturday. He's going to stay overnight in a hotel.'

Scarlet's eyes widen and a knowing smile crosses her face. '*Is* he now?'

'I won't be going back there with him after our date.'

'We'll see,' she replies.

I'm at my desk at my temp job on Friday afternoon – or, rather, I'm at someone else's desk covering their annual leave – manning the phones and cobbling together security badges and lanyards yet again. It's at a not-so-busy office block in the City, where each floor is rented out to different companies and it's interesting watching all the various people coming and going.

Actually it's not interesting at all, and that's why I'm discreetly scrolling through interior design courses on the computer in front of me. All the scrolling and clicking makes me look busy, which is one thing, I suppose. I'm over-whelmed by how many courses there are and how many are spread across London at various 'creative' campuses. And as if the confusion wasn't enough, they are eye-wateringly expensive, if I want to attend either in person or from home. After about an hour of research and taking notes about prices and colleges, I close the browser. Being an interior designer felt more like a possibility yesterday than it does today. This just doesn't feel feasible for me at the minute, financially or time-wise, if I'm going to work at the same time.

A dream is a dream for a reason, I suppose. Maybe it's best to keep it that way.

My phone dings, and it's Josh asking if I'm still on for our date tomorrow evening. I answer immediately. We've been texting back and forth a little bit here and there through the week. It's slow, casual, easy.

The same can be said of Chris, as he messaged and we picked up our conversation straight away, comparing art we like, films we hate, books we own, but haven't read. I can't text back quickly enough and I feel my face form an easy smile whenever one of his messages lands on my screen. But when Josh's messages arrive, I feel heightened too – in a good way.

On Monday evening I thanked Josh for a lovely date the previous day and then followed it up with a request for a pic-ture of him on his farm. I'm not sure what I was expecting, but I got a very early-morning selfie on Tuesday of Josh fit-ting some kind of contraption to a cow's udders. I was hoping for a pic of him chopping wood or something equally sexy.

I think I've misjudged what goes on in a farmer's world. I had no idea how to reply to the photo he sent, and instead focused on the presence of his morning stubble. And then on Wednesday I sent him a selfie of me at work, because my life is so utterly boring it was either that or a selfie of me walking *to* work.

I've got one week left in this temp job and I haven't been booked for the week after yet, so I need to make a point of nudging recruiters again. But first . . . I reply to Josh.

What shall we do?

What do you want to do? he asks. Just when I'm thinking this might be a little unimaginative, Josh types, **OK . . . tomorrow evening, dinner, obviously. And then on Sunday – you mentioned Kensington Palace last time . . . shall we give that a go? A picnic and a palace?**

I smile because I can't think of anything better. Later he suggests that for our dinner we meet at a restaurant named Daphne's in Chelsea. I practically skip home at the end of my working day.

It's only the next evening, as I'm readying myself to leave the flat for our date, that I work out that tonight and tomorrow morning means two dates back-to-back, and I'm honestly not sure what to do about this. Should I demurely say goodbye to Josh after dinner this evening and then bundle myself back to the far side of town, to meet him again for our palace picnic on Sunday?

'You should pack an overnight bag and go with the flow,' Scarlet tells me.

'Really? Feels a bit . . . you know,' I reply.

'Yes, it does,' she says excitedly. 'But also investigative. Because if he's crap in bed, then you don't have to keep waiting around all week for a farmer from the West Country to make it back into London at the end of the working week. You can get rid of him early on.'

'Hmm,' I ponder.

'Just enjoy yourself,' she tells me. 'See where it leads. Don't put pressure on anything, and if you end up back here tonight, so be it.'

The restaurant is filled with fresh seasonal flowers on every table and in open urn-style vases around the walls – bright dahlias, clematis and big blowsy heads of hydrangeas in varying shades of purples, reds and pinks. Above us is foliage, which I suspect is fresh rather than synthetic, and there's an archway leading towards a conservatory area filled with more fresh flowers. It must cost them a fortune to keep the place looking like this. Waiters in matching green suit jackets move around effortlessly and it's as if the restaurant has fallen out of a bygone era and into modern-day London. I love it.

'This is so pretty,' I tell Josh immediately as I greet him at our table. The wide bifold glass doors are open at the front of the restaurant where we're sitting and the evening sunlight filters down onto us, as conversations from nearby tables and those positioned just outside on the pavement merge into one, while Chelsea locals walk past with large handbags and small dogs.

'Hi.' Josh stands to greet me, kissing me on my cheek, the

roughness of his stubble grazing my face, but not unpleasantly so. He smells of fresh earth and countryside. I inhale him. 'I'm glad you like the restaurant,' he says. 'I asked a friend for a recommendation and this was it.'

'You don't supply the beef here too then?' I ask with a sideways smile.

'Afraid not,' he replies. 'Which means you're not obliged to order it and enthuse madly over it, if you don't want to.'

'I won't then,' I say, although I haven't even looked at the menu. I can't stop looking at Josh; his button-down shirt is rolled up at the arms and his chinos look totally in place in this neat part of London. And yet he still looks effortless. All ability to make conversation has left my body and I still don't know what to say. I'm saved by a green-blazered waiter offering us water and asking for our drinks order. Today feels like an ice-cold white wine kind of day, as the weather has picked back up again, which is encouraging given that September will be here soon. Josh leaves me to choose. I opt for a Sancerre, checking with him if the price is OK, and he seems very at ease with what are – to me – hefty sums.

I often wonder what people *do* for a living to be able to afford to eat in places like this. Being a farmer obviously pays Josh well enough that he doesn't bat an eyelid at £70 bottles of wine. I glance around. What does everyone else *do*, to afford all this? Presumably none of them are temping while secretly wishing they had a job that was more creative.

We talk for a while about our weeks, and Josh's sounds like it's been . . . intense: waking early to feed the cattle and then attend to jobs around the farm. 'Checking pipes and troughs for breakages, making sure the animals are well, milking.'

'What time do you go to bed?' I ask when he finishes. 'If you have to get up at five-thirty?'

'Nine p.m., latest,' he says and I wince. That's unsociably early. 'I've tried later and I'm a mess the next morning,' he continues. 'Thankfully, I don't have to get up early for work tomorrow, so I'm all yours for a bit longer.'

'Nine p.m., though – my evening's only just getting started after I've got in my ten thousand steps or snuck in an occasional yoga class.'

'Farming is my cardio,' Josh replies. 'Imagine I told you I lived in London and got up at that time and went to the gym. It's sort of the same.'

I make an *I'm not sure about that* kind of noise. 'How on earth did you become a farmer?' I ask as the waiter returns and takes our food orders, topping up our chilled wine.

'The route of most farmers: I was born into it. It was my grandfather's and then my father's farm, but he's retired now. He and my mum moved out in order to truly retire. Living at the farmhouse and working on the farm – it's like living above the shop. So now it's only me. And I've stayed put, other than a stint at agricultural college to learn more modern techniques, and then uni. Although experience is everything, and my dad's still just down the road for help and advice. I've been running the place on my own for so long that I feel at ease, though, comfortable with what I'm doing and how I'm doing it. My best mate works with me and is helping me to diversify. We're branching out from beef and the obvious dairy supplies, and are producing our own ice cream now too and . . . Sorry, am I going on a bit? I've just realised I might be.'

'No,' I reply honestly, straightening up, encouraging Josh. 'You're not. I think it's wonderful. I'm kind of in awe. Ice cream sounds brilliant. How many of you work there?'

'I've got a team of four, and we're more of a family than a workforce. Known each other for years now. We're happy to do pub quizzes as a team at the end of a long week, rather than stride off and not see each other again for forty-eight hours.'

'Sounds like the dream working environment.'

Josh laughs. 'I'm pleased I'm making it sound that way. It's hard work. Doesn't leave much time for anything else.'

I ponder this for a moment as our starters arrive. 'Do you get lonely?'

'I don't really have the time or the energy to get lonely, but I guess if I think about it . . . maybe.'

'Not too much time for romance?'

He smiles, shakes his head. 'Not really.'

I smile back. The universe is strange. The way Josh and I met was strange. The way Chris and I met was strange.

Being with Josh, here, like this, is easy. His gaze connects meaningfully with mine, and I have to really work hard to fight the overwhelming urge to lean forward and kiss him.

We're politely ushered away from our table at the end of the meal as we've been there for hours, and we decide to prop up the bar at the restaurant instead of lingering at the table, which they clearly want to start clearing away. We decide to order cocktails from the bartender, even though it's verging on 10 p.m.

'This is past my bedtime,' Josh jokes, stifling a yawn.

'I'm a little sleepy too,' I say as we read the cocktail menu. 'And I've got nothing like your excuse. Your job is intense. Mine ends in a week.'

'No signs of anything new?' Josh asks as we both order the signature Daphne's Martini.

'Sadly not.'

'Something will come up,' he tells me as we watch our drinks being mixed.

'I'm sure it will,' I reply with a positivity I don't feel.

We drink our cocktails and then order one more each while the restaurant slowly empties out. When we take the hint that it's time for us to move on and let the hard-working restaurant staff go home to their beds, we stand in the street, not knowing how to end the date.

Josh automatically turns, presumably in the direction of his hotel, and I walk with him, my overnight belongings rolled up tightly in one of the larger handbags I own. Josh's hand finds mine and we walk and talk about the many differences between London and Somerset. He pauses for a few moments and then laughs uproariously after I confess that I honestly thought Somerset was a London borough when he first mentioned it.

'Really?' he eventually manages to say when he's stopped laughing. I'm giggling along with him and tell him what I'd told Scarlet.

'Yes,' I say. 'One of those areas you never hear about,

like . . .' I grasp for London suburbs, 'Hillingdon or Bexley,' I finish.

'Are they in London?' Josh asks. 'I'm going to have to take your word for it.'

'See?' I say. 'See? Easily done.'

'This is me,' Josh says as we reach the end of the road. I look up to find we're at the entrance to his boutique hotel, with white Georgian architecture, sash windows and candles flickering in lanterns placed on each step.

'Oh, this is lovely.' This is either the end of the date or the start of something else entirely, depending on what happens next.

'Do you . . . ?' Josh starts. 'Do you . . . ?'

'Do I?' I tease.

'I'm not very good at this,' he confesses, dragging a hand over his forehead and through his hair in obvious despair. 'I don't know what's too forward and what's lagging behind. If I invite you up for coffee, is that the lamest thing you've ever heard?' He doesn't let me speak. 'But if I don't invite you in and I just say "bye", then . . .'

'Then?' I could save him, but I want to hear everything he wishes to say.

'Then I look really disinterested, which I'm not, and . . . You have quite the journey home, don't you? Then you have to make that same journey again tomorrow, if you still want to see me again for our palace-and-picnic plans? Oh, hang on, *do* you want to see me tomorrow?' he asks. 'It's fine if you don't want to – come in, that is – and also see me tomorrow and . . .'

'Josh?'

'Yeah?' He looks concerned.

'Be quiet.' I tip my head up and kiss him.

His kiss is warm and his hands find my back, guiding my body gently towards his as we kiss in the street. In one hand I'm holding my bag – heavy with my overnight belongings – and my other hand has reached up to touch his face as our kiss becomes just the wrong side of acceptable for this public space. It's me who breaks away first, slowly, reluctantly.

Josh's eyes open and he glances around sheepishly. 'Shall we . . . ?' he asks tentatively. 'Do you want to . . . ?'

'Come in for coffee?' I tease and he laughs. 'Yes, please,' I say, answering my own question. 'Yes, please,' is my new motto. I'm saying yes to things, pushing my life on. There's no pressure. We don't have to see each other again if it doesn't work out. It's only sex. It's a trial run. I've spent far too long playing it safe. I'm bloody going for it – it starts now.

We walk hand-in-hand through the lobby and I avoid embarrassing eye contact with the receptionist, while Josh replies warmly to her greeting. He hits the lift button with full force while I try not to draw attention to us, by purposefully *not* kissing him here, even though I want to. There's nothing remotely sexy about standing in a lobby, pretending to be disinterested. But somehow it *feels* sexy. It's the intention behind what us being in this lobby means.

Josh stares straight ahead, a smile on his face, and I do the same until the lift doors open and we enter: two ordinary people returning to a hotel room after dinner. Then the lift doors close and it's all I can do not to jump into his arms and wrap my legs around him in this confined space. He turns into me and kisses me again, and I'm backed up against the mirror as Josh's body presses into mine. The lift doors open at the first floor, surprising us both, and a couple stares at us, uncertain if they want to get in. Josh and I spring apart and they look away embarrassed, stay in the hallway, let the lift doors close. I laugh and so does Josh.

'That was awkward,' I splutter.

'More awkward if they'd have got in the lift.'

'True,' I mumble as Josh's mouth finds mine again. The doors reopen at the second floor and Josh takes my hand, fumbling in his pocket for his key card. And then we're inside his room, all muted tones of grey and beige.

'Ooh, this is nice,' I say, automatically scanning the room. 'I mean it's very predictable for a hotel, and they could have done so much more with . . .' I turn and look at Josh, who's smiling at me. 'Sorry,' I giggle. I actually giggle. Who is this girl who goes into hotel rooms with a man she's only met a few times before? This is the girl who kissed Josh at a wedding in order to win a game of bingo. Perhaps this girl needed to get over herself, after a disastrous relationship and endless shit first dates. I like this girl. I think kissing Josh is the best decision I ever made.

'Do you . . . ?' Josh asks yet again.

'Are you going to ask me if I want coffee again?'

'Yeah, I was going to.'

'No. No to coffee,' I tell him. 'Not right now.'

Neither of us moves, and I can't tell if Josh is wondering who *he* is, this guy who barely has time to date, but has managed to get a woman into his hotel room on a second proper date. We move towards each other. Just when I think he's about to kiss me, he lifts me up – actually lifts me up – and carries me towards the bed. He deposits me gently on it while he kicks off his shoes, and I do the same. And then I'm sitting up, undoing his shirt for him as Josh wrestles with his buckle before starting on my dress.

His body is a warm tanned colour all over, as if the sun reaches him through the confines of his work clothes. There are way too many buttons on my dress, but eventually I wriggle out of it, which is awkward to do. Then it starts feeling so natural and easy to be with him as we move together on the bed, Josh sitting against the headboard, nestled among the pillows. Without thinking, I move on top of him. Is it possible for sex to be both gentle and frenzied? If so, then I think we nail it, as he pulls my knickers to the side and I lower myself onto him. He moans into my mouth as I move up and down on him – his hands guiding my body into a rhythm until we're moaning louder and harder, our pace quickening and deepening. My hair falls around my shoulders, coming undone at the same moment that I do and then, seconds later, so does Josh.

We stay like that, pressed together, my forehead on his shoulder as my breathing regulates, and then he lifts my head, finding my neck with his mouth, and plants soft kisses onto my clavicle, my shoulder, the space behind my ear, making me moan again. My eyes close as I feel him harden once more inside me and instinctively I move again. I can't help myself. Who is this person? I've never had sex twice in a row before. I never thought I could. My eyes find Josh, who looks just as intense as I do. His fingers dip to the space in between us, and then his thumb finds me and he strokes me gently as I move.

I murmur something encouraging and it spurs him on as his thumb rolls against me faster and faster. I think I call his name, and then I fall against him once again as the full force of everything between us magics a second orgasm out of me.

I rest against Josh, my eyes opening and closing in shock against his shoulder.

'Your eyelashes are tickling me,' he whispers into my hair.

I lift my head, stare at him. 'Are you a magician?'

'What?' he splutters.

'I've never done that before,' I tell him.

His eyes widen. 'Sex?' he questions. 'I suspect that's a lie, because you're very good at it.'

'Thank you, but . . . I came twice. I've never— That's never happened . . .' I trail off, still in total bafflement, which ushers a low chuckle from him. I look at Josh and ask where the hell he's been my whole life?

'On a farm in Somerset,' he says in amusement.

'I thought two orgasms in a row was the preserve of people in certain types of films . . . who fake it,' I say, more to myself than to Josh. I move off him, sit up next to him in bed and pull the duvet over us both. He turns to look at me and obviously doesn't know what to say, either, but he seems fairly chuffed with himself. He should be. He's achieved with me what no other man has managed to do. This is momentous – for me at least.

I can't help it; the endorphins rushing through me are out of this world, so I reach up, touch his face and usher him towards me, so I can kiss him again. I have no idea how long we stay like that for, in his super-king-size hotel bed, but at some point we fall asleep.

When I wake up in the morning, it's to the smell of fresh coffee and the sound of the hotel door closing, a waiter instructing him to enjoy his breakfast. Josh, in his hotel bathrobe, wheels a breakfast trolley into the room.

'Room service,' he says. 'Two full English breakfasts, pastry basket, toast and a fancy-looking fruit plate full of,' he peers at the plate, 'I'm not sure what.'

'You're amazing,' I say.

He smiles shyly. 'Thanks.' He pours me a coffee and hands it to me. I inhale the aroma and sip it.

This man is incredible. He's made me come twice and has ordered everything on the room-service menu. If Scarlet was here (which would be weird), she would tell me not to give way to emotional highs after sex, or during sex, or before sex. We'll unpack all of this together later.

Josh sits on the edge of the bed and starts taking all the silver domes off the rest of the food. He looks good in a robe. He looks even better out of it. I sit alongside him, sipping my coffee and feeling pretty strange being naked next to a man whose own modesty is covered. I slip off to the bathroom, find the spare robe and return. We eat ravenously, talking about everything and anything. He tells me he's a single child, and we have that in common. He talks about his mum and dad and what they do now they don't run the farm. He tells me how in love they still are and how he wants that for himself some day.

'They met when they were young and it just worked out . . . you know?'

I nod. 'When you know, you know,' I reply flippantly as I start on the fruit plate. But there's nothing flippant in that at all – not really. 'True love is hard to find. Sometimes it's right under your nose and sometimes it can take a long time to find it,' I say, a bit more articulately. And then I think about what I've said, if it might ever apply to me.

Josh nods, ponders for a minute and starts tucking into his eggs. 'What about your parents?' he asks.

I make a face. 'Divorced, sadly. They're happier now than when they were together, though. Now they're with other people and are better off as friends. But it took them twenty-five years to work that out.'

'Then perhaps they just weren't right,' he says helpfully, and I can only agree.

'Exactly. I'm a grown-up, so I'm grateful they divorced when I was old enough to understand the ups and downs of relationships.'

Josh touches my lip, removes a tiny piece of croissant. His touch does so many things to me.

We finish our breakfast, wrapping the remaining croissants and Danish pastries in linen napkins, so we can take them to the park as a snack for later. We shower and dress, and Josh checks out and pays his bill before we venture into Kensington Palace Gardens. The sun's shining, but I notice – now we're heading towards slightly shorter days – that its strength is starting to weaken.

'I feel bad about stealing these napkins,' Josh confesses as we follow a path towards the boating lake.

'Do you really?' I ask.

He chuckles. 'No, not really.'

We walk idly and his hand slips into mine. Instead of taking a boat out on the water we continue to walk happily, working off our breakfast. We stand in front of Kensington Palace and look up at it together, before Josh gallantly purchases both our tickets and we go in.

'I don't think I've ever been here before,' Josh says as we take in the ornate ceilings and furniture, looking at Queen Victoria's childhood items.

I feel like a grown-up, doing something like this. I've never been on a date to a palace before. I glance at Josh as he spends a moment looking at a portrait of Queen Victoria and Prince Albert together, and I realise this weekend is full of unexpected firsts.

Queen Victoria's childhood doll's house is on display and I'm fascinated by all the tiny furniture, the miniature decorations and the intricate chandeliers.

Josh wanders over, bends down to kneel alongside me as we peer in together. 'Thinking of all the things you'd do to it, if you could redecorate?'

I laugh. 'Yeah, I'd rip out all this Victorian crap, for a start,' I say, which elicits a horrified gasp from an American tourist next to us.

'All those frilly cushions and doilies?' Josh asks as we share a knowing smile.

'They'd be the first to go,' I reply, playing along.

'Replace them with fake plants and Ikea furniture?'

'Obviously,' I say. 'Actually I'm more into working with what's already there. This is the problem,' I say, more to myself. 'I don't think I have a particular style. I see what's *in situ* and what can be kept that will look effortless and comfortable but is also in keeping with the style and age of a building or a room.'

'Why's that a problem?' Josh asks, rising.

'I don't know,' I reply as I stand up. 'Maybe it's not. Maybe I need to find out.'

Minutes later we're in the gift shop, playing a game of 'Guess how much this is?' I'm holding up a Christmas-tree ornament; it's in the shape of a mantua dress, embroidered with ivory and gold beads.

Josh looks at it and then at me. 'Ten pounds.'

'I wish it was ten pounds,' I reply.

He narrows his eyes, looks thoughtfully at it. 'Thirty pounds.'

'Higher.'

His eyebrows raise. 'Higher than thirty? For a tree decoration?'

'Much higher.'

'Who buys this stuff?' he asks, as the American who took umbrage at our interior-design chat steps forward to look at the range of decorations.

I put Josh out of his misery. 'It's sixty pounds.'

'Wow!' he says. 'That's a really decent bottle of wine.'

I give him a look. 'Or, if you're me, that's six bottles of decent wine.'

Josh smiles. 'I'm having fun.'

'Me too. Where next?'

We emerge into the sunlight, where a vendor is selling Pimm's with fruit and cucumber trimmings and gourmet packets of crisps. Josh orders for us both, and we walk through the parkland again until we find a spot in the sunshine and settle ourselves on the grass, talking about the most random things we saw today and opening up our strange picnic of croissants, pastries, crisps and Pimm's.

'I really like you,' Josh confesses out of nowhere as we finish eating.

My heart has just picked up pace. 'I really like you too,' I say. *It's date number three,* I tell myself. *Or still date two, if we're being technical about it. Don't go too quickly. Don't ruin it, Lexie. It's too soon with Josh, and only a fortnight ago you were considering getting on a plane with another man.* I wonder what Chris is doing right now? Things have moved on so unexpectedly quickly with Josh that it feels wrong to think about messaging Chris now.

'So I've been thinking,' Josh says.

And I wonder if *he's* about to ruin it. If *he's* about to say something silly, so I lean forward to kiss him, surprising him.

'What was that for?' he asks when we break loose.

'I don't want to go too fast,' I tell him. 'I don't want to wreck it.'

He frowns. 'OK,' he says slowly. 'I mean, we've already slept together and so . . . I'm not really sure what else would be going quicker than that? I'm not about to propose or anything,' he jokes.

'No, we're way past the seventeen-minute sweet spot,' I say.

'Pardon?'

'Nothing,' I reply. 'Ignore me.' I wish I hadn't said that. It was neither appropriate nor funny. Josh doesn't deserve me thinking of Chris. I instruct myself to stop immediately.

He continues. 'I was wondering . . . if you wanted to come and visit me for our next date?'

'Oh,' I say and then, longer, 'Ohhh.'

'I can't tell if you like this idea or hate it?' Josh says uncertainly.

'In the London borough of Somerset?' I ask.

'Ha! Exactly.'

'When? How?'

'Next weekend and by train.'

'Ohhh,' I draw out again, not thinking this through at all. 'Yeah, OK.' I smile as the implications of this swirl around my mind. 'You're inviting me to stay at your house?'

He nods. 'Is that OK?'

My smile widens and it's my turn to nod. 'You're inviting me to stay at your house,' I repeat. 'In Somerset?' This feels huge. Although if he lived in London, it wouldn't have felt huge at all. If he'd lived in London, we'd have spent last night at his place probably. Then I remind myself that no, we wouldn't have done that, because I wouldn't have seen Josh two days on the bounce and I wouldn't have spent the night. It's *because* he lives so far away that we're seeing each other for two days straight.

Aware that I've disappeared inside my mind, I refocus. We look up train times for the coming Friday and we make plans for the weekend. On the way back to the station, Josh pops into the hotel and returns the linen napkins.

Chapter Twelve

'Oh God, he's perfect,' Scarlet says after I give her the breakdown of my weekend. 'So what's wrong with him? Why is he single? You're going to arrive at his house in – wherever it is – and find a collection of axes or knives in a dungeon, or discover he's really into *Warhammer* or that he's a cyberhacker or . . . something.'

'I bloody hope not,' I reply as we sit on our sofa, feet up on the coffee table, each drinking a glass of cheap red wine. 'Although he's just so lovely and so-o-o good in bed that I could probably live with a combination of all of that, to be honest.'

'Does he have a brother?' Scarlet asks hopefully.

'Sadly, not.'

'Best friend who is single and also owns his own farm?'

'Maybe,' I say. 'He does have a best friend, but I don't know if he's in the *eligible bachelor* category or not. I'll do some digging.'

'You might *meet* the best friend. Then you can do some proper reconnaissance for me.'

'I feel it might be a bit too soon for *meet the friends*, although we are going at quite a speed, so you never know. In only a few weeks we've kissed on the night I *met* him, been on two dates – or three, if you count the two-in-a-row situation—'

'Had two orgasms,' Scarlet chimes in helpfully, which makes me laugh.

'Yeah . . . that. And now I'm going to stay at his house in the country for the weekend.'

'Here's to a roll in the hay,' she says as we clink glasses and cheers each other.

As the week rolls on, my flirtatious chat unconsciously dies away with Chris. I acknowledge any message he sends, because I'm not rude, but they're short replies, unquestioning, a thumbs-up emoji here and there instead of a full-blown conversation. I no longer start our messages back up. I'm not the kind of person who usually treats people like this and . . . it's Chris. It's *Chris*. So it hurts to be so flippant, but I need to instigate the general demise of our – whatever it is we're doing – because of Josh. I've slept with him. Twice. And we're making plans to keep seeing each other. Focusing on Josh is the right thing to do. And, slowly, I *think* Chris has got the hint, as his constant stream of messages has petered out.

By Friday afternoon I am ready to escape London. I am also unemployed again, as the multiple agencies I'm registered with have either failed to respond to my messages or *have* deigned to reply to me, but in the negative. Why is the job market so hard at the moment? I've been lowering my prospects towards doing *any* kind of office job. Anything at all. I have a degree, for God's sake, and a lot of admin roles behind me, but I can't even get a temp job now. I'm trying to convince myself it's merely a blip. It's just as well I'm escaping London for the weekend. It'll take my mind off it.

I say goodbye to the woman I've been working with on reception every day for the past two weeks. We exchange general chat, wishing each other good weekends and enthusing about what the other has going on. We'll never see each other again, unless I get a job back there, which is unlikely.

I pick up my mid-sized roller suitcase and make a beeline for the door. I've loaded the case with clothes. I have no idea what to expect. Josh and I have messaged every day this week, and my worries – about the pace of whatever is happening between us – have abated in favour of excitement about going to his farmhouse. In fact I can't wait to get out of this building and onto a train for a couple of hours. Knowing Josh is going to be at the other end of the journey makes me smile and pick up pace, as I roll my luggage towards the station.

I'm scrolling through my social media while I wait for the train to come in, when Chris messages me a simple **Hi**. My heart rises with its usual excitement when this happens – and then falls all at the same time, when I remember I have to disentangle myself from him. The guilt is only going to gnaw away at me, if I don't. I won't reply immediately. I've got a long journey, so I'll sit on this message for a bit and work out how to make it clear that we shouldn't be talking as much as we are. I wonder about the possibility of keeping Chris as a friend. We both know our messaging isn't taking us in any particular direction. But it's laced with something *additional*.

I put my case into the overhead rack after I've boarded.

With the weather changing from summer into autumn, I've brought T-shirts and jeans, cute dresses with jumpers, trainers, some nice shoes, just in case; some very lovely underwear and, of course, my older-than-old Hunter wellies, because I'm going to a farm and the novelty of this is beyond compare. I tried them on last night with a floaty white dress and felt I'd nailed that Glastonbury look – not that I've ever been. Maybe I should. Maybe I should take a leaf out of Chris's book and take myself on a date to Glastonbury. I look out of the window while we're still in the station and smile at that thought. I hope, with all of these outfits, that I will at least be able to conjure up a couple of suitable looks for anything Josh has planned this weekend.

After an hour's delay, when the train sat outside somewhere called Didcot Parkway for what felt like for ever, the sun started going down and the sky darkened to a deepening shade of blue, I finally arrive at Chippenham and follow Josh's instructions out to the car park, where he's standing by an army-green Land Rover. Of course he is.

The lights of the car park illuminate him and he looks just as he always does: button-down shirt, dark chinos, but with the addition of a gilet and some Timberland boots. It's colder down here than it was in London.

Josh smiles when he sees me. I thought I'd look out of place here, in my receptionist work clothes, but lots of people got off the train similarly dressed. Somerset is clearly a weekend hotspot and I had fun on the train trying to work out, from people's conversations and luggage, who might have a weekend house nearby.

'Hi,' Josh says with a wide smile, stepping forward to take my case. He bends down to kiss me and it's long and deep. That chemistry from last weekend hasn't disappeared. 'I'm really pleased you came all the way down here, after a long day at work,' he goes on. 'Thanks for making the journey.'

'It's obscenely long,' I joke while getting into the car's passenger side. 'I can't believe you did that back-and-forth four times for me.'

'I didn't have an hour's delay, though, so you had it worse. Sorry.'

'It was worth it,' I reply and he looks pleased as he starts the ignition and we leave the car park. 'I'm really excited,' I confess.

'Me too,' Josh says, grinning as we begin driving away from the station and out towards the countryside. 'It's a bit of a drive now, I'm afraid, so settle in. I can't believe you're here.'

'Staying in London, or visiting you in Somerset? Tough call. So what are we doing first?' I ask, and he tells me that he's got dinner cooking in the Aga already and he's brought some wine and nibbles to get us started.

'And then maybe . . . I dunno; board games or—'

'Board games?' I cut in. 'Is it Christmas?'

He shrugs apologetically. 'I don't know how to entertain a woman at my house. I've never had a woman back to mine before.'

I turn to him in disbelief. 'You've never had a woman back to your house? What – ever?'

Josh shakes his head, flicks the indicator and we turn into a country lane.

'How . . . ?'

'It's just not happened.'

'How old are you, Josh?'

'Thirty-two.'

My jaw drops, not at his age, but because he's reached thirty-two years of age and has never had a woman back to his house. I'm only a little over thirty, but I wasn't expecting Josh also to be *over* thirty and be *so* inexperienced with women.

'Like I said, I'm so busy working that meeting women is difficult.' And then he clarifies. 'I'd like to point out that I have put it about a bit over the years. Just . . . when my parents lived here, I couldn't exactly bring someone home for a casual thing. So I never did.'

OK. Phew! That makes *slightly* more sense. I suppose, if I think about it, I don't bring men back to the flat I share with Scarlet all that often. And I certainly didn't bring any home when I lived with my folks. I settle back into my seat as we continue through the countryside. We turn into a long drive and Josh tells me, 'It's down here.'

After about a minute of driving along a tree-lined avenue the house appears through the darkness. There's a series of lamps lighting up each of the windows of the ground-floor rooms – at least three long windows sprawl away on either side of the front door – which indicates that this house is not small, although I can't see in the dark how big it is. I was expecting a dinky little tumbledown farmhouse. This is a mansion, surely? Or a manor house? I'm not sure what the difference is.

Josh parks and I feel the reassuringly country-esque crunch of gravel under my feet as I get out of the car and stare around. The moon shows a series of small outbuildings, built of similar pale stone to the house, but I can't see anything that indicates an actual farm. He leads me through the front door, carrying my luggage for me, and a wonderful smell of cooking greets me.

'Lasagne,' Josh tells me. 'I popped it in before I came to get you.'

'You're a man of many talents,' I say as I glance around the large hallway.

Inside, it's like stepping back in time. The decor fits the house. It's so comfortable, with hooks holding Barbour jackets in the hallway and a series of weather-beaten wellies waiting underneath them. To the left of the hall is a huge sitting room, with casement windows and battered red-fabric sofas that look old but in keeping, providing a hint of a well-loved family home, which is now inhabited by one man. In the middle of the quadrangle of sofas sits a fabric ottoman, piled high with farming journals and old issues of *Country Life*.

'It's gorgeous,' I say. 'So homely.'

'Thanks. Come through to the kitchen. There's a bottle of red with our name on it. You hungry?'

'Starving,' I reply, giving him a warm smile. Josh puts me instantly at ease. He did so at the wedding, at the restaurant, in the hotel and in the park, and now here, in his home – where he's never entertained a woman. Until now. I feel I've a lot to live up to. I'm either about to set the bar for every girlfriend who follows me into Josh's life, or this is it. But I'm getting ahead of myself now. I've been here for four whole minutes.

He's already set places for two, and he lights candles in the middle of the scrubbed wooden table that could easily seat ten people. Heat from the Aga bursts out as Josh opens the door and presents me with a bubbling lasagne. It looks great. I've never seen an Aga in real life and quiz Josh as to how it works. He baffles me with a general level of basic science, and we sit to eat one of the most delicious home-cooked dinners I've ever tasted.

'Do you have a Labrador?' I ask as we tuck in.

He stares at me. 'Me? No. Why?'

'In every picture of an Aga I've seen, there is always at least one Labrador asleep in front of it.'

'Oh, right,' Josh laughs. 'We did have a family Labrador. Or, rather, we do. He lives with my parents.'

'Aha,' I say. And then, 'Tell me about your friends.' I want to know all about his life, his friends, but I also need to remember to find out about his best friend, for Scarlet.

'Well, there's Dan, who you've met.'

'Have I?' I ask, my wine glass halfway to my mouth.

'At the wedding? I was his best man.'

'Of course you were,' I exclaim. I've done this twice now – totally forgotten this poor man, who was inadvertently responsible for bringing Josh and me together. 'I remember now,' I say guiltily as Josh smiles. This makes me wonder. 'How well do you know Chris?'

'The usher you decided to ditch me for, after we danced?' he says with a sideways smile.

'Yeah,' I reply slowly, guilt rising even more. 'Sorry about that.'

'It's OK,' he says, and I think he means it. 'I don't know him that well, to be honest. I know Dan from school, and Chris is one of Dan's mates from uni, I think? That's the extent of my knowledge.' Josh looks at me. 'What did Chris have that night that I didn't?' he teases after a pause, but I sense real curiosity there.

'I'd already promised him I'd return with drinks. Which you paid for,' I point out.

'So what happened with Chris, in between me buying you both some drinks and you kissing me not long after?'

So many things, I think. *So. Many. Things.*

'We talked and it was nice, and then he got a taxi to the airport and went back to New York.' I've made that sound so much simpler than it was. I left out the fact that I'd felt torn in two directions, unsure whether to get on a plane with a man I'd only just met or stay in London. I've been picturing Chris and me together in his adopted city. Would I still be there now? I drag my thoughts back to the present. 'And then you coerced me into kissing you,' I say light-heartedly.

'I did *not*!' Josh laughs. 'You were up for it, as I remember.'

'I was,' I say. *I still am.*

We eat our lasagne and drink more wine, Josh opens a

second bottle and eventually we wind up in the sitting room, taking our glasses with us. There's a chill in the air and he deftly sets up kindling in the fireplace, starting a small fire and building it up into a proper roaring blaze.

'Boy Scout?' I ask.

'Farm boy,' he replies. And there's something so sexy about that comment. I wonder if he's got any hay bales and if it would be comfortable? Or if it would be itchy? Like how sex on the beach is a bit . . . grainy, and not *that* sexy in real life.

I tuck my feet under me, thinking about this for a moment as Josh and I cosy up on his sofa. I feel so content, sophisticated in this space (hay-bale thoughts aside) as I sip delicious red wine with an attractive man in his country house. This is ridiculous and I laugh.

'What?' Josh asks.

I turn towards him. 'Nothing,' I say and then, because it's probably been a whole ten minutes since I last kissed him, I lean in again. 'It's probably time for a tour of the house,' I suggest, finally pulling away and seeing the heat in his eyes match my own.

'Is it?' he asks. 'Where should we start?'

'The bedroom.'

Chapter Thirteen

When I wake up, the sun is shining and I'm alone. A note scribbled on a scrap of paper and left on Josh's pillow says: 'Gone to work. Breakfast on the Aga. Be back soon or come and find me? Look for cows.' I forgot Josh works six days a week.

I lie back on the pillow, holding the note and smiling with contentment. I can't stop smiling. I wonder if I smiled even in my sleep.

I shower and dress in jeans and a T-shirt. If Josh is on the farm, then this feels like the most suitable attire from my bulging suitcase of options. I pull on my trainers and head back into the kitchen, where Josh has left a selection of breakfast goodies on top of the warm Aga: bacon, fried eggs, tomatoes and mushrooms. I spoon some onto a clean plate that he's left on the table for me. There's also fresh juice and I spy a coffee machine with warm coffee still in the pot. I glance around at this set-up. Josh lives very well. He's also organised and thoughtful – whipping all this up for me at the crack of dawn before taking himself off to work.

I send Scarlet a picture of the kitchen set-up; she's obviously still asleep and offline and I don't get a reply yet. I remember the message from Chris, which I opened on the train, but didn't reply to yet. I wonder what I should do about that. I might just leave it a bit longer. I feel bad keeping him hanging, but I also don't want to make a snap decision I'll come to regret.

After I've eaten, I leave the house and pull the door closed behind me. Presumably Josh has got his key. He's trusting, leaving me here like this.

Now it's daylight, in the distance I see large metal farm buildings, and I'm halfway there before realising my wellies might have been a better choice of footwear. The whiter-than-white trainers I'm wearing are starting to suffer.

I stand at the open door to the building and look inside. It's a hive of activity, with two men moving around checking machinery. Neither of these men is Josh and I don't want to interrupt them, but one turns to me anyway. It's wet inside this building and I can't really enter without flooding my trainers. I feel silly now.

'Josh!' one of the men yells. He wanders over to meet me.

'Hiya, you must be Lexie,' he says in a West Country accent. 'I won't shake your hand as I'm covered in muck.'

I look at his glove. He is. 'Hi.' I reply.

Josh appears around a corner and meets me with a grin. 'You're up! Did you find the breakfast I left you?'

'I did, thank you.'

He moves forward to kiss me, before introducing me. 'This is Tony.'

Tony grins and says hello before turning off to continue his work.

'Want to meet everyone else?' Josh offers.

'Sure.'

'Shall we start with humans or cows?' he teases.

'Ha! Humans, please.'

Josh calls over to another man in his thirties, who's had his back to me in the far distance, and he turns, squints a bit, smiles and shouts hello. I wave back, say hello and then turn to Josh.

'What time did you get up?'

'Five-thirty, as usual.'

'Ugh!' I calculate: it's 10 a.m. now. 'You've been up hours.'

'I have. Remember it's my cardio?'

'Oh yeah,' I smile at him, and his gaze holds mine before he dips his head and kisses me briefly.

'Did you sleep OK?' he asks.

'Like a baby,' I reply.

'Babies sleep terribly, don't they? Screaming and crying?' Josh says knowingly.

'I wouldn't know,' I say. 'I've no clue how babies work.'

He opens his mouth, looks as if he wants to say something and then stops himself at the last second. I'm desperate to know what he's thinking. Josh looks down at my feet and raises his eyebrows. 'I thought you said you'd brought wellies?'

'I didn't know I'd need them the minute I stepped out the front door,' I wail.

'I should have said,' he tells me. 'Well, if you want to come and meet the cows, you can trek up to the house and swap your footwear or I can carry you over the threshold . . .' He looks around us at the state of the freshly washed and very flooded floor. 'Or around the whole building. What's it going to be? Leap into my arms or head back to the house?'

'I can't be bothered to go back up there, so it's arms, please,' I say and squeal with delight as Josh lifts me up and carries me, my legs wrapping around his waist. I scout around for hay bales. 'This is inappropriate behaviour for your place of work,' I tell him.

'I'm the boss. It's all good,' he replies, before depositing me in front of a series of metal pens on a slightly less-wet patch of floor.

'So what are we doing, and can I help?' I ask.

'Putting more food in here for the cows, so when they come in they can eat while being milked.'

Josh tells me what to do and lets me help. I'm intrigued by his work and excited by the prospect of helping animals eat so they can be milked, though I'll bet the novelty wears off quickly.

'Do you enjoy doing all this?' I ask as I help pull armloads of hay into troughs.

'I don't think about it,' Josh says with a shrug. 'I guess so. There are boring bits and fun bits. It's ever-evolving and I'm used to it. I wouldn't know what the hell else to do if I didn't do this. It's the perils of taking on a house and a job together. It's been in the family so long that I'm tied to it. It's all I've known. It's all I've wanted to know.' He carries on loading hay as we move along. I admire this. Josh has a job and a beautiful home and he's in charge of his own destiny, which is more than I can say for myself.

When we finish we move off and then he spins round,

remembers to pick me up again, and I distract him by kissing him on his neck while he tries to walk us both outside. He murmurs his appreciation.

'Want to meet the cows?' he asks as we head into the field. He lands me on a patch of grass and I lean against the wide metal gate and look out at his herd of black-and-white cattle.

'They're Holsteins,' he says.

'They're beautiful,' I say, a wistful expression on my face. 'And you butcher them for beef.'

'Don't start,' he continues with a smile, seeing my face. 'I know exactly what you're about to say. But where do you think your food comes from?'

'But their *little faces*,' I say.

'These are dairy,' he tries to placate me. 'Milk. That's our core business.'

'And, soon, ice cream,' I say as a cow moseys over. She nuzzles Josh and then me with her warm nose, thick eyelashes and beautiful face.

'Oh God, they're like pets,' I say softly, stroking her nose.

'Hmm,' Josh says sceptically, picking me back up again. I'm not sure that it's essential, but I enjoy it nonetheless. A cow trots after us merrily as if to follow us back to the farmhouse.

I lean towards Josh's ear and whisper, 'See? They're like pets.'

'Stop saying that,' he says with a laugh.

Chapter Fourteen

'I feel like I'm on holiday,' I tell him later that evening after we've both showered, wrapped ourselves in warm fluffy towels and Josh has ribbed me about the quantity of attire I've brought with me, as he sees how many clothes are inside my case.

'Are you moving in?' he teases. 'I thought you were only here for two nights?'

'You *wish* I was moving in,' I say jokingly as I rifle around in the case, eventually finding what I'm looking for. My packing system needs some work.

He's quiet and then says, 'Strange kind of holiday. One where I put you to work all day.'

'I enjoyed it,' I tell him as I pull on my T-shirt, neaten out my hair and pull it back into a band.

'Really?' he asks hopefully.

'Yeah,' I say, pulling on my jeans and socks and wondering if I should put make-up on or not. Ordinarily I would, when dating someone is in this early stage, but after working in the sun with Josh all day I've got a bit of a glow. It might just be the heat from the shower.

'What are we going to do tomorrow?' I ask. 'Can we feed the calves again? I loved that so much.'

'Not tomorrow. Tony will be in to do that. I don't work Sundays. We can have a lie-in, breakfast in bed and not move all day.'

'That sounds good too,' I reply before we descend the large wooden staircase and turn towards the kitchen in search of dinner.

'Shall we make tikka masala from scratch?' he suggests, eyeing up the contents of his fridge.

'I don't know how to do that,' I confess. 'I'm very good at ordering from Deliveroo, though.'

He casts me a look. 'City girl.'

'I think I could easily learn not to be a city girl,' I say absently as I watch him open cupboard doors, pulling fresh meat wrapped in paper from the fridge. He nestles some jarred spices among the bundle in his arms, and I go to retrieve a few of the glass jars before they fall.

'Could you?' he asks. 'Really?'

I'm distracted by the fresh produce, which looks like it's come from a swanky farm shop rather than a supermarket. 'Could I what?'

'Learn not to be a city girl?'

I'm not sure exactly what Josh is asking, so I don't probe further, just in case. 'I guess so, yeah.'

'Do you have to go back to London tomorrow night, as planned?' he asks.

'Er, yeah, obviously, because . . .' My sentence trails off as I think. 'No,' I say slowly. 'No, I don't. Why do you ask?'

'Stay here a little bit longer?'

I lean back against the counter and look at Josh intently. 'How much longer?'

He shrugs. 'Couple of days? Maybe more?'

'Um . . .'

Come with me. Come with me to New York. I blink Chris's words away. I said no to that. I can't say no to Josh too. I can't keep saying no to every offer that comes my way. What will happen to my life if I never say yes to anything? I feel torn, but remind myself it's only a couple of days. My confidence was knocked when Simon cheated on me. I've gone from feeling so low, to terrible dates. And now it's going so well with Josh. If it was going badly, it would be an easy *no*. And what else do I have going on?

'It's not like you've not brought enough clothes,' he teases, which makes me laugh.

'Are you sure?' I question. 'Haven't you got enough going on without me crowding your space?'

'I'll be on the farm all day, and you can come down and feed the calves or help out a bit if you want; and if you don't want . . . you can chill out here or walk into the village, or whatever.'

'I brought my laptop for the train journey, but I've not even opened it. So I can work on my portfolio a bit maybe and apply for jobs while you're working,' I tell him.

Josh nods and begins unwrapping the chicken, his attention seemingly diverted by this. 'I'd really love to see your portfolio,' he says.

'Oh, I don't know.' I say shyly. 'It's not ready, but in the peace and quiet here for a few days I could probably get my head down and get on with finally tidying it up, editing some photos, working on my thought process – you know.'

He looks back at the chicken he's dicing and then back at me. 'So . . . is that a yes?' he asks, and it's his turn to look shy.

'OK,' I reply. And then because I'm not the kind of girl who subscribes to the 'treat 'em mean, keep 'em keen' philosophy, I move over to him, take his face in mine and kiss him. 'Josh, I really like you.'

He looks at me after we've finished kissing. 'I really like you too.'

Chapter Fifteen

The next day our decadent lazy Sunday morning in bed is ruined by the heavy sound of the front door slamming closed, even though neither Josh nor I is anywhere near it.

Josh doesn't look too concerned, but I flick a glance towards him.

'Have you got a ghost?'

'What? No.'

'What's that noise then?'

'Front door.'

'I got that. Who is it, is probably more what I mean.'

'Probably Tamara.'

'Who . . . ?'

'My best mate.'

'Your best friend is a *girl*?' I didn't see that coming.

Josh nods, slowly starts moving out of bed, pulling on some clothes. 'She's a bit early, though.'

'Early for what?'

'Ice-cream tasting. Come on, this'll be a fun way to spend the morning – eating ice cream for breakfast. We don't get to do that very often as adults, do we?'

Josh leans over the bed and gives me a quick kiss, before pulling on the rest of his clothes and moving towards the stairs, giving me a grin as he disappears round the corner.

I lie still for a minute before getting up and ready. I thought we were having a lie-in. And Josh's best friend is female. No eligible bachelor for Scarlet in this direction then – she won't like that at all.

Tamara's downstairs. She's also just wandered straight in through the front door without knocking or . . . Does she have her own key?

I dress, whip on a little bit of make-up and brace myself to meet Josh's best friend.

The second she starts speaking I can hear she's posh. But being called Tamara, there were no surprises there, were there? She bounds towards me as I enter the kitchen, embracing me in a too-tight hug and masses of natural icy-blonde hair. 'Hello-o-o,' she trills. 'I've heard so-o-o much about you! Josh won't stop going on and on,' she says at a hundred miles an hour. 'Lexie this and Lexie that . . .'

'Oh. He's—' I stop myself finishing with the words *said nothing whatsoever about you*. 'I'm so pleased to meet you,' I rally back.

Tamara keeps talking at speed.

Her smile is infectious and her figure is an eye-catching hourglass shape. My gran would have made a comment along the lines of 'good child-bearing hips, those', which is what she said about Scarlet, who is similarly shaped, when they first met. She never said that about me, because I'm straight up and down. I waited years for boobs to arrive and, when they did, it was as if they forgot to appear properly.

'I chose Daphne's for you, did you like it?' Tamara asks.

'Daph— Oh, the restaurant in Chelsea.' Josh had said a friend recommended it. 'It was wonderful. Good choice. Thank you.'

'Phew! I googled for hours and hours.'

'You *googled*? I thought you'd been there?'

'No. Josh asked for help and I wanted to make sure you had a lovely time, so I looked at so many reviews for different restaurants, and proximity to the station and the hotel and . . .' she continues, and I cast a glance at Josh. He obviously knows all this information, but I'm finding it just a *little* bit odd.

Tamara moves about the kitchen, making two mugs of tea, and after a while, still talking so quickly about the farm and ice cream and asking how Josh and I got together, she goes back to the cupboard for a third mug and a teabag. She's clearly at home here.

'I think the lavender might be a bit bold,' she says, switching the chat to ice cream after she's decanted some into a variety of bowls for us. 'I think we should focus on flavours everyone recognises, or a diversification thereof . . . like this one: blackberry ripple, for example. Tell me what you think.'

She hands me a spoon and I take a bowl. I'm drawn into her captivating presence. This is all happening so quickly. Ten minutes ago I was in bed. I taste some ice cream. The lavender is surprisingly nice and I admit as much.

'I honestly don't know,' Josh says, dipping his spoon in and taking a mouthful from my bowl. 'It's a bit like perfume. But it doesn't hurt to broaden our horizons a bit, and it's not like we have a huge production line. It's small batch and artisan, so we can diversify as much as we like in as many quantities as we like and see what sells out, up at the farm shops that have already agreed to trial us. It's your baby, though, Tam, so you tell me what you want to do.'

'It's only my idea,' Tamara says. 'It's your product.'

Josh and Tamara talk non-stop. Their knowledge about dairy production goes over my head, but their enthusiasm is infectious and I nod in all the right places. They talk in acronyms, like a shared code.

Eventually Tamara stands up at a speed I wasn't prepared for, hugs Josh and then me, which is sweet, tells me how lovely it was to meet me and that she wishes me a safe journey home later on and hopes to see me again soon.

'Lexie's not going back to London just yet,' Josh chimes in. 'She's going to stay for a couple more days.'

'Oh, that's *great*,' she exclaims. 'You'll love it here. If you want any pointers about shops or whatever while you're here, I'm your woman.'

Eventually we say our goodbyes.

The front door bangs as Tamara bounds out. 'She's so nice,' I say. 'And gorgeous', because I want to sound Josh out about this in particular. I've never been in a scenario where a guy I'm dating has a best friend who's a very hot female.

'I suppose so, but she's like family,' Josh replies, and I take that at face value. He carries on, tidying away mugs and spoons while I finish off the rest of the blackberry-ripple ice cream, which is incredible. Ice cream for breakfast is the best.

'Is this a recent best friendship?' I ask.

'No. Since we were children. Babies, I guess. Tam was born the day before me, and her mum was next to mine in the hospital ward.'

'Oh,' I reply, wondering what to say next.

But Josh saves me. 'We weren't always friends. We hated each other when we were about ten or eleven. Can't remember why, though. Then we met again through Young Farmers.'

'Young Farmers . . . ?'

'It's a rural social group, and we've been hanging out ever since. Then Tamara started here when I needed more of a hand. She works hard, wants the best for the farm, the best for me – she's a great friend. I've got male friends and while they're good for banter, you couldn't ring them up at two a.m. and cry down the phone to them when something's gone wrong,' he says, laughing off his confession jokingly.

But I think he's being real. 'Have you done that?' I ask.

'Yeah. Once. I made a bit of a bad decision on the farm. It all worked out in the end, but I needed to sound off. Sometimes girl mates are just better, less judgemental,' he finishes.

'Yeah,' I agree as I think of Scarlet and how she's always there to be real with me, to pick me up when I'm down or simply to be sympathetic, depending on what I need. I hope I'm that for her too.

It's nice that Josh has got a good friend to whom he can show his emotions. I'm pleased for him.

'Is she a bitch? I'll bet she's a bitch,' Scarlet says on the phone to me later, in an outstanding show of unasked-for solidarity.

I had to break it to her that Josh's best friend was not a single handsome farmer.

Josh is in the kitchen, cooking a roast dinner from scratch. I'd helped peel potatoes, but after I sent Scarlet a message telling her I wasn't coming back home yet, she rang me straight away and demanded to know if I was being held hostage. I've snuck into the sitting room and am completing slow laps around the huge sofas, while talking. We've moved on to Tamara now, although I dropped her into the conversation so gently that I thought Scarlet wouldn't say anything. She leapt straight on it, which means I'm now worried.

'You can't be best friends with a girl if you're a guy,' she says. 'It's a fact. Look at all the shit that went down in *When Harry Met Sally*.'

'I've not seen it,' I confess and Scarlet splutters in surprise. 'Give it to me in a nutshell,' I command.

'You don't want to know.'

'Don't be silly. Tamara's not a new friend. They've known each other since they were kids. They're like . . . family.'

'Just be aware. Monitor the situation and react appropriately,' she instructs, as if we work at NASA and there's a live mission under threat.

'Yeah, OK,' I say trying not to sound dismissive and we sign off as I return to Josh, who's waiting patiently for me, candles lit on the table.

'Ta-da,' he says with a flourish as he presents a roast dinner with all the trimmings.

'Is this one of the cows I met earlier?' I sort of half joke.

'Don't start . . .' he warns with a smile, and I decide I'm

going to have to put their cute little faces out of my mind if I'm going to carry on like this with Josh. I look around the homely farmhouse kitchen and then back to him. I could get used to this.

Saying goodbye to Josh a couple of days later at the train station was hard for both of us. 'I wish you could stay longer' was his parting shot to me as I waited for the London-bound train to arrive. Then he followed up with, 'Come back next weekend?' before giving me the most delicious kiss.

How could I say no? I feel so secure with Josh in these early stages. And they are early stages. But feeling this wanted and secure in a relationship is something I didn't think I'd experience again, after having been so horribly cheated on. In a way, now, I almost understand why Simon waited for me to rumble his actions rather than confess. Yes, there was cowardice there, but also the desire not to hurt someone.

Or perhaps I'm bestowing my own morals onto him. Because, although what passed between Chris and me was brief, it was *something*. And yet I still have not replied to his last message. It's been days since his last simple **Hi**. And last night he messaged again, which makes me close my eyes tightly and put my hand over my face in embarrassment when I see it.

Big Talk round . . . whatever we're on. Chris's previous message is still sitting above this one, unanswered. I'm wrong. He hasn't got the hint at all. I feel awful now. **What would you say if I told you I think I can get you a job?**

Well, that's not at all what I was expecting. There's no more to the message. As teasers go, it's up there.

I feel terrible replying to this message when I haven't replied to his previous one. It's such a transparent motive. He'll probably be asleep now, so I send the following, knowing I've got a few hours' grace until Chris wakes up: **What kind of job? Because if it's in interior design, I am obviously going to jump at it.** Then I send another one. **Thanks for thinking of me.**

Chapter Sixteen

That evening Scarlet and I are engaging in one of our favourite evening activities: scrolling through Deliveroo to see what offers are on and what we – I mean *what I* – can afford. I spent the entire day applying for jobs and waiting for the one that Chris teased me with to land in my messages. But nothing comes. I think that's for the best. If he doesn't reply with more details about the potential job, I'm not going to chase. I wonder if he's cooling off on me, sensing I've been doing the same.

Or maybe not, as a message lands just as Scarlet and I are about to succumb to a two-for-one pizza offer.

Of course I thought of you. I can't stop thinking about you. You're kind of hard to forget.

Oh no. I breathe in, breathe out. I put the phone down, then I pick it back up again. How do I handle this? These are words I'd have fallen over myself to hear coming from Chris, twenty-four hours after he left me standing on the gravel drive of the wedding venue. But now . . . ? I can't encourage Chris. I can't. Things are moving so swiftly between Josh and me that I can't do *anything* out of the ordinary to hurt either of them.

'Back in a sec,' I tell Scarlet as I stroll, far too casually, back to my bedroom for a moment. But she's too busy placing our pizza order to notice my dilemma.

I'm online, and so is Chris. But I'm not replying because I don't know what to say. I sit on the edge of my bed, thinking. I'm trying to phrase it in my head, attempting to find the words that mean we can still be friends, but nothing more, because I'm now moving at quite a pace with the man he knows simply as his mate Dan's best man.

And then I see Chris typing. He hits send.

It is indeed an interior-design job, you'll be pleased to hear. Or, rather, it's sort of an interior-design job. You interested?

My attention is now diverted. My new plan is to deal with this potential job and then let Chris down gently, and hope he doesn't retract his offer to help me land an exciting new job.

An interior-design job? I ask tentatively. **Is this for the company you work for?** I'm pleased I've been spared having to let him down for a moment. I haven't gone off him. That's the problem. My feelings for Chris were only growing, not diminishing, and I can't forget the connection we had. Chris is kind and thoughtful and sent me a job listing. But I hold tightly onto the fact that I'm with Josh, and building something with him is my priority.

He sends a thumbs-up emoji, followed by: **We're opening a hotel in London. Our in-house designer wants someone on the ground over there. It's more of an admin/assistant role with a design-slant, from what I can work out. You might think it's a bit beneath you, but take a look?**

At this point nothing is beneath me.

He sends a laughing emoji followed by: **How are you anyway?**

Now is the time to do this, to rip the plaster off and tell him the truth. But I don't want to look crazed, so I'll lead in gently.

I'm good. How are you? This is polite. Very small-talky. Anything more than superficial small talk has *got* to be out of bounds now. Josh and I aren't serious. We're just seeing each other. It's a bit more accelerated, pace-wise, than I'd normally go with a man, but he lives so bloody far away – it's either this or snail's pace.

Chris is replying to my question, so while he types I click on the link he's sent.

The job looks great, and the role-profile describes lots of things I feel confident doing already, barring the fact that it mentions a working knowledge of a few software programs I've never used. I'll take a look at some online tutorials and see how I get on. The majority of the job involves running to and from the site in London, being present when needed at all stages of the build for the office team, who need a site liaison. There *is* an element of design involved, as the company wants to use UK-based manufacturers for the interior, so there would be some reporting back to the Head of Design. It sounds like it's a lot of admin and diary management for delivery schedules too. I can do that. If I go for this and I get it, then it's closer to any design work than I've ever got before.

I assume they want to use British craftsmen while also making this hotel look aesthetically like every other one of their properties. I take a look at the hotel chain online and happily find that I'm wrong. Each property has a different aesthetic, depending on where in the world it is. The hotels are small, fewer than fifty rooms, but they're each individual, homely, elegant, comfortable, expensive and full of tasteful soft furnishings and no sharp edges. Whoever the head designer is, we have the same taste, which feels like a sign. The job also includes occasional travel to their New York office.

· This is far too exciting for words. The position is work from home, when not travelling, and I presume that's because there's no office in London yet. I think I'm going to apply for this.

I flick back to our chat. Chris's message lands, telling me about his day, and I want to keep our conversation going, to find out *more* about his day, his life, what he's been doing since we last texted properly. I want to know about him and his world, to have deep, meaningful conversations with him and . . . I hate knowing I can't do that now. Just for a few seconds longer I bask in our exciting, flirtatious messages of Big Talk and remember that night with him at the wedding, how it felt to be near him. But this has to stop.

It's now or never. I'm about to end everything between us. I'm about to say goodbye to Chris. Again. It's the right thing to do, so why does it feel so wrong?

Neither of us types. Then we both start at the same time. I can see him typing, and so this is going to be a rush as to who can reply fast enough. I'm determined it's going to be me, because I need to get this over and done with and I can't let him say anything flirty or suggestive. It's not fair. I hit send on my message: **I'm really enjoying having you as a friend.**

He stops typing. The word 'friend' has now entered our chat and it should do the trick, because everyone knows what that means. It feels so cruel, but I couldn't work out how else to do it. I could hardly say, 'Remember Josh, the best man from the wedding where you and I met and then had to let each other go? Well, about ten minutes after you left I kissed him as part of a game and now I'm shagging him.'

No, I couldn't do that. Instead we're entering the friend-zone and no one looks grimy. Only . . . Chris isn't typing any more. I'm going to end it as nicely as I can and then I have to go, move on, call Josh and make plans with him.

I finish with: **And thank you so much for the job recommendation. It looks perfect.**

I follow it up with another message – a kiss so I don't look rude. I hit send and then, hoping he hasn't seen it, I quickly tap 'delete', remove the kiss and, in doing so, remove a piece of myself.

Chapter Seventeen

Chris

Did I just get friend-zoned?

I'm standing at my bathroom sink, ready to brush my teeth, but haven't done it yet because I messaged Lexie and that took over. She's gone now, but I'm still lingering here, staring at her words, analysing our exchange.

I reread our messages. I'm midway through telling her all about my day and . . . I did – I just got friend-zoned. And rather abruptly too. So abruptly it almost makes me laugh.

I shake my head in bafflement and scroll up our chat. And then I scroll down and . . . Where was the sign this was coming? There was no sign. Or was there? She went silent on me for a few days. Was that it?

I read through the bit where I tell her I can't stop thinking about her. This is a little embarrassing now. And why I did this is beyond me, because I'm on a mission to be single. But I haven't been able to stop thinking about Lexie. I'm drawn to her. We had an evening of perfect conversation and I asked her to get on a plane with me. She said no. And now I've been friend-zoned. She put a kiss and then I watched it disappear as she deleted it.

That was painful to watch.

But we got on so well. It was so real. That night on the terrace, it felt so real. She almost got on a plane with me. And everything after that . . . perfection. Until now. I pull a deep breath into my lungs, let it out slowly.

I stare at the phone in anticipation, just in case. But there's nothing more. She's gone offline. That's it.

I look away from the phone and stare at myself in the bathroom mirror. Under my breath I mutter the word 'Fuck!'

Chapter Eighteen

Lexie

It feels so normal being back at Josh's for the weekend. Almost as if I never left, almost as normal as if I was at home with Scarlet. Although with Scarlet this past week she was at work all day and I was on the sofa, giving my CV the kicking-into-shape it really needed for the design job that Chris sent me.

I had a call lined up this coming Monday for a temporary job with an agency and, just as I boarded the train to head to Josh's for the weekend, the agent cancelled. I cannot explain how down this is all making me feel. As if sensing that I need perking up, after we've had dinner and then after we've had sex, Josh asks if I'd like to hang out with him a bit longer again, instead of racing back on the train on Sunday.

'If you get even a hint of a job I'll have you back on that train as fast as you want,' he says.

'Really?' I ask, turning into his warm body.

'I can drive very fast,' Josh says, stroking my hair.

'No, I mean . . . you want me to stay a bit longer?'

His gaze connects with mine. 'Why not. I've got to work,

but if you don't mind the solitude during the day, we can have dinner together each evening. Take each day as it comes and see what it brings. If you get bored, or a job offer, or miss your own bed . . . hop back on the train.'

Take each day as it comes and see what it brings. It had better bring a job offer. Although being here with Josh is wonderful. I *could* stay a bit longer. A few days perhaps. We won't be overdoing things with each other, because he'll be gone all day. It would be like having a dinner date every evening. This could be fun. And I can indulge my Lady of the Manor fantasies, wafting around his supersized country house in floaty dresses, playing with the Aga and walking into the village. It'll be like a little holiday. I could really do with a little holiday.

On Monday Josh pops in from the farm from time to time to see me, thoughtfully checking on me, and while he's out on the farm I work on my portfolio. I've redesigned it a thousand times, I've edited images, I've written down my thought processes and inspirations and now I don't know what else to do. I need to go on a course. I thought this might take me all week. It's taken me less than a day.

Josh tells me to pull my wellies on. We go down to the farm and I get to pet the cows and their young. I'm so in love with these mini cows.

'How's your portfolio going?' Josh asks as I stroke a six-month-old calf, which seems to be loving the attention.

I'm so in awe, I blink a few times before answering him, telling him what I've done.

He sounds impressed. 'Show me after dinner?'

I nod. 'Shall I cook for us tonight?'

'I thought you couldn't cook?' he says.

'Hey,' I cry, and the calf bolts at my sound level. 'Sorry,' I tell Josh.

He's kneeling on the floor. 'She'll be back in a moment, don't worry.'

'I can cook when I have to,' I tell him in a quieter voice. 'I'll rustle something up for you while you have a bath, or whatever you want to do when you get in from work.'

'Shower, dinner, pyjamas, usually.'

'Every night?'

'Mostly,' he confirms.

'Oh. Well, you do that and I'll pretend to be a farmer's wife for a bit.'

'A farmer's wife?' he asks with a knowing smile. 'Sounds *good,*' he says. 'I think I'm running out of food, though. Might be cheese on toast at this rate.'

'When do you shop, if you work all the time?'

'Usually on Sundays, but I've been enjoying myself with you too much to ruin it by suggesting a trip to the supermarket.'

'Tell me what you want to eat and I'll go for you tomorrow while you're at work, if you like?' I suggest.

'Really?'

'Only if it's walkable, though. I can't drive.'

'You can't drive?' he questions, shock passing over his face.

'I live in London. I've never needed to drive.'

'Right,' he replies, thinking about this. 'Have you always lived in London?'

'No. I'm from Hertford, but I went to university in London and then stayed there. I never took driving lessons; they were too expensive for a poor student like me.'

'I guess everything's different in the country. I learned to drive as soon as possible. Dad let me drive him around the farm in his four-by-four and I learned to reverse-park in between farm machinery.'

The calf doesn't return, so Josh pulls some apple slices out of a little bag from his pocket and tells me to coax the cows over with them. 'Healthy snack,' he says, and the slices disappear out of my hands and into their soft mouths, one by one.

'So if you can't drive,' he says, 'I guess that only leaves the farm shop up the road. It's just before you get to the village. We need some top-up supplies. My mum's old bike is in one of the outhouses. It's got a big basket on the front. I'll give it a check-over and you could take that? Have a cycle around the countryside for a bit, if you want, first? Go sightseeing?'

'OK,' I smile. 'Leave the shopping to me,' I instruct. And then I remember that I'm broke. 'How much do you think it might . . .' I start.

But Josh remembers too. 'I'll give you my credit card. You can tap it.'

'Thanks,' I say, feeling embarrassed.

Later, in bed, Josh slumbers peacefully – the sleep of a hard-working farmer who's been up since 5.30 a.m. I'm restless, unable to drift off. I think it's because I've not had enough exercise today. I'm not a gym bunny, but I usually leave the flat every day and speed-walk (because I'm late and get my 10,000 steps in super-fast) to whichever job I'm at. And at weekends, when funds allow, I'll meet friends for lunch or pop down the road for coffee and a croissant. Today I've been down to the cow shed and back. And that's it.

I can't wait to get out tomorrow, ride Josh's mum's bike and shop for food. Somehow this mundane-sounding activity feels exciting. I've never been to a farm shop before. As I'm mentally planning my *I'm-going-to-a-farm-shop-on-a-bike* outfit I wonder how many days' worth of food I should buy, and how much I can bring back on a bike. I curl into Josh as he sleeps, feeling the warmth of his skin against mine. He sighs and turns into me, which feels so comforting. But for reasons I can't fathom, I still can't fall asleep.

Chapter Nineteen

After a week, Scarlet is bemoaning the fact I'm not coming home. **It's only been a week. Chill out. I'll come back soon, I promise.**

I will. I can't stay here for ever. As much as I'd love to. The job hunt continues. Scarlet and I send messages back and forth, but her job is busy and she's filling her evenings by watching all the stuff she series-links on our TV catch-up, which I'm just not that into. She says my prolonged stay elsewhere feels like a mini-divorce. Although she knows I'll be back at some point and I indicated as much to Josh, he seemed up for me staying another week. I think that's probably enough time together, so that we don't overdo things. In the meantime, Scarlet's whizzing through all those cop dramas I can't stand as quickly as possible.

It's a shame TV doesn't have a x2 speed option, the way audiobooks do, she laments one evening as I'm cooking potatoes dauphinoise and chicken Kiev for me and Josh.

I realise, in hindsight, this dinner is going to be garlicky, but it's too late now. I'm learning how to play at being a farmer's wife, even if I'm not one. I'm enjoying it. It's novel. It's nice not to be temping, and I've decided not to think about how broke I am. Not this week. I'm on a sort of holiday.

I glance at the phone as Scarlet's next message lands. I'll reply later, when I'm not willing 500ml of cream to simmer, but not burn. I've learned how to find my way around this Aga and I'm secretly very proud. It's a genius contraption. I might suggest to Scarlet that we get one, although I think the weight of this in our first-floor flat might kill the tenants below, if it ever plummets through the floor. Also, the expense of the thing. I've googled.

It turns out Scarlet can't wait for a response, as my phone rings. Josh looks up from a copy of *Farmers Weekly* as I swipe to answer.

'Are you still alive?' she asks, 'because you didn't acknowledge the genius of my two-speed comment.'

'I'm acknowledging the genius now,' I tell her with mock-seriousness. 'Although I know you can increase the speed on YouTube videos, if that's any use to you?'

'It's not. Nothing I want to watch is on there,' she says and then changes tack, whining, 'You've been gone ages. What's happening? Why are you still there? Are you sure you're not being held prisoner?'

'I'm not a prisoner,' I tell her, which elicits a snort from Josh as he turns a page. 'I'm currently cooking potatoes dauphinoise,' I say.

After a beat she replies, 'What the fuck is that?'

'Sliced potatoes in cream and garlic, basically. It's really easy to make. We have a lot of potatoes, so I thought I'd—'

But she cuts into my monologue. 'We?' she asks. 'You've been there a week and it's . . . *we* have a lot of potatoes?'

'Josh,' I correct myself and, thinking he's being addressed, he raises his head to look at me. 'Josh has a lot of potatoes.' I give him the nod to indicate that he can go back to his magazine. 'Although I went to the farm shop to buy them, and so I guess . . . *we* have a lot of potatoes.' Scarlet says nothing in return and so I follow up with, 'Hello?'

'I'm still here,' she says quietly. 'Are you coming back? Are you thinking about getting a job or . . . are you there full-time now?'

'Of course I'm not.' But I don't carry on because I have no idea what Josh and I are doing, and I don't necessarily want him to overhear this conversation. We're enjoying each other's company and I'm enjoying being here. It's only been a week. 'I need to finish dinner, can I call you back?' I suggest.

'OK. Call me after dinner. I want to talk to you about our spa day.'

'What spa day?' I ask, distracted by my inept culinary skills.

'The spa day you snogged Josh to win,' she replies, as if she can't believe how easily I've forgotten. Of course: I snogged Josh to win a spa day. And now I'm here, weeks later, cooking what I consider to be a gourmet dinner for us both. How strange this is. I can see Scarlet's point. And I know later on she's only going to use the spa day as an excuse to stick it to me again about being here, although she is sweet to remember my winnings and to push it forward, when she didn't have to because, as it turns out, I had completely forgotten.

After dinner Josh and I mosey towards the TV and sip cups of tea while we watch the news. This has become our happy evening ritual. I don't often watch the news – it's usually there in the background while I wait for the good stuff to come on – but Josh makes a point of putting it on, and I watch the various European comings and goings with glazed eyes. I glance over to Josh as a story breaks about another politician sleeping with someone they shouldn't have, and I find Josh has nodded off. I could go in search of the Kardashians on whatever channel they're on now, but I don't. I look at Josh's sleeping form and feel some sort of sense of duty.

'Let's go to bed,' I prod him, and he blinks himself awake, gets up willingly. I've already loaded the dishwasher and it whirs comfortingly in the background as we head up the stairs. I could get used to this life.

While Josh is at work the next day I ring Scarlet on what I know will be her usual lunch hour, and I apologise for being a shit flatmate and not calling her back the night before.

'Can we plan our spa day now?' she asks.

'Yes, please,' I reply, the diary open on my phone, which is a pointless thing to do because it's blank. I know it's blank. There's nothing in there, given that I've had to decline all invites due to a lack of cash.

'I thought we could tack it on to our stay in Edinburgh in February,' she suggests.

'Great,' I respond enthusiastically.

'We should stay overnight,' she says, 'or the train journey home after a day of pampering might be a bit of a downer.'

'I can't,' I'm quick to say. 'I can't afford—'

'I'll pay,' Scarlet cuts in. 'It's part of the bingo deal.'

'No, I can't accept that,' I protest.

'I want to spend time with you,' she replies. 'If luring you away from the sexy farmer's gorgeous house involves spending a bit of money on an overnight break, then let's do it. Let's treat ourselves.'

'I won't still be here in *February*,' I say.

She ignores the comment and says, 'I quite fancy a little Edinburgh jaunt. I hardly ever go anywhere that isn't an overnight stay for someone's poxy wedding, so the spa will be a nice bonus. And I've booked us a chain-hotel room nearby, rather than staying in the swanky hotel the night of the wedding.'

'Oh, you didn't have to do that for me.'

'I didn't do it for you. The wedding hotel is three hundred and fifty pounds per night per room. Even I'm not enough of a muppet to pay that. We'll get some luxury at the spa day anyway.'

'Thanks. I'm sure I'll have a job by then to pay my way, if our travel choices stay relatively frugal.' I am not sure of this at all.

'So I'll book the spa,' she says, without acknowledging my mention of being hopeful about a job. 'No arguments.'

I love her so much. 'Thank you. You are one in a million.'

'I know,' she says. 'Perhaps, as it's going to be Valentine's weekend, we can pretend we're a couple and it's our anniversary – maybe the spa will offer us a free bottle of fizz.'

'Pah! Try it. See what happens.'

'I will. I'll report back. What are you up to today, if sexy farmer is out sexy farming?'

'No idea,' I reply. 'It's halfway through the day already, so he'll be home for lunch shortly. Josh usually makes us both a sandwich. I feel like I should be doing some household chores or something. I make the bed each day after I get out of it, and the kitchen gets a once-over after I've cooked dinner, but that's only because I've obliterated it, using every single pan there is. Do you think I should be doing more? Should I change the sheets, do you think, or give the bathroom a proper clean? Or should I be the one making him lunch? What do you think?'

'You really do sound like you live there now,' Scarlet says unhelpfully. 'I thought you were working on your portfolio.'

'I've done that. And I've applied for some jobs. I'm not sure what else to do now. I feel like I need to pay my way, and this is the only way I can.'

'Does he have a cleaner? How did he do it all before you came along?'

'No idea. The house was spotlessly clean when I arrived, though.'

'Maybe his mum does it,' she laughs.

'Don't!' I say and laugh in return.

'Maybe *Tamara* does it!' She splutters even harder with laughter.

'Stop!' I tell her, but I can't help laughing.

'Do you think you'll just abandon me and stay there for ever?' she asks and the mood changes.

'No, of course not,' I reply. 'I could easily stay here, though. This life, it's easy. Too easy. But I do need to get a job, and I can't live here rent-free much longer.'

'Why not? You live rent-free with me every now and again,' Scarlet digs, but I can hear the smile in her voice.

'I know. But I always catch up in the end,' I say in a sing-song voice.

'True,' she confirms.

'Anyway, someone sent me a *really* good job listing and I've applied.'

'Ooh, have you? What's the job?' Scarlet asks and I break into a few short, sharp facts about meeting Chris at the wedding and how he sent me the listing. I don't tell her *exactly* how well Chris and I got on the night we met, that had things been different – had I said yes to his suggestion to go with him to New York – I might be there right now, living a dream life in New York with Chris, instead of living this dream life in the countryside with Josh.

So she's armed with some of the facts, but not all of them, because I don't want her to read too much into the fact that I met Chris before I met Josh and that he asked me to get on a plane with him.

'What are you doing tonight?' I ask, changing tack.

'I'm off to a gallery opening with a friend. Some singer fancies himself as a photographer, so I'm going to go and issue praise wildly while knowing in advance the photos are going to be all really arty and really shit. What about you?'

'Being jealous of your night out,' I say.

'You could come along?' she suggests. 'How long is it from Josh's farm to London?'

'Bloody for ever. I would, but I can't. We're going over to Tamara's for dinner tonight.'

'What's she cooking?' Scarlet probes.

'Don't know.'

'Can you ask her what kind of grout cleaner she uses in Josh's bathroom, please? I'm having a nightmare getting ours to—'

'Oh, piss off,' I tell her.

Chapter Twenty

'Slow-cooked pulled pork and a few unfussy sides. Just stuff I threw in the oven earlier. I hope you don't mind it's so simple,' Tamara says in response to our enthusiastic sniffing when we arrive. She leads us in through the front door of her chocolate-box cottage, wisteria vines growing around the top window frames.

'Slow-cooked pulled pork doesn't sound so simple,' I mutter as we take off our shoes and go through to the kitchen. Josh stops in front of me and I crash into him. I peer round him to see there's a man at the kitchen table, smiling affably.

'Hi,' I say from behind Josh, who shuffles forward. 'We met in the pub the other night,' I continue, pointing out the obvious after I tagged along to join Josh and the farm team for some after-work drinks.

'Hi, how's it going?' Mark, the pub landlord, replies. He's our age and very good-looking. This feels like a double date.

Tamara puts a hand on his shoulder. 'Mark's joining us for dinner. I hope that's OK?'

I laugh because it's such a strange thing to say. What if we were to say, *No, chuck him out?* 'Of course,' I reply. 'Nice to see you again.'

'Likewise,' he says, standing to kiss me on my cheek and shake Josh's hand.

'Let me check on the potatoes dauphinoise,' Tamara trills.

I cast Josh a look he doesn't understand. 'It's a popular dish,' I nudge him, with a knowing smile.

'Is it?' he asks.

'I only just made it for you,' I prod.

'Oh . . . yeah,' Josh replies absently.

'I've been making it for years. My gran taught me,' Tamara says, her back to us as she digs around in the oven. 'The trick is to add much more garlic than you think.'

'Do you think I added enough?' I look to Josh for confirmation that my cooking skills aren't that dire.

He looks trapped, as if I've asked a trick question. 'Um . . .'

'There's no wrong answer,' I say helpfully.

'Tam . . . shall I open this wine?' Mark asks, tactfully turning away from us and uncorking the bottle.

Tamara glances at me. 'Don't compare yourself to me. I've been feeding up Josh for the best part of a decade. Every few days he's here, or I'm at his, and we try to outdo each other every time – we should probably enter *MasterChef*. I take it he's managed to cook you a few decent meals since you moved in?'

I smile and then realise what she's said. 'I haven't *moved in*,' I reply quickly, assuming Josh has given his best friend the lowdown, but hasn't successfully articulated it. 'I'm just staying on for a bit. And yes, the man can cook.'

'You're welcome,' Tamara says jovially as she lifts dishes out of the oven. Mark helps carry items over with a floral pair of oven gloves and remains silent.

'Every few days?' I mutter, barely adjusting my brain to fully receive this information.

'Sorry?' Josh says.

'You're at each other's houses every few days for dinner?' I ask.

'I guess so, yeah. Usually. Not while you're here, though,' Josh replies, planting a quick kiss on my lips. 'Other than right now, obviously,' he chuckles.

I turn to Mark and, willing the conversation in a different direction, I grill him about the pub and how long he's been running it. He touches Tamara's hand every now and again as we talk through dinner. Tamara's dauphinoise is better than mine, and I catch her touching Mark's arm for emphasis when she talks about . . . anything. I keep thinking about the fact that she and Josh usually see each other for dinner every few days. Is that odd? I see Scarlet almost every night for dinner, but we live together.

The fact that Tamara and Mark touch each other so readily does rather take the edge off my paranoia, though. I wonder if she's ever fancied Josh, or if he's ever fancied her? If so, surely one of them would have done something about it by now. I wonder if they *have* done something about it previously, and this is now the friendship aftermath. I feel I may need to watch *When Harry Met Sally*.

But the chat has moved on and the in-jokes between Tamara and Josh are hard to ignore, the shared history that surfaces in their conversation with 'Do you remember when . . . ?' and 'So this one time . . .' and 'Your mum said the funniest thing to me the other day . . .'

I'm not in on any of this, and neither is Mark – we smile politely, top up our wine glasses and help clear plates, while Josh and Tamara witter on around us, politely trying to include us.

Pudding is ice cream again, which makes me laugh and sigh in equal measure. Tamara must be *drowning* in ice cream. She opens her freezer and, sure enough, there are plenty of plain white tubs in there with sample flavours scribbled on the sides.

'What do you think of all the flavours so far?' I ask Mark.

'There's been rather a lot of them,' he says quietly. 'I'm working my way through them, taste-testing what to put on the pub's menu. Currently we buy in from out of town, and it'd be nice to outsource it to someone local. Also . . . have you seen the flavours? Tamara's so creative.'

We get the tubs out and I marvel at some of the hand-scrawled labels. 'Blueberry pie,' I say.

'There's flakes of real pie crust in there,' Tamara comments proudly. 'And blueberries, obviously.'

'Rhubarb crumble,' I go on, as I pass one to Josh for him to take the lid off and put on the table for us all to dig into.

'There's home-made crumble pieces in there,' Tamara says.

I see where this is going, and so I don't comment when I take out apple strudel. I'm secretly impressed. If I saw these in the supermarket, I'd buy them, which is a comment I make aloud, and I find Mark is very invested in the blueberry pie. 'It's addictive,' he says. 'Tamara gave me a taster pot for the kitchen brigade and I had to ask for another because I ate the whole thing.'

I like Mark. He seems less high-octane than Tamara, the Yin to her Yang.

'Try the mint-choc chip,' Tamara instructs Josh, and he pulls the tub towards him and serves some out into his bowl. 'It's got locally grown mint finely diced and swirled in,' she continues. 'Although I'm concerned it's not minty enough. I think it might be too subtle, while also looking violently green . . .' She talks on and on about ice cream, and I wonder if this is what I sound like when I start on about interiors, although it's a rarity that I get onto the topic like this. Tamara's not qualified in ice-cream-making. She's just having a go. But she's doing it with far more confidence than I am with my interest. Perhaps I should be more like her. It's good to have a passion. Tamara's found hers and can run with it. She's pushed herself into a new territory. Good for her.

'So you've tried a few,' Josh says to Mark. 'Any other feedback?'

'Yeah, I'm trying to convince Tam to make salted caramel.'

'Ugh!' Tamara says.

'I know,' Mark defends his choice, 'I thought it'd be a flash in the pan too, but everyone orders it when it's on the menu, so . . .'

'OK, OK,' Tamara concedes, touching his arm. 'I'll work on a recipe and see what I can do. I'll make my own caramel, not one of those jarred sauces swirled in, and I'll use Maldon sea salt . . .' She talks on and Mark looks animated. Tamara looks animated.

I watch Josh as he watches them.

Chapter Twenty-One

Chris

I find our Head of Design, Max, in the pantry kitchen, eyeing up a fresh box of doughnuts that comes weekly and that no one eats, other than him. I'm making it a personal mission to eat everything in this pantry at least once, other than the vegan items. I'm not too fussed about those. We get so much food delivered daily, and I wonder if it's a ploy to keep us here rather than having us venture out for a proper lunch or coffee break. It works.

'If a résumé's landed in your inbox from a woman called Lexie, will you take a look at it?' I ask. Even though whatever was between Lexie and me seems to be no more – as I am 99.9 per cent sure that 'friend' comment was a thinly veiled hint to send me on my way – I still like her. And I know she wanted a job in design, so I will put in a good word and see this through to its conclusion. Whatever that may be.

Max and I are quite good mates. We bonded over our shared annoyance that there's no kettle for a proper cup of tea in this office. Americans don't do kettles. While Max is a dyed-in-the-wool New Yorker, his grandad was English and got him hooked on Yorkshire Gold. I have to buy him a big box whenever I go back to the UK. Max doesn't look up at me, so intent as he is on his doughnut selection. 'I've been looking at every résumé that's come in,' he says absently. 'Why's this one special?'

'She just is,' I say, grabbing an almond croissant. I can't eat doughnuts for breakfast. It's simply wrong. I've worked this much out about myself.

Max swivels his head and looks at me. 'Ohhh.'

'That's not what I mean. I'm recommending her . . . as part of the recommend-a-friend scheme.'

'All right,' he replies, turning back to the doughnuts. 'I'll go and look for her in my inbox. What's her last name?'

'No idea.'

'You know her well, then . . . ? This friend you're trying to get me to hire?'

Ah, shit.

Max smiles to himself, reaches forward for a glazed doughnut.

'How do you know her?' he probes.

'We met at a wedding when I was back in England and she's keen to get into design. I think she'd be good for the job. But I'm not begging for her to get the job, I'm just letting you know that if she sends a CV – résumé – which I assume she has done by now, that I referred her and . . . well, that's kind of it.'

I can see Max digging around in his mind, trying to find a way to ask me more about why I want Lexie to be considered, while also trying to stay within the realms of what's allowed to be discussed in the workplace.

I cut him off before he can get any further. 'Thanks, Max, enjoy your doughnut.' And I make a swift exit back to my desk.

Chapter Twenty-Two

Lexie

I stare at the email on my phone the next morning from Max Riley, acknowledging receipt of my application for the job Chris recommended and asking if I'd be available for a video interview today, with a selection of times offered.

I scramble into a sitting position in bed. 'I've got an interview!'

I'm talking to myself, because Josh is long gone to work. I'm excited, elated and then I'm petrified, and all these emotions happen at once, accompanied by the physical feeling of wanting to be sick.

I swallow, my mouth suddenly dry. I don't say anything more. Instead I reach to the bedside table and down the entire glass of water that I get for myself each night, but never ever drink. Until now.

I'm shaking. My hands are actually shaking and I don't know what to write in reply. I type carefully, reading my response three or four times to confirm that yes, I'd love an interview and double-checking the time they want it. I'm available all afternoon to fit their time zone, but don't know how to phrase that without sounding like I've got nothing else to do all day – which I don't really, barring helping Josh a bit down on the farm.

The head designer Max's email came in overnight, so it'll take a while for him – or maybe Max is a her – to reply as, by now, they'll be asleep in New York. This buys me a bit of time to prepare, although I've no idea what to say or what questions I'm going to be asked. I wonder if some of them might be: *So why does a fully-grown adult who's over thirty want an admin role masquerading as a design job? Why don't you have your shit sorted out already?* I hope Max doesn't ask me that, even though both of those questions would be fully legitimate. Someone from HR will probably have a rule about those kinds of questions, though, I muse to myself as I head towards the shower and mentally plan out what I'm going to wear – the nicest of all the tops I've brought to Josh's, so that on this Zoom call I will look professional.

When the time comes round later that day I have worked myself into a nervous frenzy. I have set out my portfolio next to me, so I can refer to anything I'm asked about; I've a glass of water ready to unstick my mouth with; and I'm trying to look relaxed in Josh's sitting room. The fire is lit behind me, and I hope the look and feel appeal to Max aesthetically while I'm being interviewed. It can only help, surely? I hope I don't look like I'm desperately on the scrounge for a job – which I am, and this would be confirmed if I was having this video call from my tiny little bedroom in my tiny little flat dotted with Ikea furniture.

But, in the end, the interview goes fine, other than the

stupid little wave I give Max when our video screens connect, and the stupid little wave I give him *again* when we finish and say goodbye. I close my laptop lid and stare into the middle distance. I remembered to unmute myself, and he put me at ease with a smile and lots of discussion about my portfolio, my influences and my thoughts on current trends. Other than that, I'd been so nervous that the rest of the interview has melted into my brain and disappeared from my memory, which is probably a good thing.

Later on, while I'm sitting around – the house immaculately cleaned again – and waiting for Josh to come back to the farmhouse, so I can tell him about the interview, I realise I need to thank Chris, as he made this happen. But I don't want to restart things after I cooled them down; especially after his prior confession **I can't stop thinking about you**, I'm a bit lost as to what to do, what to say. I read that message back more often than I should. I try to hear Chris's voice saying it. I know I shouldn't, but no one has ever said that to me before. Ever. I can't stop thinking about it.

I've had zero luck in relationships, zero luck with jobs. But now my luck is picking up and it's all happening at once. I take a deep breath. It's heady and overwhelming, all at the same time. It makes me feel higher when, for so long, I've felt so low. I'm going to say thank you, because I wasn't raised to ignore people when they give you a leg up. I hate the fact we probably won't talk much now, after this. But a note of appreciation is due.

I just wanted to say thank you, I type to Chris. **I've had an interview for the job you recommended.**

He appears online, begins typing. **I know,** he writes.

How do you know?

We're not a huge company, Chris types. **I sit about ten feet away from Max. I may have overheard some of your interview.**

What?! Were you earwigging?

Earwigging? What a great word. I heard your voice when your Zoom connected.

Oh God, I reply. **Did I sound like I knew what I was talking about, or not really?**

I heard you say, 'Hi, nice to meet you', then my head shot up and I thought: Oh, so she applied. Then Max remembered to plug his headset in and I couldn't hear anything else. How do you think it went?

I hope it went well, but I've been wrong about that before. He's really nice, though, isn't he?

He is, yeah. You'll like working with Max, if you get it. They're all great. I hope you get it.

Me too, I say, somewhat obviously.

Our conversation stalls for a bit. Chris is still online, and so am I, but I don't know what to say now. I should probably go. I hear the front door bang, announcing Josh's arrival home, the sound of his wellies hitting the flagstone floor as he takes them off one by one, the floorboards creaking comfortingly as he walks from the hall to the sitting room, pops his head in and waves.

Thanks again. Have a good rest of day, I tell Chris. I look at my phone mournfully for a few seconds, then put it on the coffee table, so I can give Josh a kiss before we eat dinner together and I tell him all about my day.

Chapter Twenty-Three

'I don't understand how this has happened. It can't have happened – it can't have done!' I squeal down the phone to Scarlet a few days later.

'You have so little faith in yourself,' she says and then, 'Hang on, I need to look busy for a minute. I've been on Instagram for ages and my boss is watching me.' I hear her opening and closing her desk drawers, then she taps away loudly at her keyboard and ruffles some papers. 'That's better,' she says. 'She's looking the other way now. Why are you so surprised that you got it?'

'Because I never get *anything*. Not even temp jobs these days,' I declare as I stand in Josh's garden and watch huge sunflowers bend and wave in the breeze. 'I got a job. A *real* job!'

'I know, sweetie, congratulations. It was your time. Did you think you'd be out of work for ever?'

'Kind of, yeah. I'm just . . . I can't—'

Scarlet cuts me off from my mania. 'Have you answered to confirm you're accepting?'

'Not yet. I woke up this morning to find the email in my inbox. I almost missed it. I'll bet I was the only person who applied,' I muse.

'Unlikely. You were simply the best person for the job,' Scarlet says, buoying my confidence. 'When do you start?'

'I'm not sure. I need to read the email again, but on the Zoom call Max mentioned that if I got it, he'd like to meet me in person for a proper handover of all the things he wants me to do, and asked what my availability would be like to go to New York. Although he's not mentioned it again in the confirmation email, so I'm hoping it's still on the cards.'

Scarlet squeals. 'New York! Really?'

'Maybe. I hope so. Anyway, even if not, it's still such a good job – or at least it's a bit of an "everything" job, but this is my foot in the door to interior design, surely?'

'It is. It's also your foot in the door to paying me the rent I've been covering for you, again. Although I admit you're not really living here at the moment,' she goes on, and I know she's not digging.

'I'm sorry,' I reply genuinely. 'Which do you miss more? Me or the money?'

'Don't be silly. I don't need the money as much as I need my best friend.'

'Are you OK?' I ask, realising how absent I've been, ensconced in Josh's house for a couple of weeks.

'Yes, I just miss you,' she says.

'I miss you too. I'm coming home.'

'Don't do it for me,' she replies.

'It's time. I feel as if I live here now, only I'm surrounded by family heirlooms that aren't mine. It's kind of strange, like a ready-made set-up.'

Now that I think about it, all of this is strange: inhabiting another person's house, another person's life. I look from the garden back to the house, to check Josh hasn't got a kitchen window open while he cooks, which would mean he could hear me. He doesn't.

'I think it would be good for Josh and me, because,' I lower my voice, just in case, 'I'm a bit bored.'

'Of Posh Josh? Really?' Scarlet asks.

I tut. 'Don't call him that,' I say. 'He's really down-to-earth. And no, I'm not bored of Josh. I really like him,' I tell her. 'But I don't think it's healthy to be living together after such a short amount of time knowing each other. It's not the norm, is it? It makes me worried, as we had a couple of fantastic first dates and . . . almost skipped the rest of the getting-to-know-each-other period. I know it's only been two weeks, but we've fallen into an easy way of life together and I wonder if . . .' I trail off, happy to let Scarlet surmise and jump in, as she often loves to do, although she doesn't immediately.

And then she finally saves me. 'Life in the country with Josh not all it's cracked up to be?'

'Not so quickly, it's not. Not when you're trying to get to know someone. I'm forever dusting the house, I don't drive, and Josh is busy all the time because—'

'Because he's a sexy farmer,' Scarlet says and laughs at her own joke.

'I really want to get to know him better, and I think we did that well when we were dating – I want to go back to that sort of sparkle. That's all.' And I mean this. We're in the kind of routine of a couple who've been together a few years, not a few weeks. 'It's my fault,' I say. 'I'm jobless and am basically sponging off a man in his country house. I need to earn back my self-respect. Starting with coming home, seeing Josh for dates at weekends, beginning my new job and getting back my sense of purpose. Waking up in someone else's house every day and only needing to worry about what to plan for Josh's dinner ten hours later isn't healthy.'

'No, it's not,' Scarlet concurs. 'Come home and worry about what you're cooking *me* for dinner.'

'When I come home, the first thing we're doing is having a takeaway,' I tell her darkly. 'There's no Deliveroo out here in this backwater and I miss it.'

Chapter Twenty-Four

October

'That's what I like about him,' I tell Scarlet as we dissect each other's news over a Thai takeaway and a bottle of cheap red. I've missed glugging cheap wine rather than delicately sipping the expensive stuff with Josh. 'He's so easy to be with. Everything about Josh is so . . . nice. When I tentatively told him I was making plans to go home, he said he'd miss me. I reminded him that it was always part of the plan that I'd only be there for a short while. He looked sad and just said, "Oh, OK".'

It does make me wonder if I'd outstayed my welcome a bit, though, and Josh was too polite to say so. It can't be easy sharing your precious space with someone in the long term. I ponder that while Scarlet tops up my glass.

'Were you having sex regularly?' she asks, and I blink a bit at that.

'Yes.'

'Then, trust me, he was fine with you being there.'

I laugh.

'When are you seeing him next?'

'We've been in each other's pockets, so I'm going to give him a few weeks to miss me,' I tell her. 'We might not see each other again until I'm back from New York!'

'Winter in New York,' Scarlet whoops. 'You lucky thing.'

'I know,' I squeal. 'I *feel* lucky. I still feel as if it's not real. Although I'll be stuck in an office every day, learning the ropes before they cast me loose back here, which means I'm not sure how much of New York I'm going to see. But just getting on a plane and going somewhere new, meeting new people and earning money while doing it is unbelievably exciting.'

'I'll cheers to that,' Scarlet says and we clink glasses, before she excitedly tells me she's booked our spa-day treatments already as they were having a sale, so we get two hours of treatments for the price of one.

'I'm looking forward to the Edinburgh trip, now I've got the job,' I reply. 'I might be able to pay you back some rent, my train ticket *and* half the room rate by then.

'Let's not go wild,' she deadpans.

Chapter Twenty-Five

Chris

November

Tinder: gone.

Elite Singles: gone.

Happn: gone.

Remove, remove, remove. I had littered my phone with dating apps, but barely used any of them. Maybe that's where I've been going wrong all this time. Maybe I should have been *more* invested in these recently, rather than hoping the old-fashioned way of meeting someone in real life would work better. I digress. I don't want a girlfriend right now. I've got a job to do while I'm waiting for the train, and that job is decluttering my phone.

I'm standing in the subway after work, shuffling forward in a crowd of bodies. I glance up, look round. With any luck, I might get on a train this year. People elbow each other shamelessly. There's no polite way to get on a train in New York at this time of day. I'm used to it now. I glance back down at my phone. There's no sensible method by which these apps have populated my phone, so I've gone digging in a moment of madness.

Or a moment of clarity.

Coffee Meets Bagel: gone.

OkCupid: gone.

I hover over the icon for The League. There was a waiting list for this one and it took me a few months to get on it. For a while I wasn't sure I wanted to be on it, seeing as it's designed for successful career types where, alongside your picture, age and name, you list your qualifications. Like a CV built for romance. It pretty much tells people, 'I'm a career-minded tosser, are you? Great. Let's hook up.' I wasn't really feeling it, but seeing as two of the guys from work had found some success with it *and* it's so hard to get on . . . I might *not* delete this one. I might pause my account, if that's possible. This isn't quite the commitment to the app-culling cause I'd planned, but I never said I was perfect. I click to go into my account settings and pause. I glance at the notification.

Ah, this isn't quite what I was expecting. I've matched goals with someone. She looks nice. Long, dark, swishy hair and deep-set brown eyes. Striking. Her main objective is to find a man who knows what he wants in life. Do I qualify for this? I guess . . . maybe? It's certainly what I've been trying to do. How long am I supposed to stay single? How long am I supposed to be off the market while I indulge myself in – what did Lexie call it – taking myself for dates?

All this time, knowing I needed to be single, needed to work out who I am, the kind of person I am . . . And now Lexie's friend-zoned me. And who can blame her?

Who wants to wait around for a man who lives so far away to pick up a phone, make a proper call, see what it might be like to invest himself in your life – fully invest and not half-heartedly via a free messaging system. No wonder she's done what she's done.

Although there was nothing half-hearted about it at all. That night, and every easy, perfect interaction since, Lexie had my whole heart, I'm sure of it.

It's only been three months since I began this journey of self-discovery. Am I there yet? God knows. But I no longer eat the same takeout from the same place every Saturday, and I will no longer say an automatic 'no' to foreign-language films with subtitles. I just have to make sure I'm not doom-scrolling at the same time – missing the key turning points in the film.

Maybe I do qualify for this woman who is looking for a man who knows what he wants. Maybe it's fate. I read on. She wants to visit as many countries as she can before she settles down. Don't we all? There's something about her eyes. Hard to look away from, like Lexie's, but a lighter shade of brown. She looks lovely. If I ignore this . . . then what if this woman is the one? What if, in my bid to find someone in real life one day, I purposefully ignore the person right in front of me who's landed in my inbox? This is a dilemma I wasn't expecting at 6 p.m. on a Monday.

People nudge me forward. The train is in. The doors are opening and I didn't even notice. I get on the train: standing space only, as usual. What if I click on this and see where it leads me? What if I take a chance? I tried to take a chance with Lexie and that led precisely nowhere. I've got to take a chance, though, haven't I? I'm doing it. I've simply got to make sure that I hold my own with this one; got to make sure I outline, in no uncertain terms, what I want.

Within a few messages back and forth I'll know if this is a possibility. That's all it will take – just a few messages. I begin typing. And then a notification from Max flies onto the top of my screen. I pounce on it immediately. It's brief. But it says everything I'd hoped it would.

Chapter Twenty-Six

Lexie

Congratulations, Chris messages, followed swiftly by a second text: **Max only just told me! I'm really pleased for you.**

I'm in the flat, unpacking and repacking my suitcase one more time. I've got a couple of days and I feel as if I've forgotten to pack something essential for New York, though I can't remember what it is.

I look at his message and, not for the first time, feel strange knowing I'll be working for the same company as Chris. It's going to be weird, seeing him again after everything that's happened since we met back in August, since I found it too easy to fall for him right there and then, and in every message after. But we've let our flirting come to an end, or rather I forced it to an end. And now we can simply be friends.

Come with me.

Oh God, I have to stop hearing him say that. Stop it, stop it, stop it. Why am I replaying this? I reason it'll be OK now, as we didn't even kiss and we're in the friend-zone now.

I can't stop thinking about you.

Fuck fuck fuckity-fuck. But I *did* then flat out say we're

just friends. So, I'm pretty sure he's got the hint. Chris hasn't said anything remotely flirtatious since then. It's all been job-related.

I breathe in deeply, attempt some pragmatism. He lives in New York, and I live in London. That's not about to change. But I'll be in the same office as him for the next couple of weeks, a fact I find slightly disconcerting. I genuinely believed, when I said goodbye to him and he climbed into his taxi, that we would *never* see each other *ever* again. Is this going to be really awkward?

And since Josh arrived on the scene, thoughts of Chris haven't managed to take on a life of their own. I've not let them. Not since those immediate pangs of regret after his taxi pulled away that night. And those pangs only lasted until I kissed Josh anyway. Sort of.

Thanks, I write in response to Chris's congratulations.

Chris types, **Someone's setting up a laptop for you as we speak on a desk next to Max. He says you're joining us for a fortnight before they cast you free back in London. That's incredible. It'll be great to see you again.**

Thanks. I've never been to New York before.

You're in for a treat. I love it here. I reckon you will too. Might not get you back on that plane in a fortnight.

Border Control will have something to say about that, I type.

Chris sends a laughing emoji and then he's offline. Then he's online again and typing.

I guess I'll see you in the office at some point then.

I send back a huge smiling emoji, which is a bit of a

non-committal cop-out, but also because I'm genuinely so excited about this job and not sure what else to say. I keep thinking I'm going to open my eyes and discover this has all been the most amazing dream; that I don't have a new job, am still penniless (which I sort of am anyway until I get paid) and that Josh isn't real, either.

But a few days later the flight across the Atlantic alerts me to the fact that this is very real as turbulence hits thick and fast, heralding the end of my celebratory mini-packets-of-cheese and mini-bottles-of-wine party for one.

I'm in economy, but there's still free food and drink and all the films I can watch, crammed into an eight-hour flight. I've eaten and drunk everything I've been given and have watched three movies. I've done well. I'm trying to keep my eyes off the onboard duty-free catalogue, though. All those make-up sets you can't buy on the high street are beckoning me. But I reason I'm going to be knee-high in debt by the time I return, so I shouldn't blow all my meagre spending money before I've even set foot in the US.

New York is going to cost me a fortune, if I want to do anything interesting outside the borders of what the company would normally pay for, so I have managed to get my parents to individually sub me a little bit of cash each. This is the guilt of the divorce still very much present all these years later, each of them trying to outdo the other.

'How much did your mother give you?' is always a question my dad relies on, in order to up the ante as he rifles through the notes section of his wallet.

I hate asking my parents for help. I hate looking like a

thirty-one-year-old failure, but I reason that asking for a loan one last time won't kill anyone. And I can't take any more support from Scarlet or I'll die of shame. Although Scarlet has actually transferred some money into my account, so that I can head into Sephora and buy her all the American skincare and cosmetics we can't currently get in Britain. I wonder if she'll like some of this very exclusive-looking duty-free stuff? I open the magazine again and start spending her money on her behalf.

The company has naturally put me in one of their two Manhattan hotels and it's bijou – space being at a premium in one of the most expensive cities in the world. It looks refreshed, furnishings-wise; and flicking through the huge bundle of corporate and investor info Max sent me, I can see they have a regular refreshing scheme for all soft furnishings every few years, and for fixtures and fittings every eight. For a portfolio of thirty hotels, this must keep Max on his toes. I'm keen to understand how a company that's twenty years old, and has expanded into most of the capital cities, has never yet opened a hotel in London.

Max said if I was jet-lagged I could come into the office tomorrow instead of today, but I'm raring to go now. I'm sure the need for sleep will catch up with me, but I am buzzing and want so desperately to start work. I text Josh again. He's not replied yet. I've already told him I've landed and have sent him a picture of my room, and now one of me standing near a yellow taxi. I'm such a tourist.

The office is just round the corner, off Bleecker Street in

the Village. I walk there so slowly once I've showered and changed, taking in the squat buildings next to tall ones, the traditional brownstone buildings mixed with shop fronts and pizza joints, bars and florists. Yellow cabs go past, honking horns randomly. I feel like a tourist. I am a tourist, but it's purposeful tourism. I'm going to work. In New York. For a fortnight only, but still. I can't believe it.

The area is fun and funky as I walk past gift shops and coffee bars, artisan perfumers and independent fashion stores, all draped with huge awnings and hand-painted signs, while oversized Christmas decorations shine in the bright sunshine. It's bright but cold. Winter is here. The shops are bigger, the signs bolder, the decorations magnificent. New York, to me, is as if Paris and London had a love-child and then supersized it. I've been here five minutes; but so far, so pretty, so inviting.

I pass the original outpost of Magnolia Bakery that I saw on a rerun of *Sex and the City*. I take a picture for Scarlet. Huge cupcakes and intricately swirled celebration cakes sit under glass domes in the window and, as I pass, I know I'm coming back here to load up on baked goods at the first opportunity I get.

The office is in a narrow three-storey red-brick building and, with a trembling hand, I push the blacked-out front doors and enter the open-plan, super-white but comfortable space. It's filled with sofas, fresh flowers and plants, and there are desks scattered about, with people moving to and from breakout areas, and deluxe coffee machines and platters of pastries and fruit. I cast my eyes around, but I can't see Chris.

Maybe he's on another floor. The woman on reception greets me with a smile and more enthusiasm than I ever greeted anyone with, when I worked on reception. I pull my eyes away from the impressive but small office and meet her curious gaze.

'Hi, I'm here to see Max Riley,' I say, taking off my thick winter coat.

But Max beats her to any spiel about signing in and, taking a badge and a lanyard, he bounds across the room and greets me so warmly, instantly putting me at ease. He's larger than he appeared on our Zoom and younger, in his fifties. He's dressed from head to toe in white, which is a brave move, but then he does work in design. He sort of blends in with the office, as if he's wearing workwear camouflage.

I'm now doubting my choice of denim miniskirt and tights, an oversized blazer and a pair of suede ankle boots. I didn't want to overdo it, but likewise I wasn't sure jeans would cut it. Max is a whole other level of fashion, though, and, paired with his bright-red varifocal glasses, he's giving off quite the Elton John vibe. I instantly warm to him and his infectious smile as he asks me about my flight and my hotel room, and tells me where I'll be sitting in the office and what we'll be doing for the next fortnight – including tours of the company's New York hotels and going through the core plans for London and my role there.

He talks so fast and I already feel I should be writing everything down and, just when I'm about to say that, I feel someone watching me. Out of the corner of my eye I spy

Chris, who's talking into his phone, but holding his gaze on me. I feel myself draw in a short, sharp breath and for a few seconds I can't hear Max any more. I can't hear anything.

Chris raises a hand in greeting and issues me a wide smile that turns into an *I-can't-believe-you're-here* kind of laugh. I smile back, trying to convey the same message, even though we've exchanged no words. Seeing him again is confusing, on so many levels. I wasn't expecting to be jolted in such a way. When I look at my Fitbit stats later, I reckon my heart rate will have gone into the low hundreds. I can't explain this feeling. I refocus on the conversation I'm supposed to be having.

'Come on,' Max says. 'I'll bet you could do with a coffee, after a long flight, and then we'll go round and I'll introduce you to everyone.'

Fully topped up with caffeine and having inhaled a giant cinnamon bun in a breakout area, we head back into the main office so I can meet the team. I'm a pro when it comes to meeting people and remembering names. I've been in and out of so many offices over the past few months, having to do this very thing on repeat through all my temp jobs. I know I'll ace this bit. The rest of it I'm shit-scared about. Excited and totally, utterly shit-scared.

'We'll start with the owners,' Max suggests as we climb the stairs to the next floor. 'It'd be rude not to.' He escorts me towards a large glassed-partitioned office and I'm briefly introduced to the joint partners, a woman and a man called Sybil and Jackson, who aren't dressed quite as snappily as

Max, with an easy attire of jeans and T-shirts all round. In among all my research I read that the two of them are siblings, inheriting their first property from their parents and turning it into something cooler and homelier. The hotels are more like apartment-hotels, each one curated to give a gentle nod to the location and the history of the original building, while fully embracing the new trend for working remotely and nomadic digital jobs. They're all dog-friendly with shared workspaces, and the last one they opened in Berlin has its own coffee shop – an area they want to expand, or so the info Max sent me stated. I'm in awe of them and the brand they've built, and I tell them this, while trying not to be too sycophantic or overexcited, like a puppy that's been shown its first real meal. This isn't my first proper job, but it is my first proper job doing something I think I'm going to love.

We move around the upper office before circling back to the ground floor. I bookmark people's names against their faces and where they're sitting and hope, while I'm here, they don't decide to have an office desk reshuffle, ruining my memorising system. Then we head back towards Max's desk, which is near to where Chris is sitting.

Seeing him is so different from texting him. He's really here. So am I. I'm surprised by how attractive Chris is. I hadn't exactly forgotten what he'd looked like, but the wedding was three months ago and memories wane, exact details become sketchy. If anything, he looks better than I remember. When I picture him in my mind, he's in that amazing wedding suit. But the black trousers and open-neck shirt he's wearing now fit him just as well. Has he done something different to his hair? It looks darker, like the summer sun isn't lightening it, now autumn is fading to winter.

He stops typing on his computer, rises from his chair and my throat constricts in anticipation as he walks towards me, smiling widely and moving to kiss my cheek in greeting. That incredible scent of his aftershave and of . . . him hits me suddenly. I breathe slowly, inhale him.

'Hi,' Chris says as he pulls back and looks into my eyes.

I swallow. 'Hi,' I respond, totally unaware if the expression on my face is conveying what he's just done to my insides. I feel giddy and I'm aware Max is watching the two of us as he exclaims, 'Of course, you two already know each other.'

'Yeah,' Chris replies warmly. And then he explains, 'Lexie and I met in the summer' at the exact same time as I say, 'Chris recommended the job to me.'

Max mutters something politely in the affirmative, as he knows all this.

'Nice to have another Brit in the office,' Chris says, moving away from me almost purposefully, leaning back against a desk. 'What have you got planned while you're here?'

'Careful! That's quite small-talky of you,' I reply and he immediately laughs. I love the way his dark eyes crinkle like that. I picture Josh suddenly, his blue eyes bright against his tanned face.

Max looks confused at the way this conversation has gone, so I give him a brief rundown of how Chris and I met and refused to engage in small talk, only covering huge subjects and deep personal insights into each other's lives. Max's eyes swivel between us, even more confused, and so to cut that subject dead, I tell Chris I've got nothing planned because I wasn't sure how much time I'd get to sightsee.

Max slides in with, 'Well, we finish here at five-thirty, so your time's your own after that. I'm not working you around the clock. You should go and check off all the sights you want to see.'

'I could take you to some of my favourite haunts?' Chris suggests.

'OK, yeah, thanks,' I reply excitedly, and then a beat later I immediately sense this is a bad idea. I shouldn't spend time alone with Chris. It feels disloyal to Josh. Although Chris and I are now working together, so I'm not sure I can avoid him without causing trouble. It's only a fortnight. And then he stays in New York and I go back to London. Nothing's changing. We can be friends.

Max turns to get on with work, so I automatically go with him, waving a quick goodbye to Chris.

And then I begin the first day of the rest of my life.

It's a light start to work, with a disturbingly empty inbox staring back at me on my new laptop, but Max assures me, 'Don't worry, that'll soon fill up.'

And then we're off, talking about upcoming projects, the vision for the London hotel, the kind of vibe the owners are looking for and how I'm going to help achieve it. I can see why they need someone on the ground. For a start, organising artisan samples to be sent from across the UK to New York is a waste of time and money. Max sends me over links, so I can access all the folders and immerse myself in the vision and the mood boards. I love a mood board, the way pieces of fabric sit against pictures of chairs and images of wallpaper and paint stripes. I'm in heaven as I help Max edit one onscreen for a presentation to the bosses, and I tell him this, making him smile fondly. I don't want to look amateurish, but I'm honestly blown away by how much I'm already enjoying this.

We work together all afternoon, and then my jet lag gets the better of me at about four o'clock.

'Off you go,' Max tells me. 'Get some rest. Thank you for coming in today.'

'Of course,' I tell him. 'What else was I going to do?'

'Sleep,' he says. 'Go and rest and I'll see you bright and early tomorrow.'

'Are you sure? I don't want to slink off early when you're still working.'

'Go to the hotel,' he instructs. 'Embrace your jet lag.'

'Thanks, Max,' I say, looking around to give a brief wave to a few of those who are sitting near me, who say 'Bye' in return or issue a quick wave and a smile.

Chris catches my eye and stands to talk to me as I near him. 'You off?'

'Under strict instructions from Max to sleep off my jet lag.'

'If you fancy something to eat later on, drop me a message?'

'Thanks,' I reply uncertainly, as I haven't worked out what I am going to do for dinner. 'I kind of thought I'd just hit room service.'

'You can't do that on your first night,' Chris says, appalled.

'Sleep well and I'll take you out for something quick to eat and have you back in time for another round of jet-lag sleeping.'

I laugh as I head towards the door. 'OK, thanks.'

Back in my room, I call Josh and fill him in on my day and he tells me about his. We trade information about chic offices in New York and homely farms in the country.

'I miss you,' Josh tells me.

'I miss you too,' I repeat, meaning it.

'I didn't realise how much I was going to miss you,' he continues. 'Somehow you being so much further away than London does feel different.'

'It is different,' I say. 'But it's only two weeks. Then I'll be home and I can pop down to yours. Now I've been thinking,' I say.

'Go on,' he replies warily.

'Have you got any hay bales?'

He laughs. 'Why?'

'You know why,' I tease.

'You want to have sex on a hay bale?'

'Yes, I do, farm boy. I'm going to leave the logistics of that one with you. You've got a fortnight till I get home to assemble something in a barn.'

'Specific,' he says, chuckling to himself.

Chapter Twenty-Seven

When I wake from my nap it's 8 p.m. and the sky is as dark here as it would be at home at this time of night. I look out of the window and take in the bright lights of the city, and of Bleecker Street and Greenwich Village. The English countryside is hard to beat for its lack of light pollution, but New York is beautiful in a raw look-at-me kind of way. I wonder if I could ever get used to this, as Chris has done.

I shower and put on jeans and a jumper and a quick dab of make-up. I'm hungry, so thoughts of falling back to sleep again fly out of the window in favour of finding something very 'New York' to feed on. Having never been here before, I want to try everything. Chris is right: I can't order room service on night one. Or at all, really, if I want to do New York right.

Do you still want to grab something to eat or did you already have dinner? I tentatively send to Chris, taking him up on his offer. I still feel it's a bad idea, but not because I don't trust myself, and not because I don't trust him. It's more that I wonder if that initial connection we had is going to be hard to ignore. But now we're friends, sort of. We're probably less than that in reality, given our distance, but we're certainly not more. Not now.

Yet going out for dinner with Chris still feels slightly disloyal to Josh, even though I'm trying to reason it out. Josh and Chris know each other from the stag-do. And while I did tell Josh that it was Chris who recommended me for the job, and that he'd be working in the same office as me while I'm here, we haven't really had any discussion about what might have ensued with Chris – if anything between us *had* happened. Josh knows the basics, but *not* the intensity of how I nearly ended up on a plane with Chris. I'm assuming Josh isn't concerned, given how easy-going he is. And I don't want to worry him unnecessarily.

Chris doesn't respond immediately and, when he does, I'm busy trying to force my feet into my trainers without bothering to undo the laces, because I'm going out, regardless of whether he's coming with me or not. I stop halfway through as my phone beeps, signalling his response.

Love to. I'm starving, he types. **Give me about forty minutes to get to you?**

Forty minutes? Where do you live?

Greenpoint, he replies.

Where the heck is that?

He puts a laughing emoji and then, **Brooklyn.**

OK. Cool. Meet you in the hotel lobby at 8.45?

He sends a thumbs-up and then he's offline and, I presume, either getting ready to leave his apartment and hail a cab or to get on the subway. I decide I'm going to have to snaffle all the complementary pretzel packets while I wait.

*

Dinner with Chris feels easy, friendly and natural – he takes me to his favourite pizza joint, where we order one huge slice each. He chooses pepperoni, and mine has aubergine and pesto, artichoke and prosciutto. I've never ordered pizza by the slice before. The restaurant is loud and casual.

While we eat at our high tables and faded bar stools, Chris sips a beer. I'm so jet-lagged I can't face alcohol, so I've ordered a giant Diet Coke. Everything is giant. 'These are ridiculous,' I say, gesturing to the cups. 'They're bigger than a venti in Starbucks.'

He chuckles as we eat. It's cold outside and warm in here, and condensation gathers on the huge windows. Fairy lights and displays of huge candy-canes and oversized baubles adorn shop windows and the lights have been left on after hours. Around doors life-sized *Nutcracker* soldiers in red and white greet shoppers. It's wonderfully photogenic and the whole city is already so festive, even though it's not yet December.

'I'm sure yesterday it was pumpkins and Halloween stuff everywhere,' Chris says to my observation. 'Overnight it all turned into Christmas decorations, without me even noticing.'

'It's so pretty,' I say. 'I can see why you like it here. The changing of the seasons. Must be magical.'

He grins, then takes a huge bite of pizza.

'Thanks for taking me somewhere touristy,' I tell him genuinely, trying not to let pizza grease slip down my chin.

'This isn't touristy,' Chris says, stunned. 'This is my new

favourite pizza place. It's old, you know – not hipstery in the slightest.'

'Um . . . it is quite hipstery. But it feels like how a New York pizza place should be.'

He'll take that comment clearly, as he narrows his eyes and glances around. 'Don't ruin it for me,' Chris jokes. Then he focuses on eating dinner. 'That is good,' he sighs after a couple of bites. 'I was starving.'

'I did wonder if you'd already had dinner and were just here out of politeness?' I ask.

'I purposefully *didn't* eat dinner, out of politeness.'

'In case I rang?'

'Something like that,' he says softly.

'Thanks,' I reply quickly, 'for taking me out tonight. For suggesting the job to me. For all of it.'

'It wasn't wholly selfless,' he admits.

'No?' I question warily, worried about what he might say. I dig into my slice.

'Because you got the job, I get fifteen hundred dollars.'

I stop eating. 'Sorry? What do you get fifteen hundred dollars for?'

'For recommending you to the role; if it all works out, I get a referral bonus. It saves them so much in recruitment-agent fees, so they're always on the hunt for recommendations when it comes to filling roles that open up.'

Somewhere in the street outside a yellow taxi honks its horn and my gaze drifts out of the condensation-heavy window to look, but in reality I'm processing what Chris has just said.

I feel offended, though I don't know why. 'And there was me, thinking you'd remembered me,' I say before slurping some of my Coke. I wish I hadn't said that. I hope it's not taken out of context.

'I did remember you,' he replies and then he looks back at his pizza. 'That's why I recommended you.' He munches the final bites and then, when he's finished, scrunches his paper napkin up and puts it on the plate. 'It's all part of my grand plan to get you to New York.'

I give him an uncertain look. 'Really?'

'Not really. I'm not that God-like.' He's frowning at his greasy pizza plate and looks as if he's thinking hard about what to say next, running it through his mind first. 'I don't want you to think I go around inviting every woman I meet to get on a flight with me, there and then. It wasn't a casual everyday move.'

I look at Chris and my breathing slows. Is the elephant in the room – everything that was said between us that night, and some things since – about to stomp forward and demand to be noticed?

'I still can't believe you did it,' I say gently. 'It was bold.'

'It was. And you almost said yes,' he replies softly.

'I did.' I want to say, *But now we're just friends*, although it feels like such an obviously forced comment.

There's silence between us for a beat, two beats, and then someone enters the restaurant and the door bangs shut behind them. Chris glances towards the noise, breaking our connection.

'So what have you been doing since you got on a plane and left me watching your taxi pull away?' I ask.

'I've been dating someone,' he says.

'Have you?' My voice rises an octave and I bring it back into check. 'I thought you were giving up on dating.'

'I was, but I matched with someone online.'

I roll my eyes.

'I know, I know. Hear me out,' he tells me. 'After everything we'd been talking about – meeting people in real life – I was going to take myself off all those apps, but when I logged in to do that very thing . . . there she was. So I took a risk.'

'On watching the sand-timer of your life run out, over a glass of warm wine?'

'I took a risk on *all* of that,' he says. 'But in the back of my mind I also think it was because of the other chat we had.'

I narrow my eyes. 'Which one?'

'Married at thirty, babies by thirty five.'

'Divorced by forty,' I remind him.

'Ha, yeah. So I took a chance. Sand timer and warm wine be damned.'

'And how's it working out?'

'Good,' he says, looking bashful all of a sudden. 'I mean, it's early days, but so far so good. What about you?'

I pause. I'm not sure how he's going to take this. 'I kind of . . . got together with Josh.'

He reaches for his beer. 'Who's Josh?'

'You went on the stag weekend with him. He was Dan's best man.'

Chris thinks and then says, '*Josh?* Owns-a-farm-Josh?'

'Yeah.' I smile proudly.

'*Really?*' he asks, his voice laced with disbelief.

'Yeah,' I repeat, a bit uncertainly now.

Chris pauses, thinking. 'How did *that* happen?'

'We met at the wedding.'

He nods and then, 'Hang on. The same wedding where you met me?'

'I met you and then I met him.' I tell Chris I met Josh at the bar, when I disappeared inside for so long that night, and about how, later on, I behaved in a very unladylike way and snogged Josh's face off in public. I don't think Chris'll be upset by this. He's dating someone too.

'*Really?*' he says again.

'Stop saying that,' I whine.

'So my taxi drove off into the distance, and I was full of regret about leaving you standing there and about how I had to get on a plane and how much of a missed opportunity it was, and that for the rest of my life I'd be filled with regret about – I don't know about what – because I could hardly force you on the plane, could I, so . . . what did I have to regret?' he says. 'But hours later you and Josh were *kissing*.'

'Actually it was more like ten minutes later that Josh and I were kissing,' I tease, to smooth out my embarrassment. 'I'm a fast worker.'

'Clearly,' Chris replies, but there's humour in his eyes. 'How . . . how come that happened? *We* didn't kiss, so why did you kiss *him*? I need to know this. Was it a timing thing – end-of-the-night erection section?'

'Erection what?' I splutter.

'The dancing at the end of weddings is always slow-dancing, isn't it? Everyone couples up, gets a hard-on and then they get off with each other.'

'That's grim. Actually the last dance was, suitably enough, "New York, New York" with can-can moves. Or was it "Sweet Caroline"? Ooh, I'm going to put that on my wedding-bingo grid for the next one I go to. So no, the non-existent *erection section* is not how it happened. It was the bingo game.'

'The *what*?' Chris leans forward, puts his elbows on the table and rests his chin in his hands as if he's in for a treat of a story.

I can't remember if I even told Chris about the bingo game at the wedding, and clearly I didn't because he looks slightly startled as I explain the concept.

'So, I had to kiss the best man. Josh was the best man,' I finish.

Chris makes a face like he can't believe what I'm saying, and then proves it by exclaiming, 'This is the most ridiculous thing I've heard . . . all year.'

'Really? I met a man in real life and I liked him, although that was an unexpected segue from the bingo game. I didn't have to be swiped on. The game worked out well for both me and Josh. You should try it. Next wedding you go to: give it a shot. It passes the time nicely.'

'For crying out loud,' Chris exclaims, but he's smiling and then his phone dings and he checks his message. 'I have to run in a minute,' he tells me. 'I'll escort you back to your hotel if you want?'

I nod. 'Thanks.' And now I'm nosy. 'You got somewhere to be?'

'I told Kayla, the woman I'm seeing, that I was over on her side of town tonight, so we said we'd meet for drinks. I may head back to hers after.'

'Oh,' I reply. He doesn't need to give me any more detail, and I don't want any. 'I'm a stopgap until you can get to your real date?' I say light-heartedly.

Chris gives me a look and then it turns into an uncertain smile, before he brushes aside my silly comment with, 'Maybe we can hang out a bit more while you're here. Somewhere less touristy?' he jokes.

'I'd love that. Empire State Building next?'

'Absolutely not.'

Chapter Twenty-Eight

I spend the next fortnight in New York in a whirlwind of hotel and showroom tours, budget discussions and ideas meetings, as well as strategising over lunches and coffees with Max and various others in the company. It's lovely, finally feeling part of a permanent team, even though I won't be here with them in person much longer. But working by myself in London, at something I love, is better than being in a bustling office doing something I hate.

I spend my evenings doing the most touristy things I can think of. A late-night trip to the Whitney Museum of American Art, a walk through the ridiculously busy Times Square. It is exactly as it looks in films – the ratio of neon lights to people is 50:50. I plug in an audiobook and grab some food from a vendor and have a little al-fresco solo dinner while I walk along the High Line.

Throughout my time in New York, Max comes out with me for dinner twice, choosing a fabulous little sushi place and then a Vietnamese joint, and it's nice, getting to know him away from the office. He lets his hair down a little more, tells filthy jokes.

The rest of my free time I fill by booking tickets and exploring on my own after work. I'm enjoying going out and seeing what's in this vast city, killing my credit card once again and living an amazing life for two short weeks.

Chris's offer to entertain me some evenings doesn't materialise, and why would it? He's seeing someone and I'm seeing someone. I figure his mind works the way mine does – and that the two of us being close friends is a step too far. We don't want to betray anyone. That's OK. It's for the best, and we hang out in the office and by the coffee machine. He's always getting a coffee at the same time I am.

I'm probably overthinking it and he doesn't still care about me at all. He's too busy getting laid and rejoicing in the $1,500 he gets for recommending me for the job.

I'm too busy to care anyway, as I'm shopping a ridiculous amount, it being the run-up to Christmas. I don't know why I do this to myself. But I do have lovely presents for family and friends – Scarlet is going to love her bundle from Sephora – and a few treats for myself. I venture back to the office carrying yet more shopping bags on one of my final lunch breaks, and Chris gives me a look of mock-horror.

'Shopping *again*?' he asks.

'It's Christmas,' I exclaim.

'No, it isn't. It's November,' he says playfully.

'I'm getting a head start. The shopping in New York is immense. I can see why you live here.'

'I don't live here for the shops. I came for the job.'

'Shops are a bonus, though, aren't they? If you're being *really* honest with yourself,' I probe.

He laughs. 'I don't really shop all that much.'

'Why on earth not?' I ask.

'I just don't shop much. I'm restrained,' he says.

'Are you implying I'm unrestrained?'

'Maybe,' he replies. 'You're very good at saying what you think.'

'How's that relevant?' I query. 'We're talking about shopping.'

'You're unrestrained in general, I think.' I open my mouth to speak and Chris stops me. 'I wasn't being unkind,' he goes on. 'I was paying you a compliment. It's good, you saying what you think. I like it. You being you. It's a good thing.'

'Oh.' I'm not sure what to make of that. This conversation feels intimate, but I'm not sure why. And I feel we were better friends when we were messaging than we are in each other's company. *Are* we even friends now? Sadly, it feels less than that, since our night at the pizza restaurant, despite the banter. Perhaps it's that the banter doesn't feel real, now we're not communicating properly with each other. Big Talk ended long ago.

I told Chris I wanted to be friends, and we've just become colleagues instead. This saddens me so much. We hang out in the office, eating salads and sandwiches and discussing work at our desks, or nipping to a bar after hours for a quick drink with some of the others, but we've not been alone since my first night here.

Chris moves into action, however, when I remind him, over a morning coffee on my last day, that I fly home first thing tomorrow. His face falls. 'Tomorrow?'

'Afraid so. My New York adventure is at an end. Back to drizzly London I go.'

'What are you doing tonight?' he asks after a pause.

'I've done every touristy thing going and I've eaten every possible cuisine, so I'm planning a last wander, and I'll grab some takeout from a place I've not investigated yet . . .'

'Takeout?' Chris smiles. 'See, you've been here five minutes and you're already using American phrases.'

'Fine,' I say, 'I'll grab a *takeaway*, pack my bag and then I'll get some rest, ready for an early start.'

'You *could* do that,' Chris begins. 'Or you could do something with me, and I could send you on your way out of New York in style.'

'Hmm,' I say casually. 'What did you have in mind?'

'It's a secret,' he replies and then gives me instructions. When I've said goodbye to Max and the team, I'm told to go back to my hotel and put on jeans and a jumper, gloves and a hat, and meet him at the Rockefeller Center at seven.

'O-kay,' I respond. And when I've packed up my few belongings and have bundled my new laptop up in its protective case, gone around the office and said goodbye to everyone, giving Max the biggest squeeze possible and having him squeeze me back in return, with a scheduled time for us to chat on my return, I take myself back to the hotel and follow Chris's instructions.

Chapter Twenty-Nine

Chris

'This is my second time here,' Lexie tells me as I lead her round the Plaza at the Rockefeller Center, past the tall flags and lit-up trees and down towards the ice rink.

My smile slips from my face. 'You've been here already?'

'Yep. It's the Rockefeller Center. It's like . . . item number two on the New York tourist bucket-list. I came and looked at the Christmas tree, ate a hot dog from a vendor, bought a coffee and then wandered around a bit. But I'm happy to be here again,' she tells me quickly.

I think my face is still showing my disappointment and I adjust it accordingly.

'So you've not been ice-skating?' I query, pointing to the rink.

'Ohhh, no, I don't like ice-skating,' she replies.

'Oh,' I say flatly. 'Right.'

'Is that what you had planned?' she asks tentatively.

'No-o-o,' I draw out the word. 'I did not have that planned. At all.'

'You did, didn't you? Have you got tickets?'

'No,' I say. 'But hang on a second and I'll tell you what we're *really* doing. Once I check the FAQs on the website and see if I can get a refund for these tickets I absolutely did not buy.'

'Oh, Chris! OK, forget I said it. We're going ice-skating. Come on.'

'Not if you *hate* it!'

'I didn't say "hate",' she points out quickly. ' "Hate" is too strong a word.'

'I should have checked with you first. I thought it would be . . .'

'What?' she queries.

'I thought it would be nice,' I say simply and then I shrug. 'Sorry.'

'Don't apologise. We're going ice-skating. Come on.' She grabs my hand and even though I'm sure it was an innocent reflex, it does things to me that it shouldn't. I look at our gloved hands entwined together and allow myself to be dragged in the direction of the rink entrance.

'Why is it you don't like ice-skating?' I ask moments later as we're lacing ourselves into our skating boots. It's so cold there's steam mingling together from our breath.

'I'm lying. I love it,' Lexie deadpans, giving me a wide grin.

I make a doubtful face.

'It's just stressful and painful, isn't it? One of us is going to fall over. It's cold. It looks all romantic in films, but the reality is that you could quite easily break something or lose a finger if you fall over, and then someone runs over your hand with their skate and *whomp!* . . . finger gone.'

'Whomp?' I query.

'I couldn't think of a better noise.'

I chuckle. 'Well,' I say as we walk on our blades towards the ice, 'no one is falling over, because I'm pretty good at this, so I'll hold you up or you can just . . . hug the edge or something.'

Lexie gives me a glacial look as we enter the arena, the ice beneath us immediately unsettling her, and she breathes quickly. I hold onto her by her elbow and watch her try to smile, while also trying not to grit her teeth in discomfort. It's quite an art. Her white wool beanie is slipping down a bit over her eyebrows, but she's making no move to push it back up. She's wearing a matching white faux-fur jacket over skin-tight jeans. She looks beautiful.

I *knew* this was a bad idea. But guilt at purposefully ignoring her for the last two weeks has taken hold of me. I feel a bit shit about it, but I've had to do my absolute *best* to stay the hell away from her. Other than a few slip-ups at the coffee machine, when I haven't been able to help myself, walking over there and engaging her in conversation: a little hit of Lexie in addition to the caffeine. Apart from that, it's been two weeks of making sure that whenever we're together, we're with other people. Which means I can't do, or say, anything now that will get me into trouble.

She didn't mention again my initial suggestion that I take her out most nights. Why, Chris, did you think *that* was a good idea? The news that she's with Josh came as a shock. At the wedding she hooked up with Josh minutes after my taxi pulled away. I still don't know what to do with that information.

Everything about that night we met felt so . . . *real*. And then, minutes later, she . . . ? I can't work it out. But I know I'm right about Lexie not liking me as much as I'd liked her. It took me longer than it should have done to realise that, but I got there in the end.

Mainly because she told me to fuck off.

OK, so she didn't say that, but I was fobbed off in a very polite way that made me pay attention. I made her feel uncomfortable with that **I can't stop thinking about you** text. And then Lexie used the other F-word: friend. Now I'm here, ice-skating with her and torturing myself. Thank God I started dating again and have stopped pining after this woman, who is categorically not interested in me. I don't know what I thought spending time with her tonight was going to achieve. I felt guilty about ignoring Lexie, although she probably didn't even notice or care. I am a level-one idiot.

She's halfway through saying something and I've missed some of it. 'I wish I wasn't wearing really tight jeans,' she continues. 'Because if my legs decide to go in different directions, I'm ripping these babies in half.'

I laugh, then my eyes inappropriately drop to the area she's talking about and I have to force myself to pull my gaze back up to her face.

'You're not bad at this,' I lie. 'For someone who hates it so much.' I notice she's clutching my arm tightly to try and help herself stay upright. Our upper halves must look like a tangle of arms.

'I'm concentrating,' she confesses. 'Can you push my hat up for me? I can't see, and I'm scared to reach up.'

'Oh, sure,' I say and move in front of her, fixing her beanie into place. We're near the edge of the rink and, with the twinkling lights shining off her dark eyes, I'm having to seriously resist the urge to kiss her. Instead I ask, 'You having fun?'

'Yeah. *So* much fun,' she says darkly.

I chuckle. 'Do you want to forget this and go get some drinks?'

'No-o-o.' She elongates the word. 'Let's stay to the end. Ice-skating's not as bad as I remember. How long is the session booked for?'

'An hour.'

'Oh, fuck that! Drinks, please.'

I lead her towards the entrance to the rink and we make our way off.

'I'm so sorry,' she says as we hand back our skates and head towards the wooden ski-chalet-style buildings where food and drinks stalls have been set up.

'You don't need to apologise,' I reply. 'It was funny. Your response was not at all what I was expecting.'

We buy eggnog from a vendor, at Lexie's insistence, and instead of sitting, we wander around, stopping to watch the other ice-skaters.

'This is much nicer,' she tells me, as the buzz of people and the din of early festive enjoyment swirls around us.

'Cheers!' I lift my disposable cup and she knocks hers against mine as we watch skaters whizz around. 'Well done for getting the job.'

'Well done for making a cool fifteen hundred dollars,' she counters.

'Ha, yeah. Don't quit now – I won't get it otherwise. I'm sad you're going home, by the way.'

'Are you?' she asks doubtfully. 'I've not seen all that much of you.'

Yeah, there's a reason for that, I think. Instead I say, 'I'm sorry. I've been a bit preoccupied in the evenings, but our office chats have been nice.' *What an insipid thing to say.*

'How's it going with your new woman?' she probes.

I look away. 'Yeah, it's OK . . .' Although my answer sounds vague, it's not meant to. I follow it up with, 'You can never really tell, can you?'

'What do you mean?' she asks.

I look back at her. 'You think it's going well and then, *bam!* – they dump you, and it's . . . shock and awe. Like a Michael Bay film, explosions going off everywhere for no reason whatsoever.'

Lexie issues a short, sharp chuckle.

'You'd probably see it coming, right?' she offers. 'If it wasn't going well, one of you would see it. One of you would *say* something. Although, in fairness, I didn't see it coming the last time I got cheated on and then dumped,' she goes on, gazing into the distance while she thinks about this.

'Thanks for those words of encouragement,' I joke. On the

far side of the rink, a man whizzes backwards at speed. We watch him spin and turn like an Olympian.

'How do they do that?' Lexie mutters.

'Skills. So, it's going well with Josh then?' I ask and I realise there was no sleek transition whatsoever into that question and it didn't sound as casual out loud as it had done in my head.

'It is. I really like him,' she replies bashfully.

'Good,' I say and I'm struck for a moment by how awkward this is.

'I'm having a nice time,' Lexie comments, obviously wanting to change the subject. She looks as if she means it. 'Ice-skating notwithstanding. I've loved it here. I can't believe how quickly two weeks have flown.'

'Likewise,' I reply and sip my eggnog, which is violently sweet. 'You haven't had the urge to move here then?' I test. 'New York hasn't worked its charms on you?'

'Afraid not. I do love it, though. I am a city girl at heart, remember. My love for London knows no bounds. But I'd miss my friends and my family too much to relocate.'

'How's being wedded to the city going to work, with Josh in the country then?' I ask.

'OK, I think. I practically moved in with him for a few weeks and it worked perfectly fine.' I see Lexie narrow her eyes after she says this and I wonder how true this comment is.

I feel my mouth drop open and then close again. 'You moved in with him? Already?'

'It was more of a little holiday,' she back-pedals.

I don't say anything, and we stare at the skaters.

'Anyway I miss Josh and Scarlet and my family. Two weeks is a long time to be away from home.'

'I've done it for quite a bit longer than that,' I say absently.

'And you don't feel that pull back to the UK?'

'Sometimes. Not often, though,' I muse. 'I came here for the job, and the lifestyle, and I love both.'

'Fair enough,' she responds uncertainly.

I breathe in, breathe out. I feel the conversation coming to a close.

'OK, she says, turning to me. 'Big Talk round . . . whatever round we're on.'

I give her an indulgent smile as I ask, 'Weren't we just doing that?'

'Shh,' she says. 'This is official Big Talk now. What would it take to get you to live back in the UK?'

I pause and think. 'I have no idea. Something . . . big.'

'How big?'

'Family illness or something dreadful.'

'Oh God,' she replies quickly. 'OK, never mind. Let's skip past that. What would it take for you to live in New York *for ever*?'

'For ever?' I ask, glancing around me slowly, taking it all in. It's great. It's wonderful. It's cinematic and I'm working on building my career here, but, 'I don't think I'll live here for ever.'

'What if you and this Tinder swipe—'

'Uh . . . excuse me. It wasn't Tinder,' I cut in and give her a playful shove.

She's dismissive. 'So *you* say.'

'Ha!' slips from my lips.

'What if you and this swipe are for ever . . .' she comes in with again. 'Really for ever. Would you live here?'

I blow air out of my cheeks. 'If we're for ever, then . . . I guess so, yeah.'

'Even if you didn't *want* to live here for ever?'

I think about it, but not for as long as I'd think about it if this *was* actually happening. 'Yeah.'

'That simple?'

'It is, isn't it? Love is simple. It's complicated and messy and all of that too, but really it's simple. If you're ready . . . you either make it work, come what may, or you don't.'

'If you're ready?' she asks.

'Sometimes it's the right person, wrong circumstances. Sometimes it all falls into line.' I think about what I've just said. I was trying to be philosophical, but really: what *is* love? It's two people who are right for each other finding each other at the right time. It's magic, it's complicated alchemy, but also . . . it's one of the simplest things in the world.

I look away from the skaters and watch Lexie's reaction thoughtfully, as her eyes follow two children being held up artfully by their mum and dad. She won't turn her head to look at me, even though she must see out of the corner of her eye that I'm giving her my full attention. And then her phone rings and lights up. 'Josh' is displayed on the screen. Lexie swipes to answer quickly, commenting how sweet Josh is to ring when it's so late for him, telling him she's at the Rockefeller Center. I hear him make enthusiastic remarks in the background and so I discreetly move away, pulling out my own phone and tapping away on it for a moment. I pocket it again and glance at Lexie as she talks to Josh, telling him she'll call him tomorrow when she's on her way to the airport. She tells him she misses him, that she can't wait to see him again, then says goodbye and hangs up.

All of that was more painful to hear than I thought it would be. I need to get out of here. How do I extricate myself from her without leaving her stranded? Although she's been getting on well enough by herself these past two weeks, so in theory I could.

'Do you want to go over to the chalets again and get something to eat?' she asks. 'I'm starving.'

'Sure,' I say.

As we tuck into our burgers at bench tables, we talk about what she's going to be doing for Max when she gets back home, how we're each going to be spending the upcoming weekend (sleeping off jet lag for her, dinner and a movie with Kayla for me) and what new adventures lie on the horizon for us both.

'Even though I'm potless,' Lexie starts, 'my upcoming jaunts include a wedding in the new year and a spa day with Scarlet, which I won via wedding bingo.'

'Sounds great,' I enthuse. And then I chuckle to myself, 'Wedding bingo.'

'Yeah, yeah,' she says. 'Don't harp on about it.'

I'm quiet and then I surprise both of us by saying, 'Wedding bingo is ridiculous, but it's not as extreme as getting on a plane with someone you've only just met.'

Lexie looks at me from under her lashes. She's incredibly still.

I get brave. 'Do you ever think: thank God I dodged *that* bullet?'

'No . . . I don't,' she replies as I watch her carefully.

Neither of us speaks and then slowly she forms a sentence. 'On reflection, I do think this fortnight has given me a good idea as to what it might have been like, if I had.'

I frown. 'What New York is like, or what being with me would be like?' *I can't believe I just asked that.*

'Chris,' she says lightly, but it sounds like more of a warning, an emotional reprimand, than an invitation to go down this path. 'I've wondered,' she admits slowly. Of course I've wondered what it would have been like if I'd come with you. How could I not?'

You mean you wondered all the way back to Josh, and then kissed him? I think, but don't say.

'I wondered,' I tell her, giving her my full attention because even though nothing good can come of it, I've hung on for so long I'm practically exploding to say it. 'I wondered on that flight home what it would be like. I kept looking at the guy who was seated next to me and thinking, "That could have been Lexie." Then he fell asleep on my shoulder and that's when I definitely wished it was you.'

She has the grace to smile and gives a tiny laugh.

'I got back to my apartment,' I continue, 'and envisaged

showing you to my room while I slept on the sofa, or maybe not sleeping on the sofa. I thought about where we'd go for brunch, dinner. I thought about continuing Big Talk and oh . . . I dunno.'

'You actually thought about sleeping on the sofa?' she asks doubtfully.

I shrug, but my eyes don't leave hers. 'Asking you to come with me to New York was the most romantic gesture I've ever made.'

'You're dodging the question.'

I laugh, glance down, glance back up again. What will happen if I say all the things I can't stop thinking about?

Her mouth opens a fraction. I can't help looking at her mouth. Christ, I really want to kiss her. Right here. Right now.

I force myself not to. I force myself to keep talking. 'It's not the Victorian era,' I point out, my eyes on her lips as they remain slightly parted. I need to look away, so I plant my gaze on her brown eyes. They're the same colour as mine and yet they look so different, so distinctive, so much . . . more.

'Would you have kissed me?' she asks in wonder.

This conversation is so dangerous. I can't stop. 'Yeah, I'd have kissed you – at some point on our journey to the airport and most of the long flight. If you'd have let me.'

'I'd have let you,' she says so quickly that she looks surprised at herself.

I swallow. 'And then . . .'

'And then?' she echoes.

'We'd have seen how we felt, discovered what felt natural between us together.'

A breath escapes her lips.

Lexie is not going to stop me continuing this 'what if' moment. But other than being explicit, we've probably taken it as far as we can. It's certainly further than we should have taken it. 'Perhaps sleeping together on the first date probably wouldn't have been a good idea,' I volunteer softly.

'Perhaps not,' she agrees.

OK, I've said everything I wanted to say. Almost everything. I can move on with my life now.

Lexie's quiet. For a second I think she's watching the ice-skaters and then I realise she's not. She's staring through them. Her gaze doesn't move.

'I watched your taxi drive away,' she starts slowly. 'And I *did* think it was a mistake that I didn't come with you,' she confesses. 'But I couldn't afford to.'

Her voice is soft, and I'm hanging on every word.

'But that was then. And so many wonderful things have happened since – new boyfriend, this job – that it's hard to feel remorse about what might have been between us, because it would have taken events – my life – in a completely different direction. And now . . . ?' she holds her hands out, gesturing openly at nothing in particular, 'It's not helpful going down the path of regret.'

Regret. 'Hang on,' I say, circling back. 'You couldn't afford it?'

She gives the slightest little shake of her head and looks confused that I've picked up on this, of all things. But of all the comments she's made, this is what's hit home the hardest, because *this* is what decided which way that night went.

'Is that . . . ?' I trail off as I'm not sure I want to know the answer to this question. But I'm asking it anyway. 'Is that the *only* reason you didn't come with me?'

She nods. 'Pretty much. I'd just had my credit card declined over two drinks, I'm ashamed to say. Those two champagnes I disappeared for ages to get?'

I nod.

'Josh bought those.'

My eyes widen. '*Josh* bought our drinks?'

'He was at the bar when I was suffering financial humiliation. Right place, right time.'

'Wow! OK. I was going to pay for your flight, you know,' I add – pointlessly now, I realise. I'm three months too late to tell her this.

'Were you?' she asks, her eyes rounding in disbelief.

'Yeah, of course.'

'There's no *of course* about it,' she says.

'I felt so strongly that inviting you was the right thing to do, that you coming with me would have been the most perfect thing,' I go on. 'That feeling simply took over. I was ready to dig into my savings account and book the flight on my phone right there and then. I wish I'd made that fact clearer at the time.'

She's watching me as if she wants me to say more, or less. I have no clue which. There's a huge look of regret on Lexie's face – one she promised only moments ago she wasn't going to feel.

Two things could happen right now. I could kiss her. I think she'd let me. I think she'd kiss me back. Then I'd be that shit guy who got her to cheat on her boyfriend. I'm not that shit. I'm not the man who does that. And this isn't the way to start something with Lexie. Nothing good comes of relationships that start with cheating.

The other thing I can do is shut this down. I dig deep. This is the way to end it. 'I was only going to buy you a one-way ticket, though,' I surprise her by saying.

'One-way?' she asks in a shocked voice, and then her face changes when she senses I'm joking and she gives me a shove.

'Yeah,' I say. 'If you wanted to ditch me the minute you arrived and scarper back to London, that was all on you.'

'Hey,' she replies. I can see by her face that she's struggling to work out what just happened here. The conversation was deep, revelatory, but now it's over.

I need to go. I need to say goodbye. Again. *Now*. Before anyone gets hurt. 'I've had a nice night,' I tell her. I'm not going to make a pointless face-saving joke about Lexie's ice-skating, and neither does she. 'I can take you back to your hotel?' I offer.

She looks confused that this is all ending so abruptly and shakes her head. 'Er, no, thanks. I've got it from here. I'll be OK.'

'I guess this is it then,' I say. 'Unless Max flies you back out again soon.' I can't believe I'm relying on small talk here.

'Um.' Lexie looks so confused. 'Unlikely. He's made it abundantly clear I'm flying solo for a good while until he comes over to catch up with progress. So . . .'

'So,' I say. If I don't hug her it will seem weird, so I wrap my arms around her. It lasts longer than it should, and I don't know if that's because of me or because of her. I only know it's lovely: being here, with Lexie and holding her like this. And it really needs not to be. I need to move away, and so does she. Only we don't move . . . until I make the first attempt to break free. My hands leave her back and I miss the feel of her already as the space between us widens. 'Goodnight, Lexie. Safe flight.'

She tries to speak and can't, simply stares at me with a look in her eyes I can't place. She swallows and starts again. 'Goodnight, Chris.'

We stand for a second. There's so much risk. I can't do this. I just say bye, and so does she.

And then I leave.

Chapter Thirty

Lexie

December

I replay that conversation between me and Chris over and over in my head. If I'd told him I couldn't afford the flight, he would have booked it for me. *Come with me.*

God, those words!

And then I'd have been in New York with Chris four months ago. I'd be with Chris right now, I'm sure of it. In some way or another I feel we'd have made it work. Somewhere along the way, we missed the chance.

Instead I'm with Josh. I made one decision that night that has changed everything.

I've thought about this turn of events so much since that evening with Chris in New York. If I'd gone with him that first night, would I still be there now? How would we have made it work? How do long-distance relationships function across such a wide distance? Who is the first to cave, the first to move hell and high water to be with the other person – uprooting their own lives to be with the one they love?

Why am I even thinking this? It's not helpful. None of this is helpful. I need to focus on work. Although if the pattern of events so far tells me anything, it's that in about twenty minutes' time I'll be thinking about it again.

My first few weeks of working from home in the flat are far easier than I expected. Things start slowly in the initial few days, and then pick up as different people in the company start sending work my way. Now external emails from builders and suppliers are coming in thick and fast too, as the inevitable delays and lack of materials begin to emerge.

An awful lot goes into opening a hotel, even a small boutique property. I've toured the various elements with the site manager this week. It's off Hanover Square, which gave me the opportunity to take in the Christmas lights in London. There's only a couple of weeks to go until Christmas and I have to work out my train times to my mum's in Reading and then, after Boxing Day, how to get to my dad's in St Albans. I never really enjoy Christmas because of this double transport stress. And because I don't drive, I have to plan out my expensive train journeys to the minute, booking seats weeks in advance, which I still haven't done.

Josh and I haven't spoken about whether I'll spend Christmas Day with him. He hasn't asked and I do want him to ask me, although I'd have to politely decline or risk upsetting both my parents. I guess Josh knows I'll be family-bound, although it would have been nice to be invited to his Christmas. Maybe he'll ask me in person when I see him this weekend. Or maybe it's too soon. We've only been together a few months. Although, on the flipside, Chris invited me to get on a plane with him even though he'd only known me for one evening. I'm annoyed that I can't stop thinking about this.

There's always next year for Josh and me to spend Christmas together. I wonder if we'll still be together then?

Whatever happens, I'll have people around me at Christmas whom I love, so spending most of the festive season on a train isn't a hardship. I promised my mum I'd look at train times today, but instead I'm looking at the latest set of drawings from the architect, which have just come in to address a planning condition. At least I've seen the shell of the hotel, so at this stage I've got a visual jumping-off point when I'm talking to suppliers and manufacturers about the space.

There's so much structural work going on behind the scenes. I knew there'd be more admin than design work and I'm OK with that, but I'm the eyes and ears on the ground here for the big bosses too, liaising with a lot of the departments. My role seems to have grown overnight. There's more to get my teeth into, and Max knows he's throwing a lot at me. He must think I'll be able to cope with it all.

I secretly love it. I love being busy, I love not sitting on reception, laminating security badges and signing people in and out all day. This is what I've needed for so long.

There's a huge part of me that's excited and worried about what will happen at the end of it. Will I stay on with the company and help with another hotel elsewhere, or be absorbed into the running of this one in some way? And ahead of that, I'm already mildly concerned about seeing Chris again, because when it's time to fit out the building – although that's not for ages yet – he'll be here, overseeing that. I'm concerned about how I'll feel then. I'm concerned about how I feel now.

Our conversation at the Rockefeller Center should never have happened. It was inappropriate for two people who aren't going to be together to talk in so much depth about what might have happened if we *had* got together. Why did we do that? Morbid fascination? The conversational equivalent of prodding a wasp nest to see what happens? It wasn't clever of either of us, and while I replay the conversation in my mind again and again and again, and while it felt right at the time, in hindsight it was a terrible idea. Only . . . I can't remember which of us started it. And why.

It's the last weekend before Christmas and I pack a little roller suitcase and my laptop bag and decamp to Josh's for a few days. I haven't seen him since I flew to New York. I've been so busy with various parties and drinks, friends to catch up with, as we all try to ram seeing everyone we've ever known into that tight four-week festive space in December. What with all of that, and site meetings – it's taken me away from spending time with Josh. He offered to come up and take me out for dinner, but I had a friend's Christmas dinner to go to, which I'd already RSVP'd to, so the timing didn't work. Josh didn't seem too phased.

It's been a joy not having to cook recently: Scarlet and I have either been snaffling Deliveroo or out with various friends, or warming up soup and toast because it's so cold outside and because we need to save money, after all the

Deliveroo and dining out. I've quite enjoyed resuming our life rota of cleaning and eating, shopping and taking out the bins. Scarlet jokes that we've got being a couple nailed better than most couples. I think she might be right. But after New York and now the Cotswolds and Christmas, which feels minutes away, we're slowly spending less and less time together.

I do wonder what might happen if Josh and I become serious, as in *really* serious. Would I move there properly? He'll ask at some point surely? Although he hasn't even asked me for Christmas. It's hard for him to move to London, owning a farm as he does. And, let's be frank, why would he want to give all that up to move to London for me? I would never make him do that.

On the train I think of that conversation Chris and I had about him staying in New York even if he didn't want to, just because he fell in love. I wonder how this might apply to me and Josh. I'd happily live in Somerset with him, if we get to that stage, because even though it's a *tad* boring out there, it is beautiful. And why would I give him up, in favour of my social life and access to takeaway apps?

Josh picks me up from the station and jogs towards me when he sees me, scooping me into his arms and kissing me. Other commuters are getting off the train, skirting around us in the car park, pretending not to notice the two people kissing. It always feels so lovely being back in Josh's arms. It's good to have a person. Being single is fun, but being with someone is such a warming feeling.

'That was like a scene from a film,' I tell him when we break apart.

'I've missed you,' he groans into my ear.

'It's only been a few weeks. But I missed you too,' I return honestly as I pull back, look into his eyes, picking out the haloes of grey that dance around his pupils. 'I'd forgotten what bits of you looked like.'

'Bits of me?' Josh queries with a sideways smile. 'I haven't forgotten what *any* of you looks like,' he answers provocatively. 'I've had to live off the memories.'

'Have you now?' I say seductively, wishing we weren't in a freezing-cold car park in December, but instead were wrapped up cosily in his house, his bed.

'Come on,' he says, sensing the urgency. 'Let's go home.'

There's a bottle of champagne chilling in an ice bucket on the kitchen table and the smell of something delicious cooking in the Aga when we walk in.

'Josh,' I say tenderly, eyeing the fizz, 'what are we celebrating?'

'Plenty of things,' he replies. 'I got a couple of new restaurant deals; Tamara's supplying her ice cream at a few more delis; and you got a brand-new job, which we've not toasted yet; and you and me . . . well, I think you and me are worth celebrating. The rest of it just adds to the occasion.'

I move towards him while he eases the cork free and pours us each a glass.

'I also thought . . .' he starts.

'Y-e-s,' I draw out the word.

'That we should toast the idea of me giving you some driving lessons.'

'Driving lessons?'

'You should learn to drive my car. I'll teach you. Then you can come and go more freely. It'll help you feel less cooped up here.'

'I don't feel cooped up here. Is that what you think?'

'You must feel isolated when you stay longer than just a weekend,' he states.

I notice it's not a question. 'I do. A bit. But that was when I had no purpose. I'm busy now. I have stuff to do. Work. It's going to be different.'

He makes an oh-OK-then face, and says, 'If you didn't work, there'd be stuff for you to do locally. Groups and clubs, or whatever. Only, you don't drive, so you can't get to anything.'

'So?' I ask.

'You don't want to drive?' he queries.

'I don't really *need* to at the minute. And when, realistic-ally, are we going to do driving lessons? You're tired from work each evening. Now it's winter it's pitch-black by the time you and I finish work. You want me to learn to drive your giant Land Rover in the dark? I'll kill us both! I'm not averse to learning to drive. I'm just not sure I need to do it right now. Maybe in the summer?' I offer.

'OK,' he replies. 'I don't need you to drive, Lexie. I simply thought if you're here more, you might like more of a sense of freedom, especially if one day—' He stops.

'One day?'

'You and me – you know,' he says.

I'm not sure I do know, so I try and read between the lines.

'If I move in with you, and we're in it for ever?' I look at Josh to see if he's on board with this line of questioning. He looks as if he is, so I continue, 'And maybe one day we . . .' *God, I can't say it. Why can't I say it?* I don't want to scare him. I don't want to scare myself. This is a big, scary chat that's come out of nowhere.

'Maybe one day we . . . get married and have kids?' he finishes for me. He looks as scared as I feel.

'Yeah,' I reply slowly. 'You're worried I won't be able to get them to and from school or . . . something?' I gulp. *Jesus! How did we get here?*

'I mean,' he bristles, 'I don't know what I'm thinking at this early stage. I only think – in the long run – you need to learn to drive if you're going to be here more often. Is that OK?'

'Of course it's OK. It's scary. But it's OK.'

'Which bit is scary? The thought that you and I might be the real deal, or driving?'

'I'm not scared that you and I might be the real deal, Josh. I'm scared we might *not* be the real deal.'

'Why would you think that? I've never fallen for someone as quickly as I've fallen for you.'

My breath catches in my throat. 'Really?'

'Really. It was immediate. When I was standing at that bar with you at the wedding, I could have talked to you all night. It crushed me when you left me after that first dance. And then, not long after, there you were again, and you ended up *kissing* me. Who gets a second chance like that? That kind of thing *never* happens to me. It was incredible. It scares me too.'

I move towards him and kiss him hard. Josh kisses me back.

'Come with me,' he says, in a voice that should do things to me, but instead I hear another man in my head uttering the very same phrase months ago in another place.

'What?' I ask quickly, in surprise. *Did I dream him saying that? Did I hear Chris? I need Chris out of my head. Why is he in there?*

Josh gathers our drinks and the champagne bucket. I shake myself back into the present. 'Come with me,' he repeats.

'Where are we going?'

'Outside.'

'Outside?' I question.

'To the barn, to be precise.'

'Why?'

He gives me a sexy look. 'Do you still want to have a roll around in the hay with a farmer?'

'Yes,' I reply, pulling my shoes back on quickly. 'Yes, I do.'

Chapter Thirty-One

New Year's Day 2023

I hold Josh's hand as we walk through Longleat's Festival of Light. I've never been to see Christmas lights at a country house. It's a festive cultural phenomenon that's passed me by, and I was quite surprised when Josh suggested it. I donned my wellies and we've been holding gloved hands the whole way round the trail.

Scarlet went to a party in London to see in the New Year last night and gave me permission to spend the occasion with Josh. I didn't want to ditch her, but I think she might have had a bit more fun than I did. I like a party and, in truth, it wasn't exactly wild in Somerset. We had a lock-in at Mark's pub, with Tamara and a few locals. But everything was over by half twelve. I wonder if this will be my life, if Josh and I carry on like this? As I get older, and less able to handle hangovers, perhaps this is a good way to spend the remainder of the festive season.

The trail theme is Roald Dahl and I can't help thinking, as we walk through the huge light-sculptures of all the characters from Dahl's books, that if we had children, they'd love this.

I'm only familiar with the characters from a few of the books that have been made into films, so Josh has to point out who Danny, the Champion of the World is, and The Twits. It's only when I get to Bruce Bogtrotter eating a giant lit-up cake that I know what I'm looking at. And Willy Wonka is always unforgettable. His life-sized trailing coat looks as if it's blowing in the wind.

A tunnel of open books is illuminated and we walk through hand-in-hand. It's cold, but at least it's not raining. It still feels so festive that my New Year's resolution to go easy on the alcohol is ruined when I spy a mulled-wine stall.

'How do you not know who Danny, the Champion of the World is?' Josh asks in mock-disgust as we exit the lights and make our way back to the car.

'I knew James from *James and the Giant Peach*,' I point out.

'Only because of the massive lit-up peach,' Josh observes, laughing, while opening the car door for me. 'We'll have to rectify this. We can't have kids whose mum has no idea who Fantastic Mr Fox is,' he jokes.

I turn and look at him. *Kids. Mum.* I smile. I know he's joking, but . . . we're discussing these things. *New Year, new dreams?*

Josh nods, but doesn't sense that I want to delve deeper into this. And what else can I say? Not a lot, if I want to remain cool and sane. Though I'm excited.

He plants a quick kiss on my lips and makes signs that he

wants me to get in the car, so we can join the queue of traffic leaving Longleat. 'Don't worry,' he says. 'I'll fix your lack of knowledge about *George's Marvellous Medicine* in time for our kids.'

I sit in the car and stare straight ahead, mouth slightly open in total surprise.

Chapter Thirty-Two

February

It's been six months since the wedding that upended my world. And now that it's the depths of winter, Scarlet and I find ourselves at yet another wedding – our first of this year. Here we go again.

'It is *one* degree,' Scarlet exclaims, as we enter the Scots baronial country-house wedding venue. 'Who chooses to get married in Scotland in *February*?'

'The bride's Scottish and it's Valentine's Day,' I tell her. 'It's romantic.'

'It's fucking freezing is what it is.'

'They're *your* friends,' I point out. 'I'm your humble plus-one. You didn't have to say yes.'

'We've had your fair share of friends' weddings too,' Scarlet says, trying her best to muster some enthusiasm. 'And it's always fun in the end, isn't it?'

'Until it isn't,' I reply unenthusiastically, and then I remember how I met Josh and I perk up a bit.

As if reading my mind, Scarlet asks, 'How's Posh Josh?'

'He's fine,' I say. I've given up asking her to stop calling him that.

'He doesn't mind that you're here with me on the most romantic day of the year?'

'No, he's pretty chill, so he doesn't mind.'

'Ugh, you're so loved up. It's depressing.'

'Why is it depressing?' I ask with a shocked laugh. 'I thought you'd be pleased for me.'

'I am. I *am*. Sorry. I've just really had enough of being alone.'

'It's not being alone. It's being single. There's a difference.'

'Yes, there is a difference,' Scarlet says. 'I am both single *and* alone.'

'OK, well,' I reply, trying to be helpful, 'let's work on that. Where's your bingo grid?'

'You've already set my one "out there" challenge,' she says.

'I'm changing it.'

'No-o-o – pretending to be famous and asking not to be photographed all day, whenever the photographer came near me, was going to be fun!'

I take her sheet from her and cross out the square. I draw a new one, write something in it and hand it back.

She reads it and says in a flat voice, 'I'm not doing that.'

'Yes, you are. It worked out well for me. This – *this* is how we get you a man.'

'It's seedy.'

'Hey! Snogging someone at a wedding was *your* suggestion, as I recall. I'm only turning it back on you.'

'Fine,' Scarlet says reluctantly, folding the paper up and

putting it in her coat pocket, which she refuses to take off, due to the temperature. 'I'm going to need *a lot* of drinks.'

Hours later I've lost Scarlet completely. This keeps happening to us at weddings. She takes her bingo grid seriously, and I have no idea how near completing it she is. I'm quite far off completing mine. In a moment of madness, while we were rushing to get ready in our hotel room this morning, I've given myself some squares that I don't think I can tick off. If I cross any of them through and write something else, Scarlet will notice, and I'll lose by default for cheating. Am I about to lose? We don't have any financial comeuppance this time, which wouldn't really matter now (within reason), as I am earning a fairly decent salary and am slowly catching up with my credit-card debt.

Even so, I wish I hadn't written in a square 'fight breaks out'. I'm never going to win, with that as a bingo option. I've literally never been to a wedding where a fight has broken out. 'Bloody Chris,' I mutter to myself as I remember his phrase *All good weddings end in a fight*. It had sounded so convincing at the time.

I haven't spoken to Chris since New York. We haven't messaged. But when a group email goes round the company and I watch the replies pile in, I read every word he writes, no matter how brief.

I turn my attention to the dance floor as guests start dancing a ceilidh. I have no idea how to do this and I haven't had enough drinks to try. I decide I'm going to slink off and attempt to complete a square or two.

It's a lovely venue: candles flicker inside hurricane lamps and oversized silver lanterns. There are stag antlers and deep tartan everywhere. It's dark, kind of moody, sexy, and there are plenty of nooks and crannies that Josh and I could disappear into. If only he was here. But it's fine, because I'm here with my best friend and I'm happy to be her wingman. Only she's temporarily missing.

I wander through quieter parts of the venue, trying to decide whether it's feasible to drink five whiskies back-to-back without vomiting. This is my 'out there' challenge from Scarlet that I have to tick off, and I'm really not feeling it. First, I hate whisky. Second, I hate whisky. Maybe I could ask for the lightest whisky they have. Is light whisky a thing? I'm looking down at my grid as I walk into a dark little snug-style room with tea lights flickering gently. But instead of walking into the room, I walk straight into someone.

'Sorry,' I say as I look up, register the person I've crashed into and then step back. I don't speak for a second and then, 'What are *you* doing here?'

Chris doesn't speak. He's clearly in shock. 'Wh—' he starts and then fails to finish. Then he finds his voice. 'I could ask the same of you. Why are you here?'

'I'm a guest.'

'Obviously,' he says. 'So am I.'

'Actually I'm really a plus-one,' I say, although I'm not sure why.

'I'm a proper guest.'

'That's a weird brag.'

'You started it,' he says and we stare at each other again. After a beat, he laughs and so do I.

'How are you here? Who do you know, to be here?' I ask. We're standing in the doorway and as a waiter rushes past in the narrow corridor with a tray of empties, we automatically move inside the vacant room, out of the way.

A crystal decanter of whisky has been placed on a side-table at the edge of the room with clean cut-crystal glasses. This venue is deluxe.

'Most people from uni are friends with most people from uni,' Chris replies simply.

'You didn't tell me you were coming to the UK,' I point out, and he looks at me as if to say: *why would I tell you?* This is a fair point. Why would Chris tell me he was going to be in Scotland when I live in London?

He skirts past my question. 'Do you want a drink?' He points at the whisky.

Not one of those, I think, but seeing as there's nothing else to quaff in here and I have a bingo square to tick off, I say, 'Sure. A small one. You having one?'

'Yeah.' He pours two measures and hands me a glass and I look at it.

'You don't like whisky,' he says, like some kind of psychic.

'How do you know?'

'You made that exact same face when I said we were going ice-skating.'

'Ah, crap! Sorry. I became resigned to that, and I'm resigned to this too because I need to drink five of these in order to stand a chance of winning the bingo game tonight.'

Chris looks up at the ceiling in exasperation. 'Ohhh myyy Goddd,' he says slowly. 'The bloody wedding bingo. You're still doing that?'

I laugh as he looks back at me. 'What do you mean? It's our wedding *thing* – mine and Scarlet's.'

'OK. Confession,' he says. 'Wait for it . . .' He pulls a piece of paper out of his suit jacket pocket, holds it out to me.

I breathe in sharply and then I snatch it from him excitedly. 'You're playing wedding bingo too!' I cry.

'Sure am. It's kind of silly. But my friend and I are here together and he had no idea what the hell I was on about when I suggested we do it. But I think we're playing it right.'

I look back down at the instructions on his sheet, glancing at the top few. 'This is very entry-level,' I tell him. 'Playing it safe.'

'Oh, I'm sorry,' he jokes. 'C-minus? See me after class?'

I hand it back. 'You've ticked quite a lot off already, though.'

'Because it's so entry-level?' he jibes. 'I'm doing well,' he says proudly. 'I didn't understand who had to set the really-hard-to-achieve challenge. That's the bit I couldn't explain. Do I set my own challenge or does Dan set mine? Neither of us could work out what made the most sense. So, in the end, I set his and he set mine. It felt like the right way round.'

'You're not taking it seriously, though?' I say, nudging him. 'What did you set each other?'

He shows me the back of the paper. 'I've got to get a girl alone in a room, make her fall in love with me, but not kiss her.'

'What . . . the . . . hell?' I ask. 'That's *messy*. Who sets that kind of challenge? Fancy playing with people like that.'

'I don't make the rules. This is *your* game,' he states, giving me a pointed look. 'But it is evil. I'm prepared to lose, based on that alone.'

'I think I might like this Dan,' I say. And then I remember who Dan is: the groom from the wedding where Chris and I met. And where Josh and I met. Why is Josh not invited, but Chris and Scarlet are? I ask Chris this in a roundabout sort of way.

'Josh only knows Dan through school. This is the uni crowd.'

'I can't keep up,' I say, eyeing the whisky warily.

'I worked in the Union bar part-time,' Chris explains. 'After I left, Scarlet got my job, I believe. Or maybe someone else got my job and then Scarlet got *their* job when they left? I'm not sure. I've still not met your friend Scarlet. I worked with Grey, and then I think Scarlet did after me.' Then he leans in conspiratorially. 'It's Grey whose wedding you're at right now, in case you've forgotten, like last time,' he says.

'Ha-ha.' He has a point, though.

'It'd be nice to meet Scarlet eventually,' he tells me.

'I've temporarily lost her,' I say, getting to my real point, which is, 'I thought you didn't bring guests to events. Why have you brought Dan? I thought plus-ones seriously inhibited your ability to meet new people.'

'I might have changed my mind on that. I might have changed my mind about a lot of things since we met.'

I look at him, unsure what to make of that, unsure if I want to analyse it. I don't have time to process my feelings about Chris being here, in front of me, after everything we said last time we met. And everything we didn't say. I forge on with more Big Talk. 'Where's Dan's new wife?' I ask curiously. 'Don't tell me it's all ended in divorce already?'

'Course not. He's not forty yet,' Chris deadpans. 'Five years to go,' he says cheerfully, which makes me laugh and I take a large glug of my drink, forgetting it's whisky and wincing as it burns all the way down my throat. I cough wildly.

'And you've got to drink five of those?' Chris raises an eyebrow as I finish coughing.

'I may have to fib a bit on this one,' I reply. 'Or drink five *really* small whiskies.'

'Or – heaven forbid – maybe be honest, not drink them and lose the game?'

'I'm not doing that,' I cry. 'You're missing the point of the bingo.'

'What *is* the point?' he asks, genuinely interested. 'I thought it was to make boring weddings less boring.'

'I guess it's to take you out of your comfort zone a bit. Do things you wouldn't normally do.'

He nods, sips his drink. 'Makes sense.'

'Do you like whisky?' I ask. 'Because you're not making the same face I allegedly made.'

'Not really, but there's nothing else in here and I don't want to get up and go to the bar. Last time when drinks took precedence over good conversation I lost you for half an hour and, in that time, you met Josh. Look where that got us.'

I watch him as he sips, but his gaze is on his drink. He's said it in a jovial tone, although the words hold so much truth.

'That was a brave thing to say,' I mutter softly.

'Was it? Why? I'm being honest. Big Talk, remember.'

'Fine,' I say, rising to the challenge. 'I remember how to do Big Talk. Where's your girlfriend? Have you decided nothing is ever going to match up to the wedding where we met, so you thought: *Sod it, I'll bring Dan and escort him around all night*.'

He laughs. 'You think you've ruined me for all weddings for evermore?'

'Yes,' I reply proudly.

'Kayla's working,' he says. 'Couldn't get the time off. Same as Dan's wife. So we're here together instead.'

And then I'm serious. 'Why didn't you tell me you were coming to England?'

'We're not in England,' he replies. 'We're in Scotland.'

'You know what I mean. Why didn't you say?'

He shrugs, thinks. 'I don't know how to say this, so . . . please don't be offended, but you're not on my speed-dial for when I come home.'

I wasn't expecting those words to come out of Chris's mouth. Neither was I expecting them to hurt so much. Why's he being so snarky?

'Shit, OK,' I reply and sip my drink.

'Sorry,' he says and looks as if he genuinely means it. 'I'm just telling it how it is.'

I don't know how to respond to this, so I don't say anything for a moment. I can see him clawing around for a follow-up, but I beat him to it. 'I obviously thought we might be . . .'

Chris furrows his brow, watching me, waiting for me to say something.

'I thought since that night in New York we were . . .'

'What?' he asks, his eyes penetrating mine.

'I thought we were better than this. I thought we were friends and that if you were in my city, the way I was in yours, you'd at least tell me. But I'm wrong. I'm sorry I overthought it. I'm sorry if I've made you feel weird.' I look away, genuinely saddened. I can feel the telltale sting of tears building in the back of my eyes.

'I'm not in your city, though. I'm in Edinburgh, and I didn't know you were going to be here. We *are* friends, I guess. Who don't see each other. Or talk to each other outside work. I don't have much time in the UK, and I'm in Scotland for a large portion of it. I'm only in London for a day and a half and I've got to fit in seeing my brother, my mum and dad before I get on a plane back to New York.'

'I get it,' I respond. I feel as if I've been told off. 'Ignore me.'

'I'm not going to ignore you,' Chris says. 'Would you have wanted to see me if I'd messaged you?'

'Yeah,' I say.

'Why?' he asks.

I want to scream. I can't keep saying the same thing over and over.

'You're with someone, and so am I. We have to stop this,' he says.

'Why?' I snap.

'Are you joking? We talked about so many things we shouldn't have done last time we saw each other. We have nearly-got-together-history.'

'We have what?'

'You heard me,' Chris says. 'We probably shouldn't have hung out in New York. I didn't think it was a good idea then. I don't know why I suggested it.' He makes a noise between his teeth.

I glance at my watch. I want to leave.

'It's been more than seventeen minutes, if you were thinking of proposing,' he says flatly.

But I don't laugh. I don't even smile. Neither does Chris.

'So we really can't be friends, because of that one night.'

'It wasn't just that one night, though, was it?' he persists. 'It was everything after too. I felt so much, and I couldn't let you go. And I don't think you could let me go, either. We messaged back and forth for ages and it was flirty. I loved it. I loved spending time with you that night, and I loved talking to you after. I couldn't wait for a message from you to arrive. All that Big Talk. We have such a connection. The kind I've never had with anyone. Then you got with someone else and friend-zoned me. But *you* did that. Not me. I'm merely carrying on what you started.'

'You've levelled up, though, with this horrible attitude. Is that how it has to be? Would you like to level up even further? Would you like us to block each other?'

'Don't be ridic—' he starts.

'No, no, this is what you're saying, right? We're not allowed to be friends. And this is all due to some noble rule you've made up. Really?'

'Well . . .'

'Well, what? Yes or no?' I ask. 'Are you seriously never going to talk to me outside work because we almost got together, once? Or is it that you *would* be friends with me, but you've got a girlfriend? So that's the game-changer. And what . . . ?' I grasp around for an accusation to hurl at him. 'Are you worried you might accidentally sleep with me? Are you that untrustworthy?' I admit saying this is probably a bit beneath me. Chris has made me so angry, and cheating is high on my worry list, even when it's not happening to me.

'What the fuck?' he explodes angrily, which I did not see coming. 'You've got a boyfriend and I've got a girlfriend. Why are you trying to fuck this up for both of us? I am not stupid enough to be mates with someone I fancy. I can't be mates with someone I want to kiss every time I see her. I can't be mates with someone I can't stop fucking thinking about.'

I stare at Chris, my mouth open. A guest walks into the room, senses the tension and walks back out again. At least now I can tick off the 'fight breaks out' square on my bingo grid.

Chris lowers his voice. 'Honestly, Lexie, what did you think I was going to say?'

'Not that,' I reply.

'Really? Then you're naïve. I liked you so much. Meeting

you was . . . perfect,' he says. 'As if any other way of meeting someone is ever going to match up to that. As if any conversation I have with anyone is ever going to match up to that. Two people meet each other, connect instantly, like each other enough to discuss hanging out together in another country, and it just wasn't to be. I tried to take that for what it was. Then you ended up in New York anyway, and seeing you was . . .' He can't find the word. 'But you left, and I tried not to think about you any more. And I failed. And now you're all *why didn't you ring me and tell me you were here?* Why do you think?' He downs half his drink in one go and winces. 'Ugh. This is awful.'

I watch Chris for a moment – he can't bring himself to look at me initially – and then he does so, with a pained expression that is a punch in the gut.

'I suppose I should be flattered,' I say quietly when I regain my power of thought.

He shrugs, tops up his glass and tops up mine, despite the fact that neither of us likes it.

'Two whiskies out of five,' he says, diffusing the tension briefly. 'You felt it too.'

'Saying goodbye *was* bittersweet when I first met you in the summer, and it was bittersweet again in New York, but so much has happened to us both over that time.'

'That it all fades away?' he asks.

'We have to let it fade away.'

'Exactly,' he says. 'Exactly. We need to let it go or we hurt the people we're with. Are you and Josh still together?'

I nod.

'Are you happy?' he asks.

I hesitate. I nod. And even if I wasn't, I'm not cheating on Josh. I could never do that to someone, after what happened to me.

'Why do you think I barely suggested we hang out in New York?' Chris asks.

'You were busy with your new girlfriend.'

'I *made* myself busy with my new girlfriend. And she wasn't my girlfriend then. Just someone I was dating.'

'Is she your girlfriend now?' I ask, waiting for salt to enter the emotional wound that's already open.

He doesn't answer.

'Why did you *make* yourself busy?'

'Because what was the point in hanging out with you when it won't do any good?' Chris says with a sigh. 'And don't say *because we're friends*.'

'I don't have the answer to that,' I confess.

'Neither do I,' he replies softly.

'So this is it,' I say.

'What do you mean?'

'There's no point in saying anything else, is there? You don't want to be friends.'

He shrugs. 'It's not *don't want to be*. It's that we *shouldn't*.'

'Are you that irresistible?' I attempt to defuse the tension with humour.

'I think it would be a mistake,' he responds seriously.

This is so pointless. I'm going to go. 'Fine,' I answer listlessly. I can't believe this is happening. Why did he have to say any of this? I hadn't seen Chris since New York and we're hardly likely to see each other as the years progress, even when we work for the same company.

'Are you OK? You're making the face again,' he says.

'I'm not OK actually,' I reply. 'I'm angry at you.'

'Why? I'm doing a good thing. You're with Josh and you're happy. Why are you even going to consider messing that up?'

'I wouldn't. It wouldn't be like that. And, Chris, we work together.' Then I remember. '*You* recommended me for the job. *You* put me in your path. Why? And don't pretend it was only for the financial bonus.'

'Because I'm an idiot,' he says softly.

'You're not. You're wonderful and smart and funny, and you make me laugh and you're so easy to get on with and . . .'

'If you're trying to talk yourself out of being anywhere near me, you're not doing a very good job.'

'I'm not the one who's being weird,' I say. 'I'm not the one who doesn't want to be near *you*. Why would I not want to be near you. You're lovely.'

'So are you.'

'So why are you doing this?' I cry.

'I'm not doing anything,' he replies. 'I'm trying so hard *not* to do anything.'

'I feel like I've just been broken up with, by someone who's not a friend and who I'm not even dating. This is so weird.'

'I know. Come here,' he says and I allow myself to be scooped into an embrace. Chris holds me tightly and it's bittersweet all over again. His cologne is different from when I last saw him, warm and woody to match the season. I feel his heartbeat against mine, his chest against mine, and it's more than I can cope with. His lips touch my hair and he lays the gentlest of kisses on my head.

I pull back, look up at him and I know it's a mistake. He looks down at me. He's so close to me, and he doesn't move and neither do I.

'Don't kiss me,' he whispers.

'Or you won't win the bingo?' I whisper back. 'I'm not going to kiss you.' But I feel so lost; so lost when it comes to Chris. It's too late to go back and undo everything – undo how I feel about him.

I feel his breath as he leans towards me: whisky, heat and fire. But he doesn't kiss me and I don't kiss him. Instead he lingers for a moment and then pulls back.

'I'm going to go now,' he says in a strained voice. And I can do nothing else but watch him leave the room.

Chapter Thirty-Three

'You're going to get serious wrinkles if you keep frowning like that,' Scarlet says as I attempt to relax by the pool on our spa day. I am wound up so tightly that the masseuse is going to have to be a miracle-worker to unknot me. We've checked out of the wedding venue and in Scarlet's little hire car we've bombed it, late, as usual, to check into the next hotel. By the pool it's calm and quiet, and the sound of people swimming slow, effortless laps converges with plinky-plunky spa music.

'I didn't realise I was frowning,' I say, using my fingers to iron out the creases settling between my brows. But it's no good and I feel my face crumpling up again.

'What's wrong?' she asks. 'You've been frowning all morning.'

I didn't tell her about seeing Chris when I found Scarlet last night, as she wasn't sober enough to understand. And what would I say? How do I tell her I feel as if I've been dumped by a guy who categorically wasn't my boyfriend to begin with. And now we can't even be friends.

Maybe Chris is right about us. Maybe, if we were friends, I'd find myself in a pickle, emotions-wise. Although I'm already in a pickle.

Scarlet leans over on her lounger and uses her fingers to try to iron out my creases. I chuckle at the act.

'That's better,' she says, sitting back. 'Why. Are. You. Frowning?' she pleads.

I tell her and when I've finished my rant – because it is a rant – I'm fuming. She looks confused.

'And this is the guy from the wedding where you met Josh? The same guy who got you the job?'

I nod.

'Chris, who worked in the Union bar with Grey, before I worked there? The perfect guy?'

I nod and then add quickly, 'No. Josh is the perfect guy.'

'Josh was the *second* guy,' she says. 'You told me you'd met someone who was perfect, but that it couldn't go any further. I remember that. Then you met Josh, all hell broke loose and you snogged his face off.'

'It doesn't matter who I said was perfect at the time.'

'But Chris thinks you'll fall in love with him if you go anywhere near him?'

'I . . . I think I'm phrasing this badly. He didn't actually say that. He just sort of pointed out it wasn't worth the risk.'

'Oh,' Scarlet says as she sips her ginger-and-turmeric shot. 'Well, that's kind of . . . nice of him.'

I make a face. 'Is it, though?'

'Yes. It is. He doesn't want you to get hurt. He doesn't want to get hurt, and he doesn't want anybody else involved to get hurt, either. So you're now simply work colleagues. Chris obviously thinks that's a good thing and – I'll be honest – so do I.'

'Oh,' I say, deflating.

'I feel,' Scarlet starts up again, 'that you would like to keep seeing Chris and keep talking to him,' she analyses. 'And that would mean you're open to the – hopefully very faint – possibility of it ending in disaster and a few people getting hurt.'

I swallow.

'And as much as I love you, that's dangerous and probably not very nice. For anyone,' she says diplomatically.

'You think I'm a bad person?'

'That's not what I said. I just think Chris has thought it through, and you haven't. And remember what I said about men and women being friends.'

'Chris said that too,' I point out and I curse myself for helping along his argument.

'The problem is, you sound as if you had a real connection in a short amount of time. You both felt it, but that moment has passed. And now you're trying to make it work with other people.'

'I'm not *trying* to make it work with Josh,' I say. 'It *is* working with Josh.'

'OK, then that's great. Case closed. And, Lexie,' Scarlet sounds exasperated now, 'I don't think you're a bad person. But if, after being warned off by Chris and me, you go and open that door with him again . . . then I do think you have the potential to be a bad person.'

Chapter Thirty-Four

April

'He told you he loves you?' Scarlet squeals.

'Yes,' I squeal equally excitably, when I return to our flat after another lovely weekend spent with Josh. This has become our routine over the past couple of months. I work from home midweek, because I'm in and out of the city so often. Then, on Friday nights, I head to Josh's. It's like living two different lives. I relish being so busy in my job and I love the time off I get with Josh from Friday to Sunday night. It was one of those gorgeous warm weekends when we could sit out and have lunch in his garden, surrounded by tulips and daffodils. It felt a shame to return to London this time.

Scarlet springs up from the sofa, where she's cradling her phone in one hand and the TV control in the other. We both jump up and down with excitement, hugging each other as if one of us has won the Lottery. I feel as if I *have*. I am in a relationship and it is going well. I tell myself this a lot.

'You didn't text me and tell me!' she exclaims.

'There wasn't time, what with all the telling one another

we love each other all weekend. Josh also mentioned me moving in with him.'

'You what?' Scarlet says, the enthusiasm replaced by surprise.

Best to get this out of the way now, I think. Like ripping off a plaster. 'I haven't said yes,' I tell her. 'Because it wasn't really a question, just a mention. But Josh did tentatively put the suggestion out there, as in "one day soon".'

'Wow,' Scarlet says. 'That's big.'

'I don't know,' I reply, with a level of dismissiveness I don't feel – but I don't want to brag. 'We've kind of been discussing it on and off for a while . . .'

'You're not keen?'

'I am, but not yet. I'm enjoying what we have.'

'You and me? Or you and him?' Scarlet jokes.

'Both,' I say truthfully. 'It's kind of perfect as it is, here *and* there. It's too soon to move out of here and in with Josh. Plus, I kind of don't want to yet.'

'You've got your city life here and your country life with Josh,' Scarlet agrees. 'Why mess that up?'

The question is rhetorical, but I nod and then pause. And I'm not sure I agree with it being simplified like that, now I'm thinking about it. To mix the two into one wouldn't be messing it up. It would be the next step. But now that I've got a job where I need to pop in and out of central London at a moment's notice, it's not ideal timing.

I'm getting ahead of myself. Josh and I have only just told each other we're in love. There's plenty of time for everything that might naturally follow. And I really hope it does. But I'm not in a rush, I remind myself. However, 'I was starting to wonder if he'd say he loved me at some point. That can only be a good thing, can't it – hanging on and waiting for it?'

'I always think it's so brave, being the first person to say it,' Scarlet chimes in. 'What happens if the other person doesn't say it back? Humiliation. Total wipe-out.'

I am pleased Josh said it first, and I tell Scarlet all about how it happened. 'We were sitting in his garden, basking in the spring sunshine, sipping local wine that Tamara and Mark had brought round the night before. Yet another new tub of ice cream to taste-test. Total perfection.'

'Ooh, which flavour?' she says, getting easily distracted from the main thrust of the story.

'Christmas pudding.'

'Yum,' she says. 'Though it's a bit early for that, isn't it?'

'It takes a long time to plan these things, apparently.'

'Is Tamara doing more new flavours? Can you bring some home for us?'

'I think she's doing mince-pie too.'

'Ugh, no thanks.' Scarlet shakes her head.

'It's got real flakes of pastry in it,' I say, mimicking Tamara. I feel I'm being mean sometimes, and I make up for it by saying, 'She's building quite the empire.'

I'm proud of both her and Josh, who's become more heavily involved in the business, as it turns out that Tamara's recipe skills are par excellence, but her ability to understand the concept of a profit-and-loss sheet is less so. I've warmed to Tamara quite a bit over these past few months, which is handy as we see a lot of her.

'Has her threat level diminished in any way?' Scarlet asks, always on the lookout for hefty wedges of scandal.

'She and Mark are a proper couple it seems, so yes, I'm not worried. And nor was I.' Although I might have been, a tiny bit. After my ex cheated on me, I have become more sensitive about these things.

'I was just looking out for you,' she placates.

'Thank you,' I say. 'Tamara's sweet. She always has kind words for people, makes fabulous ice cream and is very giving with her friendship. To both Josh and me. It can be lonely in a rural environment. I wonder if she feels it too, even though she's lived there for ages. She must have friends other than Josh, although she never mentions them. She works long hours. It's tough to meet new people.'

'I feel her pain,' Scarlet says.

When we finish gossiping, Scarlet tells me she has news.

'Go on,' I say, inching forward on the sofa where we've camped out. Scarlet was watching a crime drama before I got in and it's on pause in the background.

'I've met someone.'

I draw in a breath. 'This is even more exciting than Josh telling me he loves me. How? When? Who?'

'Which bit do you want answering first?' she asks joyfully.

'All of it in one go, and quickly.'

She giggles and it's lovely seeing her like this for the first time in . . . for ever.

'He's called Rory and I met him at the wedding in Scotland.'

I narrow my eyes. 'But that was two months ago.'

'I know. We messaged back and forth a bit, and I didn't

think it was going to go anywhere. I message a few guys a bit on dating apps, you know that. And because they go nowhere, I don't mention them, but . . .' She's hesitant, cautious, as if she dare not say, 'I think this has potential.'

'Ooh,' I make an appreciative noise.

'It's early days,' she's quick to say. 'But he's a gardener from Leith and we're making plans to meet up soon. I'm going to go and visit him.'

My mind is blank. 'Where's Leith?'

She gives me a look. 'Scotland. Edinburgh.'

My mouth falls open. 'He lives in *Scotland*?'

'Yes,' she confirms. 'Did you do that thing where you think somewhere you've never heard of must be an outer-London suburb?'

'Shut up,' I joke. 'OK. Right, I'm confused. How did you meet at the wedding?'

'You set me a challenge to snog someone and—'

'You did it? You said you didn't. Did you snog a gardener? And you *didn't tell me*?'

'No,' Scarlet replies patiently. 'I was nowhere near drunk enough to do that, but I was sort of on the lookout for someone to flirt with and if it led to snogging, then I was willing to get a bingo square ticked off . . .' She shrugs. 'But it didn't, because Rory's not like that. He's quiet and reserved, but he's so fit and sweet, and he sort of *wooed* me with his chat about flowers. He took me for a walk around the estate grounds and it was lovely, even though we couldn't see much because it was dark, but there were lanterns flickering, and the house was behind us and . . .' She sighs romantically. 'It was like going back in time to a bygone age when men don't try to sleep with you the minute they meet you. It was all my Jane Austen fantasies rolled into one evening.'

I sigh romantically too. 'Does he work there? At the house? What was he doing gardening at night?'

'No,' she says as if I've asked the world's silliest question. 'He was a guest of the bride, who's from there.'

'Oh,' I reply. And then I ask, 'Are you shacking up in Scotland with a sexy gardener?'

'Might be,' Scarlet cries excitedly and we both squeal with joy.

'You didn't tell me *any* of that!' I say, as we settle in and she shows me a picture on her phone of Rory from Leith.

'I was practically bursting to tell you at the spa day, but you seemed so *down* and I didn't want to brag. I also wasn't sure if it was going to go anywhere, so . . .'

'Was I down?'

She nods.

I don't remember being down. I was definitely annoyed. Annoyed with Chris. Annoyed at a missed opportunity for . . . I don't know what. Although, on reflection, I know it's for the best. I'd never have made that suggestion not to get to know each other. It's far too grown-up and mature for me to have thought of it. So I suppose I should be grateful that Chris made that suggestion, that he *forced* me into being mature.

I don't want to go over all that again out loud, so I focus on Scarlet and her new man – and this relationship, which may or may not be the start of something.

Chapter Thirty-Five

May

I hate having to be in any kind of contact with Chris now, but it is inevitable, seeing as we work together, even if we're far apart in both time and distance. My work emails are clipped and short and, far from thinking I'd have nothing to do with him until the end of this project, it seems he's currently a huge part of my working day.

At least it's Friday, so this is the last bit of work I'm doing today after a full day of going back and forth with Max and Chris over the new set of layout plans. If it frustrates Max that I finish my working day five hours ahead of him, he doesn't let on. I always log on the next day and discover a trove of emails piled up for me to get through, from those in the New York office who need on-the-ground London hotel intel. Max was right. My inbox filled up fast and it's been non-stop since. It's exhausting. I love it.

I email ever so professionally at the end of my day:

Hi Chris,

Hope you're well. Just updating you on the change of layout for the kitchen, as discussed. Drawings attached.

> *All the best,*
> *Lexie*

I hit send. Max informed us all last week that a celebrity chef – who simply goes by the name of Javier – is going to be our chef patron and has decided he needs to do more than just cook. He feels he also needs to be in charge of the layout for the hotel's kitchen. I think this is totally over the top, but apparently the New York team are used to this sort of thing, though the UK suppliers are flipping their lids.

Chef's kitchen is his space, according to Max, and heaven forbid that our talented architects should be allowed to do their job in the process. All their hard work is being undone, as Chef Javier tries to move a sink five inches to the left for no reason at all, as far as I can see. The structural engineers are having kittens, and I've been with the site manager getting the lowdown and sitting in on Zoom calls between the London team and Max, while everyone tries to manage each other's expectations.

Chris replies within two minutes:

Thanks, Lexie. I'll take a look and come back to you on Monday if I need anything further.

> *Kind regards,*
> *Chris*

Kind regards. Honestly. Thank God it's Friday. I close my laptop lid. It's 6 p.m. I'm done and I don't have any plans tonight. Josh is at some kind of farming event this weekend, so I'm staying put in London. I can't wait to run a bath, put on a podcast and anticipate Scarlet getting home, so we can decide what delights to order from Deliveroo this evening.

I start running the bath and, while I wait for the tub to fill, scroll through my podcasts, wondering if I should listen to a true-crime series about a woman who got murdered in her first-floor flat in broad daylight in the centre of London. I poke my head out of the bathroom and glance at the front door, wondering if it's locked. It isn't, so I turn to lock it and decide just to put on some music instead of the podcast. That feels safer. But before I get the chance to select any *bath music*, my phone rings.

I stand still and stare at the screen as Chris's name flashes back at me. I switch off the tap and swipe to answer. 'Yes?' I say with uncertainty.

'I wanted to grab you quickly before you finished your day over there.'

'Yes?'

'You forgot to attach the drawings.'

'Oh, sorry. I didn't think I had,' I say. 'I'll do that right now.'

'Thanks,' he replies.

'OK, bye.'

'Wait,' he's quick to add. But doesn't say anything else.

'What's wrong?'

He doesn't reply.

'Hello?' I ask.

'I'm still here. Look, Lexie, this is silly,' he goes on, with a hint of exasperation.

'What is?' I ask. 'If you're referring to the kitchen change, I think we can all do without—'

'No,' he says. 'Well, yeah, that too. But that's just people being people. But this: *you and me*. This is silly.'

'Which bit?' I question because he needs to say it, not me.

' "Kind regards." "All the best." It's stupid.'

'It's a polite way to end an email,' I point out.

He tuts. 'This isn't what I had in mind. I don't know what we're trying to achieve, but we're doing it all wrong.'

'I don't make the rules,' I say, echoing his words at the Edinburgh wedding. 'This is *your* game.'

He pauses, remembering. 'That was bingo,' he replies, cottoning on. 'This is life.'

'It's not really, though, is it?'

'It is. Lexie, I didn't envisage *this*. There doesn't need to be any drama. We can chat. You're over there, I'm over here. We need to be able to communicate over this kitchen nonsense, and all the other things that are going to start amassing soon. We can't do it if we're sending "Hope this email finds you well" to each other over and over again until one of us dies of politeness overload. It's inane.'

I chuckle without meaning to, and then I'm annoyed at myself for relenting quite so quickly. 'Yes, it is,' I agree. 'But you started it.'

'You going down that road is even sillier,' he dares.

'Er, excuse me—' I start, but Chris responds quickly.

'I know. I know,' he says. And then, more gently, 'I hold my hands up. I've caved.'

'You can't,' I tell him. 'You're not allowed to.'

'No?' he questions. 'Why not?'

'Because this was your idea, and you've only held out for three months.'

'I didn't think it through,' he says.

'Not my problem,' I reply, digging in the knife.

'You want to be rude to each other? You actually want that?' he asks. 'Because you know full well that's not what I was suggesting, when we agreed to cool it all down.'

'We're not being rude to each other. We hope each other's emails find the other well. We're being *really* polite.'

'We're being rude now,' he snaps. 'Or, rather, you are. You're being rude while we discuss the fact that we're being over-polite.'

'It's quite the mind-fuck, isn't it?' I declare, proud of myself for having found a way to shoehorn this word into our conversation, because I've been thinking all of this is a mind-fuck for quite some time.

Chris sighs. I can picture him, his head thrown back in his chair at work, shirt sleeves rolled up as he stares at the ceiling in frustration.

'Where are you?' I ask.

'I'm working from home today,' he says.

'Oh, I pictured you at work. I thought this is quite an interesting conversation to be having within earshot of everyone.'

'You pictured me?' he asks. And then, 'Forget I said that. How's your day been – kitchen nonsense aside?' he asks.

'Fine,' I answer, a bit taken aback at this change in direction. And then I remember. 'I'm not used to small talk from you. You've thrown me a bit.'

I hear him laugh softly. 'I want to make sure everything's OK.'

'With me?'

'With us,' he says. 'That we're OK. That I can hang up and we can both go off and have our weekends and it'll all be OK.'

'Chris?'

'Yeah?'

'It'll all be OK.'

'Thanks,' he says.

You put your head on mine and you kissed my hair. That's what I really want to say. *You leaned in to kiss me, changed your mind and told me we couldn't be friends. I really liked you*. But I don't say any of that. Instead I ask, 'What are you and your Tinder swipe up to this weekend?'

'Pah,' he laughs. 'You just made me snort coffee. And it wasn't bloody Tinder. But let's change names to protect the innocent. Tinder Swipe and I are going to the Rockefeller Center because there's an exhibition she wants to see.

'That sounds lovely. Did you ever take her ice-skating there, like you did with me?' I ask.

'Er . . . no.'

I immediately pick up on his caginess. 'Why not?'

'I'd pre-booked those tickets.'

'I don't understand,' I say.

'I pre-booked those tickets for Tinder Swipe.' He laughs briefly at how he's started using that name.

My mouth drops open. 'What?'

'You were going home and I realised I'd been neglectful,' Chris goes on. 'So my grand plan to take her ice-skating got replaced by an emergency night out with you and, because I had the tickets already, ice-skating seemed like a good idea.'

'You took me on a date that was meant for *someone else*?'

'It wasn't a date. With you, I mean.'

'You know what I mean,' I tell him.

'I felt guilty that we hadn't spent much time together. I had ice-skating tickets. It wasn't meant to be anything more than that. Please don't read anything further into it.'

I inhale and exhale. 'I think I preferred it when we were saying "kind regards" to each other. Can we go back to that?'

'Yeah,' he sighs. 'If you want to.'

'I don't want to really,' I say.

'I'm sorry I suggested we go radio-silent on each other. It was a rash decision. We need to be able to communicate.'

'It was done with good intentions,' I spring to his defence, although why, I'm not sure.

'My gran says the path to hell is lined with good intentions,' Chris muses.

'Your gran is a wise woman.'

I can hear the smile in his voice. 'She is,' he says, then tells me how she used to love photography when she was young and how she met his grandad, who was a picture-framer. I'm grateful Chris is switching up the conversation, that we're continuing on so naturally. I don't think I realised how much I missed him until now. He asks about my grandparents, and I tell him how they grew up in the same town in Hertfordshire and met each other at a bus stop. I tell him about where I was raised, and he does the same, until we've been talking about anything and everything for hours. The bath I had planned to run never gets run, Scarlet comes home, clanging the stiff door lock and waves at me, before disappearing into her room to FaceTime the gardener from Leith. When I next look at my watch I see it's 9 p.m. and I tell Chris as much. I'm starving.

'We've been talking for three hours,' he exclaims. 'I need to get back on with some work. What are you doing with the rest of your Friday night?'

'That was pretty much it,' I say. 'It's a rare weekend off from Josh, so I'm in my flat.'

'A weekend off?' he queries. 'Like day-release?'

'No,' I reply. 'He's at a farming event. I have no idea what it entails.'

'Are you at his every weekend?' Chris asks.

'Mostly, yeah, or else we wouldn't see each other.'

'Oh,' he says. 'Which do you prefer now? Country or city?'

'Both equally now.'

'You've changed your tune,' he comments.

'Yes, I have. I love the freedom of both. In London I love coming and going from a pub or a bar, to the cinema or theatre; a gallery at the weekend with Scarlet, although we don't do too much of that any more. And I love how easy it is in the country. I don't feel any pressure to do too much. I can just be, relax, spend time with Josh, cook a bit, help him feed the animals or whatever. I understand why city types have weekend homes now.'

He chuckles. 'Idyllic.'

'Yeah, I suppose it is. Like a dream. A good dream. I feel as if I'm leading two lives.' I'm not sure why I've told Chris this.

'Sounds like you are,' he says without judgement. But what would he judge? 'So you're happy,' he continues, and I can't tell if he's stating it or asking it.

'I am. Are you?'

'Yeah,' he says, but there was a split-second pause before he replied.

We have to be able to talk. I have to be able to hear about his life. I have to get over my regrets, move on.

'So tell me about Tinder Swipe,' I ask, and I'll bet he's rolling his eyes.

'I can't believe you're making this stick,' he says before continuing, 'It's good. Yeah. I like her, Kayla. No thoughts of moving in together, though, I hasten to add. It's all very easy and it's only been a few months, so we're enjoying each other's company. Getting to know each other.'

'Ah, I'm really pleased,' I reply, and I mean it. I do. 'And I'm pleased we're friends again.'

'Me too. Sorry for being such an idiot in Edinburgh.'

'You weren't,' I say, though I want to respond with, *You were. You really, really were.*

'Let's forget that ever happened,' he says.

'Deal. It was nice,' I say, 'chatting like this.' It was. It wasn't emotionally fuelled or dramatic. It was easy. I'm sure we can keep this up. If we both put our minds to it and try really hard.

'It was nice,' Chris agrees. 'I've had a nice afternoon, even though I should have been working.'

'I've had a nice evening,' I reply and then tell him I'll send those drawings over in a few minutes.

'Speak to you soon,' Chris says. 'Have a good weekend.'

'You too. Kind regards,' I trill.

He chuckles and then deadpans back, 'All the best.'

Chapter Thirty-Six

August

'Surprise!' the room full of people shouts at Josh as he walks into the farmhouse sitting room after work on Friday evening.

He looks genuinely surprised as party-poppers spray around him and thirty-four people shout and cheer his arrival.

'Happy birthday!' I call over to him as people start surrounding him and wishing him the same.

I watch his reaction go from surprise to happy confusion, and then he glances at me as his dad puts a glass of red wine in his hand. Josh narrows his eyes. 'Did you do this?' he mouths from across the room.

'Might have done,' I mouth back, and he holds his glass up in the air to cheers me from the other side of the room. Next to him, his father misunderstands and lifts his glass high to clink it against Josh's, which makes Josh and me laugh together conspiratorially. And then I lose him to the crowd as he's engulfed in birthday wishes.

*

'You make my son very happy,' Josh's mum, Cassandra, says to me later that evening. 'I hope you know that.'

I'm sure I'm blushing. 'I do. I think I do. He makes me very happy too,' I reply as we're hovering over the remaining canapés by the sideboard in the sitting room, hoovering them down together, one after the other.

She gives me an encouraging smile and then says she's off to talk to my mum again, as she's remembered the name of the book she was trying to describe to her earlier.

I'd invited my mum and dad along to the party, which in hindsight was a brave move, considering Josh has never met them before. But then, even though they live in the next village, I'd only met Josh's parents a few times for some kitchen suppers now and then. Josh has been so protective of our time together, seeing as we hardly get any. We've been together nearly a year. A year ago this month I met Josh. And Chris. Two different men and two different stories. My life has changed so much since that day.

Today, at this party, I have killed all the birds with all the stones. Everyone's met everyone. Scarlet and her boyfriend Rory travelled separately from London and Scotland respectively, and are shooting off for the rest of the weekend to explore the Cotswolds as he's never been to this part of the world.

Scarlet was desperate to meet Josh again, after that one time on the terrace at the wedding back in August, and he was excited to see her again too. He confides in me later, when we're standing in the hallway as the last guests are trickling out the door, that he thinks he's passed the Scarlet Test, and I don't pretend not to know what he's talking about.

'Yeah, she likes you. Sings your praises from afar. Liked you from the wedding where we met, and I leapt on you and snogged your face off.'

'Oh, you've admitted it was you who made the first move then, have you? Even though I allegedly "goaded" you into kissing me.'

'Yeah, yeah. I'll let you have that win, but only because it's your birthday.'

'Thank you for this.' He gestures around us at the detritus from the night. 'No one's ever thrown me a surprise party before.' He pulls me into his arms and kisses me deeply in the hallway until Tamara appears, coughs loudly and laughs, hand-in-hand with Mark.

'Happy birthday for yesterday,' I tell her as I remind myself again that she and Josh met after being born only a day apart.

'Thanks,' she says. 'We're off now,' she smiles warmly.

'Great party,' Mark says.

'Thanks for coming,' Josh and I both say together and then laugh.

'You two are just too cute,' Tamara replies as she and Mark hug us and leave.

'I think that went really well,' I say to Josh when we're alone. 'It was such a good way for everyone to meet each other and, as a bonus, you got loads of presents.'

'Mostly wine, I think,' he says happily as he heads towards

the collection of bottle bags lined up. 'I'm glad our friends and family had a good time. They're all so generous.'

'You're very loved,' I tell him.

'I feel it,' he says, moving away from his new hoard of wine bottles and coming back over to me. He looks at me for a long time, as if deciding something.

'What?' I ask gently.

'Would you like to move in with me?'

My eyes widen. Although I'd been wondering if this sort of invite might eventually be dispensed, as we'd talked about it briefly a while ago, I wasn't really expecting it – not now, not after Josh had had rather a lot of wine. Surely this sort of chat should be reserved for a sober occasion?

He asks me, 'What's wrong?' as I continue to look at him.

'Really?' I ask.

'Really,' he confirms. 'Do you think I'm not being genuine? It's a very big decision to make, asking a woman to move in with me. I've never done this before. I wanted to wait for the right time.

'And that time is now?' I ask warmly. I'm fishing for compliments, clearly.

He smiles. 'It is, yes.' With that he reaches into the pocket of his jeans, struggling to retrieve whatever it is he's looking for. For one tiny fraction of a second, I wonder if it's a ring. That would be two shocks in one night and I'm not sure I could cope with that.

But it's not a ring. It's a key, on a key chain with a huge glittery L on it.

I beam as he passes it to me. 'I don't need this,' I joke. 'Your front door's usually unlocked – which, to me as a Londoner, is just asking for it.'

'It's for those rare occasions when it's locked,' Josh says, playing along. 'Consider it a symbolic gesture. We're moving along, you and me. You know my parents, and now I've met yours. It's been almost a whole year of us going back and forth, back and forth,' he goes on. 'Or, rather, it's been nearly a whole year of you doing this. I've stayed right here. And every time you go back to yours to appease Scarlet, I miss you.'

'I miss you too,' I reply and then realise what he's said. 'I don't appease Scarlet. I have meetings.'

'Which you spread out across the days you're back in London, Monday to Friday. Why not condense them into one day and commute from here for that one day? Plenty of people do it.'

'I know,' I say. 'I've seen them getting off the train with me on a Friday night.'

'In fairness, some of them might be second-homers,' Josh replies, undoing his own argument.

I'd worked that out for myself, but don't like to say so.

'But not all of them,' he's quick to point out. 'Being with me, here . . .' He shrugs, lets his sentence hang in mid-air. 'I mean,' he continues, 'I'd love that. And it'd mean you're not paying rent with Scarlet for a flat you're only living in half the week.'

'I live there for *most* of the week,' I say. 'And I'm not going to move in with you just so I can pay less rent. I'd be moving in with you because I *want* to move in with you.' Josh looks pleased at that until I say, 'Hang on, how much rent do you want?'

He's taken aback. 'I don't want any rent.'

'Why not?' I ask.

'The house doesn't have a mortgage.'

'That's the dream, right there,' I say, glancing around at my surroundings. Faces in portraits a hundred years old glance back at me, and I silently thank them for doing whatever it was they did that got this giant hulk of a house mortgage-free in time for my arrival.

'My grandparents paid it off years ago,' Josh tells me. 'Mum and Dad got the benefit of that when they raised us here. And now it's my turn to make a life here with someone.'

'Someone?'

'With you.'

'Oh my gosh, Josh,' I say in awe and then try not to laugh as I realise that rhymes. He notices it too and emits a brief chuckle.

'I love you,' he continues. 'And this is the next step. We know it works when you live here, because you practically moved in with me five minutes after we met.'

I thump him playfully, 'It wasn't five minutes, and it was only for a few weeks.' I think of all the things we do together – there's quite a bit of sex, and he's taking the time to teach me how to drive. He's been gradually letting me into his world and now he wants me to live in it fully. It's going to be such a change from my own world. I make jokes about becoming a country bumpkin, though I'm not sure I am one at heart. I'm going to have to learn how, if I move to Somerset full-time.

I reason it's not the other side of the world. And then my mind flicks to the alternate life I could have had on the other side of the world in New York with Chris. I force him from my thoughts and bring myself back to the here and now. Somerset is a train journey away from friends and family – that's it. And moving in would be the perfect next step. But it still feels like such a *huge* step for me. I'd be leaving Scarlet, for one thing. I wonder if I need time to think about it. I can hardly say that, though.

'I'll need to talk to Scarlet about it,' I respond, buying myself a little time, and Josh adopts a look of confusion.

'Why?' he asks. 'You want her permission?'

'No,' I say, slightly taken aback. 'We share a flat. I can't leave her with all the bills. We'd need to discuss how me moving out would work – if she would want to sublet my room or if we'd end the tenancy together. Either way, it'll take time, so I can't just move out. Not that quickly.'

'Ah, I see,' Josh says more gently, now he understands.

'It might take a while to sort,' I say.

I watch hope rise on his face as it dawns on him. 'Does that mean . . . Are you saying yes?' he asks. He looks so concerned that I might say no. This handsome kind man, who I do love – I do – has asked me to move in with him.

'Yes,' I say, realising this at the same time as he does. 'Yes, I am.'

Chapter Thirty-Seven

November

'This is still one of the most boring bits, in my opinion,' I tell Chris after he arrives in London to oversee the next stage of the interior hotel fit-out. I'm glad this bit is his job, because it's a total snooze-fest. He's tried – and failed – to jazz it up to me over the phone whenever we speak.

I'm watching him do his thing: measuring, issuing instructions and checking over all the materials that have arrived onsite, despite the fact that I've checked them over already, as has the site manager.

'It's like watching someone give a really boring Ted Talk on how to assemble flatpack furniture, only on a bigger scale,' I tease. Chris has got his serious face on, and I'm trying to get him to crack a smile.

He's pretending not to laugh as he walks away to talk to a supplier, holding the coffee I've gone to get him from the artisan place round the corner. His jet lag is setting in and he's yawning.

The hotel is still a building site, and we've been given hi-viz jackets and hard hats, as usual. Chris blends into a sea of neon yellow as he moves around, inspecting the space and talking to the fit-out team.

We're a little bit behind schedule, but Max and Chris both assure me this is usual, so while the fit-out guys are hovering with their instructions and drawings, boxes and toolkits, the painters and decorators are working as fast as they can to finish and make space for the next crew. The site manager looks harassed, so I hand him the coffee that I've not drunk from yet and he goes off to bark instructions at someone.

I can't wait to see it all finished. Max allowed me a lot of input into the fixtures, fittings and furnishings aspect of the design, whittling down hoards of samples into a select few of my favourites for each item of furniture or furnishings. I'd discuss with him why something would or wouldn't work in the space, how it would affect the overall aesthetic of each room and fit the hotel's brand. Part of the large building was once the home of a prominent map-maker working in the late nineteenth century. Given that the hotel brand loves to nod to what the building was once used for, I've had great fun buying old maps from eBay and Etsy. I've learned so much from Max. I've decided I'm going to do a proper interior-design course as I want to learn so much more.

Until then, I can't wait to see how the items Max and I have chosen together will look. After seeing a first mock-up of how a space will appear, nothing compares to watching it finally come to fruition before your eyes. All those colours on a mood board converge into a room. A space becomes cosy, habitable, desirable, real.

At the end of the day I suggest that we take the site

manager for a well-earned drink and Chris recommends a bar round the corner. Only the site manager cries off at the last minute, so Chris and I stand at the bar, a bit uncertain what to do. This contravenes our rule not to be alone.

'Do you think we should—' I start at exactly the same time Chris says, 'Oh yes! They've got a Happy Hour.'

'Uh . . . OK,' I reply. Looks like we're doing this, then.

We order two drinks each, to take advantage of the remaining fifteen minutes, and Chris pays.

'I'll get the next ones,' I offer when we're sitting on our tiny back-less bar stools.

'They'll be full price then,' Chris warns me.

'Oh, well played,' I say, looking at him properly for the first time since he arrived in London.

He laughs, suggesting, 'We can split the bill for all of it.'

I realise I've missed seeing him in person, although we've spoken quite a bit for work, and we manage to tack on a friendly conversation or life update occasionally too. We've at least been adult about that recently.

We hold up all four of our drinks, one in each of our hands, and clink them together. 'Cheers!'

He looks good. Chris always looks good. He's tanned as if he's been on holiday, and I ask him if he's been away. He nods and tells me he went to Palm Springs for a week. That explains why his out-of-office was on the last time I sent him a new set of drawings. The tan suits him. Everything suits him. I refocus, as Chris is telling me he saw an offer in the *New York Times* and went for it.

'You and Tinder Swipe?' I probe.

'No. Just me.'

'Really?' I ask in surprise. 'By yourself?'

He pauses for a second. 'By myself.'

'Are you still doing that?' I enquire in awe. 'Finding yourself?'

He makes a gagging noise. 'Yeah. Sort of. I've never been on holiday on my own before. It was great. Strangely great. No pressure. I needed a bit of no pressure. Because there's a lot of pressure, now I'm over here.'

'How long are you over for?' I ask after we've winced at how strong our drinks are.

'A week. I'm in an Airbnb,' he says. 'But I'll be back once a week every month from now on, to get this all over the fin-ishing line. In December I'm here for two weeks back-to-back at Christmas. One week for work and then one week with my family. I've not spent Christmas in London in . . . for ever.'

'Nice,' I say absently and then I realise. 'Oh, you'll be here for my leaving and Christmas party all-in-one. Do you want to come? It's the week before Christmas, which is a busy time for everyone, I know, so we're booking people in now.'

'Leaving?' he asks with surprise. 'What are you leaving? Not this job, surely?'

'London,' I say. 'I'm moving in with Josh.'

'Oh,' he replies simply. I watch his expression. 'Congrat-ulations, I guess, is the right thing to say.'

We're friends now. We can do this.

'Thanks.' I sip my cocktail. 'Scarlet and I had some fast decisions to make,' I continue.

'I'd imagine it's tricky when one of you wants to move out and the other doesn't,' Chris says.

'She's leaving too.'

'Where's she going?' Chris asks conversationally.

'Scotland, would you believe?'

He raises his eyebrows, his eyes wide. 'Cool. Why?'

'She's going freelance, and her boyfriend lives near Edinburgh.'

'Is she doing what you're doing? Is she moving in with him?'

'No. It's too soon for that, and Scarlet knows it. But this is the closest she's got to a long-term relationship since the dawn of time and she's giving it her all. So is he. They're well suited and want to make it work. Rory lives near his family, and Scarlet's is a bit like mine: scattered all over the place. She's got no real *need* to be in London, so she's renting a little one-bed place and seeing how she gets on up there. She hates the cold, so that might be a bit of a shock, but she's willing to suffer it for love.'

'Good on her.'

'Yeah, I think so too.'

We sip our drinks and I'm already halfway through my first one, a Raspberry Bellini – I wish I'd ordered something bigger, as it's quite small.

'So if you went on holiday on your own,' I start, 'does that mean . . . ?'

He takes a deep breath. 'I've broken up with Kayla.'

'Have you? I'm sorry to hear that.' I'm not sure if I

mean this or not. I feel strange about it. Although . . . why? 'I must stop thinking of her as Tinder Swipe, although I guess if you've broken up with her, I won't be thinking of her again.'

He rewards my light-hearted jibe with a slow chuckle.

'What happened?'

He shrugs. 'Incompatibility, to quote your words.'

'When did I say that?'

'The night we first met. About your last boyfriend. "Incompatible enough for him to cheat on me after only eight months" was, I believe, your phrase.'

'Oh, yeah,' I agree slowly. 'I did say that. Thanks for reminding me. Is that what happened? Did she cheat on you?'

'No. I just realised our relationship wasn't the type I wanted.'

'Ouch!'

'I know what I want now. This is progress for me. It's not fair to keep someone hanging when you know there's no future.'

I listen to his words. Chris is right. They do make me think, though. 'So you ended it?' I question.

'I'm of an age—' he starts.

'Please,' I splutter. 'You're thirty-six.'

'Thirty-seven' he says.

'Have I missed your birthday?' I'm easily distracted.

'Yeah, it was in October.'

'Oh, sorry. Happy belated birthday.'

'Don't worry about it. Can I continue?' he asks.

'Go on.'

'I'm of an age . . .' he goes on, and I keep quiet, but he stops, changes tack. 'I know I'm *the one* for someone out there. But it wasn't Kayla. And she wasn't the one for me. And as you head towards the end of your thirties . . .' He lets that hang there. I know what he's saying: time is running out. God, that's bleak.

I'm quiet and so is Chris.

'What are you thinking?' he asks me.

I don't know how to say what he wants to hear without putting myself in danger, slipping up in some way. I shrug in response.

He continues. 'I know what I want. I know I want to be with someone – really be with them, give them my all. I want to build a life with someone, fall in love with them, marry them, have children one day.'

Wow, I think. My heart just flew all round my chest.

'But it's not happening,' he continues. 'Dating apps are a no. Real life is a no.'

Real life was almost a yes. I don't say it, though. I don't dare.

'You've not quite found what you're looking for yet,' I tell him and I want to choke on my own insipid words. 'But one day, when you do, it's going to be mind-blowing. And the wait will have been worth it.'

I imagine Chris finding *the one*. I don't like what that thought does to me. I feel uneasy.

He looks at me, but doesn't reply. *Don't say it*, I think. I have a fear he's going to say something – reference what nearly happened between us. But he doesn't. When we last spoke about this, it was at the wedding in Edinburgh nine months ago. Perhaps Chris doesn't feel it any more. So much time has passed since we first met.

'Anyway,' he says, 'I'm back to being single and making sure I don't invite people to events with me, so I can meet hot single women.'

'Women? Plural?' I ask.

'No. Not plural.'

'I should hope not,' I reply. 'You're too much of a perfect gentleman for that.'

'Maybe next time I won't be a gentleman and will see what happens.'

My eyes open wide. 'Next time?'

'The next woman I meet that I think might be a potential winner, I'm putting my tongue down her throat there and then. It worked for you and Josh. And I'm proposing within seventeen minutes. It's all going to happen on that first night. I won't invite her to come home with me. *Instead* I'll miss my flight and *I'll* stay here.'

'Bloody hell. Stand back, Chris is on a mission,' I joke and I'm pleased we've managed to claw back some humour into what could quickly have turned into a loaded conversation. 'No chance of you being divorced by forty at this rate,' I continue.

He smiles, holds my gaze. 'Or of proposing to someone within seventeen minutes, either. Where *are* all the single women?'

'We're all taken, I'm afraid. Every now and again one of us emerges, fresh from a failed relationship and blinking into the glare of the sunlight. And there you'll be.'

He smiles. 'Like some sort of messed-up rebound hero.'

'No, like you,' I say meaningfully. 'Just . . . you.' I smile and so does Chris. I need to move this conversation out of dangerous waters. 'Hang on, old man,' I say, and he rolls his eyes. 'It'll happen. Just not today.'

'I'm pleased it's happened for you,' he says.

I pause briefly and then reply, 'Me too.'

Chapter Thirty-Eight

December

'Welcome to our house-cooling party!' I cry as Josh and Tamara arrive at mine and Scarlet's flat, clutching three bottles of wine to add to the bar.

'House-cooling?' Josh queries, as Scarlet moves forward and she and Josh exchange a kiss on the cheek.

'I'm guessing it's the opposite of a house-warming,' Tamara says.

'Of course it is,' Josh mumbles, giving me a smile I didn't know I needed. I'm nervous about moving out. I feel more nervous about this than I did when I moved out of my parents' and took myself off to London. I was so young then. Young and full of confidence.

Scarlet takes Tamara off towards the bathroom, so they can stow their booze in the bath, which we've filled with cold water and ice, and Josh envelops me in a hug. The party hasn't quite got going yet – a couple of early guests mill about in the kitchen, munching crisps and nibbles and pouring themselves healthy doses of punch, which Scarlet and I have put together with every single bottle of half-used alcohol we had remaining. It's surprisingly good. I've had two glasses already. I'm not sure we should have added the Pernod and crème de menthe, though.

'You taste like toothpaste,' Josh says when we part.

'Where's Mark?' I ask.

'Tamara and he are a bit . . .' He shrugs, searching for the right word. 'On the rocks.'

My eyebrows lift. 'Oh, I didn't know that. I thought he was coming along tonight.'

'So did he, I think.'

'That's a surprise. Has Tamara told him not to come? Have they had a row?' I'm as bad as Scarlet for gossip. 'I didn't think Tamara had it in her to have a row with anyone.'

Josh gives me a look and glances round to where Scarlet's introducing Tamara to the kitchen gang. 'That's not very nice,' he says quietly.

I feel a bit checked. 'OK. Well, it's the truth. She's so . . . nice all the time is what I mean. Are they breaking up?'

'They've not broken up,' Josh clarifies. 'Just cooling things down a bit, I think. I haven't dug into the ins and outs.'

'But she's your best friend,' I say. 'Isn't this something you'd talk about?'

'You can go and ask her if you like?' Josh offers.

'I might,' I reply. 'I'll have a couple more drinks and then I'll grill her.'

'Go on then.'

I try to work out his expression. Is Josh annoyed? At me?

What's going on? Because of the conversation we've just had? Or something else? I start to ask him, but behind us the front door is being pushed open from its ajar position.

'Hi,' Chris says as he enters, and so does the woman he's arrived with.

He's with a woman. Only last month Chris was single. He's moved swiftly, for someone who doesn't even live in London.

'Hi, I'm Victoria.'

Victoria is gorgeous and tall and . . . everything.

'Hi,' I reply as she smiles widely. 'Nice to meet you. Are you and Chris . . . ?'

She furrows her brow and then realises what I'm on about.

'Oh no,' she says, 'We met right now in the hall. I work with Scarlet.'

'Oh,' I respond, and I sense the relief in my voice. I think Josh, Chris and Victoria can sense it too. Everyone's looking at me strangely. Chris, in particular, has eyes as wide as saucers. I'm mortified.

'Is . . . um . . . Scarlet here?' Victoria asks.

'I'll grab her. Do you want to put your booze in the bath?'

'Sorry?' she asks.

'It's our makeshift ice bucket.'

She laughs. 'In that case, yes.'

The two of us move off, so I can show her where the bath and Scarlet are. In doing so, I realise I've left Chris and Josh alone together.

Two men could not look more awkward if they tried. I glance at them out of the corner of my eye as I dash to fetch them both drinks. When I return with two glasses of punch, they look grateful.

'This smells nuclear,' Chris remarks. 'What's in it?'

'Everything we had left in the cupboard and neither of us wanted to take with us,' I say. 'We're moving out, remember.'

'Why's it green and . . . fizzy?' He sniffs it dubiously.

'It's yum – just drink it,' I tell him.

Both he and Josh sip their drinks and look a bit concerned.

Josh runs his tongue up and down the roof of his mouth a few times. 'I'm going to grab that bottle I brought,' he says and leaves Chris and me alone.

'You OK?' I ask Chris.

'Yeah, you?'

'You and Josh looked awkward as fuck,' I say.

He cough-laughs on his drink, which I triumphantly notice he's taken another sip from.

'See, it's not that bad, is it?'

'Did you make it?' he asks.

'Yes.'

'Then it's lovely. I shall keep drinking and definitely not throw up later.'

'Ha-ha,' I say, followed by, 'I thought you'd arrived with Victoria.'

'I did arrive with her.'

'No, I mean I thought you were together.'

He looks at me. 'So what if I was?'

'OK, calm down,' I say. 'I'm just making conversation.'

'You're being weird.'

'I'm not. What were you and Josh talking about?' I try again.

'We didn't have time to talk about anything,' he tells me. 'You were gone for one whole minute. We basically said hi and then you strong-armed us into drinking this paint-stripper.'

'Fine. Be like that.'

'Like what?' he asks. 'What's wrong with you? You invited me and now you're being all . . . strange. Not like you at all. What's up?'

'Nothing,' I say.

'I don't believe you,' Chris replies, his eyes searching mine. We move out of the way of the front door as another of Scarlet's work colleagues arrives, says hi, squeezes past us.

'Josh is being a bit odd,' I tell him. 'Only a little bit.'

'OK. Are you going to talk to him about it?'

'I was going to and then you arrived. And it's only a little bit,' I say, defending Josh one second after putting him down.

'All right then,' Chris says. 'Why are you even mentioning it to me?'

'Because you asked what was wrong?' I reply in a voice much whinier than I usually sound.

Chris sighs audibly. I sigh too. And we stand like that for far too long. 'I'm going to go and get a proper drink,' he says and walks away.

'I can't believe this is happening. We're growing up,' Scarlet says on our final evening together.

'We're thirty-two years old,' I say.

'And haven't we done well,' Scarlet chuckles as we clink

our plastic cups of Squadka – vodka and orange squash, both of which were left over from the house-cooling party, although neither of us knows who brought the orange squash. We're sitting on the floor in our flat. Scarlet's shipped all our crockery, glasses, cutlery and furniture up to her new flat, with my blessing, as Josh has plenty and she's starting out from scratch. Plus all the flatpack Ikea stuff we bought together is about ten years old, so I was hardly going to put up a fight.

'Can we still do Deliveroo on Fridays sometimes?' Scarlet asks as I glance around at my cases and boxes filled with clothes, books and far too many cosmetics. I can't believe my life packs up into such a neat arrangement.

I look back at her, focusing on what she's just said. 'How are we going to do Deliveroo on Fridays at such a huge distance? Our train fares are going to be out of control.'

'I'll order it in Edinburgh and you order the same thing in Somerset and we can FaceTime.'

'That sounds great. Only I'll have to cook or run out to the local fish-and-chip shop because there's no Deliveroo in Josh's village.'

'Soon to be your village too. Do you think you'll miss London?' she asks.

'Yes,' I say. 'You?'

'Yeah,' she nods. 'I think I will.'

'Do you think we're making a mistake?' I ask.

'Both of us are moving to opposite ends of the country, for men,' she points out. 'Do you imagine Emmeline Pankhurst will be spinning in her grave?'

'Who?' I ask and Scarlet gasps in horror. 'I'm joking, I'm joking. No, I don't think she would be. We're making a choice. We are in charge of our own destinies. And you're not moving in with your guy; you're just making yourself available in your own flat, and with a fab new job to boot. I'm the one moving in with a man in his ready-made set-up, like some kind of freeloader.'

'You know that's not true,' Scarlet chastises, leaning over and stealing a slice of pizza from my side of the box. 'Our lives are changing,' she says. 'For the better. And we've done that. We could hardly live together for ever, could we?'

'Imagine how amazing that would have been, though.'

'It would have been fricking awesome,' Scarlet replies as we clink our cups together in our flat, one final time.

Chapter Thirty-Nine

February 2024

It's Valentine's Day and I've cooked Josh and me the most amazing dinner. I feel like a proper country housewife these days. I'm fully settled in here and, even though I had a bit of a panic before I was due to move in, about how everything might be between Josh and me, it turned out to be groundless on that score. I wasn't sure how things might change if I was a permanent fixture. Would I take him for granted? Would he do the same to me? Would the fun we'd had getting to know each other dwindle away?

But it was just like it was before, a year and a half ago, when I accidentally found myself staying for what I considered far too long for a new relationship, even though it was only a few weeks. Josh is right. Back then, it laid the foundations for the start of us living together.

We had Christmas Day together this year with his family. It would have been a bit strange if we hadn't, given that we live together now. And then Josh drove on Boxing Day as we set off early, making the whistle-stop tour towards my parents' houses. We're a proper couple. Who live together. It still feels so strange to think it.

Tonight we're having boeuf bourguignon, with Josh's wonderful beef and all the other ingredients we had in the pantry. It meant I didn't have to get on the push-bike in the depths of this icy winter and dice with death on the country lanes. I'm nowhere near passing my driving test and the only real downside of village life is that if I'd felt isolated before when I was part-living here, I'm really feeling it now.

I had half-hearted ideas about joining bookclubs and yoga classes, but they haven't come to anything. I'm so busy with work, and I can't really get around unless Josh drives me. Public transport is a dud out here, and taxis are hit-and-miss. Plus Josh is so busy with work that he's too tired in the evenings to run me around like a very sexy chauffeur. I asked him once and he was practically asleep on the sofa after a gruelling day. I don't want to ask again. The guilt would ruin me. Instead, when he has a spare bit of time, we're going to keep working on my driving lessons. Then, when I pass, I can take myself to these social activities and make some friends.

Tamara pops in every now and again, but I notice she's being respectful and not bashing the front door open without invites, in her cute but clumsy way. She texts first and checks it's OK.

Josh seems put out when she texts me and not him, and we hang out just the two of us more often now. Josh wonders how his best-friendship with Tamara can have morphed into me and Tamara hanging out together loads instead.

'Am I the third wheel?' he asks with a sideways smile as we discuss this over our Valentine's Day dinner.

'Sadly, yes,' I joke. 'In the divorce I get custody of Tamara.'

'Divorce?' he asks and then narrows his eyes.

'I'm joking,' I reply. 'Not actually suggesting we get married, so I can take Tamara with me when it all ends.'

He laughs, but it's an uncertain laugh, sort of nervous.

I can't work out what he's thinking. Josh has not been getting my sense of humour much these days. Maybe I'm not funny any more. Maybe he's distracted. I make Scarlet laugh. I made Chris laugh, often when he was trying to drink something.

'We've been together a year and a half next month,' I say.

'Have we?' he asks. 'That's flown.'

'I guess it has, yeah. That's a good thing,' I reason.

'Yeah,' he says.

He's quiet, staring at his food. Then he looks up at me. Candles flicker between us, and I wonder . . . it is Valentine's Day after all. A year and a half is too short a time in which to get engaged, surely. What would I do if Josh asked? Would I say yes? God, I've no idea.

This silence lasts too long. Josh looks away, sips his wine and I sip mine. I dig around in my mind for something to say. 'Do you think you might be able to come to the hotel opening next month?'

'I know I said I'd try, but as it's midweek it makes things tricky here. If I can, you know I will.'

'It's fine,' I say. 'Don't worry. I know your time isn't your own. The farm is the other woman in our relationship.'

He gives me a curious glance.

'I'll bore you rigid with how it all went after the event,' I tell him.

'Please do. And take pictures?' he asks. He reaches out across the table, holds my hand for a moment, before we go back to eating our food.

Chapter Forty

Chris

Hi, it's Victoria. I hope you don't mind me messaging so long after Scarlet's house party. It was really nice to meet you. Don't suppose you're in London again anytime soon? If you are, let me know. Maybe we can get a drink together? V x

This is unexpected, given it's been a couple of months since Victoria asked for my number at the party, and I was so stunned that I blurted it out to her. It didn't occur to me to ask for Victoria's, after I gave her mine. But she was fun to talk to, and it would be nice to see her again. Nothing serious can come of it anyway. It's the proverbial problem of meeting someone just before I leave to go back to New York. Is London where all the good women are? Am I missing a trick being in New York? My career took me there, kept me there. But maybe I need to rethink my strategy. I've been in the US for a few years, and in this job ever since I arrived. I love it. But it's not always beneficial to play it safe when it means letting life and love pass you by.

I've been thinking for a while that it might be time to move jobs and country. I've done it once before. It could be time to look for something more senior. My CV looks good. Where would I go? London? Somewhere else?

I'm excited to find out what the next stage of my life entails, though I'm not an impetuous person – other than that one time with Lexie. This will need some thought. Until then: **Hi, it's nice to hear from you. I'm in London right now. I fly home tomorrow, though. Don't suppose you're free tonight? Chris x**

Chapter Forty-One

Lexie

March

Today is the day when everything I've been working towards over the past year and a half finally comes to a head. From the tiny details to the big last-minute things . . . today is the day.

Everything's finished, although there have been so many delays that I thought Max was going to flip his lid. But now – now we're ready to open the hotel, so I should be feeling fine. But I'm not. I'm so nervous. Max has been over from New York for the past week and it's been fun tweaking the finishing touches just the way we'd visualised them. The thrill is out of this world.

I knew I was going to love sinking my teeth into the design element, but the final portion is by far the most rewarding. I loved the whole process when I decorated my nan's house, but this is on another level, with so many different designs for suites and rooms, bathrooms and entranceways, the lobby, the bar, the restaurant. It's been such an amazing experience, barring the input from Chef Javier, who very much had his own unique vision that needed toning down, but also appeasing. I've had to learn the art of diplomacy like never before.

Chris has been back and forth with the fit-out team and I feel like we've been chasing him around and hurrying him along. I've been staying in an Airbnb in Soho this past week while Max has been here, as the days are long and it was too hard to go back and forth from Josh's. When I spoke to Josh late one evening on the phone, he joked that I must be following Chris around, waiting for him to put a sofa down so I can put a scatter cushion on it. I didn't like to tell him he's only half-wrong, though I thought he'd rather oversimplified what I've been doing since I got this job.

Now we're here, exhausted and with champagne glasses in hand in the main lobby, while the publicity team does its thing, ushering celebrities along the red carpet outside the front doors. I watch them getting their pictures taken, dressed up in their finery. I'd felt pretty sexy tonight in my little black dress and silver ankle boots, but against celebrities – well, it's impossible to ooze serious glamour next to them, isn't it? They radiate sexiness on a whole other level, as if they've got a camera filter always on them.

'I've never heard of half these people,' Chris says as he stands behind me.

'Is it because you don't watch *The Real Housewives of Cheshire* or *The Only Way Is Essex* or anything like that?'

'Do I look like a *TOWIE* fan?' he asks coolly as he sips his drink.

I swing round, stare right at him. 'You know its abbreviated name, though,' I accuse. I'm so close to him. I didn't realise how close we were to each other.

'OK,' Chris says as I step back a bit, 'I might have watched one or two episodes. You?'

'It's my guilty pleasure,' I confess. 'When Josh isn't watching the news or curled up in bed for an early night, I'll be all over shows like *The Kardashians* and *Selling Sunset*. There aren't enough hours in the day to keep up with all the reality programmes, though.'

'Reality?' he remarks. 'You do know it's not *real*, right?'

'Shut up,' I hiss playfully, turning back to people-watch. 'It is definitely real. Don't start on at me about scripted reality. I won't hear it.'

Chris laughs behind me while we watch the red-carpet photographers do their thing. His proximity feels heady and intoxicating. He says, 'Cheers!', so I turn back to him. He clinks his glass against mine and then stands back. I can feel a spark of energy between us as he says, 'Well done, Lexie.'

Eventually I find my voice. 'Likewise. And I don't think I deserve any real credit. Max is the design superstar.'

'He couldn't have done it without you on the ground, running all over the place. He said as much.'

'Did he?'

Chris nods, and I glow with the energy of a job well done.

We automatically start moving further into the room and I swipe us two more glasses of champagne. And then Chris and I lose each other for a while, but every now and again I spy him across the room. I move around, greeting everyone

I know and making introductions to some I don't. The sibling bosses are in, and we talk for a moment or two before they move off to continue basking in their well-earned glory. I don't think I could be any more high on life if I tried. This moment is everything I've worked for, and although I know I'm only a bit-part, I genuinely never thought I'd ever get this far.

I do hope this is the stepping stone to something more within this company. I love working with Max and with Chris, and I've got over how odd it is that we keep being re-united, on and off. It's friendly now – good vibes and nothing more. Maybe something tiny more, but we're going in different directions. I wonder if Chris is keeping a lid on anything further. I wonder if I am?

There's no danger of either of us doing anything we shouldn't, though. We're good people and everything's worked out in the end, but if you'd asked me – only minutes after Chris reluctantly got in that taxi and left me standing on the gravel drive that first time we met – if I'd see it all panning out like this, I'd have been horrified.

Funny how things never go quite as you expect. But that's OK. That's life. Things were meant to work out this way, clearly.

Chris finds his way back to me and we talk about work, New York, the Cotswolds, how well Scarlet is settling in up in Edinburgh, his family, Christmas and slowly, bit by bit, the night wears itself away until I declare, 'It's nearly pumpkin hour.'

'What?' he asks.

'You know the time when Cinderella has to get to the coach, before it turns into a . . . Never mind. It's late – and I should probably go, is where I was going with that.'

'Fair enough. I might sneak out as well. I've got an early start and a flight home to catch.'

'You're running out on me for a flight . . . again?'

He gives me an interested glance. I wish I hadn't said that.

'I didn't know you were going back so soon,' I say.

'Disappointed?' Chris questions, with a glint in his eye.

It's my turn to give him an enquiring glance.

'Yeah,' I reply, but it's kindly meant – nothing more. 'Of course.'

'I've got a big week coming up,' he continues, obviously deciding he's not going to take that line of questioning any further.

'Go on,' I prompt.

He glances around, checking that no one can overhear us. 'I'm leaving,' he whispers.

'What?' I whisper back. 'Your job? Are you? Why?'

'I've been there years,' he says. 'And now this project's done, I fancy a change. Change is good,' he goes on, as if convincing himself and not me.

'It is,' I say blithely. 'Where are you going?'

'I've got a job lined up here.'

I open my mouth in surprise. '*Here?* In London? Are you moving back?'

'Shh,' he whispers. 'I haven't told anyone yet.'

I look at him, waiting for more.

He obliges. 'Yes, I'm moving back. And I've been . . . kind of . . . seeing someone in London too,' he says slowly.

My smile falters and I don't know why, but I have to force my face to lift it back into place. 'And it's serious enough for you to move back here for?' My voice has suddenly gone really high.

'Shh,' he says again. 'No. Not yet. But getting a new job here and kind of seeing a woman from here have coincided and have forced my hand into making decisions. I realise I'm letting my life pass me by. I've had my life in New York for a few years and it's been a blast. But the way I see it, I can move back, work here for as long as it suits me, rent somewhere and I'm only as tied in as I want to be. If I stay, then so be it. But if not . . . it's not a big deal. While I'm young and free, I might as well let my feet take me where they want me to go.'

'You were moaning last time how you felt old, you nomad.'

'Being a nomad's not a bad thing. I'm a suit-wearing nomad,' Chris fires back conversationally. 'So not a real one.'

'Big life-decision.'

'Yeah. But one I'm excited about.'

'Who is she, then? This woman who's making you reassess your life?'

'You're misunderstanding me,' he says. 'I'm just seeing someone and she happens to be here, and I happen to have accepted a job here. I'm not sure why I mentioned her now. She's a by-product of what's happening.'

'A by-product? What a lovely description.'

'You know what I mean,' he dismisses my comment.

'I'm not sure I do, but we'll go with it, if you like. But you haven't answered my question.'

'What question?'

'Who is she?' I ask again. It shouldn't bother me this much, but it does. Chris and I let living in different continents get in the way of anything that might have happened between us. But whoever this woman is, she's special enough to make him reassess. I'm not buying the by-product story.

He looks as if he doesn't know how to say this. 'Her name's Victoria.'

'More, please,' I prompt.

He smiles. 'We met at your anti-house-warming party.'

I give him a blank look and then it dawns on me. 'The woman you arrived with?'

He nods. 'Yeah.'

'Scarlet's boss?'

'Yeah, I think so. At the time. But now Scarlet's in Edinburgh going freelance, I'm not sure Victoria's her boss any more.'

'Semantics,' I say. 'How did you guys . . . ?'

'The usual way, or rather the unusual way these days. I met her the same way I met you: at an event where I didn't have a plus-one. We got chatting while in the kitchen, pouring ourselves some of that lethal poison you concocted. It was quite the talking point.'

Ordinarily I'd have laughed, but I don't. 'Did you get drunk on it and kiss her?'

'What? No. Of course not. But we got on, and she knew my deal. She knew I lived in New York and wasn't in London very often and she was cool, laid-back. She didn't have any grand expectations. So we just messaged a bit, arranged to meet up whenever I've been here for work. And it's been nice. It's not serious. And we've only really had a few dates. But I guess, now I'm moving back, we'll be seeing if we can – you know – go for it.'

'Oh, right,' I reply, mostly as a way to fill the gap in the conversation that's ripped a void between us.

'Anyway, that's my news.'

'You've kept everything so quiet,' I tell him. 'All the times we've spoken and caught up . . . and . . . tumbleweed from you.'

'Well, the job thing I couldn't really go bleating about. I still can't, actually.' He glances around, checking no one's listening. 'I've got to formally hand in my notice this week, so please keep quiet, won't you?'

'Of course,' I say.

'And with Victoria – it's just messaging and the odd phone call and, like I said, it's really a by-product of me moving back.'

I roll my eyes. 'You can't keep calling her that. She seemed really nice, from the few minutes we spoke at the party.'

Chris smiles, looks self-conscious. 'She is. She's really easy to be with.'

'When are you moving back?' I ask.

'Not sure yet. A month?'

We're silent while I process this before realising I need to talk or risk looking abnormal. 'Congratulations,' I say. 'I'm really pleased for you.'

'Thanks. I appreciate that.'

His alarm beeps on his phone and I'm drawn back to a similar night talking to Chris for the first time, that same hateful alarm sounding from his phone.

'Shit,' he says. 'I've got to go.'

I don't know what to say at this point, so I don't say anything. He leans forward, embraces me in a hug and I'm sure I stop breathing. I'm far too close to him. He smells faintly of mint and bergamot. And for some reason I feel a bit empty, as if he's drifting further away from me than ever before, even though he's moving back home to England. He's going in a different direction, as if he's picking up the pace and running with it.

But I'm also in my stride now. It's taken me for ever to get here, but I'm in a job I'm enjoying, living in a home I adore with Josh, whom I love, and we have a life together. Chris wants that for himself too, so why do I feel so put out about the whole thing?

I say goodbye and so does he. And it feels that little bit too final, laced with something bordering on regret.

Chapter Forty-Two

May

Scarlet hands me a big mug of tea and we curl up on our old sofa in her new flat in Edinburgh. It's a crisp morning, only fourteen degrees, despite the fact that it's May. I've only brought one jumper with me, so it's going to get well used this weekend. Today is Scarlet's birthday and it's the first time I've managed to get up to Scotland to see her.

I've seen her flat on a video tour she filmed for me, but nothing compares to being here in real life, in Scarlet's space with her, finally. I love seeing how at ease she is here, how relaxed, how at home and settled she is. Also I notice now that our jointly purchased old Ikea furniture looks small and out of place in this giant-ceilinged Georgian space. I half-seriously recommend that she invests in some serious, oversized antique furniture the minute she can, so it looks a bit more normal in the flat. And artwork – I have ideas about artwork. After I've finished inspecting all the wonderful period features, we sit back and position ourselves on our old, battered was-once-white-but-isn't-any-longer sofa.

'Can I ask you a funny question?' I enquire, as we place

a plate of Danish pastries between us. 'Ooh, can I have the cinnamon roll or do you want to split it?'

'It's yours. Was that your question?' Scarlet asks as she gulps her tea. I change my mind and reach for a croissant, knowing that in a few minutes she'll regret letting me have that cinnamon roll. It is her birthday after all.

'No. My question is this . . .' I realise I'm not sure how to phrase it, how to tackle the question about her old boss hooking up with Chris, without alerting Scarlet to the fact that I'm fully invested in Chris from afar, even though I can't have him and don't want him, because I'm with Josh and I'm perfectly happy. Scarlet will only tell me off and say something like, 'Just because you can't have him doesn't mean no one else is allowed to.' I can already hear the words. If she knows something, she'll volunteer if I lead her there, and then I won't have to look desperate for information about Chris.

I adopt an innocent expression and go for it. 'How's your friend Victoria?'

She pauses while reaching for a Danish. 'Was *that* your question?'

I nod, playing it cool.

'I don't know,' she replies, confused. 'I only really speak to her about freelance work.'

'Is she . . . dating anyone?' I ask casually.

'Why? You found someone to fix her up with?' Scarlet asks. 'That's very generous of you. Where was this benevolence when I was on the hunt for a man?'

I chuckle. 'I tried setting you up with many single people.

You didn't like them and . . . I'm just curious. You don't know if she's with anyone?'

'No, I don't. Why?' she asks, her eyes narrowing to suspicious slits.

'I thought she was really nice and I wondered why she didn't have a boyfriend.'

'Oh,' Scarlet says, obviously completely perplexed by this conversation and why we're having it. It's clear she knows *nothing* about the likelihood of Victoria and Chris still being together. It sounds as if she didn't even know they'd got together in the first place. 'Want me to do some digging?' she volunteers. 'I can message and ask if she's single.'

'No, that's weird. You can't do that. Forget it. It's not important.'

Victoria and Chris have probably fizzled out by now. It's not even worth mentioning my concerns to Scarlet. And I don't know what my concerns are. I don't want her to dig me out over it. I sit chewing and thinking.

'You're being odd,' Scarlet says slowly. 'Why are you being odd?' I wish she didn't know me this well. She could at least *pretend* not to know what's going on in my head.

'Chris is moving back to London,' I say.

'That was quite the subject change,' Scarlet replies. 'Is that why you're being weird?'

'Yep,' I reply.

As predicted, Scarlet reaches for the cinnamon bun. 'Why's he moving back?'

'Applied for a job and got it,' I paraphrase.

'That's quite impulsive. Mind you, he asked you to get on a plane with him. That's impulsive.'

'Why would you mention that?'

Scarlet laughs, tears the cinnamon bun in pieces and hands me half.

'He's not normally an impulsive person, I don't think. Although he seems to be turning into one.' I'm trying to reason it out in my head. 'He's moving because he's got a job and it's a good jump up the career ladder.'

Her eyes narrow again. 'Are you bothered he's coming back, even though you're happy with Josh?'

'What? No.'

'Are you worried something's going to happen between you and Chris, now he's coming back to London? Are you worried you don't trust yourself.'

'No!' I exclaim and throw a bit of pastry at her. I sigh, long and loud. 'Can I be honest?' I start.

'No. Lie to me. I feel that's a safer conversation.'

'Ha-ha,' I say flatly. 'I *am* bothered.'

'Knew it.'

'But not because I don't trust myself. I know it's wrong to be bothered. There's just something about him. I've never dated him, never kissed him, never even . . .' I trail off. 'It doesn't make sense, I know that.' I can't believe the words coming out of my own mouth.

Scarlet looks at me, her lips parted. 'You two didn't even kiss?' she asks.

'No.'

'I didn't know that. I thought you kissed at that wedding.'

'I kissed Josh.'

'I knew *that*,' she says. 'But I thought you'd kissed Chris first.'

I shake my head.

'He asked you to go with him to New York, but you hadn't even kissed each other? I'm not sure if it makes the connection between you stronger or . . . weirder.'

'Oh, shut up,' I reply as I hurl a second bit of cinnamon bun towards her and it hits her on her right boob.

'Good shot,' Scarlet says, lifting up the pastry and eating it. Then she looks serious again. 'You know what I mean, though – not kissing, but it all still being so intense . . . that sort of look-but-don't-touch vibe. It's hot without being hot.'

'Stop,' I beg.

'It doesn't matter now anyway,' she goes on quickly as she works out the intricacies of all this. 'He's not yours. And you're not his. And you can't do anything. It's too messy.'

'Yeah, I know.'

Poor Josh. If he could hear me talking like this . . . I feel an overwhelming need to move this conversation on. I glance at my roller suitcase, in which Scarlet's gift sits. 'Want to open your birthday present now?'

'Yes, please.'

I go towards the suitcase and retrieve her present: a small sterling-silver letter S on a chain. It feels like a proper grown-up gift, and I've not been able to buy one of those for her in years. She puts it on immediately and tells me she loves it and that she's going to wear it every day.

We're spending the day sightseeing and walking – so much walking. And I'm amazed by how beautiful Edinburgh is. I've only been to this main bit once before and that was for the Fringe festival with my ex-boyfriend, when we basically saw a lot of theatre and drank a great deal of booze. I'm not at all into the Fringe, but went with him because . . . Edinburgh. Scarlet has a day of history planned, as we're going to do Edinburgh Castle at the top of the street and then the Palace of Holyroodhouse at the far end later on, after the obligatory pub lunch that she's booked halfway between the two.

'And then tonight we've got a ghost walk booked, and Rory is going to join us for that when he finishes work,' Scarlet says as we walk through the town, passing the Georgian sandstone buildings, elegant in their fine lines and uniformity.

'Sounds fab. Look at us in our thirties. If you compare how we previously spent our birthdays throughout most of our twenties . . .' I start.

'Getting trashed, overdoing it and throwing up?' Scarlet sniggers.

'We can still do that tonight if you want?' I suggest uncertainly, pulling the sleeves of my jumper down a fraction to cover my chilly hands.

She makes a face, shakes her head. 'No, it's OK. A few drinks, but let's not lose our dignity.'

'Do you think we're behaving like we're getting old?' I ask.

'Yes,' Scarlet says. 'I love it. I'll be ready for a National Trust membership for my birthday next year,' she jokes.

'I think I'm ready for one of those right now,' I reply as we walk up towards the castle, with a bagpiper playing at full force to all the other tourists and us, as we immerse ourselves in history and culture.

Chapter Forty-Three

On the train home from Edinburgh two days later I'm reading through my assignment for the design course that I finally enrolled on and getting ready to watch the accompanying video. Today it's planning and drawing out a living room, measuring spaces and furniture and placing everything freehand onto grid paper to check it all fits. I've invested in pretty stationery and mechanical pencils, and I click one with purpose to get started. I realise, after I've begun drawing, that I've forgotten to include plug sockets to go with my table, lamp and armchair situation that I've drawn by my imaginary window. A lamp with no socket to go into is no use to anyone, and as the Scottish countryside merges into the English scenery, whipping past me at speed, I draw a socket and reference it at the side.

In the end I knew that, with a full-time job and trying to maintain some sort of romantic life with Josh in the Cotswolds, I wasn't going to have time to attend a structured in-person course. Neither was I going to have time for a full-on degree, so I picked a go-at-your-own-pace online professional course and am dipping in and out when time allows. It does mean that I've had to be really disciplined about not automatically switching on *The Kardashians* in the evenings. Instead I've been plugging into the course videos and reading reference materials during every spare moment I get.

After nearly seven hours that involve a train, a tube and another train, I arrive in the Cotswolds late at night. The taxi I pre-booked to pick me up from the station drops me a little way down the farmhouse drive. I don't want the sound of the engine and the car door closing to wake Josh up, given how late it is. He's long since stopped volunteering to pick me up from the station because I always politely decline at this time of night. I know how much he needs his sleep, given the unthinkable hour at which he has to wake up.

I enter the house, but it's dark, which is unexpected. When I've travelled home late before, Josh has usually left a couple of lamps on downstairs so I can find my way in. I do my best not to knock into anything. I'll never get used to how dark it is at night here in the countryside. I'm still programmed into the always-present street lights in London.

I managed a little sleep on the train and so I'm feeling quite alert, despite the hour. I make myself a cup of tea and head into the sitting room, closing the door gently behind me, so the sound of *The Kardashians* doesn't travel up the stairs and wake Josh. I've done enough coursework today so I can treat myself to a bit of easy TV. I hammer my way through two hours and then am forced to call it a night as I'm yawning and have so much admin to catch up on tomorrow for Max, so I can't be late to my laptop. Our next hotel project is in Dublin and I'm excited to have another start-to-finish job to get to grips with. I feel like more of a pro now, though, no longer shit-scared of my own job description.

I unpack my laptop from my case and place it in the kitchen, all ready for me to leap onto it first thing in the morning while I'm floating around in my pyjamas and making my first cup of tea of the day. Then I go upstairs, taking care to avoid the creakiest of all the creaky stairs on my way up and heading into one of the guest bathrooms, rather than our en suite, so that I can faff around without waking Josh.

I change into the pyjamas from my overnight bag, so I don't have to rifle around in the huge chest of drawers in our room, and slowly open our bedroom door, tiptoeing tentatively inside. I move round to my side of the bed and slide in. But, despite the fact it's summer, it's cold. Adjusting my eyes to the gloom after I've lain down, I glance across at the other pillow.

I look to where Josh sleeps.

And discover our bed is empty.

Chapter Forty-Four

I'm at my laptop the next morning, my leg twitching up and down, as I'm unable to concentrate. I rang Josh three times last night after I discovered he was nowhere to be found. I left a voicemail each time, which is silly, because if he'd listened to any of them, he'd have found they all said the same thing. And I followed each one up with a text.

I didn't know if I should be worried or not. It was too late to ring his parents, too late to ring Tamara or any of his work crew. I didn't want to look deranged. But equally, Josh hadn't said he'd be away. Or had he? He hadn't spoken to me all day when I was travelling back down from Scarlet's. But then I hadn't messaged him, either. We're past that phase of checking in on each other every hour on the hour. Not that we were ever there in the first place. That's a bit extra, even for new couples, I think.

Visions of Josh mangled and dead in some kind of farm-machinery accident suddenly fill my mind and I pull my wellies on in the boot room, heading out now it's daylight in search of Josh. He'll have been up for hours ordinarily, and hard at work, but he's not on the farm, either, and his work-mates look equally baffled by his absence.

'He was here yesterday evening when we finished,' Tony says. 'Are you sure he's not at home?'

I shake my head, now even more confused, and go back to the farmhouse where, incredibly, I find Josh sitting at the other end of the kitchen table, facing the door, head in his hands. He's nursing a cup of tea and wearing crumpled clothes. He looks up at me as I enter.

'You're here,' I cry and move towards him.

He smiles thinly and then uses his knuckles to rub his forehead.

'What's wrong?' I ask, stopping midway to him.

I watch his Adam's apple move in his throat as he slowly swallows.

'I don't know how to say this, so I'm going to just say it, and it's not going to be articulate or . . . anything like that,' he tells me.

'OK?' I say. I still haven't managed to throw my arms around him and tell him I missed him. Josh's body language is off. He's stiff and blocking me emotionally, without blocking me physically.

'Last night I . . .' He shakes his head, clearly unsure how to phrase whatever it is he wants to say. 'I . . .'

'Say it,' I urge, but I realise I've snapped it, in my haste to hear whatever it is. I want to hear it. I don't want to hear it.

'Last night Tamara and I . . .'

I remain in a blissful moment of ignorance before everything goes wrong. As I work out what has happened, I crumble in devastation. 'Oh God,' I cry, working it out.

'You have to hear me out,' Josh says quickly. 'I didn't mean for it to happen.'

'Oh God,' I cry again. I pull out a chair and slump into it. 'I'm such an idiot.'

'You're not. I am. I'm the idiot,' he says. He doesn't stand up, doesn't try to move towards me. He doesn't do anything, but looks less stiff now, as if he's free now that he's said it – the heavy weight of guilt marginally less, now his words are out. 'I didn't know it was going to happen. It surprised me. All of it surprised me. And even as it started, I thought: I'll regret this. In the morning I'll wake up and I'll regret this.'

'And do you?' I ask helplessly, because what does it matter, either way.

He can't look at me. 'I regret hurting you,' he replies.

My voice comes out laced with tears. 'But you don't regret doing it.'

'I . . . I didn't know I felt like that – about her.'

I want to be sick. I don't know what to say. I've been cheated on. I've been cheated on again. Lightning has struck twice. This can't be happening. I need air. I stand up and go outside into the back garden and gulp down huge lungfuls of fresh country air.

Josh follows me and stands at a distance. 'I'm so sorry,' he says. 'Tamara and I have been friends since for ever. It was all just . . . so confusing, so spur-of-the-moment. We were having dinner and then we were watching a film and then we were kissing, and I don't even know how it started, but then we were—'

'No,' I say, 'I can't hear this. I don't want to know how

romantic it all was. I want to clarify that we're talking about the same thing, though. You fucked Tamara while I was in Edinburgh?'

Josh nods and at least has the good grace to look ashamed. 'I didn't ruin what you and I have for something inconsequential.'

'Oh, that makes it all right then,' I say. I can't look at him. I look into the distance at the tall purple alliums, waving back and forth drowsily. Summer blooms around me. But inside my head it's a storm.

'Please let me explain,' he pleads before taking a breath. 'I love her.'

'Oh God,' I cry. 'Stop talking.'

'I think I've always loved her. I just didn't know it,' he says quietly, more to himself than to me. I swing round and stare at him. 'Can you come back inside, so we can talk?' he asks.

'No. I can't be here,' I reply.

He nods, looks at the ground. 'I'm not expecting you to forgive me or . . .'

'Good,' I cry between sobs. 'Because I never will. Who does this to someone? I'm leaving.'

'Don't go,' Josh begs. 'Not like this.'

'What else am I supposed to do? We were building a life together,' I shout.

'I know,' he says.

'But you wanted her more than you wanted me.'

'I don't know,' he goes on. 'I've not had any time to process what happened. I thought you were coming back today, not yesterday. I saw your messages this morning and I felt awful.'

'While you were still in bed with her? But you didn't feel awful up until that point?'

'I did,' he replies, but I don't believe him. He was too wrapped up in shagging his best friend to feel anything for me. How is this happening? I trusted him. I thought I knew him. But clearly I didn't know Josh at all. I'm an idiot, in so many ways. Scarlet told me from the outset that Tamara was trouble, and I didn't believe her. I just . . . trusted Josh. I trusted Tamara too – we were building a friendship. And then the two of them betrayed me.

'I crept around the house last night, trying not to wake you, and you weren't even here. You were in bed with her,' I say. I want him to feel guilty. He needs to feel guilty.

'I'm so sorry,' he says.

Tears stream down my face. I want to tell Josh I hate him, but I don't. And now I hate myself because of that. The pain in my throat, from trying to hold all the sobs in, is hurting too much.

'I can't say anything that will lessen the hurt I've caused you,' he says, so woodenly that I feel he's read it somewhere, or that Tamara's coached him to say it.

I can't believe I've been cheated on again. I can't believe this. Why? Why? I hate him. I hate them both right now. 'I can't be here,' I reply and move past him, ignoring his pleas for me to stand and listen to him justify his actions. Ordering Josh not to follow me, I phone the local taxi company. And while I wait for them to send a car, I throw as many things as I can back into my case.

Chapter Forty-Five

Scarlet's lips are clamped together tightly as we sit in her flat analysing everything. I'd only left Edinburgh yesterday and now I'm back again. I feel sure she wants to explode with the words 'I told you so.' Only she doesn't. She's nodding, listening, restraining herself magnificently, yet again, while I pour out the hatred and sadness that have built up inside me. I could hardly stay in Josh's house. I couldn't deal with the fallout from going to either of my parents' houses, as they adored Josh, and my sadness would be their sadness. Plus, they'd want to be calm and adult about it all. So Scarlet's seemed the safest place for me to spit pure venom until I calmed down. I knew she'd encourage me – which is what I want and need.

Scarlet has had the chance to get over the initial shock of it all, after my intense phone call from the train station telling her what had happened, and begging to come and stay again through epic amounts of racking, heaving sobs. I have not got over the initial shock, but I have had a seven-hour journey back to Edinburgh in which to torture myself by imagining Josh and Tamara together, wondering how they started, how they finished, whether he felt any guilty thoughts, whether he even tried to stop himself, or if she did. Every time I think about it, it hurts so much. I can't stop seeing them in bed together. While I was climbing into bed, expecting to find Josh there, they were on the other side of the village having sex. Thank God they didn't do it in our bed. I can't imagine coming home to find that in front of me.

I think of the first time I had sex with Josh: how good it was, how much effort he put in. That will have been Tamara. He's in love with her. Josh is in love with Tamara. I hate them both.

Days later I make a long, drawn-out noise while trying to plan out the seating arrangements of one of the communal working areas. I'm on the floor with my laptop. I've done something wrong on this drawing, only I can't work out what. The chairs I'd almost settled on don't look right at all. I need to talk to Max and see what he thinks. Papers are spread out in front of me. Scarlet's in her boxroom of an office and her head pops out of the door. She gives me a sympathetic look.

'Do you want to drown your sorrows in another cinnamon bun?' she asks. 'Or the biscoff bun? I got the good ones with all the icing from Mimi's Little Bakehouse.'

'Yes, please. Both, please,' I say quietly, and she goes to the kitchen to fetch them for me.

When I first arrived, Scarlet asked if I wanted to drown my sorrows in ice cream, as is traditional for a break-up.

Ice cream.

I could have screamed. Instead I cried. I don't think I'll be able to eat ice cream ever again. Bloody Tamara. Now I'm on a perpetual rotation of buns. The good ones. With all the icing.

I'm trying to work and, in truth, it's helping to take my mind off Josh for a little while, though I'm struggling to match Max's effervescent enthusiasm as we bat ideas back and forth for the upcoming Dublin hotel. We were having a conversation about how much green we should incorporate and, in my grief at my failed relationship, I missed the fact it was a joke and have started pulling together ideas for a mood board with far too much emerald. I sort of think it would work and be regal, elegant, refined, but Max is horrified I've gone down this route. I'm really off my game.

We've got a call scheduled later on, when I will have to either plead insanity for not cottoning onto his joke quickly enough or confess what's happened to me, so he goes easy and doesn't fire me for having suddenly turned into a moron. It could go either way. I love working with Max, but I'm dreading this call.

I don't even have Chris to moan to at work any more, because he's long gone. I miss our emailing and work calls, which always segued into other subjects. When Max let it drop that they were on the hunt for a new fit-out manager and asked if I knew of someone suitable, he mentioned that I'd be able to get a bonus as part of the recommend-a-friend scheme. I thought I'd ring Chris and bask in the fact that the tables had turned, but somehow it felt odd calling to tell him this when we were no longer working together. Now we're not colleagues, we haven't spoken since he said goodbye. Again.

Chapter Forty-Six

Chris

June

I pull out my phone and hover my finger over her number. I've been mulling this over for a while. This isn't the kind of thing I can say in a message. This has to be in person. But as I want to say it right now, and as I can't physically see her, I might just have to ring her.

Back and forward, back and forward. *Make a decision, Chris.* I always get there eventually, it simply takes me a lot of time. There was a brief period when quick decision-making was my *thing*. I'd open my mouth and the right words would come out. *Come with me*, for example.

Why is Lexie in my head now? There's so much I want to say to her, but can't. I said far too much over the past couple of years. And now I'm back living in London, it's somehow more complicated than ever. And there's Victoria. Perhaps it was easier when I was in New York and she was living here. Expectations on both sides were lower. But now . . . there's no avoiding that life is speeding up, cruising away from the dock. Only I'm in danger of being left behind.

If I carry on like this much longer, I'll be forty and not even married, let alone divorced. I smile. *That conversation. Her.*

I hit the icon to call, breathe in deeply and brace myself, because I'm either going to look a fool or it will turn out to be a well-constructed plan. I'll know in a few moments.

'Hey,' Victoria says, with warmth in her voice, when she picks up.

'Hey, you. I haven't spoken to you today and I wanted to check in.'

Victoria breathes in. 'I love how you do that. I love how you seem to *know* when I want to hear from you.'

I hear the sound of her chair creaking as she gets up and closes her office door.

'You busy?' I ask.

'Yeah,' she replies. 'I've just had some sketches back from Scarlet and there's a couple of tweaks I want her to make. Remember Scarlet, whose party we met at?'

I'm jolted into a state of high alert. Lexie's friend. 'Yeah?'

'Well, she's doing this project for me and . . . oh, I don't even know if Scarlet is aware we're together,' Victoria continues. 'Anyway . . .'

I quickly realise there's no information relating to Lexie about to be shared in this conversation, so every now and again at suitable moments I say, 'Uh-huh,' and 'Oh, right, that's nice.'

'Well, she's . . .' Victoria continues talking about the project Lexie's friend is working on. Only Victoria doesn't know anything *about* Lexie or how we met, or why I was even at that house-cooling party. I zone even further out, glancing around my Airbnb for my charger cable. Where did I put it? I need to check out and move into my next rental, as I only had this one for a month. I've really got to find somewhere more perman-ent to stay, although I quite like being nomadic. I might keep Airbnb-hopping until I work out where in London I want to finally settle, and whether I want to settle here long-term at all.

Victoria is still talking about whatever this project is that her company's working on, and I wait for a break in the con-versation so that I can say the thing I want to say. There's silence. Oh, she's finished.

But I open my mouth and I freeze. This isn't the time. And I wonder – just a little bit – if I should maybe . . . *not* say it. The implications of asking someone to be your girlfriend when it turns out you're not sure are damaging to everyone involved. And why would I do this on the phone? I should see her, face-to-face, and work out how I feel about everything then.

Instead I say something else. 'My brother's in town this week and you know we said we'd go and see the *Jersey Boys* musical and catch some dinner, but as we didn't buy tickets yet, can I invite him along?'

'Of course,' she says warmly. 'You like me enough to intro-duce me to your family,' she continues meaningfully.

I smile. 'Yeah,' I reply. 'You OK with that?'

'I am,' she says. 'Big step: meet the family.'

'Yeah . . . I guess so,' I say. I was about to ask this woman to be my girlfriend. I suppose meeting my brother is a big deal.

Chapter Forty-Seven

Lexie

It's the middle of June and I've been camping on Scarlet's new sofa for the past month, as she needed a new one and decided a sofabed was the safest option, especially seeing as I'm still hovering around. It's a huge, flumpy green-velvet affair. I may have had a hand in helping Scarlet choose it, based on the size of this giant room that she needs to fill. The black leather one she was looking at was vile and didn't work in this space at all.

She keeps telling me I need to get myself straight mentally before I even so much as think about leaving Edinburgh, which poses a problem. Where do I go? I'm finally in a position where I can think about it, and she's caught me looking on rental websites at flats in London. I'm just seeing what's available for a sad, lonely woman who isn't relishing the thought of living by herself in one of the world's most expensive cities. Rory has stayed over here a few times and Scarlet goes to his place quite often too, but she's a loyal, lovely friend and stays in with me on the nights when I don't have anything else on. I think they'd be seeing a lot more of each other if I wasn't here. I need to make a decision soon because I'm sure I'm outstaying my welcome.

'Of course you're not,' Scarlet insists when I tell her this as we cook dinner together. 'It's exactly like it was before, when we used to live together. Plus you've learned to cook a bit since then, so it's even better. I'm in no hurry at all to see you go, trust me. But until you work out what you're doing, you should really think about rescuing your stuff from Josh's before the guilt wears off and he throws it in a skip.'

I gasp, spin round from the cooker where I'm stirring our risotto and look at her. 'He wouldn't do that!'

'He shagged Tamara. His moral compass is iffy.'

I slump briefly and then try to rally. 'When I work out what I'm doing and where I'm going next, I've decided to let him pack it all up for me. Josh can be trusted to do that, even if he can't be trusted not to cheat on me. Plus he can shoulder the cost of it all, and the burden. I can't go back and do it. I can't go back ever again.'

'I'm still impressed you just turned on your heel and ran,' Scarlet says.

I didn't exactly do a runner. I bundled a few items into my case and called a taxi. I stood outside for ages, drowning in my own humiliation while I waited for it to arrive eventually. Josh tried to offer me a lift and then tried to make me stay, so he could explain in more horrific detail, in an act to appease his own conscience. Or get it off his chest. I'll never know now. He won't give me another thought. He's in love with Tamara – Tamara who's been right under his nose the entire time. I was the usurper who stood in the way of them being together. Scarlet called it from day one. She smelled trouble from the moment I told her about their friendship. I'm an idiot. I'm—

'I'm the other woman,' I say suddenly.

'Sorry?'

'*I'm* the other woman. I'm the one who stood in the way of two people who love each other getting together for the past two years. I'm the one who thought this was the real deal, when really it wasn't. If this were a book or a film, I'd be . . . I'd be the one you'd hate. I'd be the one you wanted to fall down a mineshaft or get a work placement in Timbuktu, so the hero could be with the real love of his life. Fucking hell, Tamara is the *heroine*.'

Scarlet blows air out of her cheeks. 'Oh, shit,' she exclaims, which says everything without saying anything. 'No,' she replies quickly. 'No, no, no. That's not how this works.'

'Yes, it is,' I say. 'Tamara is the heroine. I'm not. Tamara is the real love of Josh's life, and I am the evil crone who needed defeating so that Princess Tamara could get her happy ending.'

'You're kind of ranting now,' Scarlet tells me and wrestles the wooden spoon off me, so she can stir the risotto that's sticking to the bottom of the pot.

I can't say anything that's not already been said, and silence descends on the kitchen. 'It's quiet here,' I point out, my tone still gloomy and depressive. I appreciate that we're in a residential street, but there's no noise and no sign of life. It's like that scene in *28 Days Later* when a young Cillian Murphy wakes up from a coma, walks around alone and can't find a single person. 'It's quiet for a city,' I point out.

'Yeah, this bit of Edinburgh is, compared to where we lived in London. It's really residential,' Scarlet says. 'Not always quiet, though.'

I'm still staring out of the window. A delivery van pulls up at the house across the road.

'It's not a massive city,' she goes on. 'Anyway, my point earlier – before we went off on a tangent – was this: Rory says you can store your stuff in his garage if you want. It's where he keeps all his work tools and lawnmower but, unless you've accumulated loads more stuff, it should all fit. It's an easy solution to your problem . . . to one of your problems,' she clarifies, making me smile. I love Scarlet for saying the truth, no matter how hard it sounds. Her lack of filter is one of her finest qualities.

'But his garage is in Leith.'

'Yes, it is,' she says. 'It's not far from here.'

'That's the point I'm making. His garage is in Scotland.'

'Yes?'

'Why would I want my stuff in Scotland?'

'Because you're *in* Scotland,' she replies slowly, as if I'm stupid. She's silent then, looking at me as if waiting for me to get there by myself.

I smile properly for the first time since Josh blindsided me. 'You think I should live in Scotland?'

'Edinburgh,' she tells me. 'I'm being really specific about

this because, selfishly, I like having you around. Don't move to the Hebrides or anything.'

'Why would I move to Edinburgh?'

'Why wouldn't you? You could move here for a bit. Find a furnished flat – there's plenty of them, so I don't have to hand over half this lot.' She gestures around to all our old furniture. 'Where else were you planning to go after you'd finished licking your wounds?'

'London,' I say automatically.

'Why?' she fires back.

'Because . . . it's where I live.'

'You *lived* in London. Then you *lived* in the Cotswolds. Now you're homeless.'

I laugh. 'I'm not *homeless*.'

'You can't live here. You can't graduate from the sofabed to the boxroom. I need that boxroom for my computer. My monitor is huge.'

'Your monitor *fills* that tiny room and no, I wasn't suggesting I live here. Am I outstaying my welcome? You told me a minute ago that I wasn't, but is that why . . . ?'

'No,' she replies. 'I love having you here. Ooh,' she starts, 'we could maybe look for a flat together? Although I'm locked into this one for quite a while.'

'I feel we might be a bit beyond that now, don't you?' I say gently.

'Yeah,' she agrees. 'I was just testing the water. Possibly we're going backwards if we do that. And also I'm learning to love my own space.'

I haven't learned how to love my own space yet. Perhaps

that's what I need to do. Maybe I do need a change, a new adventure. Maybe I need to be somewhere new, work out what I want from my world. Maybe I need to do a Chris.

'Moving to Edinburgh is only a suggestion. A selfish suggestion,' she says. 'Though it's great here.'

'I know it is,' I agree.

'You work from home, and now the London hotel's finished . . . I've missed you, and you need to find a place to live.'

'I've missed you too.'

It's my turn to take the spoon from her and unstick the rice. It's ready and I remove the pan from the hob.

'All the things you loved doing in London are here: shopping, eating, Deliveroo.'

'Deliveroo?' I question. 'Now you have my attention. I'll think about it. I'll do some research.'

Scarlet holds out the bowls for me, so I can start serving up our dinner.

'You do that,' she says. 'And meanwhile I'll start bombarding you with links to the flats I've already found for you.'

Chapter Forty-Eight

August

I stand with a mug of tea in front of one of the huge sash windows in my new rental apartment. I throw the window wide open, letting the summer air breeze through, which whips the long almost-not-there white curtain into the room. This space looks so elegant that I take a picture and pop it on Instagram. My social media accounts are a bit less about all my nights out now and more design-centric. I feel professional, showcasing goals I've achieved publicly. I'm making things happen for myself.

This flat is the first home I've lived in where I've been able to put a bit of my own stamp on the design. I look out across the tree-lined street towards the central-square garden – access to which comes with the tenancy of my flat. I'm slowly settling into this new life in Edinburgh.

Living in London, it would cost me at least twice as much for a flat in a central city location such as this. And I've got so much more space here than I could ever afford in London. The flat is recently refurbished with a new kitchen and bathroom, contained within a Georgian town house similar to

Scarlet's: all high ceilings and original cornicing. The Georgians knew how to build a decent-sized room, not like the rabbit hutch that Scarlet and I were previously living in at Edmonton Green. I can't imagine going back to that life now.

Edinburgh feels fresher, purer than London. I breathe differently here. I can walk to Arthur's Seat and drink in the clean air while looking down at the city I'm learning to call home.

The only downside has been having to live off the scant belongings I brought with me, and some basics I got in an emergency trip to H&M a few weeks ago. Having barely any of my belongings here has made it feel like I was in an Airbnb. It felt temporary, as if I hadn't really occupied the space – which I hadn't. And I kind of liked it, knowing it was temporary: only for six months, with the option to extend. But I think I'm going to stay a bit longer and make a life for myself here. I've already gone some way towards achieving that, allowing myself to buy some ornaments and wall art for my apartment. Just a few bits here and there to make the space feel more mine.

I'm going to get the train to and from my parents' respective houses in Reading and St Albans every now and again, and they're excited to come and visit me in a few weeks. I plan to fly back and forth from Dublin when required – which the company will pay for – as the new hotel project gets off the ground; and Max has hinted at a promotion, as he's keen to move up the ladder and is determined to drag me with him. I'm not far off finishing my design course but, even when I do, I'll have the training wheels on for a long while yet. Max won't let me run riot on my own. Nor am I confident enough to do so. But being able to input ideas, with the benefit of having been educated in the subject properly, means I'm more confident in my choices, my designs, my abilities. I'm getting there. I'm closer than I've ever been, for someone who didn't even start a proper career until post-thirty.

I've joined a yoga class in a new studio round the corner, which I visit in my lunch hour some days. Every couple of weekends I go swimming with some new friends I've made through a co-working space. And I've signed up to a monthly book club. These are the activities I wanted to do when I moved to the Cotswolds, but never managed to, mainly due to not driving. But I've done it here. It's easy.

It's a rare Sunday when I don't have too much on. I'm alone, but not lonely. I'm without Josh, learning to resent him and Tamara less as each day goes by and . . . it's OK. We weren't perfect. And although I don't expect perfection in a relationship, I think I had high expectations based on how keen he was at the start. But neither Josh nor I met these expectations jointly. Cracks had started to appear, but I didn't want to see them. Looking back, I can see them all now – hairline fractures that grew and grew. I wish I'd paid more attention to them. I wish I'd seen the end coming.

I was lonelier living with Josh than I am living by myself now. I tried not to admit it to myself at the time. And then he was hesitant about so many things. So was I. There was so much brewing beneath the surface. I've always wondered 'what if' about Chris. Maybe Josh was feeling the same about Tamara. Maybe he'd had feelings for her long before he met me. Maybe I'll never know. Perhaps he didn't even know himself. If Tamara and he hadn't got together, how long would Josh and I realistically have carried on like that for? A few months? Years? Maybe we peaked too soon.

Despite my gently waning resentment, I can't bring myself to answer his occasional phone calls. I can't speak to him. I don't want to. Josh rings me again while I'm uploading my window picture to Instagram, presumably to find out where I am, so he can send my belongings to me. It's not the first time he's rung, and I've ignored him, but my reaction is the same. Every single part of me tenses. But I don't cancel the call. I let it ring while I stand stiff and still. He's tenacious, but then the ringing stops. I can't answer. I don't trust myself not to cry or scream at him.

Instead I wait two days before messaging him my address, and asking him to send all my belongings up to me. I don't sign off with a kiss. It's a perfunctory message. It says what it needs to.

Josh rings me again straight away, but I don't answer or follow up with a message. Neither does he.

And then, just under a week later, a collection of boxes arrives. I guessed they were coming, but it still takes me by surprise when a courier buzzes via the main front door and tells me there's a large delivery for me. I help him carry them upstairs and feel partly renewed, partly sad that this has all happened in the way it has. The courier and I put everything inside my front door and I look at the boxes with mixed feelings . . . A little piece of me was still in Josh's farmhouse. Now that's no longer the case.

Josh didn't ask me to cover the delivery charge (maybe that was what he was ringing about again, after he discovered how much it would cost to courier eight full-size packing boxes the length of the British Isles). And I didn't offer. Paying to deliver my life to me after he'd ruined it was the least he could do.

I didn't tell Josh I was living in Edinburgh, but having him send my belongings to this address must have confused him. I want to confuse him. I want him to wonder why he's sending all my things to a city so far away from anywhere I'm connected with. I assume he thinks I'm staying with Scarlet. And if he does, I'm not going to correct him. It's not worth my time. A little bit of mystery is never a bad thing.

That afternoon I feel spurred on to join a women's social club so that I can continue to make friends in a new city, which is something Scarlet hasn't even done yet. I'm going to force her to come with me, so I don't have to go alone. I'm a brave, independent woman, but I'm not *that* brave and independent. The social club organises dinners and now that I can afford to do a bit more socially, I intend to go to some of them.

I peruse the list of social events and spy a day's wellness retreat coming up. I'm not sure what Pilates is or how it differs from yoga, but I do know it's £50 for an hour's class, plus a lovely-looking brunch and a glass of fizz, so I click the booking link. I'm going to go. I'm going to keep making new friends in the city I now live in, and I'm going to enjoy it.

I glance at the boxes one more time and decide I'm not

ready to open them yet. I've lived without my piles of unread books and 7,000 different shades of Kylie Jenner's Matte Lip Kits for the past few months, so I'm sure I can do without them all a little longer.

Chapter Forty-Nine

Chris

October

I get home from work and find a very thick envelope waiting for me in my flat's post box in the communal hall. It's nestled among the takeaway leaflets and notices from estate agents about how they want to buy my property. I'm renting, so I can't sell it even if I wanted to. I'll be a perpetual renter at this rate, but I'm enjoying it. I feel different these days. Chris in New York wasn't the Chris I wanted to be. I'm not going to say I found myself. But I feel . . . better, renewed. I don't have this need to do stuff all the time, see things all the time, find new places to go. I don't need to *try* to be by myself any more. I feel free. Of what I'm not sure. But I'm more at ease these days. With who I am, with work, with my relationship status. That reminds me: I promised I'd message Victoria about her birthday.

I throw all the post into the recycling box that one of my clever neighbours set up down here, but keep hold of the thick card envelope, which I slice open with my key.

It's a wedding invite. I've been invited to Max's wedding. 'Oh, that's nice,' I mutter to myself as I hit the button summoning the lift. I weigh up whether I can go. It's on 28 December. That's a strange time to have a wedding, although it's nice of him to invite me. We've spoken a bit since we stopped working together. But now that I don't live in New York, maintaining old relationships can be difficult. I could go back for the wedding, though.

I quite fancy it actually. I wonder if Lexie might be there? Last time I checked, she was living with Josh in Somerset. It's been so long since we last spoke, I wonder if I should message her now, break the ice again before we meet in New York. I feel we're forever breaking the ice and then letting it settle back in place as the months drift by.

I stab the button for the lift again and see it's still on the fifth floor. Someone's probably got it jammed open while they unload their food shopping. I look down at my phone and stare at Lexie's number.

Maybe I'll text her later, after I've RSVP'd to Max's wedding.

Chapter Fifty

Lexie

December

'Is this the invite?' Scarlet asks, spying it on my mantel and moving over to take a look. 'That's lovely. *Very* good paper quality.'

I chuckle to myself as I make us both dinner.

'Shame I can't be your plus-one for this one,' she continues, placing the invitation back on the mantel. She and Rory are going on their first proper holiday together while I'm away. 'New York would have been amazing.'

'Who am I going to play wedding bingo with now?' I ask.

'It's finally happened,' Scarlet says mournfully. 'We aren't plus-one-ing each other to weddings. That's it. It's ended.'

'No, don't say that. There are always more weddings. Always.'

Why Max has chosen to have his wedding in between Christmas and New Year is beyond me. It's a ridiculously busy time of year for most people. I've personally got to get from Edinburgh to my mum's in Berkshire, then to my dad's in Hertfordshire and then catch a flight on 27 December from Heathrow. I'm only in the US for two days and then I'm heading home. It's going to be a fast turnaround, but I suppose it's nice to have all these places to go to. And when the time comes, I'm bubbling with excitement to return to New York and celebrate Max's wedding. Although I won't have anyone to play wedding bingo with this time.

As I exit the terminal at JFK the ice-cold air hits me like a tidal wave. Christmas in New York is as exuberant as I remember it, but the weather is no joke. Seeing the twinkling lights and skyscrapers of Manhattan, I can't work out if it's the change of location, the fact that I'm hardly ever here and excited to be back or whether I'm bowled over by New York generally, but I feel so buoyant about everything. Life is good. I love it here. I love my life in Edinburgh. I think of Chris and how easily he moved from England to New York five years ago. And then back again a few years later. I wonder if I could do the same thing with New York. Maybe I'll move from Edinburgh in a few years' time. Who knows? I'm enjoying the not knowing.

I haven't spoken to Chris much since the last time I saw him at the hotel opening in March. That's about eight months, but who's counting? We said goodbye over a long call when he was sending out his farewell emails during his last day at work. I wished him luck for his leaving drinks, and thought then how strange it would be not knowing what his new office would look like, where he'd sit or how he'd spend his days. I couldn't picture him any more in his daily environment and it bothered me. I don't know how or when we'll speak properly again. He's gone a bit off-radar – has activated stealth mode.

I found him on Instagram and followed him. Chris followed me back. We've liked each other's posts a few times. And that's as far as it's gone. I miss him, though. I miss his conversation, his sense of humour, his openness. I wondered about messaging him, but decided against it. I've been in too strange a place emotionally, after everything that happened with Josh, to consider talking to Chris at the moment. And he hasn't messaged me, either. But I hope we will soon.

Men and women being friends *is* kind of weird if there's an added layer of obvious chemistry. And he's got a girlfriend. *I am not stupid enough to be mates with someone I fancy. I can't be mates with someone I want to kiss every time I see her. I can't be mates with someone I can't stop fucking thinking about.*

I think about what Chris said at the last wedding we were at together. I think about a lot of things he's said over the years. The intense words he and I have shared are the kind that Josh and I should have been exchanging. Josh rang me again this morning. But I can't talk to him. I don't want to. What is there to say? I let it ring and ring. He's tenacious; he hung on for ages. But *he* ended it with me. I've moved on. We got together so immediately and fell into being a couple so quickly, so easily. There was physical chemistry between Josh and me, and I wonder now if that was the main cut and thrust of our relationship.

But Chris . . . we barely even touched, never kissed. Our

connection was based on a personality fit. You can't fake that. You can't replicate it with another person, either.

Most of our recent interactions before he went off-radar were work-related, but Chris was there, in my life, hovering in the background. And now he's not. At all. I really miss him.

Max's wedding is at Glasshouse Chelsea, a high-rise building where views of the winter sunset across the city are a thing of wonder. The light is so red, setting across the buildings in a horizontal bright flame. It takes my breath away.

He and his partner Michelle are having a glamorous but laid-back sort of wedding. While the venue is stylish, the atmosphere isn't staid, or as formal as I'm used to in the UK. Max is very 'New York' and so is his wedding. He and Michelle wrote their own vows, including how he promised to refill the coffee machine with water each night, and how she promised to stop putting the remote control in random places. Michelle is wearing bright red rather than white, and she's sporting a baby bump. There's so much happiness in the air, there's no formal seating plan and the pianist is playing Billie Eilish. If I was playing wedding bingo today, I'd have lost as I'd have had none of this on my grid. The wedding's fabulous and it's proof you can get married and enjoy the happiest day of your life however you want.

My jet lag is catching up with me. It comes in fits and starts and, to counteract it, I've been drinking Espresso Martinis all night. The mix of caffeine and vodka is making me feel wired, but mellow at the same time. My eyes are wide open, but my brain is exhausted.

I reflect on how another wedding has been ticked off a seemingly endless list. Each one I've attended over the years has been different, but only one of them do I live over and over again in my mind. Only one of them was truly stand-out. I found Chris and then lost him, all at once. And then I met Josh. Which, in hindsight, I really wish I hadn't.

I did wonder if Chris would come to this wedding, but there's no sign of him, and I felt strange grilling Max about Chris in the run-up. He had more important things to think about as the happiest day of his life loomed. Chris not being here takes the shine off this trip, dulls it in some way. But I put a huge, happy smile on my face, congratulate Max and his new wife and enthuse wildly about their cool, fun wedding. Max confirmed excitedly what I'd already guessed, that they're expecting a baby, before being ushered off to speak to other guests.

I make small talk with the colleagues I rarely see and then, when that's run its course, I hang out at the bar and try to order a final drink before I leave. I might not make it an Espresso Martini. But I'm struggling to get served – it's so busy.

I glance at my watch. It's half eleven and I wonder if there's any point going to sleep now, given that my flight is so early. I should think about going back to my hotel to start packing. I'll count to ten and, if I don't get served, I'll take that as my cue to say goodbye and thanks to Max, give him the biggest hug I can and leave.

Ten, nine . . .

'Can I get you a drink?' a man asks me. 'I've got the bartender's attention and you've been standing there a while.'

'Thanks,' I reply quickly, all thoughts of counting down my exit gone. 'Vodka tonic, please.'

He echoes my words to the bartender, who mixes my drink. I pull out some dollars and try to hand them to the man, but he politely declines.

'I've wanted to introduce myself to you all evening, but I didn't know how,' he confesses coyly. 'This seemed like a good way.'

'Sneaky,' I say, immediately drawn in.

He smiles, looks down at his drink, glances back at me and we're suddenly jostled out of the way by a couple who clearly want to get to the bar. I'm pushed into him and he looks shocked, but catches me. 'You OK? You want me to say something to them?'

'No, it's fine. They didn't do it on purpose. They're drunk. They're happy,' I tell him. 'I'm Lexie by the way.' I extend my hand and he shakes it. His grip is warm, his eyes blue.

'Xander.'

'Nice to meet you, Xander. Shall we move away from the drunk people, so we don't get caught up in the fight that's probably about to break out?'

'Good idea,' he says.

All good weddings end in a fight. I smile to myself.

'You're English?' Xander asks.

'Was it the accent that gave it away?' I tease.

'It was, yeah. It's a cute accent. You live here or are you just over for the wedding?'

'I'm over for the wedding. Max is my boss.'

'Oh, cool. Max is my best friend's brother.'

'Oh, brilliant,' I say conversationally and then try to work out that line of connection – best friend's brother. OK, I'm there now.

'Where are you staying?' he asks.

'At The Curated. The rooms are heavily discounted.'

'How come?'

'Because I work for the company.'

'Right, yes,' he replies. 'That makes sense. If Max is your boss, then of course you work for the company.' I can see him clawing around for something else to say. I'm doing the same.

'Is this the most boring conversation you've had all day?' I ask and then smile wide in recognition as I remember this exact line from another conversation, soaked in so much small talk we were in danger of drowning until we cleverly lifted ourselves free. I'm in danger of drowning in small talk now.

But Xander isn't smiling. He looks affronted.

'I didn't mean to offend you,' I continue quickly. 'I'm implying that I'm boring.' I'm not implying anything like this, actually. I'm implying that our conversation is boring, but Xander looks even more startled at my words and now I don't know how to bring it all back to normality. I toy with the idea of suggesting we ditch the small talk and start on Big Talk, but I don't. I don't want Big Talk with this man who is devoid of humour. It wouldn't be the same. And deep down, I don't want it to be the same.

This is going to look like the quickest about-turn in history, so here goes, I think, steeling myself. 'Xander, it was so lovely to meet you,' I say. 'But I need to drink this swiftly and then say bye to Max. I have a flight to catch in . . .' I glance at my watch, 'a matter of hours.'

'Oh, right. I see. OK. No problem. It was nice to meet you, Laura.'

'Lexie,' I reply.

'Lexie,' he repeats. 'Have a great flight.'

'Thank you.' I give him a polite smile, neck half my drink and go in search of Max, so I can say goodbye and make my way home to Edinburgh.

Chapter Fifty-One

Chris

January 2025

I look at the engagement ring as it sparkles on Victoria's finger. She looks the happiest she's been since I've known her. That should tell me everything, shouldn't it? This isn't a mistake. None of this is a mistake. Her happiness means so much.

My happiness means a lot to me too, and I haven't overlooked that. I am happy. It was strange at first, the way this all happened. A chance encounter that I didn't know would have such an ending. But I am genuinely overjoyed.

'Are you OK?' Victoria asks me.

'I'm perfect,' I reply.

'Honestly?' she asks, with meaning in her eyes – I forget how kind she is, how thoughtful, checking on me when all the attention should be on her.

'Honestly,' I say. 'I couldn't be happier. Any ideas about a date?' I ask tentatively, so I can get more used to the idea of what's going to happen.

'September maybe? I don't want to wait too long. Are you OK with that?'

I chuckle. 'Victoria, you need to stop asking if I'm OK. I need you to enjoy this. Whatever you want is fine by me. I cannot stress this enough.'

She smiles, kisses me on the cheek and pulls me into an embrace. 'I knew you were a good one,' she replies, before moving off to rifle around in her bag for her diary.

I take the opportunity to glance at my phone. Max posted pictures of his wedding on Instagram. I feel kind of bad for not going, although I did RSVP a polite and regretful no. On reflection, it was too much to fit in around everything that was going on here, plus Christmas. But seeing the pictures of Max and his new wife, and a smiling Lexie talking with a guy at the bar (I zoomed in), has made me antsy. I have no right to be. But the feeling is there all the same.

If I'd gone, I'd have seen Lexie, spoken to her, been near her. I'm kicking myself that I didn't go. Being near her would have been enough. I think. It would have had to be enough. I've looked at this picture a hundred times over the past week and I'm sure I'll look at it a hundred more.

What might have been.

Chapter Fifty-Two

Lexie

The new year has arrived and with it a promotion, which Max hinted at but I didn't like to hold him to, as the job needed to be advertised externally too. I love the bijou size of the company, as it's not so large that there are people in the same department to fight off for a promotion. Because I've proven myself in the job and finished my course with a predicted high grade, I am now listed on the company website as Interior Designer instead of Design Assistant. I cannot believe it. The feeling is incredible. When my new business cards were delivered, I couldn't tear the packaging open fast enough and stared at them for ages. I wanted to message Chris and show him and, in part, thank him again for helping me get here, for kick-starting the possibilities and opportunities. But I didn't.

I've managed to prove my worth since starting in my role and now, as our Dublin hotel plans ramp up, I've flown out for the week to get the lie of the land.

This hotel is in an old factory from the 1950s, and Max and I have been debating whether we should venture into the expected, design-wise, with exposed steel beams, or whether we warm it up. I have this urge to brighten the space with pinks and greens and give it a faded 1950s Palm Springs vibe. It'll be different, cool, inviting.

'Gone off the idea of going totally emerald then?' Max teases. I give him an embarrassed look and he casts his gaze around the huge space. 'Like a Slim Aarons photograph?' he suggests after a pause.

'Exactly that. It was the rooftop pool on the architect plans that gave me the idea,' I tell him as we stand in the gloomy space, hard hats on and notepads in hand. Max is here on his honeymoon: a grand tour of Europe and – in between drinking as much Guinness as he can while he's in Dublin – we've arranged to meet for a quick afternoon of work.

I'll join Max and Michelle later for dinner, and then tomorrow they fly off to London before moving on to Paris. I'm offended they haven't included Edinburgh or Glasgow in their travel plans, so that must mean I'm feeling some grounding and loyalty towards the place I now call home.

'I'd throw in some golds to neutralise the look, but also add some glamour,' I say to Max. My words echo around us in the cavernous space. 'These downstairs rooms are all going to be huge, so it'll need softening,' I muse as I look around, taking pictures on my phone. 'What about pillars? Even though we don't need them structurally, it's so big in this main lobby and restaurant that we could add some to break up what the eye sees, create different spaces around them.'

'I *love* that. Draw up some ideas,' he tells me and then his gaze softens. 'Can I be patronising and tell you I'm proud of how far you've come?'

'You can,' I say, trying not to blush. 'Thanks.'

Max squeezes my arm. 'Right, that's enough work for one day. Pub?'

'Definitely.'

Chapter Fifty-Three

February

'You are now an interior designer with a Distinction certificate and all sorts of brilliant skills,' Scarlet declares in an excited ramble, as we sit on the sofas and she pops the cork open on the bottle of champagne she and Rory brought round to celebrate. It feels too cold outside to drink champagne. It's one degree and is threatening to snow.

'I know!' I squeal. I'd been told my predicted grade was going to be good, and I'd worked so hard, but a Distinction still surprised me. This is the first time Scarlet and I have found a free evening together when we can celebrate. 'Thank God it's a Friday. No early starts for work for any of us,' I say.

'Hello-o-o,' Rory says, raising a hand. '*I* have to be at work tomorrow.'

'Poor you,' Scarlet replies and makes a sad face that Rory doesn't buy into. 'Scything in a garden while hungover? Like some sort of brooding, shirtless Scottish Poldark?'

Rory raises an eyebrow. 'Shirtless? In this weather. And . . . a scythe?' he questions. 'A lawnmower more like.'

'Lawnmowers aren't sexy,' I tell him. 'Could you just play along about the scythe . . . for Scarlet.'

He laughs, takes the glass of fizz that I offer him. 'Christ, you two are a nightmare together,' he mutters. 'Congratulations again.'

'Thank you,' I tell him, as Rory automatically rests an arm over the back of the sofa and pulls Scarlet into him, where she nestles comfortably. The movement sends a jolt of happiness through me for my friend. But it also reminds me how I have no one to do that to me. I breathe in, breathe out. I'm strangely OK with this. I have so much going on, such a good life now. I'm happy.

Alongside celebrating my new educational milestone and promotion, I am also commiserating about failing my driving test. It was too soon to take it, given the infrequent lessons I'd been having, but a space came up and I thought I'd try and wing it. I'd been doing so well in general recently that it has been grounding to fail in something.

'Reversing round a corner is the most unnecessary driving skill ever,' Scarlet says knowingly as we commiserate together.

'I also clipped a kerb,' I confess.

'Kerbs are overrated too,' Rory declares in solidarity.

'Apparently the car could have bounced all over the place and maybe have mounted the kerb and then hit a few pedestrians,' I say.

'Fuck off,' Scarlet says, scoffing. 'That would literally never happen.'

'Bit late to argue it now, and I'm not sure I'm supposed to. Got to roll with the punches,' I tell her.

'Here's to next time,' Rory says.

'Not sure I can go through with that again.' I shudder.

'That's what people say about childbirth,' Scarlet declares. 'But those babies keep being born. A driving test is pain-free. Suck it up. Book another test. And maybe a lesson or two to brush up, before you go in.'

'Just in case next time I flip the car over on the kerb and take out an entire town?'

She nods. 'You can't have everything at once, so perhaps we could focus on the good news of the day and how much money you'll be earning, now you're qualified, with a promotion.'

'A couple of thousand more,' I say, 'essentially to do near enough the same job I've been doing, with more freedom over the design process. Although Max has trusted me since the start not to mess it up. It's nice to be rewarded while doing something I love – having a voice that's listened to, while still technically having my learner plates on.'

'Not for long, though,' Rory chimes in. '*All* those learner plates will be off soon enough.'

Although today was a bit of a fail in one department, it came on the back of success in another. I now have a bit of paper that proves I know what I'm talking about when it comes to interior design.

I'll get there in the end on that driving test. It's not like I *need* to pass. Now I'm living in a city again, I drive precisely nowhere, and I don't own a car. I can't see myself buying one when I pass, either. But I'm *determined* to do it. I'll book a few more lessons and take it from there.

After they go home I close the front door and tidy up the shoes scattered around the packing boxes, which have by now gathered a lot of dust. They've been here for months. Scarlet glances at the boxes pointedly every time she comes round, but I haven't opened them yet. I like to joke they're a permanent design feature, but in the end I had to confess and tell her my secret fear was that all those photos Josh and I took in our two years together, then spent time diligently choosing frames for, would be in those boxes.

'It's not just my things,' I told her. 'It's *our* things.' I wasn't ready to be confronted with Josh's face smiling out at me from a photo frame, reminding me of a time when I thought I was happy. I also didn't want to be confronted with my possessions; items I owned and wore when Josh and I were together. Each one would remind me of our shared memories. It wouldn't have been so bad if everything in these boxes hadn't been at his house, if I had never have moved in. Now they contain the relics of my two years of being happy, coupled and loved, or so I thought.

For ages I wondered if it might hurt, seeing the way Josh packed up our photos with my things and sent them away, deleting me from his shiny new life with Tamara. I half wondered for a while if I might be better off taking all the boxes to the charity shop and letting them enjoy the fruits of my failed relationship. But I couldn't bring myself to do that, either. So the boxes remained.

But six months is a long time to have left all my stuff piled up. I've been in relationships that have lasted less time than these boxes have been here. I go to the kitchen, fill my glass with leftover wine and return to the hall. Only this time I've brought a pair of scissors, because I think I'm going to do it. I'm finally going to slice open the packing tape holding the boxes closed. I'm ready. I'm over it. I'm over Josh. My life has moved on, for the better, in so many ways. I'm happily single and I've not felt that way in for ever. Is it right to do this on a Friday night, after drinks with friends and a failed driving test behind me?

I psyche myself up. 'Let's do this,' I whisper to no one, then cut open the packing tape on the first box.

I pull out clothes, wellies and all the outdoor gear I'd purchased, including a Schöffel gilet, hiking boots and a Barbour waxed jacket. I remember my old life at Josh's, my old clothes. A few issues of *Country Life*, bought when I imagined this was the life I'd have, are bundled into another box, along with the entire contents of a Superdrug store. I forgot how much make-up I owned and left behind when I fled – or escaped, depending on how you look at it.

Literally anything I took into that house is now in this flat, 400 miles away from Josh. I stand back and assess the damage, spread all over the hall floor. Then I start carrying books towards shelves, and putting shoes I'd forgotten about into the spaces that were occupied by the now-empty boxes.

'My silver ankle boots are here!' I say to myself excitedly. I forgot about those. The last time I wore them was to the hotel opening. Which was also the last time I saw Chris.

And then I see something else as I pick up the empty boxes. At the bottom of one of them is a sealed envelope with the word *Lexie* written on it, in Josh's handwriting.

My heart stills, my breath slows. I wonder if it's a bill for the courier. I wonder if it's an apology, a further explanation of everything he and Tamara did and why he thought it was OK. I open it carefully and pull out the letter: two sheets of A4 lined paper in Josh's neat handwriting. I take a deep breath, start reading and only get halfway through before I'm floored by the contents. I can't bring myself to finish it. I stare into the middle distance. 'Oh. My. God.'

Chapter Fifty-Four

Scarlet stands in the hallway the next morning, unable to make it into the flat all the way before she demands to see the letter. I hand it over and close the front door, while she kicks off her shoes and devours Josh's words.

'He can't be serious?' she baulks as she reads.

'I think he is. He sounds serious.'

'He wants you back? Where does it say that?'

'Keep reading,' I say as we walk towards the lounge.

She scans it. 'Bloody hell,' she exclaims. 'He's made a mistake,' she paraphrases, 'he wants you back, he can't sleep at night, he knows he's made the worst mistake of his life. He doesn't love her.' Scarlet looks up at that one and stares at me. 'He doesn't love Tamara!' she exclaims again.

'Yeah. I did not see that one coming.'

'Me neither,' she says. 'He's in love with you,' she continues and looks up at me in shock again.

I'm not as shocked now as I was when I read the letter yesterday, so my expression doesn't mirror hers. I feel strangely emotionless. And confused about Josh's U-turn. Was this what all those missed calls were about?

'He's in love with you. He's the worst person on Earth for doing what he did. You're the best thing that ever happened to him. He bangs on about how much you loved him, and the surprise party, and . . . blah-blah-blah,' Scarlet says. She scans the rest, which is more or less a varied repeat of the contents that come before it, and then she looks at me, shakes her head, folds the letter and hands it back.

I don't need to scan through it again. I've read it nine times. I place it on the coffee table and step back from it, as if it's a nuclear weapon and should be left well alone.

'What are you going to do?' she asks.

'I don't know,' I say. 'That letter has been in the box for six months, so . . . I guess I'm going to do nothing.'

'Damn right. After what Josh did to you.'

'I know,' I reply. 'I can't believe he wrote that. I have to believe he's telling the truth. I have to take it at face value. But it was six months ago, and yes, there have been a couple of calls since then, but it's probably because I refused to answer the phone to him that he's stopped since. He might *not* feel the same way now as he did a few months ago. And I don't feel the same way about Josh as I once did, so I don't have to do anything about it, right?'

'No, you don't. What a twat!' Scarlet says.

I smile.

'I wonder what would have happened if you'd read this when Josh sent it all those months ago. What might you have done?'

'It's not worth thinking about, because I only know what my reaction is now and . . . anything I felt for him has gone.'

She looks a mix of surprised and impressed. 'I really want

to know what happened between him and Tamara, though, don't you? I need the gossip on that.'

'It's one of those things we're probably never going to know. Because I'm not going to do anything about this.'

'Good for you. Shall we set light to it?'

'No, I don't trust that smoke alarm not to go off.' I look up at the blinking light, which has been going at a rate of knots this week.

'Throw it in the bin?'

'Yeah,' I say. 'I'm just going to give it one more read though, you know, to make myself feel good.'

'And smug?' Scarlet suggests.

'Very smug,' I reply. 'And then we throw it in the bin.'

'You know what this means, don't you?' Scarlet continues, as we stand ritualistically over the bin moments later and look at Josh's letter as it soaks into the wet kitchen roll I threw in earlier. 'You're the heroine again,' she says, in revelatory fashion.

I frown. 'What?'

'Tamara's the evil crone who just got defeated. And *you* are the princess. You are the heroine.'

I stand a little taller, unpicking her words and resisting the urge to laugh. 'I forgot I said that. Did I sound like an idiot?'

'Yes, you did, but it was a memorable speech all the same.'

'I'm the heroine again,' I muse.

'Yes, you are,' Scarlet agrees enthusiastically. 'Yes, you bloody well are.'

354

Chapter Fifty-Five

Chris

March

The wedding invitations are in. I'm sitting at the dining table in my parents' kitchen and hold one in my hand, running my fingers over the calligraphy letters. My parents and Victoria's parents *invite you to the wedding of* . . .

They're jointly on the invitation as they're very generously jointly contributing. Victoria is talking about the swirly font and I'm trying hard to be interested, but fonts and typefaces, or whatever they're called, are not my bag.

I still can't get my head around the fact this is happening. I am really happy, even though everything seems to be moving so fast. When Victoria wants something, she goes all out to get it.

'Are these invites more expensive than the dress?' I ask.

'Nothing is more expensive than the dress,' she replies conspiratorially.

'I can't wait to see it,' I say.

'You're not allowed,' she tells me. 'No one is. Oh, while

I think of it, are there any other people you'd like to put on the guest list – anyone you want to invite? Speak now or for ever hold your peace!' she jokes.

My immediate thought is no. And then my mind goes somewhere it shouldn't. How odd would it be if I invited Lexie?

I haven't seen her in a year. I didn't know that time I said goodbye to her at the hotel opening would be our last goodbye. But I can't imagine standing at the front of the church and seeing Lexie there. I don't know what that would do to me. I'm not sure being in contact with her is wise anyway, especially since she moved in with Josh. By now they're probably getting ready to make babies and live happily ever after in his ancestral home, or whatever it is they're doing. I wonder if she'll invite me to her wedding when it happens? Probably not. And that's wise too. I'm glad I cooled down our friendship. It would only lead to danger. I knew it then and I feel it now.

'No. I'm OK.'

'You're OK?' Victoria queries.

'I mean I don't need to add anyone to the guest list. I'm all good.'

'So long as you're sure.'

I smile reassuringly.

'I'll leave a couple of spaces in case you decide you want to add someone else later,' she says. 'We've got a one-hundred person package and there's a few spaces left to fill.'

This is too much for me and a huge smile spreads across my face. I stand up as a distraction, move to the sink, fill a glass with water so that Victoria can't see my face, and try desperately not to laugh. Is it inappropriate to draw up a bingo grid now? It probably is, given that I know everything awaiting me at this wedding.

'What's so funny?' she asks.

'Nothing,' I say. A 100-person guest package and not enough friends to fill it. That's kind of tragic.

And also very funny.

Chapter Fifty-Six

Lexie

Six months later: September

'Here we go again,' I say. 'Another wedding. Lexie and Scarlet. Scarlet and Lexie. Until one of us dies.'

'I wouldn't have it any other way,' she replies, as she hares through the country lanes. 'Though I really thought these days were over.'

'I'm pleased they're not. It's like the good old days.'

'The good old days were only two and a half years ago, when we last did this at Grey's wedding in Edinburgh. The one where I met Rory,' Scarlet sighs with happiness.

I've driven the first half of the journey and she's on the final leg. I've only just passed my test and I'm far too nervous to negotiate tight lanes. The motorway was frightening enough and, because I refused to go above seventy miles per hour, we're even later than we normally are for these occasions. Scarlet's a pro, though, whizzing through the tight spaces. She's been driving since she was eighteen, unlike me. We're dressed in our wedding finery, although we really should have checked in with each other first, because we are both in pale pink.

'Now we *really* look like a couple,' Scarlet noted when I picked her up half an hour late in our little rental car. 'It's going to be *just* like before.' This wedding is for Scarlet's friends. And as this year's wedding season is in full swing, Rory is on a stag-do, so I'm Scarlet's plus-one.

'All my friends are married now,' I tell her. 'And all your lot must be close to being married too? Surely next year we'll get our summer weekends back.'

'Probably,' she agrees. 'Although just when you think everyone's finished, it'll be divorces followed by second marriages, and the weddings will kick-start again. We really could be each other's plus-ones until we die,' she says.

'Dear God, I hope not.' I cough pointedly, as I would like her to put both hands on the wheel in the ten-to-two position, and not check her make-up in the rear-view mirror.

The GPS tells us we've got about ten minutes left on the journey, and Scarlet asks me to get the card out of her bag and write it.

'What are their names?' I ask as I rest the card on my knee.

'Victoria and . . .'

'And . . . ?' I query.

'Bugger, can't remember.'

'Try and remember.'

'Just put *To the Happy Couple*.'

'That's such a shitty cop-out. And I've already written the

word "Victoria". I can't cross it out and write something else now. Where's the invite – it'll be on there?'

'I left it on the mantel, but I've written the time and the church address in my diary.'

I stare at her, but as Scarlet's driving, she has to glance quickly at me to see my face.

'What?' she asks as her eyes dart back to the road.

'That's no help,' I mutter as something awful strikes me, like a lightning bolt of recognition that brings with it a sense of fear and horror. 'Scarlet, how many Victorias do you know?'

'Er . . . two.'

'Is this one your graphic-design friend?' I ask carefully.

'Yeah . . . *friend* is a bit of a stretch, though. She gives me work every now and again, so it's good to keep her sweet. I sort of felt obliged to RSVP with a yes—'

I cut her off suddenly. 'Is the groom's name Chris?'

'I can't remember,' she says again, dismissively.

I'm quiet, the cogs in my mind turning.

'You OK?' she asks.

'Yeah,' I reply slowly. *No. No, I'm not OK. This cannot be what I think it is.* We cannot be going to Victoria and *Chris's* wedding. That level of awfulness cannot find its way towards me. But it wasn't *that* long ago that Chris and Victoria were dating. So—

'When you say "Chris".' Scarlet interrupts my thoughts. Her face frowns. 'You don't mean *Chris*?'

'Um . . .' I don't know what to reply. The whole idea that I might be on my way to Victoria's wedding, and the groom is *Chris* – no. Just . . . no.

'Do you know something I don't?' Scarlet asks, simultaneously trying to keep her attention on the road and on me.

I'm frowning so much I can see my own eyebrows.

'Tell me,' she urges. 'Is Chris – *your* Chris – the groom? Why would you even *think* that?'

'He was never *my* Chris,' I say, although I really wanted him to be.

'He sort of was, though,' Scarlet replies, somewhat unhelpfully.

'He and Victoria were dating,' I say. 'He told me.'

'What? When?'

'They started messaging after our house-cooling party.'

'Why didn't you tell me that?' Scarlet asks.

'I didn't want to look deranged and obsessed.'

'Are you? Are you obsessed with Chris? Is that why you asked me ages ago if Victoria was still single? Were you grilling me as to whether the two of them were together, in case I knew anything?'

'I just . . . I don't know. I really liked him – more than that. And then,' I shrug. 'It wasn't to be. There was Josh and . . . now Chris has Victoria. I think.'

'*No*,' she aims to placate me. 'I'm *sure* it wasn't his name on the invite.'

'Are you?' I ask desperately.

'I don't know,' Scarlet wails. 'I can't remember.'

'I don't want to go now.'

'Let's get there and see,' she tells me.

I put my head in my hands and close my eyes. I know what's going to happen. I can feel it deep in my bones.

Scarlet's quiet as she drives, pulling up on the grass verge outside the church in front of a *No Parking* sign. A sense of dread has settled itself in the pit of my stomach. I feel a wave of nausea.

All the guests are inside, and the wedding car with the bride and her father is pulling up behind us.

'We have to be quick,' Scarlet says, and I follow her across the grassy churchyard, past some thirsty-looking hydrangeas.

The door is open and we slide into the back of the church silently, and it's only now that I realise I didn't have to do this to myself – I could just have sat in the car, knowing Chris and Victoria were getting married. I look over the heads of people as we work our way towards a pew. I can't see him.

Suddenly it hits me. I'm in love with Chris. I think I was always in love with him. Since that first meeting. We let it slip away – that instant connection. And now . . . it's too late.

As we squeeze ourselves onto the end of the row, I see him at the front of the church and all my worst fears are confirmed. It is him. Chris. My stomach knots. There's so much pain. Oh my God, my heart. I let him go before and now I'm about to lose him for ever. He's smiling, talking to one of his groomsmen. He looks like this is the happiest day of his life. And I'm the most miserable I've been in a long time.

I thought Josh had broken my heart, but this is on another level. With Josh I was angry, hurt, embarrassed. With Chris I'm devastated. Why? And why didn't I do anything about it sooner? Now it's too late.

Scarlet sees my pain and reaches down to hold my hand. Her jaw is tense and she looks at me. She knows. I can feel tears forming in the back of my eyes and I give her a sad smile, resigning myself to what's about to play out. I don't think I can do this. I think I might be physically sick when he says *I do*. I might be physically sick now.

And then Chris is halfway through saying something to his best man and turns, his gaze connecting directly with mine, and the smile falls from his face, to be replaced with confusion and then . . . a look I can't place. His mouth closes and he stares at me.

I let out a breath I didn't know I was holding as his mouth opens again and makes the shape of my name.

Chapter Fifty-Seven

Chris

I can't believe what I'm seeing. Lexie is here. How is she here? I *purposefully* didn't invite her. And then I work it out: Scarlet.

Victoria invited Scarlet.

Scarlet brought Lexie.

But why would Lexie come?

I should have seen this coming but, with hindsight, I realise I paid zero attention to the guest list.

'Lexie,' I say out loud and my dad steps forward.

'You OK?' he asks, putting his hand on my shoulder. 'Everything all right?' He looks at me as if he's worried I'm about to have a breakdown.

'I'm OK,' I say. 'I just . . . someone's here and I didn't expect them to be and it's thrown me a bit.' So I *can* still string a sentence together then. 'I have to go and talk to—'

But I can't do anything. The 'Wedding March' has started and the door that was being held ajar opens. The vicar is primed and ready at the front of the church, and Victoria enters. She looks incredible.

As Victoria gets about halfway down the aisle, I find my

gaze is drawn back to Lexie, just for a second. Or it would have been – only she's gone. Why did she come? And why is she leaving so quickly?

I only needed a few more minutes before Victoria walked down the aisle, but now . . . it's too late.

Chapter Fifty-Eight

Lexie

Scarlet's given me the car keys. I'm in so much emotional pain, even though I don't have any right to feel like this. But I can't sit and watch him marry her. I can't. I'll go to the Premier Inn we've booked and I'll nurse a pot of tea and a huge slice of cake, or even a whole damn cake, for hours in my room and cry until Scarlet wants picking up from—

'Lexie!' I hear my name being called and Chris is running across the churchyard towards me.

I breathe in sharply. His black suit jacket is undone, his hair is shorter than when I last saw him and he's smiling at me. This is everything I wanted.

But all I can say in return, in disbelief, is, 'Get back inside that church. What the *hell* are you doing? What are you *doing*?'

He stops, yards from me, staring at me. 'What am *I* doing? What are *you* doing? Why have you left?'

'Why have *you* left?' I call back to him. He can't do this. I want Chris. I love him – I know that now. I knew it so long ago, but I couldn't admit it. I love him, but this is not OK. I walk towards him. 'You can't do this. We can't do this. It's

366

her wedding day.' Tears fall down my face. 'You're ruining Victoria's life!'

I push him, his chest warm through his shirt, and he staggers backwards in surprise. And then Chris stands his ground. He grabs my hands, holds them away from his chest.

'What are you doing?' he asks. 'Stop. Just stop.'

I stare at him, my hands held tightly in his. I can't move. He looks as agonised as I feel.

'You can't do this to her,' I cry. 'You can't walk out of the wedding and do this to her.'

'Victoria doesn't care that I'm out here,' he says. 'She probably hasn't even noticed.'

'Of course she's noticed,' I cry. I'm in hell. Or at least I'm going there. Why isn't he in hell too? 'The man she's marrying has left her at the altar. How could you do this to her? I thought you were a good person, Chris. Get back inside the church! Now!'

He stares at me intently, his brown eyes piercing my heart. 'What?' he says. '*I'm not marrying her.*'

'You have to. You can't leave her standing there.' I'm really crying now.

He's quiet. And then he says softly, 'Do you even know whose wedding you're at?'

'What?'

He loosens his grip on my wrists. 'She's not marrying *me*.'

'What?' I'm going to say this on repeat until Chris starts making sense.

'Oh my God, Lexie. She's not marrying *me*,' he says. 'She's marrying my brother.'

'What?'

'She's marrying my brother, Ben. I'm his best man.'

'What?'

'You have to stop saying that,' he continues, warmth returning to his eyes.

'No,' I reply. 'You're getting married. You're with Victoria and you're getting married to her, and my heart is breaking.' Am I dreaming all of this? I must be in a nightmare.

He's quiet, looking into my eyes, into my soul. 'Your heart is breaking?' he asks softly. 'Because you think I'm getting married?'

'Yes,' I say between sobs. 'Yes. I . . .'

'Lexie,' he goes on, and his voice is pained. 'Lexie, I'm not getting married. I was never getting married. My brother's getting married. And I'm standing here with you, which is exactly where I want to be.'

I can't see him through my tears, and then my eyes clear as they fall down my face. Chris wipes the tears away gently. I've missed him so much. I've missed everything about him.

'How?' I ask. 'How is she marrying your brother?'

He blows air out of his cheeks. 'I made the error of introducing her to him when he was in town. But it wasn't an error in the end. They *really* hit it off,' he says with a laugh. 'More than I'd hit it off with Victoria. It was immediate. I could see that. There were no hard feelings. I watched them together that first night they met. They talked so animatedly about a musical we'd just seen, which they'd both loved and I'd hated. I knew it then. I could see what they couldn't. I was the one who suggested they might like to hang out and see what happened. I gave them my blessing and conceded happy defeat, let's put it that way.'

I put my hand over my mouth to stop a sob. There's so much I want to say. So much I want to reveal – that I wish so much I'd got on that plane with him three years ago, that I love him. That I fell in love with him a little bit that first night we met and it's never gone away since. That I'd made a huge mistake in letting him go, in letting our friendship go. I thought I was doing the right thing in pursuing things with Josh. It's all my fault.

Chris's eyes are still on mine. He's watching me intently as if he can hear my thoughts. 'Are you and Josh . . . ?'

'No,' I say. 'It ended. Ages ago.'

'Oh,' he replies simply. 'OK then. Well, Lexie?'

I nod.

'You need to stop crying,' he urges softly.

'I can't,' I answer honestly. Tears of sadness have merged into tears of joy.

'You need to stop crying because I can't kiss you when you're crying, it's too weird,' Chris says, moving towards me and making me laugh, the way he always has. Then his mouth is only a fraction away from mine, and then his lips are on mine and I fall against him as he lifts me out of the regret I've been in, ever since that first moment we said goodbye and I let him go. I press myself into him, desperately, hungrily, letting him kiss me and kissing him back – his arms around me, and mine around him. This is a level of intensity I never thought I'd feel, with a man I never thought I'd have, at a time and in a location I could never have imagined.

Chris kisses me for what feels like for ever and then I pull back from him and look into his dark eyes. I love him so much.

'Be my plus-one?' he asks and I laugh. 'Please don't leave.'

'I'm not going to leave,' I say, and his hand finds mine.

'I need to go back inside to watch my brother get married. Come with me?'

I said no to this man when he uttered those three words once before. I won't make the same mistake again. 'Yes,' I reply as I kiss him again, followed by, 'Do you think they've noticed you've gone yet?'

'Oh yeah,' he says regretfully as we make our way back towards the church door. As we reach it, he kisses me once again. 'I snuck out down the side while the vicar was talking, but by now they'll have definitely noticed I've gone,' he says, tapping his jacket pocket, 'because as the best man . . . I've got both of their wedding rings.'

Chapter Fifty-Nine

The rest of the wedding blurs as Chris deposits me at the back of the church and he slots back into the front pew, resumes his seat and then stands when told to, passes the rings to his brother and Victoria, who place them adoringly on each other's fourth fingers.

Then we sit, we stand, we sing and I'm here without being here, in a cloud of my own happiness until I find myself being swept along outside with the other guests, walking into the sunlight and the temperate, lulling heat of the churchyard. Now that we're in the open, Scarlet demands a full debrief (there was only so much I could convey silently with my eyes and my wide smile) and I tell her everything that passed between Chris and me, as we're directed to throw confetti. The photographer snaps away and, when he's finished, guests break away to talk and offer congratulations. Scarlet squeals with excitement as I tell her that Chris and I are . . . I don't know what Chris and I are, but it's certainly not what we were before. I look across to where he's talking to his brother, his gaze finding its way over to me every now and again, and his wide, knowing smile matches my own.

And then Scarlet says she's going to thank Victoria on my

behalf for casting Chris free and shacking up with his brother, so that he and I could come back to each other.

'Please don't do that,' I say, flying with happiness, when only an hour earlier I was sinking in misery. 'Not on her wedding day, for God's sake. Save that chat for another day.'

'No, I'm going to,' Scarlet says and scurries off.

And there Chris is, next to me again. It's as if the world has grown silent, and although there's the jubilant noise of a wedding crowd in full confetti-throwing mode, I barely notice. It's as if it's only Chris and me. His fingers find mine and he looks down at our hands. His smile reaches his eyes, making them crinkle in a way I hadn't realised I'd missed.

'Hello again,' he says softly, his gaze thick with meaning.

'Hello,' I reply in a tone that matches his. 'Fancy meeting you here.'

'Go on then, how much of this did you have on your bingo grid?' he starts with.

'Ha! None of that, I can assure you.'

'Oh, I had all of it. I've won then.'

I smile, his hand finds mine and then he kisses me.

'Big Talk round seven,' Chris says.

'How do you know we're on that number?' I query. 'Or are you just chancing that I won't call you on it?'

'I worked it out,' he says, pulling me towards him and stroking my bare arm absent-mindedly.

'Really?' I ask, attempting not to be distracted as his hand moves up and down my arm deliciously, over and over again.

His eyebrows lift and he nods. 'Really. I replayed every

conversation we had, every Big Talk and every minute I was with you, and I worked out we're on round seven, although I think there were a lot of unofficial Big Talks in between, and we didn't bother labelling them.'

'I'll have to take your word for it.' He still has the same effect on me that he had that first night I met him three years ago.

'I never thought I'd see you again,' he says. 'And I can't tell you how desperately sad that made me.'

'Likewise,' I answer honestly. 'My heart did all kinds of things when I first saw you today. I thought I'd lost you for ever.'

'How do you think *I* felt?' Chris asks. 'I couldn't believe you were here. I'd been thinking about you so much, but I assumed you were still with Josh, so I kept out of the way. And then there you were. I thought I was losing my mind. But you looked as shocked as I was.'

'I was shocked to see you at the front of the church, let's put it that way.'

'Oh, I don't know,' he teases. 'Married at thirty, divorced by forty. Plus, remember I'm massively behind age-wise. It's not too surprising, surely.'

'I'm so pleased it wasn't you getting married,' I say.

'Is that a massive understatement?'

I laugh. 'I'm *ecstatic* it wasn't you getting married. Is that better?'

'Yes,' he says, inching even closer to me.

'You running out of the church like that was very impulsive,' I point out.

'And not at all like me,' he agrees. 'I'm only ever impulsive when it comes to you.'

My face forms a smile. 'That's not a bad thing.' I glance around. 'What do we do now?' I ask.

'I think we should enjoy the wedding reception, I think we should talk Big Talk all night long, I think you should dance with me—'

'And kiss you hard during the erection section?'

He chuckles, reminded of his own words. 'And kiss me *really* hard during the erection section. And then . . .'

I watch him thinking. But it's my turn to ask Chris what he once asked me so long ago. And so I say it. 'Come with me,' I dare.

'Where?' he asks, but he's looking at me with an intense good humour, so I can see it doesn't matter. I could say somewhere miles away, such as Nova Scotia, and he'd agree.

'Edinburgh, where I currently live.'

I watch his face spring towards shock. 'You live in Edinburgh?'

'Yep. Or we could go back to London, if you're still there . . .' I continue. 'Dublin, New York. I don't mind.'

'I don't mind, either,' Chris says genuinely. I'd go with you anywhere, Lexie. I'm not letting you go ever again.'

'Neither am I,' I tell him, kissing him in the middle of the churchyard. 'Neither am I.'

Acknowledgements

This time around first thanks should go to you, lovely reader, for buying a copy of *The Wedding Game,* or downloading it on e-reader or audio, or even borrowing it from the library. Did you know that authors get paid a little sum for every library 'borrow'. No? Neither did I, until I became an author. So to all of you telling me with a little blush that you borrow my books from the library . . . you keep going!!! Libraries need our love and support and are such a community asset. Likewise, if you've been gifted this copy and enjoyed it, or if you intend to gift it on, recommending my work to friends and family is music to my ears. There's nothing like being recommended a book. It keeps the world moving. And if you'd like to leave an Amazon review, that helps keep my world moving too.

My fab family are everything and I couldn't have written this, spending my days buried in my office day in and day out without Steve, Emily, Alice, Mum and Dad. Thanks also to Luke and Cassie for support and love. Having grandparents willing to do school pick-ups is also a total life saver, meaning I can do a full day's work. Oh the luxury. So thank you to Colin and my mum. The two of you are racking up those land miles but it's so appreciated by me, Steve and the girls who love spending time with you even if it is them in the back of the car asking, 'What snack did you bring?'

Bestest buds Natalie, Sarah and Nicky, thank you for always being at the end of a like-minded WhatsApp rant. It's heaven to know I have friends for life: come what may.

I've been so lucky to make some fantastic writer friends in this industry, and having sounding boards and first readers in Write Club (Peter, Snoops, Nic, Sue, Tracy, Karen) and fellow partners in crime, Rayleigh Writers, is everything. Thanks for always being there to dispense advice: Lizzie, Sam, Emma, Julie and Tracy. My WhatsApp has never been so busy but I love it and wouldn't have it any other way. Thanks to super Savvies who freely dispense advice in this mad old world. To Chelmsford RNA chums: our monthly lunch meetups are a balm to my soul. And to good chum Mandy Robotham . . . a like-minded soul (who lives far too far away from me for my liking).

Praise be for the goddess that is Becky Ritchie, agenting like a total boss as always and finding wonderful homes for my books. Finalising contract renewals on maternity leave and then giving birth twenty-four hours later must be worthy of some sort of industry award for dedication! And to the ever-fabulous Oli Munson, thanks always for the year-where-you-had-no-choice-but-to-field-Lorna's-ever-present-emails. You did it with gusto and remain a star. Thanks to Jack who always goes above and beyond, and to Harmony and Gosia and the rest of the wonderful A.M. Heathers who look after my books.

To my wonderful editor Emily Griffin: thanks for being so smashing at everything you do, making the editing process a total dream and honing hooks, characters and meet-cutes into effervescent books. Thanks to all at Century who work on my novels and sell them around the world with special thanks to Jess Muscio, Laurie Ip Fung Chun, Mandy Greenfield and Hope Butler.

And finally, saying thanks again to my lovely readers feels just the right thing to do. If you've loved *The Wedding Game* please do leave a review online and tag me on social media in any pictures you share of my books. I get such a thrill when I see you all on your sun loungers by a hotel pool or in your gardens or curled up on your sofas with your pets or a cup of coffee, clutching a copy of one of my novels. And if taking pics of books isn't your cuppa tea, then do give me a little follow online instead as social media is where I post all my bookish news. With two books a year under two names there's always something to chat about. Or simply join for pictures of beaches, wine, cake, dogs and my terrible attempts to make things grow in my garden.

With love,
Lorna/Elle

www.lornacookauthor.com
Facebook: LornaCookWriter
Instagram: LornaCookAuthor
X: LornaCookAuthor
TikTok: LornaCookAuthor

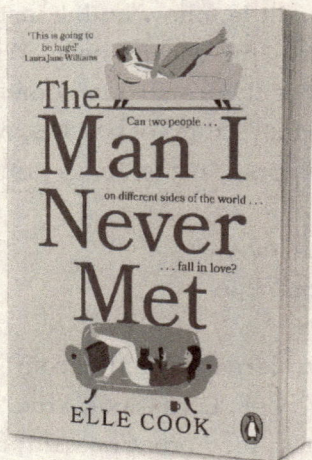